# FOR ZION'S SAKE

## *I Will Not Keep Silent*

By Gary Kosak

**Xulon PRESS**

Library of Congress Control Number: 2003092693
ISBN 1-591608-25-2

www.xulonpress.com

# ENDORSEMENTS

"Once I began reading this book, I could not put it down. This book is delightful, inspirational and filled with love and sensitivity for the Jewish people. This book truly fulfills the biblical injunction to Gentiles to "comfort ye, comfort ye, my people." As I read it cover to cover, I kept thinking, if only there were more Christians like Gary Kosak. Such people give hope to the Jewish people and reassure us that we are not alone, that we have true friends. They are the witnesses of God's love in the world. I felt as though I was walking with him on his journey. I recommend it heartily for Christians and Jews alike. He sheds light on the stories of the miracle we are witnessing in our own time, of God's ingathering of His children to the land of Israel. He also addresses with special sensitivity and emotion the trials and tribulations Jews have endured this century, particularly during the holocaust."

Rabbi Yechiel Eckstein, Founder and President
International Fellowship of Christians and Jews

"What a wonderful book...profound, moving, wise, insightful and passionate about those people and that land so close to the heart of God. I urge you to read this book and rejoice in the people you meet here. This is a book that could bring you to the place where you think God's thoughts about God's ancient people. Read it...and you'll thank me for recommending it."

Steve Brown, Author and Teacher
Professor, Reformed Theological Seminary
Key Life Network

"It is deeply encouraging to read the words of a Christian whose heart beats for Israel and our people. Author Gary Kosak connects the reader with some of Israel's ordinary people and the incredible price they have paid to survive and live in the land of their fathers. This book is a "must read" for both Jews and Christians who want to expand their understanding of each other and of Israel."

Zvi Givati, Brigadier General (retired)
Deputy Prison Commissioner
Israel Ministry of Police

"...a skillfully written and engaging volume which reflects the heart of God; it exudes with a genuine love and concern for the people of the Book and their historic homeland. A committed Christian Zionist, Kosak is passionate about his subject yet thoughtful and balanced in his approach. His work displays many years of study, travel and personal interaction with Israeli Arabs and Jews. Amid the vast spectrum of voices crying to be heard in the Middle East today, don't miss why these words from Isaiah have been so meaningful and life changing to Kosak, 'For Zion's sake, I will not keep silent'."

> Marvin R. Wilson, Ph.D.
> Professor of Biblical Studies
> Gordon College
> Wenham, Massachusetts

"For Zion's Sake", written by Capt. Gary Kosak, is refreshingly different from many other volumes written about Israel and the Jewish people in that it brings us into contact with an old and new people in a way that we are profoundly moved and challenged to re-examine our attitudes to them. The book is based on Scripture, written from the heart and inspired by love. Those who read it will be enriched."

> Malcolm Hedding, Executive Director
> International Christian Embassy, Jerusalem

"...I know that the Lord has not forgotten His people, the Israelites. "And so all Israel will be saved, so it is written; 'The Deliverer will come out of Zion, and He will turn ungodliness from Jacob; for this is My covenant with them, when I take away their sins'." This will be a great day for Israel and God's people. Your heart will be touched as you read this well-researched book."

> Joe Ivey, Founder and President
> Fellowship of Christian Airline Personnel

# ACKNOWLEDGMENTS

**To my wife**, Hellen, whose encouragement, prayers, suggestions, helpful editing and occasional prodding helped spur me on to finish this book.

**To my children**, Chris and Kathy who were there hoping for me, and especially to my daughter Kim who created a beautiful needlepoint "For Zion's Sake" which hung on my wall for years as a constant reminder to stick to the task of finishing this special labor.

**To my friends**, Bob, Dick, Irit, Jamie, Marvin, Sally, Shirley, Tanya and Yechiel, who read this manuscript and gave me suggestions, encouragement, and support.

**To a special cadre of Israelis**, some of whom are of Arab descent, each of whom spent many hours with me telling their special experiences and histories and giving me a solid background of understanding on which to write this book. As much as I would like to publicly acknowledge and thank them before the world, in the interests of their own safety and privacy, I have chosen not to reveal their full names. I am deeply indebted to, Avraham, Batya, Bertha, Dalit, Chaim, Daniel, David, Eleanora, Ellen, Irit, Isaak, Isidor, Izak, Jan, Joel, Johann, Lucien, Margot, Michael, Miriam, Moshe, Nadia, Nasser, Pola, Rafi, Sarah, Saul, Shlomo, Shmuel, Uri, Uzi, Walter, Yitzak, Yehudith and Zvi.

**To the Jewish people at large**, who have born the rejection and wrath of the nations on their own bodies, souls, and spirits. They have persevered through the ages to give us the Bible, to contribute in thousands of ways to the betterment of mankind through law, medicine, arts, music, physics, chemistry, and a host of other disciplines.

**To those Jews** who never had the joy of annexing to their names the title, "Israeli". Their lives were stolen from them in many nations. Their untimely deaths became the paving stones of inspiration for their own brothers and sisters to return to and rebuild the land of Israel, according to the prophecies of the Book.

**To those Israelis** whose own lives of suffering are laid bare in this book.

**To our Heavenly Father**, Who through His people, both Christians and Jews, is carrying out every jot and tittle of His great plan of redemption for mankind.

*For Zion's sake I will not keep silent, and for Jerusalem's sake I will not keep quiet, until her righteousness goes forth like brightness, and her salvation like a torch that is burning.*

Isaiah 62:1—NIV

# FOREWORD

Zion. It is a name that provokes passionate response rang-
ing from bloodthirsty hatred to deep-seated love. Mt. Zion
is the pinnacle of Jerusalem, which in turn is the pinnacle
of Israel; a land, according to the Bible, that is destined to be home
for God's chosen people.

Zion was the backdrop for Abraham and Isaac's long trek up Mt.
Moriah, and where Abraham raised his knife over his only son. If a
mountain could hear and feel, Mt. Zion would have sensed the
struggle raging within Abraham as he obediently led his only son to
the altar of sacrifice. His innermost being was purposefully obeying
the voice of his God, while his rational mind reasoned that it was
not possible to slay his son as a sacrifice and still have him be the
son of promise for the Jewish nation whose numbers would be as
uncountable as the stars.

Zion has been the scene of centuries of prosperity, but more
often has known the parched dryness of burned out dwellings, over-
turned walls, and the trampling feet of outsiders who had come to

conquer. Zion has witnessed the most outrageous acts of mankind as well as the greatest.

There are many that lay claim to Zion, who zealously desire to possess it. But Zion seems more able to possess than to be possessed. Zion attracts the best and the worst of human efforts...those to build...and those to annihilate.

It would be from Mt. Zion that one could have observed the agonizing steps of Jesus, a Jew, carrying the cross, not unlike Isaac, who carried the wood on which he would have been sacrificed centuries earlier. And only meters away, on the hill called Golgotha, one would have heard the cry of a pleading voice which has echoed for nearly 2,000 years, "Father, forgive them for they know not what they do," as Jesus hung in agony on a Roman cross.

It is Zion that has had to bear the weight of tradition that Mohammed, the prophet of all Islam, was said to have ascended to heaven from its heights. It is on Zion that the Dome of the Rock stands obtrusively over the site of the Second Temple, as a defiance to the God of Abraham, Isaac, and Jacob.

Zion, especially in more recent years, has had its meaning enlarged to refer to more than simply the mountain in Jerusalem. The tent cords of this word have been stretched to the limits, from Dan to Beersheba, over Judea and Samaria, and the Golan. As tightly as a real tent cord would have to be pulled to encompass such an area, so is the strain and tension upon the people of Zion, the Jews.

Zion has become another of the "isms" of the world. But Zionism is more than philosophical, or political, or economic. Embedded in its roots are the very oracles of the **Torah** and **Tenach** (the Old Testament), the words of which are holy and powerful, spoken by the God of Abraham, Isaac, and Jacob through His people, and recorded meticulously through the ages. They are words, which have come true, are coming true, and will continue to come true. As numerous prophecies of God's Word continue to be fulfilled, the unfolding brings new heights of joy, as well as depths of suffering.

As a Christian, I have come to observe that the people of Zion have been the subject of much attention, especially in recent days. The attention has sometimes been deep...but more often superficial.

Many of us Christians have often viewed Israel as "a place where the Jews live", a "trouble spot in the Middle East", or "God's time-piece in end-time prophecy." In so doing, we have lumped together the Jewish people as an impersonal mass with whom we have little personal interaction or understanding. We vaguely know who they are, or what they have suffered individually.

This book is being written primarily to the Western Christian. So many from this community are only superficially familiar with Israel. My hope is to impart more vision for Zion's people, to foster understanding and support. It is a book, which will introduce some new terminology to those who are just learning about Israel and her people. I hope that any present "head" knowledge about the Jewish people, will flow from the intellect and into the heart as you, the reader, enter into the lives portrayed in this volume.

Israel is not just a "place where the Jews live." It is not simply the geography for the working out of God's end-time plan, and it is not only "some trouble spot in the Middle East." When we speak of Israel or Zion, we are speaking of PEOPLE...individual lives that have been lived in great suffering to build and to survive in that small patch of land no larger than the State of New Jersey.

You will be introduced to some of Zion's people, each of whom have paid dearly...far more than most of us in the West can imagine...simply to survive. Their stories are absolutely true...as accurately as I can report them. Names have been changed to protect and preserve the privacy of those who have so generously shared their experiences with my wife and me.

My own life serves as a thread, which ties together the lives mentioned in this book. The first two chapters describe in some detail how I became linked with the Jewish people. I describe events in my own life which led me to God, His people and His land. He is the same God who led the patriarchs and who restored the many individuals who today call Israel their home.

Indeed... undergirding Zion, or Israel, are people—ordinary people. Not to know any of them personally is to miss some intimacy and details that cannot be conveyed with the cold facts of a news story, or a group history. You will meet only a few...but hopefully in meeting these special Israelis through this book, your insight will be expanded and your empathy and support for Zion's future will increase. If that support develops, you will be giving aid and comfort to those that the Bible calls the "apple of God's eye".

If you are a Jew and this book falls into your hands, it is my hope that you will be inspired to do more than write checks to your synagogue or a Jewish organization. I hope that you will be motivated to empathize with your people in Zion, and that you will develop greater vision for the Land of Israel. May you further be encouraged to trust that God—the God of Abraham, Isaac, and Jacob—is a God of the living, and is faithful to the utmost. His Word says that He Who watches Israel neither slumbers nor sleeps, and as He has promised, He will fulfill His Word to the very jot and tittle. I pray that this book will allow you to feel the pain of your own people who have not had the opportunity to live in the American Diaspora. I want you to meet some of those who have been seared by the fires of the Holocaust, and who have overcome British blockades, malaria, Arab terrorists, the iron curtain of communist Russia, as well as a world of indifference.

To the Christians who discover this book, I pray that you will also discover the debt that we owe to the Jewish people. Remember, that it was the Jewish people who recorded the Bible for all of us. Through the ages it was their scribes who meticulously copied letter by letter, the very oracles of God, and kept passing them down through the generations. It was the Jewish people who gave us Jesus, the New Testament and who comprised the roots of Christianity.

A strong admonition to the Gentile Christian church is recorded in the biblical book of Romans. The Apostle Paul, using a metaphor of an olive tree to refer to Israel, writes:

> "Do not be arrogant toward the branches; but if you are arrogant, remember that it is not you who supports the root, but the root supports you."
> (NAS—Romans 11:18).

Our roots are JEWISH! This fact has always been present in the pages of Scripture, but too seldom expressed in day to day Christian life. Perhaps this realization will now take hold, and bring forth a gratitude and a sense of indebtedness toward our senior brothers and sisters, the Jews.

To both Jews and Christians who may read this book there may be things which occasionally create discomfort. For example, I may be accused by some Jewish readers of trying to proselytize or convert. Likewise, I may be accused by some mission-minded Christians of not "tellin' 'em about Jesus." In this regard let me be clear: I am a Christian. I really do believe that Jesus is the Messiah for all humanity. I love to share this good news with others; however, despite this conviction, I have also come to the place where I can remain peaceful, knowing that God is also capable of revealing the truth about His Messiah with little help from me. My job is to love, to comfort, and bless all of God's people, and to live my life so as to reflect God's will as I seek to be obedient to Scripture as a true disciple of Jesus of Nazareth. I can leave the rest to Him.

I believe the people who have been interviewed in the following pages were brought into my life by God Himself. There are no ringers or counterfeits designed to prove a point or to fit snugly into anybody's theology. You will meet hardened atheists, many agnostics, and even some Jews who firmly believe that Jesus is the Son of God and their Messiah. I did not design it that way. I did not know these people before I began this project, and certainly did not know their beliefs.

Finally, before I proceed to share with you my experiences with the people of Zion, I must acknowledge that I have precipitated pain in the hearts of those I interviewed. As I asked for details, stabbing recollections flowed forth from the catacombs of their memories. I was part of exhuming that which had long been buried. With the same sorrow that one might experience while standing next to the re-opened grave of a loved one, I was able to begin the process of understanding, sharing as best I could the painful moments that could only be described in words.

I am truly sorry for any pain that this surely caused to some of those whom my wife and I interviewed. I, as a Christian, felt I had to know and understand what my elder brothers, the Jews, had experienced. This journey confirmed that it is important that I speak out for Zion. In order to do that I had to enter in, however slightly, to the pain and suffering endured by so many for so long. It was equally important and even comforting to many of the Israelis, who shared their lives so intimately, that someone else even cared.

I cannot express in words my gratefulness to those, whom you will meet in this book. They taught me so much, and were God's instruments to bring me a step deeper in understanding and compassion. As I interviewed and listened, I wept with many.

An El Al flight steward sank in the despair of tears as he heard for the first time new details of his mother's story, which he translated from Yiddish into English so that I could understand. On another occasion, a young Israeli soldier clutched me tightly and wept deep sobs as he recounted twenty or so years of a fatherless life which was filled with terror and the violent and premature deaths of many friends. I also sat with a Russian *refusenik*, pain contorting her attractive face, with tears in her eyes, as she strained to speak the words describing her own mother's death at the hands of "Mother Russia."

The time is long past due for all believing Christians to give comfort to those who have given them their heritage and begin to repay the love debt owed to the Jewish people.

> Comfort, O comfort My people, says your God. Speak kindly to Jerusalem; and call out to her, that her warfare has ended, that her iniquity has been removed, that she has received of the Lord's hand double for all her sins."
> (NAS—Isaiah 40:1)

I am grateful for the privilege to meet, to know, and to share with those you will be introduced to in these pages. As I entered into these lives I learned much, and it is why...for Zion's sake, I will not keep silent.

# 1

# ISRAEL IN MY HEART

The teletype clattered away with a steady beat filling the communications center with yards of paper. A U.S. Air Force sergeant read the documents, stamped the pages "TOP SECRET", and hand-carried the information to the command post, where I sat as the Emergency Actions Officer of the 48th Tactical Fighter Wing.

The command post was a flurry of activity as senior ranking fighter pilots—colonels, lieutenant colonels, majors, and a few captains like myself—pondered the significant events taking place. They could conceivably place us all in the cockpits of our fighters and send us to war. We were a Tactical Fighter Wing of F-100 pilots; capable of waging either conventional or nuclear war if called upon to do so. We all wondered if this might possibly be the time.

At the East End of the Mediterranean Sea, flights of A-4 Skyhawks and Mirage fighters streaked close to the desert floors of the Sinai in a blistering attack against the Egyptian army. The attack was fast, furious, and successful. The Egyptians hardly knew what hit their confused forces. Russian-built Migs fell from the air like mosquitoes zapped with the deadly fog of Black Flag aerosol. Most aircraft never even got off the ground and were burning before their pilots were even out of bed. It was all out war around Israel, and thoughts of Armageddon flashed through the minds of many who had once read a Bible.

In six days the war was over, and little Israel, like a feisty bull-dog had managed to clean the neighborhood of the Dobermans who wanted to devour her. As I sifted through the battle reports and eventually saw some of the gunnery film taken from behind the gun-sights of Israel's fighters, I was awestruck at how this little nation was able to completely take over the Sinai, and neutralize the entire Egyptian army and air force. It was done with such precision and with significant but not intolerable losses.

The Israeli commander with the patch over his eye, General Moshe Dayan, had led his men brilliantly, and his face began to grace posters that were sold with the humorous caption, "Hire the Handicapped." He was the hero of many a military officer and corporate underling who had a can-do attitude, but who found himself bound by the maze of bureaucratic regulations that encumber almost any large organization.

As Israel fought, American fighter pilots all over Europe and North Africa were on the alert. Command posts such as the one at RAF Lakenheath, England, where I was on duty, were placed throughout the NATO countries, and were filled with generals and colonels making plans for all the contingencies. Commanders researched their inventories of parts, planes, men, and weapons. Leaves were canceled, and those of us who were combat-ready were within minutes of being able to launch. Much to our relief, the war ended almost as fast as it had begun.

Months after the 6-Day War was concluded in June of 1967, I was sitting in the living room of my rented English bungalow in the village of Beck Row, Bury St. Edmunds. It was a five-mile drive from RAF Lakenheath where I was based. The phone rang and I answered.

A superior of mine asked me if I would be able to fly the T-39 Sabreliner to Israel. This was a small business-type jet used to carry high-ranking officers, government officials, and an occasional fighter pilot that was deploying to another location. The little Sabreliner could carry a crew of two pilots plus an additional 4 passengers and luggage. I was qualified to fly the little bird, as well as the F-100 Supersabre—a shark-like fighter which was the backbone of America's tactical air force at that time.

This mission would take me to Lod Airport, (now called Ben Gurion) just outside of Tel Aviv. My refueling stop would be in a remote corner of Naples Naval Air Station in Italy. I would not be allowed to wear a uniform, but was to dress in a business suit.

I packed my bags and drove my 1947 black Jaguar "Saloon" to the RAF Lakenheath flight line. It wasn't long before I was lifting the landing gear lever in the black of early morning and heard the clunk of the wheels as they snuggled themselves into the wheel wells. My little Sabreliner streaked through the English skies, appearing as only a flashing red light accompanied by the roar of two Pratt & Whitney engines.

I made my refueling stop at Naples, and continued on to my destination....Israel. As I cruised at 41,000 feet over the azure Mediterranean, my navigation radios eventually picked up the signals that indicated that it was time to start my descent. I soon saw the hazy coastline of Eretz Israel as I heard the voice of my Israeli air traffic controller, "Air Force Jet 24474, cleared to descend to flight level one-one-zero. Report leaving flight level four-one-zero."

My mind filled with anticipation as I viewed the ancient Jewish homeland that had felt the footsteps of foreign conquerors as well as returning refugees. Though not in my consciousness then, I later came to realize that there were thousands upon thousands of Jews who would sell all they had to be going where I was. I had only to nose my jet over, pull back the throttles, and I would be in Israel. Later in my life I would come to meet inhabitants of Zion who crawled, clawed, staggered, stumbled, cried, and even swam to reach their homeland. Little did I know that this short visit would plant a small seed in my heart that would come to fruition a decade and a half later.

As I landed at Lod Airport, the sun was shining brightly and the day was a warm 75 degrees. I was escorted to my car and brought to my hotel, which was only a few blocks from Dizengoff Circle, the "Times Square" of Tel Aviv. The plan was for me to be in town only for a night.

As "fate" would have it, I went out to crank up my little Sabreliner the next day to fly back to England. One of the engines, although running, simply would not respond to throttle commands. The engine would not accelerate above idle thrust, and I had to shut down and send the appropriate communiqués for maintenance support. I was now "stuck" in Israel for a few more days.

Along with another pilot friend, we rented a car and a guide, and made a whirlwind tour of the local area. I was completely embarrassed when our guide would make a statement such as, "I'm sure you know about King David and his son Solomon," or "I will take you to the Western Wall of the Temple now," looking at me as though I would know what I would be seeing. Though I am sometimes ashamed to admit it, the plain facts were that I didn't know King Solomon from a roller skate, and Israel was still just a little "bulldog" that had some competent fighter pilots that knew how to clean the Dobermans out of the neighborhood. That's what I knew about Israel.

Simon, our guide, did not have to be very perceptive to note the vacuum that existed in my knowledge about his homeland. He was very patient in trying to fill some of that void. He was a walking encyclopedia and taught me some of my first lessons about Zion.

We drove the old road to Jerusalem, (the new one had not yet been built), and along the road I saw the evidences of the battles that were waged in the Sinai and around Jerusalem. In one place we passed a storage area, where thousands of half-tracks, trucks, tanks and vehicles of all sorts lay silent, some upright, some on their sides, some simply a pile of disassembled parts. Many were broken and burned, and had been dragged off the desert as the spoils of battle. I wondered about the outcome of the Egyptian soldiers who had driven and ridden in these vehicles. I was to find out later that though many died, and many had fought valiantly, many simply abandoned their vehicles and ran from the advancing Israelis.

As our car climbed the hills to Jerusalem and wound its way through her narrow streets, we came upon a road that led to the Old City. Along the wall that bordered the road, a pile of stones broke the symmetry of the wall's masonry. Lying upon the stones were a few wilted wreaths of flowers with a few fresh ones. It was here that a Jordanian bullet had snuffed out the life of one of Israel's sons. He had fallen in the battle for Jerusalem. He was but one of the myriad of Israelis who had paid the full price to live in the Land of Promise. This place was simply the most recent of the many battles in history that had been fought over the Holy City. The victorious Israeli commander of that battle was General Uzi Narkiss, a man with whom I would sit face to face some 19 years later in my life, as he shared some of those moments in history with my wife and me.

I was immediately aware that I was not visiting just another place on planet earth, or simply the city of Jerusalem, but I was riding over a battlefield that had been the scene of much bloodshed only months before my visit. I was walking in a place which up until the Six-Day War had been "off limits" to the Jews. Although others in the world were able to obtain visas to visit Jordanian-held Jerusalem and the holy places, Jews were only allowed to look from afar at Mt. Zion and the Temple site.

I was taken to the Western, often called "Wailing" Wall. In the brightness of the Middle East sunshine beating upon the light colored stones, my eyes ached from the glare. I saw pilgrims from all over the world making their trek to the Wall—the West Wall of the Temple—the same Temple that Jesus had walked through almost 2,000 years ago driving out the moneychangers, and the identical site where King Solomon had sought the Lord 1,000 years before that.

Bearded, black-hatted **Chassidim**, ultra-orthodox Jews who tried to live up to the 613 laws derived from the Holy Book, were praying. I later was to learn that their bobbing-bowing-rocking motion that adds a physical rhythm to their recited prayers is called **davening.** At the time, I had real questions as to whether there really was a God who was listening. I also saw a self-appointed "prophet" pacing the area nearby with a sign stating "The end is near." Nearby merchants who were selling everything from **kippot** (small skullcaps) to rosary beads beckoned us to buy.

Afterwards, I was taken to Bethlehem, where I visited the Church of the Nativity, erected over the stable where Jesus was believed to have been born. I bent low to enter the purposefully constructed doorway of the church, designed to humble the visitor with its short height. Down the stairs and into the cave-like stable I went, where I was greeted by the light of hundreds of candles that had been religiously lit by dedicated people. They evidently believed that they were pleasing a God who would look with favor upon them, or the cause for which the candle was lit. Even I, the cynic, lit one in honor of a relative who had fallen in the rice paddies of Viet Nam.

A woman stood there staring at me with a sad painful expression. It appeared to be a practiced look, which acted as an incentive for the unwary to add to the collection plate which she extended to me. I added to the plate. She bowed silently, and waited for the next visitor.

I lunched in the cafeteria of the Hebrew University, and visited King David's tomb, still unaware of who he really was, or what role he had played in the history of Israel. I was made aware of the Dead Sea Scrolls, never quite grasping their significance. Through all the sightseeing I was still pondering how those Israeli fighter jocks managed to do their job so well.

In a couple of days, I had seen the old and new city of Jerusalem, the Temple Mount, the Wailing Wall, Hebrew University, Bethlehem, a couple of other shrines, Dizengoff Circle and some of the Tel Aviv night life. Another surprise waited me when I returned to my Sabreliner and had the opportunity to meet one of Israel's test pilots. We had a beautiful visit while leaning on the wing of my Uncle Sam's jet. He introduced me to the concept of the **kibbutz**, a collective of people who joined together and shared their talents and labors. They divided the fruits of those talents and labors so that all had their needs met. It was a Spartan and tough life.

The closest thing that I could compare it to in America, was a commune, but most of the folks that would have lived in an American commune at that time, were usually flower children and hippies who had dropped out of life. Now I was face to face with one of Israel's finest, a test pilot, and he lived on a kibbutz. I would later learn that the *kibbutzniks* were the backbone of Israel's agriculture and the spawning place of her surviving spirit. There were no flower children and hippies here—maybe a doctor, a few engineers, accountants, and a test pilot or two—but no flower children. Dropouts don't make it in Israel, and unfortunately for the past fifty-plus years since Israel's rebirth, there has been precious little time to sniff flowers. I left Israel with more questions than I had answers, and the seeds of my first visit settled into the soil of my heart, waiting to spring forth....a decade and a half later.

My life during that decade and a half went through a lot of turmoil. The priorities of my life were misplaced. I loved flying more than I loved people. The same life focus that caused me to think about airplanes and air forces while I was standing near the Wailing Wall, took its toll in my personal life. In 1973, I was stripped of almost all that I had when I walked out of a Massachusetts courtroom, divorced. I had lost my family, a wife, three beautiful children, and the material possessions of house and furniture. I left the Northeast, driving away in my car and with its trunk full of clothes, to take up residence in Miami, where I was already employed as a pilot for Eastern Air Lines.

It would be another 5 years of struggle and failure before I had a personal encounter with the God of Abraham, Isaac, and Jacob. It was a day that I shall never forget. The **Ruach Ha Kodesh** (Holy Spirit) touched my life as I wept deeply, asking God for help and deliverance from a life that I knew was a lie. The airplanes didn't fulfill me, the travel and the parties left me dry, and failed relationships had turned me into the empty vessel that God wanted to fill. In the brokenness of that moment, a transformation began, as I handed my life over to the God of Israel, through His Messiah, Jesus. Christians would call my experience that of being born again.

Some years later, in 1982, I began a trip to Israel to celebrate the **Feast of Tabernacles** or **Succoth** as sponsored by the International Christian Embassy in Jerusalem. As an airline employee, I have the liberty of purchasing airline tickets at greatly discounted prices. Although this is a wonderful privilege, it also means that I must travel on a "standby" basis.

As I had prepared for my trip to Jerusalem, I had called many of the overseas carriers, only to find out that all of them were overbooked. On top of this, Israel's national airline, El Al, was on strike. Thus, I was given the opportunity to exercise my faith.

I was traveling alone. I wanted this to be a journey that would allow me to smell the smells and see the sights without the encumbrances of rigid schedules and fellow travelers who would slow me down in accomplishing my goal of experiencing Israel. I now knew that this was not just a trip to another nation of the world, but was the land where Abraham, Isaac, Jacob and Jesus had walked. The tug in my heart was irresistible.

I flew from Miami to JFK Airport and made it to the Swissair counter where I would continue on to Zurich. From there I would continue to Tel Aviv. Because of my affiliation with the Fellowship of Christian Airline Personnel, I had met other Christians from all over the world who are employed by the airlines. I knew a few members of our ministry who worked for Swissair. It was a pleasant surprise when I met my friend Matthias, a Swissair steward, who just happened to be working the flight to Zurich. He assured me of a place to stay in Zurich, should I need one.

The flight from New York to Zurich was a pleasant one where I enjoyed an occasional chat with my Swiss friend and indulged myself with Swiss chocolates, which are given out in flight. We landed right on time. I said good-bye to Matthias, and headed for my connecting flight to Tel Aviv.

I was among several "standby" passengers, all of whom had higher boarding priority than I. The full fare passengers boarded, and the standbys were being called one by one. I was soon standing at the ticket counter alone except for the ticket agent. "I'm sorry, Mr. Kosak, there are no more seats," she informed me.

I instantly shot a prayer to heaven. "God.....What have you in store for me? Am I really to go to Israel? Lord, Please show me what I'm to do." I prayed quietly as I walked through the expanses of Zurich's Airport. It was about noon, and I had been up for most of the night flying from New York, catching only an occasional catnap.

My assumption up to that time had been that because El Al was on strike, that there were no flights being flown by Israel's national airline. I was informed that El Al had hired some charter airlines to fulfill their contracts to passengers who had booked flights many months earlier. I approached the El Al manager, presented my pilot credentials, my discount ticket, and asked if I might ride on the cockpit jump seat to Tel Aviv. Access to this seat is strictly controlled and is generally used only for pilots and flight examiners.

While my request was innocent from my point of view, it was only minutes later that I was standing between two Israeli security men with walkie-talkies. They asked me a lot of questions.

"So....you're a pilot eh? What kind of airplane do you fly? How fast will it go? Why do you want to go to Israel? Do you have friends there? Where will you be staying? ....and after all that ....."Just sit over there for a while, and we will be back with you."

A conference took place between an El Al official and security men. The security agents once again came over to me. More questions. Another conference with the manager. A third approach to me with more questions.

"Hey guys", I said. "Would you be kind enough to help me out?" I reached down, opened my suitcase, and withdrew a twenty-foot banner, which was rolled up like wallpaper. "Would you check the Hebrew on this sign?" I squatted and gave the roll a shove, unfurling its full twenty feet on the floor of the Zurich Airport.

On a white background and in blue letters were the English words from Psalm 33:12..."Blessed is the nation whose God is the Lord." The same Scripture was painted in Hebrew just below the English. I had the sign specially painted in Miami and I did not know if the Hebrew had been painted correctly. I would carry it in the Jerusalem March with Christians from all over the world, expressing their solidarity and love to Israel.

A couple of security agents and an El Al station manager stood over the sign, one with his hand on his chin, another pointing out a small flaw in the Hebrew, but no problem. "What's this all about?" asked the security agent.

I told him about the 7,000 or so Christians who would be coming from all over the world to basically say, "We love you Israel, and we stand with you." This sign was simply one of the ways that we were expressing it.

"I think we can do something." A few more questions were asked, a thorough security check followed, and I found myself at the boarding gate ready to climb aboard a chartered Boeing 707. I was the last passenger to board the flight. "Thank you, Lord," I prayed.

I sat down in the tourist section in the only remaining seat. At once I met Moshe and Rifkah. He was in his early 70's, and she in her early 60's. We introduced ourselves and immediately began to learn about each other.

"You know, offered Moshe, "I was talking to my wife, and I was saying to her, 'I wonder who will be sitting in this empty seat next to us?" The question had been answered for both of us, and I sensed that my missed connection with the previous Swissair flight had been ordained.

We were absolute strangers only three hours before, but by the time we approached Tel Aviv our hearts had been knit together in a special way. Moshe extended an invitation for me to visit their home in Afula, a town in northern Israel not far from the Sea of Galilee. Rifkah sincerely concurred. My plans were loose, so I agreed to call them within a couple of days.

The next day in Jerusalem, I placed a call. On the other end of the phone, I heard Moshe's Israeli-accented English. "Yoffi"..... "Wonderful"........"Of course"........"Come tomorrow!".......'"We are only a short walk from the bus station in Afula."

I arrived at the crowded Central Bus Station in Jerusalem. Hoards of young Israeli soldiers carried their M-16's, Uzi's, and duffel bags. They elbowed their way through the crushing crowd. Ultra-orthodox Chassidic Jews sprinkled the olive drab background of army uniforms with the jet-black garb of their religion. White beards of the old and wise, and black beards of the more youthful accented the array of humanity. Only the most essential of travel information was posted in English. The rest was appropriately done in Hebrew, a language that is still a mystery to me. Having its own exclusive characters, I was unfamiliar with even the simplest letter.

I boarded the bright red bus for Afula. We headed through East Jerusalem, and out through the Judean hills toward Jericho. Up the Jordan Valley we roared, paralleling the Jordan River, which was off to our right. It was a muddy stream lazily making its way south to the Dead Sea, providing a natural border between Israel and Jordan. On this bus I observed first hand the deep interest that hourly news programs commanded for Israelis. There was a radio playing over the bus speakers. When the news came on, all conversation stopped, and full attention was given to the words being broadcast from radio antennas around Jerusalem. Although things were "peaceful" now, it was only because there was keen awareness and vigilance on the part of all Israelis. Any news program might bring the announcement of another attack, perhaps from terrorists, or even a whole army from Syria, Jordan, or Egypt.

We slowed dramatically as the bus driver maneuvered our large red bus through another checkpoint. Alert, but bored Israeli soldiers waved us through the "S"-turns required to get around the barriers. They were dressed for war and were quite alone out in the middle of the hot desert, sitting under the shade of some canvas secured by ropes. The blue and white flag with the **Magen David** (Jewish star) waved in the hot desert breeze. It was evident that Israelis love their soldiers. Hands waved gently from the bus passengers, which in essence said, "Thanks guys, we're glad you're here."

We breezed by little villages and settlements with names like Netiv ha Gedud, Gilgal, and Mahola as we passed through Judea into Samaria or what the Western press most often refers to as the West Bank. Inhabited almost solely by Arab populace, it is controversial but beautiful land with its color spectrum of burnt oranges, ambers, and browns, sprinkled with wild cactus and flowers of every color. The colors and shapes of nature were unfortunately disfigured by the graffiti of rusting automobile bodies or carelessly discarded trash.

My rendezvous with Moshe and Rifkah was made after the 3-hour bus ride. Although Rifkah had other things to do, Moshe fired up his Fiat, and we headed out for a **kibbutz** where his daughter lived. We drove northeast out of Afula, passing through the village of Deverat Illit and close to Mount Tabor. This is the mountain where many believe was the site of the Transfiguration of Jesus, which took place in the company of Peter, James, and John, as recorded in the New Testament. We descended through beautiful farmland and scenery. We came to a sign on the road that said "sea level". We had many hundreds more feet to descend before we would be at the level of the Sea of Galilee, and to the level where I would visit my first kibbutz. I would finally experience what was first introduced to me many years earlier in a conversation with an Israeli test pilot.

As we approached the living quarters of the kibbutz, we drove past a few kilometers of lush fields of banana and date trees. Barbed wire fences lined the fields, and an occasional watchtower loomed above the fencing. They were necessary structures left from earlier years when the *kibbutzniks*, had to pull their share of guard duty at night to maintain their safety. By being vigilant and warding off terrorists in the night, it helped guarantee that there would be another day to work in the fields.

We greeted Moshe's daughter, Edna, who brought us into her little cottage. It was small, but comfortable. As I would learn later, most kibbutz layouts are similar. There is a main dining hall, with a mass kitchen, and the *kibbutzniks* go there for their meals. In addition, there is most often a children's house, where the kids eat, sleep, and learn, supervised by a few mothers. At one kibbutz that I visited, I also saw young men pulling duty in the children's house. I watched a 25-year old, ex-soldier on his knees, helping a group of toddlers get dressed. This co-operation allows most of the mothers to work instead of having to take care of their kids individually.

In each of the cottages, a kibbutznik had a small living room, bathroom facilities, and a small kitchen. I learned that there were only one or two telephones on the entire kibbutz, although later more *kibbutzim* had phones installed in every individual cottage. Unlike the city, there was plenty of grass, flowers, and trees, however amongst that cultivated beauty, hard physical labor was evident.

Moshe next took me to a part of the Jordan River where many visiting Christians have baptism ceremonies. It was also a place where hot and tired travelers often stop their cars and jump in for a swim. A short ride up the western shore of the **Kinneret** (Sea of Galilee) brought us to Tiberias, a fishing town dating back before the time of Jesus. We then drove to the supposed place south of Capernaum where Jesus fed the 5,000 people by multiplying five loaves of bread and two fish. I was amazed that I had only met this man and his wife for the first time in an airplane. In that short time, I became their honored guest, and here was a Jew with a loving heart, taking me, a Christian, to places that he knew would have significance to me. He was fulfilling part of the Jewish law to bless the stranger. I was lavished with real Israeli hospitality.

Moshe's appearance was one that bears evidence of some hard years. The lines in his face revealed character molded in the crucible of much hardship, and his expressions exhibited the ability to hang tough and hold the line where necessary. When he smiled, the room lit up.

Although he was born in Poland, he came to the land of Israel as a young boy. This disqualified him from being defined as a *sabra*, a person born in Israel. However, he had all of the characteristics of the *sabra*, a wild-growing cactus found all over Israel. It is a cactus, which is hard, and thorny on the outside, but when cut open, reveals a soft and sweet interior. It is a natural metaphor, well designated to depict the Israeli. There are many variations in the balance between the soft delicious interior, versus the hard thorny shell of an exterior, but there are some of both in all Israelis.

Moshe drove me back through the hills toward Afula in his little Fiat. He had taken an entire day to show me some of the sites around his corner of Israel. As we wound our way along a narrow road woven between the hills, a majestic sunset greeted us, painting the surroundings with burnt orange rays. The hills, trees, and farms took on a new glow, and the sky was a kaleidoscope of reds, yellows, and oranges reflecting off majestic cumulus clouds. I cannot begin to express the feeling that I had in those few moments. It was as though God Himself was flooding our little Fiat and the land of Israel with an out-pouring of liquid Technicolor love.

We returned to Moshe and Rifkah's modest second-floor apartment, where we dined. Rifkah had already been preparing the scrumptious salad, fresh olives, fish, mushrooms, fruits, and nuts, all harvested in Israel. We spent the evening learning more about one another. Moshe told me that he had been in Afula when it consisted of 3 or 4 families and a hand-dug well. He was there when Israel, as a re-born nation was still a hope of biblical promise, and a gleam in God's eye.

As I spoke with Rifkah, I learned that she was a survivor of the Holocaust. She spoke in general terms, and it was easy to ascertain that this part of her life held painful memories. It was much easier to speak of other things. At this meeting with my new friends, I had no thought in mind of ever writing a book. I was interested only in learning as much as possible about Israel and her people. It was because of Moshe and Rifkah that some of my first lessons were made easy. Their hospitality and their willingness turned a casual meeting on an airplane to where I was now an overnight guest in their home.

The next morning I was treated to an abundant breakfast before I had to make my way back to the bus station for my return to Jerusalem. Although I had spent only about 24 hours with these gracious people, I felt very close to them, and was sad to leave. However, I knew that there was more to learn and more to experience back in Jerusalem. The big red bus wheeled out of the Afula terminal and thundered down the narrow road which was bordered by lush cotton fields, fruit orchards, and many kinds of agricultural endeavor. What was once arid and dry land was producing rich and abundant crops. Was I not seeing the very reality of fulfilled biblical promises?

"The desert and the parched land will be glad; the wilderness will rejoice and blossom. Like the crocus, it will burst into bloom; it will rejoice greatly and shout for joy.

(NIV—Isaiah 35:1-2)

Back in Jerusalem, I joined with thousands of Christians from around the world, at the Christian Celebration of the Feast of Tabernacles, sponsored by the International Christian Embassy, Jerusalem. The Feast of Tabernacles is the third of three major feasts mentioned in the Jewish Law (Deuteronomy 16:16) where the Lord called for Israel to appear before Him. The Feast of Tabernacles is a celebration of ingathering and harvest and a celebration of God's faithfulness to His people during their wilderness wanderings. There are many other implications and interpretations of this biblical celebration.

As part of the celebration of the Feast of Tabernacles, the

Christians who had gathered together in Jerusalem desired to show support to the people of Israel. Banners and signs proliferated among the several thousands of us who took part in the Jerusalem March. Norwegians, Swedes, Finns, Canadians, Americans, South Africans, Dutch, Germans, Australians, New Zealanders and representatives of some forty other nations of the world, marched through the streets of Jerusalem. My twenty-foot banner was stretched across the road and held by three other Christians and myself. "Blessed is the nation whose God is the Lord," it announced in English and Hebrew. Other, more simple signs appeared. "Israel....you are not alone!" "Savannah Georgia loves Israel." *"Por Israel, con El Dios de Israel."*

It was a heart-rending experience for me. As I marched through Jerusalem, on both sides of the street I saw Israelis laughing, singing, and yelling "Shalom".....,"Shalom".....,"Shalom" (Peace). "Welcome!" Tears ran from the eyes of many. Flowers flew through the air at us, and handsful of cellophane-wrapped candy were showered on the marchers.

From this simple demonstration of love, the people of Zion were being soothed. The eyes of those viewing us from the sidelines were enjoying and fully receiving the long overdue support from the Christians of the world, who had too often remained silent. Many of those eyes, which were receiving comfort, had spent long years looking upon persecution and tragedy. They had seen the world in dark grays, blacks, and browns, splashed with the crimson of their people's blood. Before them now was festivity. Bright colors from flags, banners, and costumes undergirded with a love that emanated from the throne room of God toward His people.

To have been a small but special part of this event was worth far more than any sacrifice in time, effort, or money. I was beginning to understand how extremely important it was and is to "Comfort ye, O comfort ye My people, to speak softly to the heart of Jerusalem." (NAS–Isaiah 40:1)

During a similar march in a subsequent year, celebrating again the Feast of Tabernacles, I carried the Polish flag. Since I am of Polish ancestry and had made it a priority in my life to visit Poland and to walk upon what I consider to be the holy ground of Treblinka and Auschwitz, I felt minimally qualified to carry the red and white banner. There were no other Poles who were able to get out of their country, or who had the resources to make this historic trip to Jerusalem. This occurred before the collapse of communism.

As we marched streaming through the streets of Jerusalem, there were many stops along the way. One group would get too close to the group in front of them, and would have to halt. This would set off a chain reaction all the way to the rear of the assembled marchers, and so it went....stopping, starting, stopping and starting.

During one of these stops, a man on the sidelines to my right noted my Polish flag. He said something to me in Polish, a language that I do not speak. I knew from the inflection that it was something like, "You? You came from Poland to do this?"

I walked over to him, the Polish flag flapping next to me. He was a man in his late 70's. I looked him in the eye, and told him that I was of Polish descent, and that there were no Poles who were able to come, so I was standing in their stead expressing what I knew were the heartfelt feelings from many Polish Christians. The man not only spoke Polish, but also excellent English. He stated that he lived in Poland at one time. The way that he said, "I was there" needed no further explanation. I knew that he had survived the Holocaust. Although some of the greatest heroes and protectors of the Jewish people came out of Poland, the facts are that some of the worst Nazi sympathizers and anti-Semitic acts also came from the Poles.

Continuing to look him straight in the eye, I said, "Look, I'm a Christian, a Polish-American Christian. I think I understand some of what you went through." I groped for the right words, and with as much tenderness as I could muster, spoke. "I am asking for your forgiveness. Can you find it in your heart to forgive me for what my people did to your people?" Although I was personally not involved in persecuting the Jewish people during those terrible years of World War II, I am still part of some of the same wider family that did, and I meant what I said in the question that I posed to him.

He continued to look at me, and after a few moments his head began to move in small shaky nods, and the tears began to flow from his eyes. He was unable to speak, but his body was saying to me, "I forgive the Poles.....I forgive." His jaw trembled. In his eyes and in those little nods, a dozen thoughts were also being expressed. "Is what I am experiencing, REAL?.... It is still too painful to talk about"....."Where were you folks 50 years ago?"......"Oh why did it have to happen?" His nods and his frail appearance melted into a formless collage of colors, as tears welled in my own eyes and we continued to clutch each other's shoulders in a brotherly embrace.

Each time that I have returned to Israel, I have met another and another, each person a jewel in a land of promise. The seeds that had been planted in my heart from my first visit to Israel as an Air Force pilot were poking their heads through the soil of my soul. The roots have reached deeper into my being, watered I believe, by the Spirit of God Who is saying to all Christians, "Thou shall arise, and have mercy on Zion; for the time to favor her, yea, the set time has come." (KJV—Psalm 102:13)

It was after several visits to Israel and after having met and come to know so many of her citizens that an idea began to grow. I discovered many stories that must be told. It also occurred to me that there have been hundreds, even thousands of books written about the Jews, their suffering in general, and the Holocaust. Did the world need yet another book? And, who was I to write it?

In asking the question, "why me?" I also had to ask the other one, "Why NOT me?" I had been to Israel several times. I was a Christian who knew many of her people, and in whose heart the idea kept growing and "kicking". I had the provision of a profession which allowed me to travel inexpensively and fairly often in order to see the task through, and so I reached the conclusion that the project must be attempted.

It is significant that I am a Christian, and not a Jew. I have heard the moans and groans of the Gentile community in tabloids and private conversations. "Oh, those Jews! Can't they just forget about the Holocaust or the struggles in Israel and get on with life?" Or...."I'm tired of hearing about it."

I have come to the conclusion that the non-Jewish community is "tired of hearing about it" because it has done precious little to help heal the deep wounds of Israel's spirit and soul. It has been the Jews for the most part who have had to tell their own story and have had to be vocal, sometimes very vocal, in order that their story not be buried, as have 6,000,000 of their people, in the soil of the nations and the sands of time. Often they have had to yell, because we as Christians or Gentiles DO not or CHOOSE not to hear.

No one likes to be reminded of his past failures and sins. When there hasn't been a real repentance for past cruelties which sometimes took the form of inaction or non-involvement, the sin comes back to haunt, both to individuals and entire nations. To ignore the need for dealing with our sins against the Jewish people in the Gentile or Christian community is like trying to spray perfume upon a corpse. For a while the scent may be palatable, but until the rotting flesh is disposed of, the stench will come back, and be a continual prod that something must be done to deal with the root of the problem, OUR problem in the Christian community. It has been an ongoing problem of insensitivity, lack of courage, ignorance, and even plain hatred. Who is better to vocalize this problem, than a member of that community?

As I have come to realize my debt of gratitude to the Jewish people, I am humbled at the precious gift that God has given me in allowing me to meet them in great numbers, from retired pensioners to army generals, to high officials of government. As He has allowed me to touch the "apple of His eye", I have come to realize that this very act must be with great gentleness and humility as I apply any healing salve to this sensitive organ of God's own body. A wrong thrust or insensitivity might result rather in "sticking" or "poking" my finger in His eye, resulting in more injury and pain, rather than the healing for which the Jewish people long.

My spiritual adventure with God and the Jewish people continued to incubate as I pondered and prayed about my next steps. Where would these steps take me and how would they unfold?

# 2

# BACK TO ISRAEL

It was October 1986 and I was walking with my wife among the cottages and trees of a kibbutz near Ashkelon, Israel. In the early 70's, Hellen had spent several months of her life here as a volunteer. She had worked among the fruit orchards, and also in the cafeteria and kitchen of the kibbutz, doing the difficult chores, which are dramatically compounded when serving several hundred kibbutzniks. She had made several friends, one especially who to this day is as close as a mother. Hellen calls this friend affectionately her "Yiddish Mama".

It was during this walk that I was inspired to seek out other Israelis whose life stories had to be told. My wife was in agreement with me as we surveyed the arable fields of the kibbutz and contemplated with awe how in such a short time, Israel had become such a beautiful and productive land. In that same time however, individual lives had been lost, broken and twisted in thousands of agonies. As we thought about the people, I began to make plans to meet more of them, and to collect their stories so that they could be

35

told to others. Even on the trip home, I began making notes about this project, which would take me more years to complete than imagined.

From my home in Miami, I began to write to some of my friends in Israel, who I knew had unique stories to tell. I asked them if they would be interested in becoming part of this project by granting me an interview at some future date. I lined up a few people who were willing to tell their stories to me and record them on a little battery-operated tape recorder. I had some vacation time coming to me which I asked for and received in February 1987. I planned for another trip to Israel to learn more about Zion's people.

The day finally came when I kissed Hellen good-bye, and headed for New York, to connect with an El Al flight to Israel. She would follow me about a week later. It would once again be a step of faith, traveling on a standby ticket as the bookings were reported as "full." I arrived at the El Al counter at Kennedy Airport, and once again stood before a couple of Israeli security agents who looked me over very well and asked a lot of questions. Having passed that part of the maze in getting to the airplane, I was filled with joy when my good friends, an ultra-orthodox rabbi and his family came to see me off.

We had met a year earlier, as a result of a "wrong" telephone number being dialed. He called from his home in Brooklyn, looking for some long lost "Kosak" in Miami, and he reached me. When he asked the question, "This is Rabbi Segal in New York, do you know a Rabbi Segal?" I answered, "No....but I certainly would like to!"

We continued a conversation, which lasted a full hour....on his dime! We had a few more telephone conversations, and eventually my wife and I sat face to face with this wonderful man and his sons in a Miami Beach hotel, as we celebrated a Sabbath dinner together.

Our friendship grew quickly, and here he was again, having driven through the traffic, having found a place to park, and having made his way through the crowds at Kennedy Airport just to see me off as I went to Israel. We had discussed my planned project both in person and by phone, and he was an encouragement to me, as was the rest of his family.

Although I was very glad to see the Rabbi and his family, I was disappointed when the boarding agent informed me that there would be no more seats available on the flight, and that I along with about a half-dozen "standbys" would not be boarded.

I tried to look at it from the larger perspective. The same God who created all of the heavens and the earth, had dominion over El Al's seat count, and it was not His plan to seat me on this particular flight.

It mattered not. As the Rabbi and his family saw the problem, I was simply enfolded as a member of the family, plopped in their big brown Buick, and away we went, zooming along the expressway to Brooklyn, where I was to be a guest in the Rabbi's home for the evening. Barry, the Rabbi's son, wove the big Buick through the snarled New York traffic, and the big Rabbi rode shotgun in the front seat, his long black beard complimenting the black "uniform" of his ultra-orthodoxy.

On arriving at his Brooklyn home, I was made to feel immediately at ease. Mrs. Segal, a dynamo of hospitality, hustled around the kitchen and brought us some tea, fruit, and some other snacks to eat. Her manner very much reminded me of the central character of a TV show that I watched as a youngster. The character was "Molly" and played by Gertrude Berg. She was a picture of warmth and love as she took charge in her kitchen domain. We sat at the table eating, laughing, and discussing Israel and life in general before we all went to bed.

I awoke to a dreary gray New York morning. The Segal household however was alive with activity. The Rabbi had already been to the synagogue to pray and had come home before I showed my face. We breakfasted, and I had the opportunity to make some rounds with him, as we first went to accomplish some *mitzvot* (charitable acts), and then visited some other friends. As we drove through the Brooklyn traffic, little white flakes of snow began to float from the heavens. In a few hours, there was a good six inches on the ground, and there seemed to be no let-up. My mind wandered to Kennedy Airport where I envisioned delayed flights, closed runways, and snarled reservations. My anticipations were confirmed a few hours later when I called the airport to find that it was indeed closed, and that there was no estimate as to when it would open again.

As we sat in the Rabbi's home, I was speaking with his daughter, a 19-year old with a vision for Israel, and a love for God. As we shared our mutual trust in the God of Abraham, I looked out the window at the snow, and worried out loud, that "perhaps I had missed the Lord's will, and that I really was not to go to Israel."

"Oh no," came the encouraging reply, "God's just testing you!" My innermost sensing was that this 19-year old was right, but my mind still wondered if I had not created my own wild-goose chase.

The snow finally stopped, but there was quite an accumulation and no vehicles were moving. I called the airport and got the runaround. How can anyone REALLY know when an airport will open? The best estimates are often many hours in error. As an experienced pilot, I knew that from having hung around in turbulent holding patterns, watching my fuel gauges make their way toward empty. While I was flying circles in the "soup", some snow committee was surveying the situation from the windows of their offices while they had conversations by radio with the guys who were pushing the mounds of snow around with their plows. As to when a given runway or airport would open under such conditions was anybody's guess.

That's the kind of answer I got as I phoned El Al's operations and reservations. If the snow committees didn't know, how was some reservations agent going to know? So, the "if's" and "maybes" were sprinkled liberally throughout any conversation spoken from the airport end of the line. I gave it one last shot, about two hours before the scheduled departure of El Al. "Yes, Yes, We are flying tonight! You must come to the airport right now if you want to make the flight!"

It was a real "fire drill" to head out to the airport. The big Buick slid and drifted all over the residential streets of Brooklyn, as Barry blew his way through the slush and ice on the back streets and finally to a main artery. The Rabbi fired a few orders from the right front seat, and I hung on for dear life in the back seat as we maneuvered our way around other traffic heading in the same direction.

Quick hugs, thank-yous, and promises to call were the last interactions as I ran quickly to the El Al counter, went through the security check, and dashed for the airplane. There were enough seats tonight! I found mine, put away my carry-on bag, and began thinking about what was in store for me in Israel. I continued to wait but the flight was not departing. The hour was getting late.

The Orthodox Jews on board began to get restless. I noted that it was Thursday night, and if the plane did not take-off within the next hour, we would not arrive in Israel in time to observe the laws of **Shabbat** (the Sabbath). One of those laws is that you are not to travel on Shabbat, unless you walk. In addition, you are not allowed to carry a load, therefore an observant Orthodox Jew would not place himself in a position to be carrying a heavy suitcase from an airplane that had landed after sundown, and then climb into a taxi. It would be a serious violation of some of the 613 laws of Jewish Orthodoxy.

The Jewish Sabbath begins at sundown on Friday evening, and lasts until sundown on Saturday evening. Because Tel Aviv time is seven hours ahead of New York time, and the fact that it takes about eleven hours to make the flight, 11:30 PM in New York would be the approximate cut-off time. If we were unable to move by then, the flight would be canceled.

The men driving the snowplows were unable to get the job done before the time, and it meant that everyone would now have to depart the airplane. Because El Al had anticipated the airport would open on time and had told passengers to come at once to the airport, they felt responsible. They ordered up the buses that would drive us into Manhattan to a hotel.

Tired and frustrated, we who had been airplane passengers suddenly became bus passengers. Almost everyone slumped in their seats as they listened to the El Al representative over the bus intercom. "I've got good news, and I've got bad news! The good news is that we have some hotel rooms for you in the City. The bad news is that because of the snowstorm and other canceled flights, there aren't many of them, and we are asking those who are traveling alone to double up with someone."

There were a lot of moans and groans, but I was grateful that I wasn't left to walk around an airline terminal for the next 24 hours, as would have been the case with some of America's airlines. We disembarked from the bus and crowded around the hotel desk. An

Israeli businessman standing next to me looked at me. I looked at him. We both shrugged our shoulders and said, "Why not?" The clerk handed me the key.

The businessman's name was appropriately, "Israel". We would have to put up with each other for the night. As we walked for the elevator, little did I know that this man would become one of my best friends. As I shared with him my commitment to his nation and people, and told him that there were thousands of others in the world who had this same concern, he expressed further interest. Thinking about his brother-in-law, an Orthodox Jew in Israel, he said, "You are going to have to meet a man in Israel who will be very interested in what you are doing." I had also told him about my attempt to gather the life stories of Israelis for the purpose of creating a book.

We exchanged information about our families, jobs, life in general, and soon fell asleep. I found out later, to his chagrin, that I snored like a buzz saw while he fought the urge to clobber me with a pillow or a phone book. In the morning, Israel had to make a few calls and decided to do a little last minute shopping. It was now Friday in New York, and it also meant that El Al would not be able to fly that night because it was now the Sabbath. Thus, I had to stay in New York for yet another day.

I called the Rabbi's home and spoke to his wife, Vered, telling her what had happened. I explained to her that I did not have the heart to call the Rabbi back to the airport at such a late hour after the flight had canceled, and thus I had chosen to go into New York with the rest of the El Al passengers. "Well, don't just stay in the hotel. Come to us and you will have Shabbat dinner with us," she invited.

I left a note for my newly found friend, Israel, who had already gone to run a few errands. I checked out of the hotel. I made my way on the subway where I followed the directions given to me over the phone. I *schlepped* (carried/dragged) my suitcase along with me and got aboard the #3 train to Brooklyn.

As I boarded the train, I still felt a little unsure about being on the right one. I spotted a young *Yeshiva* boy, complete with his black wide-brimmed hat and his *pais*, the long curly side-locks of hair. I quietly approached him on the semi-crowded train. "Excuse me, but I'm trying to get to Kingston Avenue in Brooklyn. Am I on the right train?"

As I held on to the pole and the train rolled away, swaying and clattering, this young man (probably about 14 years old) looked at me and with an enthusiasm written on his face, calmly and in a soft but inflective voice responded to my question with, "Messiah is coming! Messiah is coming!" This was no "crazy" that you might see around the subways of New York. This was a well-groomed intelligent young man who spent hours each day studying the Holy Scripture.

I smiled, and my spirit inside leaped for joy. "I agree with you. I know that He is coming, and soon." It was refreshing to speak to this young man, dedicated to God, studying and anticipating the coming of Messiah. With many of my Jewish friends as I have discussed this subject, I have pointed out that our differences can be boiled down to one word.

I have said, "You believe that Messiah is coming, and I believe that Messiah is coming... AGAIN." Or, as Teddy Kollek, the world-famous former mayor of Jerusalem once said to a group of Christians, "We believe that Messiah is coming, and you believe that Messiah is returning."

I continued to speak to this Yeshiva boy, and learned that we would both be getting off at the same stop. We left the train, and walked a couple of blocks together as he directed me to my destination. "God bless you mightily," I said as we parted company.

I arrived at Rabbi Segal's home and was again greeted warmly. Much seemed to have happened since I had left 18 hours ago. I would remain as the Rabbi's guest, and would celebrate Shabbat dinner with him and his family. I had the opportunity to meet other members from the Jewish community, and was able to take part in the Friday pre-Sabbath rush to get all the chores and traveling done before sundown. The Jewish community in Brooklyn was a flurry of activity, as each observant Jew went here and there accomplishing those last minute tasks, so that the Sabbath would be exactly what it is supposed to be, a day of rest. An observant Jew will not even carry money on the Sabbath, and certainly there would be no business transactions on that day. In today's modern living, the Mosaic Law which forbids the lighting of a fire on the Sabbath, is extended to mean that to start an automobile engine or to turn on an electric light, is to build a fire, and thus forbidden.

There are devices in most Orthodox Jewish homes that turn the lights on and off automatically, so that its inhabitants will not have to be part of "building a fire" on the Sabbath. It is also forbidden to write on the Sabbath, as it is considered to be a form of work. There are many laws of this nature, and I as a guest in the Rabbi's home had to try very hard to observe them so as not to dishonor his tradition. I have to admit that I stumbled on a couple of occasions, but the Rabbi was able to smile and forgive me. I was like a young colt trying to walk in a place where I had not the equipment. My "legs of orthodoxy" were very weak. The Rabbi and his family were most understanding and forgiving.

As the Friday sun disappeared over the western horizon, the flurry of activity died in the Brooklyn Jewish community, just as it had seven hours earlier in Jerusalem. A peace began to settle over the household, and the rigors of the previous week were placed on the back shelves of each person's mind. There was plenty of food and warm conversation that brought relaxation and joy among those of us gathered together. My frustration of having been delayed for four days in New York had been laid to rest, and I drank thirstily of the gracious fellowship that was offered to me by the Rabbi and his family.

As we delighted in the Sabbath meal, the *kiddush* was prayed over the wine, the *challah* bread was broken and passed around the table, and once again, the peace of God settled upon yet another Jewish home, as it has for thousands of years. In spite of all the persecution and the ravages of evil men driven to annihilate the Jewish people, I was witness to yet another Sabbath, and yet another example of God's faithfulness to His people.

As darkness fell on Saturday, the Sabbath was officially over, and it was now permitted to drive, to fly, to cook, and to re-enter the realities of life in the world. Once again, I was treated to a ride in the big Buick, and soon found myself aboard the El Al Boeing 747 waiting to take its precious cargo of hundreds of lives to the Land of Promise.

The departure was uneventful, and as the flight leveled off at altitude for the long overnight flight, the movie began. As a preliminary to the main feature, there was a short segment depicting a day in the life of an El Al pilot. A mention was made that this pilot had survived the Holocaust as a young boy in Europe, but I did not catch his name.

I reached out and grabbed an El Al flight steward as he hurried down the aisle to serve the passengers. "Excuse me, do you happen to know the name of the El Al captain that was featured on the video only a few minutes ago," I asked? "No, I'm sorry, but I can probably find out. Why do you want to know?" came back the reply, half-caring, and half-suspicious.

I explained my project to Amos, and he immediately responded, "You MUST talk to my mother. She has a story that you will hardly believe." I gratefully thanked him for his suggestion, we exchanged addresses, phone numbers, and schedules, and I once again turned my thoughts upward to Him, the One who knows all things. I silently thanked Him and realized that He was more than able to ordain the crossing of two lives, perhaps using even a delaying snowstorm for His purpose. Amos, the flight steward, also obtained the name of the El Al captain for me. After our arrival in Israel, he was kind enough to place a note from me in his company mailbox.

After a couple of phone calls and confirmations, I received the directions to meet Amos at a large intersection in Holon, a suburb area of Tel Aviv. I zipped down the mountains of Jerusalem in my rented Mitsubishi and met Amos on a rainy day. I followed him in his car as we wound our way through the narrow residential streets of Bat Yam to where I would meet his mother.

We walked into the modest but comfortable upstairs apartment, and I stood face to face with Zelda, a woman who had love in her eyes, but whose outward appearance revealed a long life of struggle and hardship. She stood barely five feet tall. Her hair had long ago grayed, partly because of the natural process of aging, but partly I am sure due to the experience of life. She was fluent in Hebrew, Yiddish, Polish and some Russian. Amos would interpret for us.

After feeding Amos and me, Zelda humbly sat down on her living room couch, politely scoffing in Yiddish at "why her life would have any importance, and that she was like so many others. Why would I be interested in her?" I looked at her, studying her, trying to see inside, trying to note any expression or body language that would help me to know her better. As she spoke in Yiddish to her son, he would then translate her words into English. I pressed the "record" button on my little recorder, asked some introductory questions, and began to listen.

# 3

# ZELDA

In 1920, Bilgoraj was a simple town not far from the city of Lublin, Poland. It was a place where the horse and wagon did the work of today's vans and automobiles. Plumbing was almost non-existent and Yitzak eked out his living as a water carrier in the Jewish quarter. He was familiar to all, shuffling through the streets with a rugged pole hanging over his shoulder, balancing two heavy buckets filled with water.

There was always the need for water, and for a *zloty* or two, the backbreaking labor of dozens of daily trips from the well to individual households allowed him a meager subsistence. In addition to being a human mule who brought water to numerous households, he hauled live animals to the butcher for the local residents and brought them back as meat to the households. He was also a local messenger, carrying about with him the good and the bad news, which fed the spirits and souls of Bilgoraj's inhabitants.

Bilgoraj was Zelda's birthplace. She was the eldest of six children....two girls and four boys. Her father was a local merchant whose buying and selling transactions earned a small percentage for his family and himself. Zelda was Jewish and a part of a community within a community. There had been a Jewish community within Bilgoraj since the 17th century. It was here that many Jews perished in the anti-Semitic massacres of 1648-49. According to the poll-tax records, there were 661 Jews in Bilgoraj in 1765. By 1920 there were about 3,800 and by the outbreak of World War II, Bilgoraj was home for some 5,000 Jews.

Life was basic and Spartan and in the Jewish tradition almost everything took second place to obtaining an education. A family would do without the right food and sacrifice almost any material possession so that there would be money for another book or tuition. Most of the Jewish children already knew how to read before they entered school.

There were no TV's or radios, no VCR's or health spas to while away the time. While father was out making his last transactions of the day, mother would spend a few minutes with the children teaching them another letter of the alphabet, or explaining a newly discovered word, while preparing the meals the "old-fashioned" way.

To be a Jew in Zelda's home was not to be totally religious nor completely secular, but the two aspects were interwoven. There was no question that God was watching over her family, that He existed, and that He was to be honored, although she does not remember the strict observance of religious tradition or frequent trips to the synagogue.

Although there were those in the Jewish community who had fairly high standards of living for the time, the majority had to be satisfied to make ends meet on a day by day basis. A new dress for Zelda would be a major family event, and a decision to spend the money would have taken some careful deliberation. Such a purchase would mean that some other area of family need would go unmet. Even a "new" dress for Zelda was usually second hand but would be adequate, appreciated, and always meticulously clean. Zelda still remembers the smell of her clothes as always being fresh and clean.

She attended a public school in Bilgoraj, and some of her first unpleasant memories were experienced in that setting. There was no question as to who was a Jew and who was a Gentile in the classroom setting. Zelda remembers one particularly cruel teacher frequently punishing the Jewish boys in his class for infractions that were done by others. These young kids would be made to hold out their palms, and would be whacked repeatedly with a stick or a ruler.

One Polish teacher held the Jewish children of his classroom for ransom. He would tyrannize the children in school, and then go to the Jewish shops where their parents labored for their meager livings. He "charged" the items that he took from the display counters, never paying what he owed for the goods received. He would then ease up on the children in the classroom. Everyone was afraid of him. He could make life miserable for the little ones, holding the power to physically punish as well as grade them low on their report cards. To hold power over someone else's children was to tyrannize the parents as well. When he would visit a shop, the food or the trousers that he "needed" were given without resistance by the Jewish owners, with the hope that their little Yossi or Miriam would not suffer at school.

One young Jewish pupil, a boy, had a particularly nice head of hair. The teacher did not like it, and ordered it cut. The message was sent home to the parents. The parents sent back a polite but firm reply, "Please inspect our son's hair, and if it is not clean and tidy, we will do something to correct the matter, but if his hair is clean and neat, we would like to leave it as it is." A few days later, a barber brought into the school by his teacher held down the Jewish lad, and his head was shaved. The explanation was that it was not the "style" of the other children, and it was improper for a Jewish boy to have long hair.

There was little or no justice in the class. Whenever something was broken or missing, the words of accusation were spewed. "You Jews......you Jews......Look what you did now!" The meaning of scapegoat was learned long before the word itself.

Instead of being a foundation for improved education the schooling that the Jewish children brought from their homes merely provoked jealousy and resentment, seemingly more from the teachers than the students. When a Jewish child would walk into an elementary school classroom already able to read, he was resented and usually received poorer grades than his Gentile counterpart. Such was the lot of the Bilgoraj Jews of the 1920's, although these persecutions were really blessings in disguise that trained many of them for that which was to come a decade later and beyond.

Life continued in Bilgoraj. Yitzak, the water carrier continued to wear out shoes and boots as he shuffled around the town bringing his payload to his customers. The few coins that he collected would get him through another day. Zelda continued in public school and made it through in spite of some hate-filled and arrogant teachers. She would go to the Jewish schools in the afternoon, where she would learn Jewish tradition.

In 1939, Zelda, as a teenager, peered from the window of her home and saw the mountain people of Czechoslovakia identified by the unique style of boots that they wore. They were rugged walking shoes that did not fit the style of the footwear worn by the folks in Bilgoraj. The tired refugees began trickling into Poland in small numbers at first, increasing the flow as time continued. She remembers the shoes, the many faces, and the strange language. They were people running away from the Nazis, some from having faced them first hand and others from having heeded the warnings of their fellow citizens. They had made the difficult decision to leave home and property and flee with their lives.

There were others who slogged through Bilgoraj from Germany and Hungary. The refugee business began to flourish among many of the Poles. People would arrive from one place with a note from someone else. This would be their passport for further help, for which the fleeing refugees, many of them Jews, paid dearly with money and jewelry. They would be smuggled to any number of towns, cities, cellars, and hideouts, where they would hopefully survive the Nazi machine which was filled with fuel and already moving fast through Eastern Europe.

At times, the hoof beats of horses clopped all through the night, as waves of humanity streamed toward some place, any place that would hopefully provide refuge from the war machine which was not far behind. Although some of these refugees were not Jews, most were.

News traveled slowly in the late 30's, and Bilgoraj was not Warsaw. As the streams of people trudged through Zelda's town, her teenage mind was easily able to understand that there was trouble behind. Although her parents spoke no words of fear, they knew that difficult times were ahead. Their body language communicated their concern.

Their two-room household though crowded, was home. It was where countless Sabbath meals were prepared and eaten. It was where Dad would enter the door and bring the security of his simple presence to his family. It was where Mom was always anchored, cooking the food, doing the laundry, kissing bruised knees, and issuing instructions which would train her brood to cope with life for the day. It was one of the stops for Yitzak the water-carrier.

It was Yitzak who would sometimes carry a chicken or a duck to the *shochet* who would then butcher the animal, examine it, and pronounce it as either kosher or non-kosher. Yitzak would also bring the prepared animal back for cooking at the home. On one occasion, the job fell to Zelda. She brought a duck to the butcher. It was not an event that happened every day, and the thought that a meal with real meat was soon to be a reality stirred her appetite.

Zelda brought the live duck to the *shochet*, Rabbi Rockach, and waited while he did his job. As he inspected and found the nail in the duck's stomach, he had to condemn the food as non-kosher. "Zelda, go and tell your mother that the duck is no good. It's non-kosher." To Zelda, the thoughts of missing that meal caused her to suggest to her mother that they might find a more lenient rabbi who would give a better pronouncement. Rabbi Rockach, however, was the respected authority, and his word stood firm in Zelda's household. The duck would not be eaten.

Rabbi Rockach was a deeply loved man in his community, and had the appearance of being a man of learning and leadership in the Bilgoraj Jewish community. As the Nazis closed in, tradition had to take back seat to necessity, and his followers convinced the Rabbi that he would be better to bear the shame of being beardless, rather than have the Nazis grab him immediately if and when they came into town. He listened to reason, and reluctantly submitted, shaving his beard. This act probably saved his life, and he was able to escape

Poland and find his way to Palestine before the Holocaust was spooled up to full throttle by the Nazis.

The "if and when" day arrived, and Nazi soldiers appeared in Bilgoraj, many on horseback. They had been preceded on September 11, 1939 by the German *Luftwaffe* as they bombed and set fire to the Jewish quarter. To Zelda, the Germans looked fat. However they looked, they were cruel. They continued the process of burning the entire town. Zelda's Uncle Mordechai stopped in the street to observe, not believing his eyes. Those same eyes would provide vision for only a few more seconds. A German soldier raised his arm, took aim, and squeezed the trigger of his Luger. Uncle Mordechai collapsed on the cobblestone street, robbed of life, no longer of value to anyone except as a memory. The fires continued to spread, and more were lit. People ran everywhere, looking for their fathers, mothers, sisters, and brothers.

Screams of fear echoed through the streets above the roar and crackle of raging flames. Mothers and fathers yelled for their children, and children cried for their parents. Cocky German soldiers shot and burned mercilessly. A few resistance soldiers around Bilgoraj fled and had to give in to the mighty Nazi *blitzkrieg*. Zelda's mother and father gathered the family together in a desperate huddle. Decisions had to be made immediately!

Zelda, the oldest, now 18, was paired with her brother Yankel, only a year younger. Zelda's father and mother knew that they would not be able to move themselves and the younger children away quickly enough. The parents decided that the heritage of their family must be carried by Zelda and Yankel. "Go!....Run!.....Run away!.....Rescue yourselves!" They were the last words Zelda heard from her parents as they pressed what little money they had into her palm and sent her and Yankel on their way. There was no time for long hugs. There were no tears. The floodgate that would allow them to run was dammed up by fear and terror as Zelda and her brother Yankel ran for their lives before a backdrop of their burning town.

With only the clothes on their backs, and the small amount of money pressed into her palm, she and her brother began a journey which would last for years and which would be punctuated with a thousand tribulations. The hideous sounds of war raged behind them as darkness fell. Bilgoraj was aflame and thousands were massacred.

Zelda and Yankel made connection with one of the Polish "rescuers" who had a wagon. This particular man's rescue operation, like many others, had an admission charge however. If you wanted to ride, you paid. Along with other fleeing Jews, they sat in the back of his horse-drawn wagon and headed for Przemysl, about 40 miles south of Bilgoraj, and right on the Russian border.

The two teenagers huddled in the wagon, frightened and alone. No conversation was allowed, which turned everyone inward to the corridors of their minds. As the refugees dipped into the well of their own thoughts, more terrors greeted them as they thought of those left behind. Would they see their parents, sons, and daughters again? What lay ahead for them? Exhaustion and fear gave way to sleep as many dozed off for moments at a time, only to awaken to renewed terror. The wagon kept moving ever slowly through the night and through or around the villages of Tarnograd, Adamowka, and Sieniawa. They paralleled the San River, a lazy stream that emanates in the mountains of Southern Poland, and later joins the Wisla River, which runs north through Warsaw and empties into the sea at Gdansk.

The steady clopping of the laboring horses, the scraping wheel bearing, and the squeaks and sways which confirmed to the dazed inhabitants that their little ark was in motion, came to a stop. They had reached an intermediate waypoint short of the Russian border. Another "rescuer" stood there ready to help.....for a price!

"After all, there is a war, and it is dangerous, and a man needs to eat, right?" "Thank you, Miss." "Thank you, Sir." "Is that all the money you have young man?" "Well, that will do.....Just head over there with the rest of your bunch, and I'll be with you in a few minutes to lead you to the border." While there were many opportunists who enriched themselves and took advantage of the Jewish plight, it must also be said that there were many Poles who risked and even lost their lives in attempting to help the Jews in one of their darkest hours.

The wagonload of Jews had climbed down from their wooden

chariot, and paid their "toll" for getting across the next obstacle on their way of escape. The trip had taken two nights and a full day in between. There had been no food. This cartload of Jews who escaped with only their lives began to ponder whether possessing life alone was worth the agony.

There was not one complete family among them. Everyone was missing someone. Others arrived at this "jumping off" point, and they soon confronted the Russian soldiers at the border. "You cannot cross! Go back!" came the shouts in Russian. Zelda does not remember how it happened, but eventually, she and the others ran across the border, through the woods and were taken prisoner by the Russians.

Prior to leaving their Polish guides and running the border, the Jews were warned by their rescuers to tell no one of how they escaped or who helped them. Naturally, it was to the rescuers own benefit to have this information locked up in the mind and not spoken out to someone else's ears. The rescuers might be able to make a few more runs, with the reward of more money or jewelry, but on the other hand, perhaps more Jewish lives would be saved. No one talked.

After crossing the border, the Jews were huddled together outdoors and made to sit on the ground for about 48 hours more. There still had been no food available to them. Russian guards stood around the group and for a long time offered no assistance. The suspicious Bolsheviks eventually compiled a list of names and began to deal with the tired and hungry Jews who had made it this far.

The September nights were cold, and Zelda and Yankel, along with the hundreds of escaping Jews, who had crossed the border into Russia, chattered and huddled close to each other. They were hungry, without water, warm clothing, or shelter. The only thing surrounding them was a cadre of Russian guards, who were not allowed to engage in conversation.

After this initiation to mother Russia, Zelda and Yankel were brought into a large room—men with men, and women with women. They were made to strip off all their clothes, and they were examined very carefully. Zelda had to run around and jump up and down, just in case this new "spy" that had been caught crossing the border into Russia, had tucked some hidden secrets into the private orifices of her body. This group of Jews was being officially treated as spies.

She was weighed, what few personal possessions she had were confiscated, and she was moved to a place where she could at least wash herself and her clothes with small bits of soap that were provided. She was given some water and a few pieces of bread. She and Yankel were now prepared to head east to the city of Lvov.

The city was part of the Soviet Ukraine, and had not yet been assaulted by the German Nazis. That assault would not take place for another two years, in July 1941. To the horror of some 150,000 Jews who had fled to Lvov from other parts of Europe, the Nazis were welcomed by the local Ukrainian population. Local Ukrainians joined forces with the Nazis, and stirred up hatred toward the Jews, torturing and murdering thousands. In the **Aktion Petliura**, (July 25-27) over 2,000 Jews were shot.

Zelda and Yankel entered the converted school building in Lvov in October 1939, which would serve as their quarters for a short period of time until their "trial". Zelda was called for her private interview. "Where are you trying to go, Zelda?", asked her interrogator. "I want to go home to Poland," she replied.

The young teenager and her brother had been on the road for a couple of weeks. It had not been a high school excursion with knapsacks, hamburgers, and chewing gum. It had been an excursion of terror, sleepless nights, unknown dangers, thirst and starvation.

"I want to go back to Poland," she said again. "Please....help me to get back to my home."

"Who is this.....this.....Yankel, that you are traveling with, Zelda?" Her interrogator took notes.

She did not know it, but her answer would perhaps spell the difference between life and death for her younger brother.

"Yankel is my brother. We came together, running away from the Nazis."

The information was duly noted. As a result of her answer, her life and that of her brother would take different directions.

After the interrogations were over, they were kept in the school building in Lvov. Zelda and Yankel, along with other Jews were allowed some privileges to leave the building during the day. Their heads however, were filled with warnings that they were to pick up nothing that was not their own. They were told that there were "booby-traps" all over Lvov, and that they were designed to blow up if someone touched them. How was a Jewish brother and sister team from the unsophisticated town of Bilgoraj, Poland to know any different?

They had to check back at the school building each night where they would sleep, and they did so. There seemed to be no other option other than to obey. They were able to go to the market and do a couple of odd jobs for small amounts of change. Stories continued to proliferate as to how people were maimed or killed as a result of touching a "booby-trap". It was enough to dissuade Zelda or Yankel from attempting to steal any food or clothing.

Zelda had her "trial," and she was charged with what in essence meant, "breaking into the country." The sentences were handed out to her and her fellow prisoners.

"You....three years in prison for crossing the border without permission!"

"And you....five years for breaking into the country."

No longer were they awaiting trial, but were now convicted criminals of Soviet Russia. She and Yankel were now separated, and their individual journeys would begin. Yankel was sent to Dombas, Russia....a slave labor camp built around coal mining. It is estimated that 90% of the prisoners never lived to see their freedom. If the hard labor and the starvation did not kill a man, then the dampness, cold, and resulting diseases did. Yankel would also meet his own uncle at Dombas, where they would both dig coal for Josef Stalin.

One day, the orders came to march. Zelda and the rest of the prisoners started to walk....and walk....and walk. For miles they continued until finally coming to a railroad station where a train awaited them. Exhausted, starved and thirsty, the desire to live ebbed from the hearts of many of her fellow prisoners.

Zelda was now on her way to Sverdlovsk, Russia. The train ride lasted for a couple of weeks, starting, stopping, waiting, and starting again. There was little or no food. Periodically, the train would stop and the prisoners were allowed off to relieve themselves and to get some water. The train whistle would blow, and that was the signal to get aboard. If a prisoner did not comply he would be left, out in the middle of Russia somewhere. The train would begin to roll slowly and the prisoners would climb aboard sometimes running as fast as their weakened limbs would carry them.

Zelda did experience some acts of kindness from the local citizenry. When she and others would disembark from the train, some of the Russian peasants would give little tidbits of food from their own meager supply.

The long train ride eventually ended and she was taken to her quarters, a prison filled with prostitutes and criminals of all sorts. Her large cell, shared with many other prisoners, was on the fourth floor...BELOW the ground. What was left of clothing was taken from her and she was issued her prison uniform. This wardrobe, with an occasional replacement, would last her through years of hard labor.

As with any prison, Zelda had entered a new society with its own rules. The rules were imposed by the prisoners themselves, and often to make a newcomer feel out of place and uncomfortable, the rules would not be revealed until one was broken. Then, the wrath which was pent up in the depths of their souls would have an excuse for expression. The newcomer would be the recipient.

These petty rules helped to establish the pecking order and the seniority of the old-timers. The greenhorn, who had a lot to learn, suffered until he discovered and understood the rules on his own. Zelda experienced this when she did not wipe her feet on a towel that had been tossed on the floor of the cell. Not knowing that the towel was set there for that purpose, she had broken the rule. In the humiliation, it was surely established that she was a mere newcomer, and she became part of the system that established a superiority among the older prisoners and kept the new ones down.

These rules were not college pranks. They were taken seriously and there was so much terror associated with them, that a prisoner was afraid to sleep at night in a cell with others who had had their rules broken. One dared not become an offender of the code. Things happened at night to those who did.

Her bed was a small mound of straw. She saw daylight only for a few minutes daily when she was allowed to climb the four flights of stairs to ground level and walk about the prison yard. Her other experience with daylight was when she was months later moved out in a work crew, to take her part as a slave for the ruling Russian pharaoh.

Her day began at 5:00 AM. Zelda and her fellow prisoners were allowed about 10 minutes prior to this to wash, dress, and prepare for the coming workday. If a prisoner was not able to "bull" her way in a fight with other prisoners to use the inadequate facilities, it was just too bad. On such a day, one simply did not wash.

It was during this critical 10-minute period each day when a lot of communication took place. In the common shower facilities, messages could be passed to and from other prisoners who would not be available for contact at any other time during the workday.

Breakfast was a cup of weak tea, a small piece of sugar, and a small piece of bread. The sugar came in a hard, "rock" form, and breaking it into equal size pieces to share with each cellmate, usually provoked a fight. Someone would always get too much, and someone else, too little. An occasional rotten potato would find its way into the available food...and according to Zelda, it was truly rotten!

At first, Zelda was unable to force herself to eat such food, but she began to lose weight rapidly. She quickly learned, that even if something was rotten or in terrible condition, you ate it. She would watch to see if other prisoners would turn down the rotten food, and if so, she would eat it. She had made up her mind to live!

The suspicious Russians were still not satisfied to leave Zelda and the other Jews alone. Convinced either by their own paranoia of the Germans, or the lies of Mother Russia, they continued to interrogate her daily when she first arrived at the prison. At first the footsteps of the guard would strike terror into her heart, as he would call out her name for questioning. She would be escorted by two guards with dogs and brought to a room where she was grilled under high intensity lights.

"Who is the leader of your gang that was sent over to spy on us?" The Russians wanted to know the entire hierarchy of this "diabolical plan" to undermine their great social movement. So great was the pressure, that often the Jews would admit to doing something. The interrogators would often open up the questioning with, "Zelda, there is no sense in hiding the facts now. One of the other prisoners who was caught with you has told us about your leadership in the plan. Why don't you just confess everything right now?"

The interrogations went on every night for four months! "What is your father's name? Tell us about your family! What organization do they belong to? Why are you here to spy on the Russian people? Who gives you your orders?" The lights glared in her eyes. The questions pounded away at her senses. There were often two interrogators and only one prisoner in a given session. There were countless numbers of rooms with the same process going on, leveled at the Jewish prisoners.

"Zelda, are you a Zionist?"

"A what?"

"Are you a Zionist?"

Up to this time in her life, she had never even heard the word, "Zionist." She did not even know what it meant, although she had a vision for Zion, because of her father and other Jews who had expressed their desire to go to the Promise Land, and to see Jerusalem.

"How many languages can you speak?"

"Only one.....Polish. I learned from the elementary school. I did not go to high school."

"Who is your leader? Who sent you here? What did the Nazis teach you? What is your agenda?"

The questioning went on for hours and hours....every night, with guards and dogs, interrogators and lights. Zelda had a very strange calm about her throughout. Although she was totally strained and exhausted, she continued to maintain the truth. She refused to capitulate and refused to receive the accusations being fired at her.

"I know nothing. You can do anything that you wish, but I did nothing to the Russian people! I only ran away from the Germans!"

When the session would finally conclude, it would often be daylight. Zelda and some of the other Jewish prisoners would be led back to their cells. There, they had to put up with accusations from the Russian prisoners, who slept through the night and now had the strength to badger the Jews in any number of ways. Zelda would fall asleep, and out of hatred, would be awakened by one of the Russian cellmates.

Zelda and four other Jewish prisoners in the large cell had remained strong in their hearts. They had not given in to the thugs who interrogated them. They decided to go on a hunger strike. They did so and demanded to see the prison leadership, all the while demanding to be moved from their present cell.

She was also picking up the Russian language from the prisoners around her, and was better able to communicate with the Russians in charge. The hunger strike worked. Zelda was moved out of her dungeon cell four floors underground, to a cell on the first floor above ground. She would no longer have to put up with the hatred of her former cellmates, four floors down, but there was also a change in the daily routine.

"Here are your trousers, your work dress, a hat, and these are your pick and shovel," announced the prison clerk as he doled out these supplies to Zelda. She was now assigned to a labor team. The idea seemed to be better than rotting in an underground cell. She would soon see that comparing the above ground labor to the below ground rotting, was like trying to decide if you wanted to be beaten with a whip or a club. In either case it is a horror.

Work began at 5:00 AM. The prisoners would don their work clothes, pick up their tools, and begin their march of several miles to the rock pits where they would work grueling long hours digging and shoveling by hand. The job was a seven-day-a-week ordeal. There were no days off. If it rained or snowed, there were no umbrellas or raincoats. You marched, and you worked! If you lost or broke your shovel or any other tool, you were given another year to your sentence, no questions asked.

The day came when Zelda and her fellow Jews would hear their names called. They were lined up and marched to trains once again. The trip would not be to the Black Sea for rest and recuperation, but to another prison, another 900 miles into the heart of Russia. In most modern countries a 900-mile train ride might last 15 hours or so, but in Russia at that time it was almost another week before she arrived in Karaganda. Bilgoraj was becoming a blurry memory of long ago. Mother and father, Yankel, and Yitzak the water carrier seemed light years away, packed into the recesses of Zelda's mind. It had only been about 6 months since she began the flight from her burning town, and she was now alone......very alone.

Was there anyone alive who would even be thinking of her? Memories of her mother's love, her father's attentiveness and provision, her crowded but love-filled two room home tried to find a place in her life today, but the thoughts were too far up the spectrum to weave them into the tapestry of horror which now surrounded her. She was like the fallen tree in the philosophical argument where it is debated if there is no one to hear the sound of the tree when it hits the ground in the middle of a forest, did it really make a sound? She had to remain in control and be strong. There was enough to be concerned about simply to survive, without giving place to memories that would only discourage her. To lose any energy wondering who might be alive or dead of those who were left behind on that fateful night in Bilgoraj, was of no use.

Five o'clock in the morning came too soon. The march to work would begin. The prisoners started their day, sick, hungry, and exhausted. They were escorted to and from the work area by armed Russian guards. It was several miles from the prison to where the work was performed, and the Russians soon discerned that the prisoners were drained physically from the walk to and from. No doubt, the efficiency of their work could be increased if they were moved closer to the work area.

The Russians erected little huts with tin roofs, which served as prison quarters. They were located near the railbeds where Zelda and her fellow prisoners labored to move heavy trap rock and gravel, railroad ties, and steel rails as they reconstructed much of the track and built new rail lines. Because the prisoners did not have to walk a couple of hours to and from work, they could now spend more time on the job.

A few of the prisoners were allowed to keep some of their personal possessions, which had been confiscated at the time of their arrest. Unbelievably, Zelda was even given back a watch that was taken when she was first incarcerated just after crossing the Russian border from Poland. With these few meager possessions, deals would sometimes be struck with Russian guards, who would take advantage in a game where they were in the catbird seat. They had the food, the guns, the sleep, and the health. The prisoners had no food, no guns, little sleep, and were often ridden with disease and infection. Their judgment was also distorted, influenced by deep fears and terror, as well as an unquenched desire to be free from their circumstances.

A guard would take a watch or gold ring as payment to look the other way. The deceived prisoner, dressed in a prison uniform would disappear off the job in an attempt to escape, from 2,000 miles inside of Russia! The guards knew that it would be a short time before they would be able to start out after the escaped prisoner, and then have the pleasure of shooting him. For those whose hearts were filled with greed and avarice, they were rewarded double, first with the trinket of jewelry, then with the perverse pleasure of killing.

Zelda, a petite and attractive girl with long curly hair, drew the attention of one Russian guard. He became fond of her as he escorted her labor team to and from their huts, and guarded it while they worked. It was a dangerous weakness on the part of the Russian soldier. He could have been severely punished for this display of compassion and breach of Russian military discipline.

As Zelda's labor team was hiking to work, Lev, the Russian guard found his way to where Zelda was marching and whispered a word or two to her.

"Zelda, I saw in the Russian newspaper that the Jewish prisoners will soon be released."

"Yeah, sure...and we will all be invited to the Kremlin to be Stalin's guest for dinner. Lev, tell your stories to someone else!" She continued to march with her eyes cast down, looking at the sweaty garments of her fellow prisoners who marched ahead of her.

Lev, trying to persuade her that it was true, and also trying to win her favor, removed the slice of bread that he had tucked into his armpit. When he felt that no one was looking, he slipped it to Zelda. He began to bring food to her daily, a slice of bread one day, a potato the next.

"Zelda, I have to serve for more time in the army. Here is the address of my mother. When you are released, go there, tell my mother that you know me, and she will take care of you. When I get out of the army, I will come and marry you."

Zelda's mind raced with conflicting thoughts. "Is this some kind of trick? Does this man really love me? Do I matter to anyone? Perhaps my family is going through a trial like me, and I will see them again in Bilgoraj. Lev has been so kind and has taken many risks to bring food to me. Perhaps he is compassionate and his overtures are real."

As all of these conflicts and questions stampeded through her mind, she was too weak and broken to have any romantic inclinations. Lev could have had the looks and charm of Clark Gable or a modern-day Tom Cruise, the tenderness of the most gentle rabbi, and it could not have aroused any interest within her, so deep were the wounds of her spirit, so great was the mountain of unknowns and fears in her soul, so weak was her physical body.

As the days and weeks continued, there was no let up in the labor. Every single day, rain or shine, in spite of snow, sleet, or hail, and with no raincoats, the prisoners marched from their temporary tin-roofed huts over to the railbeds that they were constructing. There, they would find yet another pile of trap rock and gravel to shovel and level, and a new supply of heavy wooden railroad ties and steel rails to lay. While they collapsed in their mats of straw at night, and hoped that their clothing would dry from the sweat and rain, a train would roll up to the place where they had stopped laying track, and would dump more tons of rock and gravel. Zelda, along with the hundreds of other "guests" of Stalin and his lieutenants, would march each day at 5:00 AM and this suffering, but not-yet-defeated gathering of humanity would continue to do the work of payloaders and bulldozers.

"Zelda, please....you can go to my mother in Uzbekistan and she will take care of you." Lev was still trying to convince her that she should marry him once she was released. He continued to hide the bread in the armpit of his uniform, and would hand it to her when the coast was clear. As his overtures played upon her heart, it became clear over time, that this Russian soldier, perhaps bruised in his own emotions, was not speaking his words out of a heart of compassion and love. He had a Babylonian heart that wanted to buy his wife with the few slices of bread that he dispensed. Zelda had no interest in this man, and the call of Bilgoraj and her family was still loud in her mind.

The year was now 1941, and Zelda had been in prison for almost two years. The project on the railbeds was completed and she was moved about 10 miles to another place where the male prisoners would smash rocks all day with sledge hammers, and the women would carry the rocks and stones to a designated area where they would be piled up for who knows what. The hard labor went on. People died.....but rain or shine, Sunday or Monday, they marched....and they worked, they lived, and they died.

There were small displays of compassion from some of the Russian guards. Even they were disenchanted with the revolution, and began to distantly befriend some of the prisoners.

"Take it easy.....don't work so hard," would come the whisper. "Slow down....save your energy.... it's going to be OK!" But while there were voices of empathy, there were still others that came right straight from Stalin's cookie-cutter. They were the ones that would beat or shoot, just for something to do. One never really knew which of the guards might be nice today, or which one would need to curry some favor with a superior tomorrow. Which one would change philosophical colors according to his mood, from compassion to cruelty?

Food was still at a minimum, and there were times when Zelda would work an entire day and would only have one slice of bread to eat. She, along with the others, lost substantial amounts of weight. No longer was there any sign of health and vitality among the prisoners. They were now like walking skeletons, barely able to move, not caring whether they lived or died. At one of the lowest points in her prison experience, she lost almost all hope. The 5:00 AM march would continue, with no let up, no days off, no food, and no rest. She and many of the others were transferred. Apparently enough stones had been carried and piled, and they were put to work on farms.

The farms however, were not located anywhere near Karaganda, and the prisoners were loaded on another train and sent hundreds of more miles into the "breadbasket" of Russia, to a town called Juma in the province of Uzbekistan. It meant more days on the train, stopping, starting, swaying, starving, and fearing. Bilgoraj, Poland and her family were now further from her, not only in time, but also in geographical distance.

As the women worked in the potato fields, some of their fellow Russian prisoners would build small underground fires that would produce no smoke. They would quickly dig a pit, get the fire going, and would take some potatoes that were being harvested, and would cook them slowly in the field. The women would now be able to eat. They began to build back their long-lost strength.

An underground economy began to thrive. Russian guards would trade some bread for a piece of jewelry, or perhaps some luxury item would find its way into the barter system. Now there was even a Russian doctor assigned to them, and there was also a clinic where the sick could recover. A small gift twisted out of the barter system would move the doctor's heart to the point where he would prescribe a day in bed. Zelda remembers that on more than one occasion she showed up with concocted stomach pains and other ailments. On occasion, she would be rewarded with a day of rest, a Sabbath, wrenched from the arms of the great Bolshevik revolution.

The farm work continued. It was never easy, but far more bearable than lifting railroad ties and shoveling trap rock. And, on a farm, one could almost always find food. Unknown to her, the war was winding down in Europe. The viper that had led Germany to commit some of the most heinous crimes in history, had also led an entire nation to destruction and would soon perish as a coward in a Berlin bunker.

As the official war ended, other personal battles were still going on. Negotiators and diplomats exchanged offers, and in one of these dialogues there was an effect, which resounded even as far as a Juma farm. Zelda was informed that she and the other Jewish prisoners would be released.

The non-Jewish Russian prisoners began to cry, perhaps out of empathetic joy that they felt for the Jews who would soon be released, but many out of bitterness at the fact that they would have to continue to endure life as a slave to Stalin's Russia. To know that someone near would be released, adds pain for the ones who were not so fortunate. They would have to continue bearing the shame as well as the physical hardships of human slavery.

It seemed unbelievable, but with all of the moving around, there really was a file on Zelda, papers that proved she was a person. A clerk filled out a few forms, lifted a stamp from the desk to the inkpad to the paper and back to the desk. In three fast practiced motions, the "pom, pom, pom" of those stamps hitting the paper became a trumpet that announced that Zelda was free!

But free to do what? She was given the choice to go to one of three places, Tashkent, Alma-Ata, or the place where she now stood....Juma. It was 1946, and she had been a prisoner since 1939. She had the clothes on her back, a piece of paper that proved she was free, and the choice to go to one of three towns in Southern Russia.

As she and many of the other Jewish prisoners opted for the more familiar Juma, they took a short train ride from their release point. On their way to Juma, they met ordinary Russian citizenry on the train. Most avoided the newly released and disheveled prisoners, but some began to help, offering food and clothing from their own travel bags. They disembarked at the Juma train station, and began to limp into the town. Citizens saw the walking skeletons draped with decrepit prison garments, and most turned their backs and walked or ran away in fear.

Others however, with hearts of compassion, gave them small amounts of change and some food. Zelda remembers the kindness of some of them. "They were very kind, and we did not even have the strength to show how grateful we were."

Many of the prisoners went to where they could obtain food in any fashion or form. Unfortunately, those that gave or sold the food to the newly released prisoners were no more aware of the dangers than the famished and severely weakened former prisoners. Little did they know that many of their body mechanisms and chemistry had almost shut down, and had to be built up slowly before there would be a physical capacity to digest normal food. Hundreds died from trying to eat a normal diet. Having come so far....having survived years of slavery where hundreds of others succumbed to disease and hopelessness, the very freedom that had been so longed for, ended their lives. They died in agony, their bodies overloaded with the protein and carbohydrates that could not be processed.

Zelda came across people who were extremely kind and generous.

This demonstration of kindness, the first in over 6 years was like turning a key which unlocked a compartment of the soul allowing her to express gratitude, anger, grief, and a full spectrum of emotions that had until now been brutally incarcerated in the recesses of her mind.

"God....who did I kill? Who did I murder to deserve all this punishment? What did I do that was so harmful?" Until this time, all of her energy was directed to survival. Now, for the first time in 6 years, she sat down and cried. She wept from the core of her being as she thought back to Bilgoraj, to her Uncle Mordechai whose life was stolen by a Nazi bullet, and to her mother and father, and Yankel, and the others.

"God....What did I do!!!? What did I do!!!?" The festering infection of her soul had been opened, and the spiritual pus began to flood from within, bringing more pain, but at the same time, relief. Though free from a physical prison, she was now still captive by the walls of confusion and fear. She was still thousands of miles from Poland with no place to live, no job, and no money. Zelda was barely able to speak Russian, and nothing changed the fact that she was still Jewish.

"Why are you crying?" came the gentle question. Zelda explained her circumstances, and received some comfort from this woman.

"I have a son, an only son, and he is away. Perhaps God will help my son if I help you now." She invited Zelda to her meager home.

"Do you mind sleeping in a little room where we do some of our chores and washing?" asked the lady.

"Oh, I don't care. I am just grateful for a place to stay." And so, Zelda had her immediate needs met. The woman had a horse, a cow, some pigs, a dog and a cat. She took care of them well, feeding them before she fed Zelda or herself. When these chores were done, she and Zelda ate.

Perhaps she had been recently infected. Or perhaps her body had been so held captive by a resisting fighting spirit to simply survive, that what struck now was unable to manifest until Zelda began to relax and believe that she was out of the prison.

She began to shiver, and break into a malaria-like fever and symptoms. She would be at her worst about twice a day. The lady continued to feed her, and wrapped her in animal furs and blankets, keeping her warm. It was not long before she took Zelda to the hospital, where she was received and brought back to health. The woman came to the hospital regularly to visit and to comfort Zelda.

Leaving the hospital, Zelda found another place where she was able to live. She performed chores around the house and farm in exchange for food and shelter. There was no money paid to her, and so although she had her basic needs met, there was no way to begin saving for a trip back to Poland.

Zelda ran across a friend from prison. They had been together from their first days of incarceration in Sverdlovsk and Karaganda. They were reassurance for each other, and began to look for work together. They approached the village leader, and told him that they would be willing to do anything. They told him of their plight as Jews, but he did not know what it was to be a Jew. He understood only that they were Poles, and he admired their willingness to work.

As Zelda and her friend worked the odd jobs that were available, more good news came their way. Negotiations between the Polish and Russian governments paved the way for repatriation of thousands. Through cumbersome and bureaucratic procedures, Zelda at last possessed the official paperwork that "proved" that she was a person. Without the papers, she did not exist in the eyes of officialdom. Her departure date would be in two weeks.

Other signs that the war was over greeted her daily as she watched the Russian wounded make their way back to their villages and homes. Streams of battered soldiers flowed from the battlefields of a vicious shooting war, to little private wars of isolation and handicap in a nation starving of food, order, and compassion. They brought with them, graphic accounts of the Jewish *Shoah* (annihilation), the Holocaust. Zelda's worst fears were beginning to receive confirmation.

Stalin's victorious but bloodied army haltingly disembarked the dreaded trains, many without an arm or a leg, others blind and maimed in hundreds of ways, all of them glad that it was over, but suffering within the ravages that war does to all. They would now have to fight the battle of rehabilitation under a government that had no ability or real desire to help.

During those days, the conflict of wanting to return to Poland

and being afraid of what she might find, tore at her. There was no question as to whether or not she would make the trip and leave Russia, however, the fears that had been tucked away in the folds of her memory for the past six years faced her head on, and there was no getting around them.

"Will I see Yankel? I wonder if Father and Mother are alive? What will I find in Bilgoraj?" These questions and a hundred more whirled in her mind. A monster of fear would frequently express itself, tearing with its claws against the inner core of her being. But through all of the pain and uncertainty, she would go back and would face whatever was in store.

As Zelda waited in Juma, she would watch an occasional government train come through and stop. The open freight cars would be heaped full of sugar beets and other farm products. Gangs of young men and old would leap upon the train, and begin to throw down the sugar beets and potatoes to whoever was on the ground to gather them. They looked upon themselves as "Robin Hoods", taking from the rich government and giving to the poor peasants. The train would begin to roll and the potatoes and sugar beets would continue to flow over the sides of the train cars, as human hands worked as fast as they could to keep the flow going. At the very last minute, as the train would pick up speed, the band of men would leap over the sides of the moving train, head back along the tracks and gather up their newly acquired "windfall". These were trying times for everyone living in Europe or Russia, and the hunger among the people spoke with far more volume than any morality that would dictate the lawful behavior of not taking something that is not one's own.

The day arrived when Zelda and hundreds of other former Jewish prisoners would take their last Russian train ride. As she boarded in Juma, papers in hand, it was a day over which to rejoice. The ride was not much different than those of the past, except that the train was heading in the right direction. The psychological desire of the passengers was to get out and push to accelerate the process, the exact opposite of the feelings that prevailed on the inbound trips. They were going home!

The trip was normal for a Russian train at the time. It was slow, tedious, and uncomfortable. Stops would be made along the way where the passengers could obtain a drink of water or tend to other needs, but as before, the stops were shorter than the food supply, and once the train whistle sounded, it meant that one must board immediately or be left behind. Many who were riding in the first car would find themselves running to hop on the 20th car as the big machine pulled away.

With the final paperwork accomplished, and every person accounted for, the train was allowed to cross into Russian-controlled Poland. Zelda was almost home. An excitement gripped her, as did the tentacles of fear over what she might face.

After living on the train for two full weeks, she finally rolled into the station at Breslau, (now Wroclaw) Poland. There were many Jews waiting for her.....really waiting for her and the others. Their arms were open in celebration as their lame and broken brothers and sisters weakly descended from the train. This was the best day in Zelda's life....in her own words, "Someone was waiting for me!"

"Who is willing to stay in a kibbutz at Pilava, and then go on to Palestine?" came the call. Zionist Jews who saw the vision for a Jewish homeland, were there at the station, waiting to welcome those who were barely able to think beyond their next slice of bread. There were kibbutz organizations started among many in Poland, where Jews could join and be trained in the fundamentals of farming, guard duty, language, and a host of other talents, all of which would be needed in Palestine.

Zelda had to have some questions answered first. She had to know about Bilgoraj and her family. Unlike the *kibbutzniks* who waited at the Breslau railroad station for her and the hundreds of others, her parents did not wait...neither did her brother, Yankel...neither did her sister and three other younger brothers...neither did Yitzak the water carrier.

It was through no fault of their own. They had been denied not only the privilege of waiting for their daughter and sister and friend to come home, but they had been denied the right to live. Their train rides had no return trip. The truth of what had all along been feared was now confirmed. Beginning with her Uncle Mordechai who died in the street of Bilgoraj, the victim of a Nazi bullet, the Nazis were thorough enough to annihilate her entire family. Her only hope was that Yankel was on a Russian train somewhere, on his way back to Poland as had been the case with Zelda.

It was not to be. Yankel, along with his uncle, had made it to Dombas, Russia, the slave labor camp built around coal mining, and they were simply worked to death. Zelda's nightmare was reaching its conclusion, although there were many more hardships and disappointments yet to face. She was to find out later that what little was left of her grandfather's bakery, which should rightly have gone to her by inheritance, was claimed by a distant relative, sold, and the money spent. It mattered not. What good were the bricks and mortar of a bakery building when all life of its owners had been extinguished? How could a few *zlotys* soothe the emptiness and pain that assaulted Zelda as each day unfolded with more news of murdered family members and neighbors?

And then there was the haunting memory of her Russian interrogators at the beginning of the nightmare. She clearly remembered telling them that Yankel was her brother. Would he still be alive had she used the word husband instead of brother? Would he have been sent to someplace besides Dombas had his captors thought that he was married to Zelda? Guilt gnawed away at her, as she sifted some of the choices of the past 6 years.

Fortunately, she had the ability to remember the little acts of compassion along the way, which saved her life. For some reason, Lev the Russian guard chose her to be the recipient of his little gifts of bread. An occasional word or thought of encouragement....a sip of hot tea and a warm blanket, ministered by a Russian woman at a time when Zelda was so sick that she would have died had it not been for these small acts of kindness. Even groups of Russian peasants gave the emaciated Jewish prisoners some food parcels to sustain them on the long train trip home. And....at the end of the journey, Jews who "waited for me". Zelda remembers tearfully these small tokens of compassion sprinkled into a life of horror always at just the right time. They are deeds that will never be forgotten. Zelda vaguely acknowledges that to trust it all to some impersonal strokes of "luck" or "fate" would require more faith than to acknowledge that despite all of the suffering, there was an order or a control in her life that was higher than any Stalin or Hitler.

Her new family began to train her for life ahead. Her kibbutz organization at Pilava, Poland provided Hebrew instruction, how to properly guard a kibbutz, and how even to care for a gun. Although unaware, Zelda would soon face those who wanted to finish the job that Hitler was unable to accomplish.

As these new Zionists began to plug their lives into the new order of the kibbutz, Jews from all over Europe wandered to and fro looking for what was left. Central bulletin boards, and walls set aside for the same purpose, contained thousands of notes, tacked, taped, and pinned as a message to a lost loved one.

"Dear Bernie Ostrinsky, If you get to this bulletin board, I am alive and am heading for Warsaw. Josef our brother died at Birkenau. Love, Sarah"

"To Molly Yevschey, If you find this note, know that your beloved husband wanted you to know that he loved you very much but he had not the strength to continue. I was his friend at Buchenwald. If you want to contact me, I will be at Targova 33 in Krakow. Sincerely, Ben Rubin."

There were entire walls of such notes, fluttering by the thousands.....little messages of hope or of stark truth that would help knit back together immediate families, and the Jewish people as a whole. Here and there a note would be recognized, torn from the wall and slipped into a pocket to act as a clue to finding someone lost. Sadly, thousands of notes hung and weathered for months, the addressee having perished in one of the 6,000,000 acts of barbarism.

Small groups of Jews would form and meet on a regular basis to establish a communication net, which would gradually confirm the death and/or the facts surrounding the death of a particular person. Little by little the truth was being established, and the survivors gave comfort to one another. In this manner it was confirmed that Yankel would not come home. Someone who knew someone who knew someone else eventually made the contact with Zelda and her question about Yankel was finally answered.

To step back into the living room situation where I was listening to these details first hand from Zelda's own mouth, and translated by her son, a flight steward with El Al Airlines, it was decided that we all needed to take a time out. Zelda had been pouring out her heart, pulling from a repressed memory, the painful details of the distant past. Amos, her son, had been straining to translate every word from Yiddish into English, and I had been hanging on every word, every gesture, every inflection, so as to fully as possible assimilate what was being said to me.

Zelda walked slowly to the kitchen of her modest apartment in Bat Yam, Israel where we had all gathered. This left me alone with her son Amos. He looked at me, and I could see the strain and the pain on his face. His words quavered from his mouth......"You know?.....I have never heard many of the details of my mother's story." His memory went back to his childhood, and he continued, "When I was a child, I always remember looking at my mother, and feeling sad.....and I never knew why....all I felt was deep sadness.....sometimes I would just cry as a young boy, not knowing why.....and today I am understanding." His head sank into his hands, and this forty year old man with a wife and three children, wept. I sat there with tears running from my eyes as well, feeling helpless to comfort. He had understood the grief that his mother, like so many other Israelis, had tried to hide for all these years, not wanting to remember, and not wanting to burden their children with worry or fear. But, that which had been unspoken with lips had still sent a message from the spirit, creating a wound even in her son's soul, unexplained, but deeply felt.

In my own sadness in being part of this intimate pain being experienced by both mother and son, I yearned and sensed that the words of the prophet Isaiah would soon be fulfilled:

"He will swallow up death for all time, and the Lord God will wipe tears away from all faces, and He will remove the reproach of His people from all the earth; for the Lord has spoken."
(NAS—Isaiah 25:8).

After a short break where Zelda prepared some snacks and tea for us, we continued, she remembering and telling, Amos translating, and I asking and listening.

The horror of Russian labor camps was over. The return to Poland had been accomplished, and the stark cruel facts that all of Zelda's family had been annihilated had been faced. She had to go on. She could not live in the past or on wishes of fantasy. Along with others she began the difficult choices of restructuring her life. There was little feeling or emotion; simply decisive acts that began the training for a new life. Decisions to learn, study, and even to hope again became the foundation stones for a new sanity. The pursuit of new goals, ones that were freely chosen, enhanced the healing process in the soul for those who had been devastated.

Despite the fact that the Jewish community had been dealt such a death blow in Europe, others too had been devastated, and there was little, if any sympathy for the Jews. People were looking after themselves, and there were still plenty who lamented that Hitler did not achieve his goal of eliminating the Jews from the face of the earth. In short, the Jews were still unwelcome in most communities.

Although most national governments in the world were giving lip service to the plight of the Jews, few really did very much to help their cause. The Jewish people themselves had to draw upon every resource possible to help their brothers and sisters who had survived the worst, and had come back to face more hatred and rejection.

Zelda made her way with others from her kibbutz organization to Palezzi, Italy. It was another arduous journey that took her by truck and bus from Poland, through Czechoslovakia, Bratislava, Austria, across the Alps and into Italy. Palezzi was a Spartan military-like barracks, and there the Jews existed on some rations provided by an arm of the United Nations. It was now near the end of 1946. Zelda worked in the kitchen facilities of the camp that was there to prepare food especially for the sick. The days were long, but slowly her people began to regain their health and their hope as they awaited the chance to sail to Palestine. While survivors like Zelda were waiting in camps, the worldwide Jewish community worked feverishly to raise funds, to buy or lease ships, to lobby Congresses and Parliaments throughout the free world to acknowledge the need for help for the Jews and a sovereign homeland.

Zelda met her husband-to-be in Palezzi. It was love at first sight for him. Ezra wanted to marry Zelda immediately. He was scheduled to be aboard the *Exodus*, the ship that would sail to the Jewish homeland, and would several years later be the subject of a movie. Because Zelda could not decide to marry Ezra in 24 hours, he relinquished his spot on the Exodus, and stayed behind at Palezzi to further woo his bride-to-be.

She half-heartedly insisted that he go on ahead, and they would pursue their relationship on reaching Palestine. He refused, continuing to stay behind, and after knowing each other for a grand total of 21 days....they were married on May 28, 1947 in Palezzi, Italy.

They remained in Italy for another year, working with their fellow Jews, and hoping for a homeland. They were one couple out of millions who heard the news which flashed all over the world, that Israel had been granted her charter to "exist" by the United Nations. That great and hallowed day was May 14, 1948 on the Julian calendar. Zelda and her husband set sail in August of that same year.

Although Americans are today inundated with TV ads describing a week at sea on a cruise ship, Zelda's journey was not one of swimming pools, caviar, or midnight strolls on the deck in an evening gown. She was on one of several re-outfitted liberty ships. Most were anything but sea-worthy, and had little if any rescue or emergency devices if anything went wrong. The people packed aboard like commuters on a Manhattan subway.

The trip took about seven or eight days as best that Zelda could remember, and it was not an easy one. It was brutally hot. The families with children were on the upper deck, and the people who were without children were on the stuffy and overcrowded lower deck. There was inadequate food, and on the last day of the trip, they ran out of water. Many were seasick, and there were few functional toilet facilities on board. The stench of un-showered, vomiting passengers made the steamy hot journey all the more unbearable. On top of all this Zelda was pregnant with her first child.

At last, the famous port of Haifa came into view, and hope abounded for those aboard ship. The day was August 28, 1948, and Zelda stepped off the ship with Ezra, her husband. Her feet had now touched Israel. She was home!

Israelis who had preceded her, waited for her again. There were sandwiches with white bread and even cheese. Some small provisions were given her, and even a drink of cold water, from a real refrigerator. After the perilous journey, it was heaven on earth. She received a baby bed and even some diapers for the baby that still rested in her womb.

One day later, on August 29th, her son Amos was born...a *sabra*, born in the land. What a gift! What a hope!

> "For the Lord has called you, like a wife forsaken and grieved in spirit, even like a wife of one's youth when she is rejected", says your God. "For a brief moment I forsook you, but with great compassion I will gather you."
>
> (NAS—Isaiah 54:6-7)

And so as the Almighty gathered His people, Zelda and Ezra were some of the early ones of millions who came and will continue to come. Upon arrival, Ezra was immediately put into uniform, and sent into the army for service. Zelda and their new son, Amos, settled in Tel Aviv for a time. They had come home, but home was not yet without peril. Israel had been born again, but she still fit one of the descriptions of the prophet Ezekiel:

> "No eye looked with pity on you to do any of these things for you, to have compassion on you. Rather you were thrown out into the open field, for you were abhorred on the day you were born. When I passed by you and saw you squirming in your blood, I said to you while you were in your blood, 'Live! I said to you while you were in your blood, 'Live!'"
>
> (NAS—Ezekiel 16:5-6)

There are no mistakes in the Word of God. The passage certainly pertains to Israel's first birth out of the womb of Egypt and through the birth canal of the Red Sea. However, there is plenty of reason to believe that as the Lord repeats His command, "Live!" a second time, that He refers to Israel's re-birth thousands of years later....and so Israel will live! It is His Word.

Since walking into the land of Israel, Zelda has endured five shooting wars. Her sons have served in the army. She has seen the developing of the land and she continues to have hope. Although she confesses a great lack of knowledge about God and His ways, she is certain that it is He who has brought her through, and will continue to sustain.

Zelda continues to live in Bat Yam, a suburb of Tel Aviv. Her husband, Ezra, since the time of the interview has passed away. Amos continues his work as a flight steward with El Al, and it was Amos who dropped my note into the mailbox of El Al pilot, Captain Arieh Oz.

# 4

# ARIEH

Before beginning this history, it is necessary to explain that Captain Arieh Oz is one of the few Israelis interviewed whose name has not been changed in this book. His life story involves a few events that would easily identify him anyway.

In spite of the affinity that I had with the many inhabitants of Zion, I had a special affinity to Arieh. He is a pilot, and I am a pilot. For those of us within the profession who have known the thrill and sometimes the terror of flight, there is a bond and an understanding that transcends words. Although humble and kind, Arieh is one of Israel's very best pilots. I did not ascertain this information from him, but had it confirmed to me by other Israeli pilots who knew his name. I did not ask questions about Arieh's professional abilities. I simply might ask a pilot that I met, "By the way, do you happen to know Arieh Oz?" If a pilot knew him, there was always great admiration and professional compliment expressed, totally unsolicited. There is no greater credential than the positive testimony of those who share a man's profession.

Pilots tend to have personality traits that are similar. Although there are always exceptions, and each of us is unique, these traits run through most of us. Pilots are generally, "in control." Although we have emotions and feelings like everyone else, the very nature of our profession does not allow us to fret or "come apart" when there is adversity. We do not have the luxury of making it halfway through a problem, and push our chair back for a cup of coffee while we ponder what to do next, as would an architect or engineer. Our "problem" may be 300 tons of aluminum whistling through the sky at 600 mph, and circumstances will not allow for the nap or the rescheduling of action until we feel better.

Because of these traits, it is usually VERY difficult to speak to pilots about those "touchy-feelie" things like love, compassion, fear, etc. We are usually much more comfortable speaking about barrel rolls, thunderstorms, inoperative engines, etc. These are things that can be seen or done, measured or quantified. Although we may not be comfortable with the squishy things of life that involve emotions, they are nevertheless there, and it takes a very secure man to discuss them. Arieh is such a man. He shared generously from his heart and though I have spent only hours of my life with him, I love him like a brother, and admire him immensely.

⟋⟍

Harry Klausner was born in 1936, a name which would be shed in favor of Arieh Oz later in his life. Adolf Hitler was a known political figure at the time, and his philosophies were beginning to make their way into the minds and hearts of people all over Germany. The Germans had suffered heavily from their defeat in World War I, and the restrictions of the Versailles Treaty kept the nation in bondage. It was time for some relief. Adolf Hitler, Germany's new god, would provide it. Even the word "Heil" which was used to adulate him, means in German, "salvation".

*"Mein Kampf"* (My Fight) had been published and widely read. It was Hitler's view of the problems in Germany and the world along with some of his solutions. Hitler explained the injustice that the Germans were suffering for the economic crimes of others. It

was "the Jews who caused all the problems," so the lie would be spoken. There were those who would heed its warnings, but there were far more who would consider it as wasted rhetoric and that the philosophies expounded would become no more than the paper and ink comprising each book.

Harry's father, Wolf Klausner, was at peace with the world around him, and lived on the edge of the "good life" in Germany at the time. He was a man of logic. He ran two shoe stores and dealt with the realities of measurements and sizes, attributes that could be easily classified. He was not ignorant of the philosophical changes that were flowing through Germany, and was also quite aware of his Jewishness. Although he was not a religious Jew, he was an active supporter of the Jewish community and had a Zionist vision for a Jewish homeland. However, at the time, as with thousands of Jews, Berlin was his Jerusalem.

Whether it was the negative forces arising within Germany, or whether it was the positive magnetic pull of the Promise Land, Arieh's father had made a decision that he would move himself and his family there. By the time Wolf Klausner was able to put legs to his vision, the doors closed in 1936. It was no longer possible for a Jew to pack up and take a trip to Palestine from Germany.

As it became more and more apparent where Germany was headed under the guidance of the new *Führer*, more intricate plans had to be made to move himself and his family out of Germany, despite the government's decree that it would not be allowed. Wolf Klausner, in July 1939, booked himself on a Mediterranean cruise, which would take him no closer to Palestine than Alexandria, Egypt. When the ship docked in Alexandria, Wolf ingested a pill designed to make him ill. It was part of his plan to make his way to the Promise Land.

He was evacuated from the ship, and brought to a hospital in Alexandria. After a long stay, he was released and nursed back to health by a Jewish family who lived in Alexandria at the time. After checking out the possibilities around Alexandria, and knowing that his cruise ship had long since departed, a now-strengthened Wolf Klausner teamed up with a couple of other Jewish men who had the same goal, to get to Palestine. In partnership, they scrounged around and were together able to buy a small boat. It would be their ark to the Promise Land. After days at sea, hoping not to be spotted, they beached the boat in the blackness of night near Tel Aviv. They had not been caught.

While Wolf had gone to Palestine to work out a plan for his life and that of his family, Hitler had already been ranting and raving before crowds of hundreds of thousands. He had built the Nazi war machine into something that could not be stopped by the horse and wagon militia which surrounded Germany at the time. He had already greased the skids for the *Anschluss*, (annexation or connection) enslaving Czechoslovakia and Austria to his maniacal kingdom. He had invaded Poland and his war machine devoured people and land like meat in a grinder.

It was a painful dilemma for Wolf Klausner. He had reached Palestine, but was now in no position to return to Germany, nor could he get the rest of his family out. For his wife, Rosa, and his children, Harry and Ruth, the dilemma was far worse. Not only had they lost their husband and father to a land far away, but they were part of a chosen people—chosen by God throughout all of history to represent Him and to be a light to the world, and chosen by Hitler to vent his own insane fury and to annihilate them.

It was no longer a matter of economic hard times in Germany. It was now war against the surrounding countries, and war against the Jews. *Kristallnacht* (Crystal Night) had already occurred, where synagogues and Jewish shops all over Germany had been defaced, smashed and burned. Jews had been questioned, publicly humiliated, beaten, and killed on a daily basis. Rosa Klausner had no choice. She had to save herself and her children. She gathered her 10-year old daughter Ruth, and her 4-year old son Harry, and she headed for Holland by train to stay with her brother. Her plan worked. At the time it was not difficult to cross the border to Holland without meticulously proper papers. The train trip was uneventful, and they felt safe from Hitler's Germany, at least for the time being.

Although inconvenient, Harry, his sister Ruth, and his mother lived with his uncle until 1941. The Nazi tentacles were reaching out in all directions. At first, the move was eastward, but now an invasion of France, Belgium, and Holland were part of the plan for world domination.

Harry's uncle was a respected man in Holland, and was quite prominent in the Jewish community. Deportation lists had been drawn up, and the Jews were already being singled out and brought to the trains which headed east to the hells of Auschwitz, Bergen-Belsen, Dachau, Buchenwald, Treblinka, and dozens of others.

Because of his prominence, he had good relationships and connections in the Dutch community. The Dutch underground came to him and informed him that Rosa Klausner and the children were on a deportation list. It was time to act, and act fast. The deportation lists were not drawn up weeks in advance, and when a name came out on the list, it meant that the people on it would be rounded up and sent to the trains within a very short time. There had been no arrangements made to hide "underground" yet. At present there was no place to go. They needed time.

The Dutch were already prepared for such eventualities, and had innumerable creative methods to stall things or to accelerate them. In this case, a Dutch physician made a short visit to 4-year old Harry's bedside. He gave young Harry a small dose of Diphtheria, enough to make him sick, but not so sick as to harm him. It was enough to be able to legitimately place a quarantine on the house, something that struck fear into the Germans. As a consequence, they left the household alone for a while. It provided for time to make arrangements for Mrs. Klausner, Harry, and his older sister, Ruth.

Although there were collaborators in every country, the Dutch as a nation behaved fairly well toward the Jews. However, in the years after the war it was discovered that a significant percentage of the population collaborated with the Germans. Many became members of the Dutch Nazi Party or NSB. However, there was also an underground in Holland second to none that frustrated the Nazis militarily, and that spent untold effort rescuing and hiding Jews. Their methods were strict and tough, but they worked. It was not a time for sentimentality, and trying to keep families together. It was a time for hiding them as deeply underground as possible, to save their lives. In order to do this, families had to be separated. Mothers went here, fathers went there, and children, often one by one, went somewhere entirely different.

As the Dutch made arrangements with Mrs. Klausner, she knew that she would have to give up her children to strangers, and worse yet, to *goyim* (non-Jews). Although she was not so prejudiced as to think that others could not help, it was still a factor which made parting with her children all the more difficult.

The questions raced through her mind. Would she ever see them again? Would they be loved....taken care of? They are simple questions when printed on a page, but when applied to the reality of one's own children, and the possible answers which might transpire, the uncertainties could only create terror in a mother's heart. It was the kind of terror that only a parent would understand.

The day came. Arrangements were complete. The kids would go to the country side village of Zeist, near Utrecht. The family with whom they would stay were simple farmers, but loving, courageous, and creative people. They were Christians in the truest sense of the word, praying daily, sharing from the Scriptures together, and doing what the Good Book commanded.

The year was 1941. Harry, about 5 years old, and his sister Ruth, age 11, were now in the company of their new family. They would be there until May 14, 1945....to a child, an eternity...for a mother, perhaps longer.

Because Harry was from an upper middle class family, he had been taught some of the "finer" things of life. He had been in the habit of dressing for dinner, and using all the proper utensils at the dinner table. His new Dutch guardians were simple people. They ate everything with a spoon, and it was doubtful that the father had ever worn a tie.

As a 5-year old, changes like this were usually greeted head on with embarrassing questions, embarrassing to even an 11-year old sister who had matured enough to be sensitive to others, and to be at least outwardly grateful for whatever was put in front of her. She now had to be the teacher for her younger brother, trying to explain to him yet another finery of life, that of being silent and gracious, in the absence of special knives or forks, eating with wooden spoons on wooden plates.

Harry was taken aside by his courageous older sister, and

instructed. As he sat on the corner of the bed, and received Ruth's "grown-up" instruction and admonishment, she concluded her lecture with a statement that until this day is riveted in his mind.

*"**Ab, Elul, Tishri**......remember......you are Jewish!"* His older sister knew only three Hebrew words....three months of the Jewish calendar. What could this young girl have meant as she instructed her little brother? Might it have been "not to forget to represent your people well?" Or...."don't listen to too many Christian stories?" Or perhaps, "we are here in a difficult place without mother or father, and it is part of the lot of the Jew to stand tall in the times of difficulty...to walk proudly and with dignity." To this day, that seven word statement with three Hebrew words impacts Arieh Oz deeply.

These three Hebrew words were all they had to connect them with their Jewishness. Their father was trapped in Palestine. Their mother was hidden underground with a Dutch family somewhere else in Holland. The Dutch farmer and his family were Christians. These three Hebrew words would have meaning to Harry much later in his life. At five years of age, being a Jew or non-Jew had little academic or theological meaning. A present and understood reality however, even for a 5-year old boy, was that by belonging to the Jewish people it meant that there were a lot of Germans who would kill you if they found you. It was meaning enough for a mind at any age.

The Dutch family were hard working, but poor, and they endured life in an atmosphere of terror. There was very little to share. Consumer goods were scarce during the war and there was little food. There were no new shoes or boots to be bought. Everyone had to make do with what they already had, for it was not known when a supply of anything might be replenished. German Nazis intimidated the Dutch mercilessly, and it meant immediate death for anyone caught hiding a Jew. It was a time of deep testing for all. In the case of this Dutch family, their lack of material goods was more than made up for in their richness of spirit and their willingness to risk their very lives, that someone else might live.

Oepke and Jitske Haitsma maintained a low profile among their little Dutch community. They carefully instructed their three children, regarding the gravity of the German occupation and the possible results of a careless word spoken to a classmate or shopkeeper.

Because they were hiding Harry and his sister in defiance to Nazi authority, every precaution had to be taken, and the slightest mistake could mean that all would lose their lives. Their mission in life at this point would have no immediate reward. There would be no pats on the back or plaques to be hung on a wall, only sacrifice, which would last for years.

The smallest of details had to be thought out and planned for. It was a favorite tactic of the Germans to come bursting into a home at two or three o'clock in the morning. If a household was in the service of protecting and hiding Jews, and there had been a laxness allowed to develop, it was often discovered in the dark hours of the night. As the Nazis would storm into a house, they would look for unmade beds. If the number of unmade beds exceeded the number of family members who were lined up in their nightclothes, a thorough search would begin. The Nazis would often break walls, wardrobes, or any structure that might have the slightest capability of concealing a human being.

Oepke and Jitske Haitsma had already given this much thought. It would mean sacrifice for their children. Harry Klausner would be made to sleep in the same bed with their 9-year old son Sieds, and Harry's sister would sleep in the same bed with Lucie, their 12-year old daughter. In the event of a surprise search, Harry and his sister would dash quickly to their special hiding place, and the Haitsma family would line up. The unmade beds would match the number of family members, and generally the search would be stopped at that point.

The Nazis were as methodical as machinery, and Oepke knew this about his adversaries. It would not be good enough to have his little Jewish charges hide in a closet or under a bed, in an attic, or cellar. The place had to be cleverly disguised so as to require great effort to discover its whereabouts. He had put his talented hands to work, and had built a wooden turret-like structure which was accessible from the second floor of his Dutch farmhouse. It hung down from the ceiling of the first floor, blending well with the cabinetry of the room, unobtrusive to even a skillful Nazi searcher of Jews.

By moving a bed aside, and turning up some carpet, the small hatch would be discovered. When the Nazis would perform their house to house searches, Harry and Ruth would run quickly to this room. Oepke and his son would hastily move aside the bed, peel up the carpet, lift the carefully crafted hatch from the floor, and Harry and his sister would quickly descend into the darkness of their little turret-like box. The hatch would be replaced, the carpet laid flat and the bed lifted back in place over the carpet. The operation could be done in moments, and Oepke could then answer the hammering of the Nazis at the door, allow them into his home, and the unmade-bed count would match the family count.

One night the Nazis showed up, and began hammering on the door. *"Raus....Raus.....Auf machen! Auf machen!"* (Open up!)

Fear struck at the hearts of the Haitsma family, and Harry and his sister. It was time to move, and move fast, just as they had been instructed and had rehearsed. Harry and Ruth stood quietly as they watched Oepke and his son lift the bed aside, peel up the carpet, and remove the well-fitting lid of their hiding place in the floor. They quietly stepped into the little pit of darkness, and felt the lid fall in place above them, the "flop" of the rug falling down over the wooden hatch, and solid but quiet clunks of the bed being replaced to cap off the job.

The hammering continued on the front door. "Open up! Open up!" Other Nazi soldiers circled the farmhouse to make certain that there were no Jews running out the back door, as happened in many searches of the less clever and the less disciplined.

*"Ein moment.......*coming......coming," Jitske yelled with a prac-ticed nonchalance, knowing that the Germans would hear her through the door. When she knew that all preparations were com-plete, she would open the door and invite the uninvited into the Haitsma home. The search would begin quickly, German soldiers looking everywhere for any sign that there were more than only the family members present. Even the hair and eye color of the children would be compared to the parents by evil and calculating eyes. A child that didn't seem to match the general characteristics of the family would be singled out and questioned. Few were clever enough to avoid detection when confronted in this manner.

On this search, the Germans were rather quick and superficial in their search. They looked the house over, and the officer in charge made his decision.

"*Ja......Ja......*this will do nicely. We will use this place for the search."

The Nazi and a couple of his cohorts made themselves comfortable and spread out their maps and notes in their new "headquarters" for the village search. The Haitsma home had been chosen. The Nazis stayed for two full days in their house, sending soldiers out from its location to search the other homes and buildings for hidden Jews.

Meanwhile, six-year old Harry and his sister hunched in their little dark box. They could not speak, and were left alone in their terrorizing thoughts. It was pitch black, and little Arieh laid back against his 12-year old sister's stomach, her legs wrapping his little body as the two of them waited out the storm that raged only a plank's width away from them.

Authoritative German voices barked orders, and familiar Dutch voices responded in kindness and graciousness to their uninvited guests. It seemed as though Oepke Haitsma had thought of everything. He knew that there might be a possibility of a somewhat prolonged visit of the enemy, and had prepared his well constructed "turret" with a supply of water and bread, as well as a little pail which would serve as a "potty" for his invited guests, Harry and his sister.

It is difficult to imagine how a 12-year old girl, and a little 6-year old boy could manage in what could be described as life in a wooden box. How in its pitch-blackness were they able to keep from panic, or to keep from having a brother-sister squabble, which might produce enough sound to cause discovery? But it was done. Their needs were met. They had disciplined themselves well, far beyond the maturity of their years.

The Nazi soldiers finally finished the village search and left. Quietly, and without a rush or surge of noisy emotion, the Haitsmas moved the bed, lifted the carpet, and removed the lid of Harry and Ruth's little world. It had been silent victory. They had been threatened, but they were safe. It was a quiet reunion with their Dutch foster parents. Thoughts of what might have been, surged through the Haitsma's minds, but peace flooded them as they enjoyed the immense victory of knowing that they had preserved two precious lives.

Arieh remembers being a quiet boy, and does not remember consciously being afraid. With airline pilot precision he states today, "there was no place for fear," but at the same time acknowledges that it was not until years later that he started to get in touch with his real feelings of early boyhood, when he answered to the name, Harry Klausner. One could easily ask, "was it God's sovereign protection over this little guy and his sister in the midst of this ordeal, or was it the self protective mechanisms of the human personality that insulated them from the threat of capture and death? "

Arieh's recollection is that in general he did not feel afraid, but that he was greatly envious of the Dutch children who were able to go outside, go to school, and play with others around the village. Oepke Haitsma would take no chances. Despite the fact that he was able to see the ache in a child's heart, and was able to discern the need for a young boy to have the companionship and fellowship of other children his own age, he had to make the seemingly cruel, difficult, but right decision in not allowing Harry or his sister to associate with other village children. As such, his orders were that his Jewish charges would not be allowed to even set foot outside the house.

The orders were carried out. Little Harry Klausner did not step outside for more than four years! There were no errands to the local shops, no taking out the garbage, no walks, and no outdoor games that allowed for normal social development with other children. An allowed transgression from Mr. Haitsma's rule might too easily place into the hands of the Nazis, two more Jewish children for their ovens. Although it was secondary in importance, it would also surely mark the end of the Haitsma family.

In Harry's four-year stay with the Dutch family, one exception was made to this rule. Little Harry had been boasting, "I'm not afraid of the Germans. I'm not afraid of the Germans." He was now a well-established member of the Haitsma family, and addressed Oepke Haitsma as "Uncle."

"Uncle, I'm not afraid of the Germans. I can go outside!"

"Alright Harry, I will let you outside." Oepke had chosen a bitter cold January night, in the middle of a snowstorm. He knew that no German would be outside on a night such as this. He allowed Harry to walk out the back door into the howling wind and falling snow. It was his first and only time outside the house. It was cold, dark, and the back door of the house was closed behind Harry.

In fatherly wisdom, Oepke wanted Harry to experience a taste of the freedom he had been previously denied, and perhaps also to allow him to touch his boyhood fears, in order to silence the childish boasts about his lack of fear. Arieh confesses that to this day, he was sure that his boyhood trip to the outdoors lasted only minutes, but that it seemed like an entire night. However, it was an opportunity to breathe fresh air. It was a little glimpse of a hoped-for freedom, one that would not come for years.

In addition to the rule that would not allow the children outside, there was another rule—not to go near the window. It was one that was occasionally broken by a young boy, longing to be free. Living near the Protestant Christian Haitsma family, was a Catholic family. There was great animosity in their minds against Protestants. Someone in that Catholic family had seen little Harry's face peering from the window of the Haitsma home.

The Germans knew that the Dutch were hiding Jews, and they kept up their surprise searches hoping to catch them unaware. All too often they were successful, nabbing one or two here, another there, and executing the Dutch family that harbored them. If a reported sighting of a hidden Jew came to the attention of the Nazis, there was certain to be a search, and perhaps a bone of favor tossed toward the collaborator who reported the "crime" against the Third Reich.

Harry knew that a member of the Catholic family had spotted him. He drew away from the window, not knowing what would happen. As a young boy he was not anxious to report his transgression to Uncle Oepke, and he hoped that nothing would come of his having been seen by a neighbor. Only a day or two later, Sieds Haitsma was in school, and heard the chatter of his classmates.

"The Germans are in town again, and they are searching for more Jews...I saw them myself on my way to school!"

The classroom chatter continued, and young Sieds suddenly became "ill" asking his teacher for permission to leave school. He held his stomach and contorted his face in mock pain, as he walked slowly out of the classroom. As soon as he was out of sight from the teachers and his fellow students, Sieds ran as fast as his legs would carry him. He reached his home.

"Mama...Father...the Germans are in town! They are looking for Jews!"

As they had so often done before during the searches, the Haitsma family went through their routine. The bed was moved, the carpet was lifted, the little hatch was removed, and a little Jewish boy and his sister climbed into their little dark refuge to wait things out again. The all too familiar feelings and sounds of the hatch being dropped into place, the "flop" of the carpet over the hatch, and the solid clunks of the four legs of the wooden bed being replaced, etched themselves deeper into the memory of Harry and his sister.

With successive victories over one's enemy, it provided the food for confidence that victory would be enjoyed again. At the same time there was the gnawing fear that maybe.... just maybe...this time...a more careful search, a more observant Nazi might discover the little children. Perhaps a cough, or an unwanted sneeze at the wrong time, would produce the clue that would uncover their hiding place.

The Germans were not to have their way. The search produced nothing, and the Catholic lady that reported seeing Arieh had to re-evaluate her memory. Had she really seen the face of a strange youngster in the window? Perhaps she was mistaken. Perhaps her thinking fell more into line with the Germans. She knew that the Haitsma family were hiding Jews...but where?...and how to catch them?

Neither the Germans nor the mean neighbors had time to figure out the answer. On the 10th of May 1945, soldiers wearing different uniforms appeared. They were Americans and Canadians patrolling the streets. It was the liberation! There would be no more Nazi searches! Life could begin again!

Oepke Haitsma was not a man who moved quickly. The sighting of a robin does not make a Spring. He reasoned that those Americans and Canadians who walked and rode victoriously through the streets of his village, might just as easily be pushed back by a Nazi counter-attack. For him to reveal his hidden treasure right now, would be a grievous error. He waited. He held his family and his little Jewish children in check. There would be no celebrating until it was sure. Uncle Oepke had come too far with his little treasures to allow for a fatal error to be made as a result of any premature emotional decision to celebrate.

On May 14, 1945, four days after the official liberation, Harry Klausner walked out of the Dutch farmhouse...free! A young boy and his sister had hidden right under Nazi noses for over four years and had gone undetected. He had not been to a kindergarten, first, second, third, or fourth grade. Because he had been initially nurtured on German, he still knew the language, but had picked up Dutch from his protecting family. He did not know it then, but he would eventually add two more languages to his arsenal, Hebrew, and English.

As my wife, Hellen, and I sat in Captain Arieh Oz's home in Ramat-Hasharon, we were deeply moved at having been allowed to share these moments. It was not without emotion that this man, a true son of Israel, shared the immensity of meaning that May 14th of 1945 had on his young life as Harry Klausner. To someone who had been caged as an animal, albeit for his own protection from the beasts that roamed the nation of Holland, freedom had acquired a meaning that only a few like Arieh Oz could understand. How genuinely prophetic would this anniversary day be...for unknown to anyone at the time, in exactly three years to the day, an entire nation would be born from the ashes of Europe's holocaust, and would experience a birth of freedom on a national scale, such as that which had been experienced on an individual scale in Harry's life.

Up until that time, Harry had no friends, no schooling, and no socialization during some of the most crucial and formative years of his life. His friends were the members of the Haitsma family, farmers, certainly heroes, but nevertheless disciplinarians who saved his life by keeping him bound, and in this sense, his captors. Because of these past circumstances, there was a giant vacuum in Harry's soul, a void of learning and social development which would cause problems later, but which also would contribute largely to his success today.

The Dutch underground and the countless numbers of their supporters had done their jobs well. Thousands of Jews were spared from concentration camps and gas chambers, hidden in closets, attics, cellars, and haystacks. Harry's mother was one of them. She too, had avoided detection, and was reunited with her little ones, who had grown up so much in the last four years. It was time for more change, readjusting to each other's presence, the authority of Harry's real mother, and a new place to live.

With the help of the Dutch, Rosa Klausner was able to procure a home, which would serve her and her children for the next several months. Communication was re-established with Wolf Klausner, who had to sit out the war in Palestine, unable to get to his family or to help them in any way. Although it is easy to dismiss Wolf's role in this drama as non-significant, his was probably as painful as anyone's. There is no more helpless a feeling than knowing about a danger, especially to a loved family member, and to have to stand by and watch...or in his case, imagine, unable to help. Ask anyone who has ever watched a child perish in the blaze of a house fire, or a rescuer who has watched a victim swirl away in flood waters only a few yards away, so close and so desirous of giving aid, but prevented by forces or circumstances beyond his ability to overcome.

Plans were prepared, and Rosa Klausner, Ruth, and Harry boarded a train for Marseilles, France on the southern coast. On April 10, 1946 they would board the ship, *Champignone* and set sail, stopping in Libya, Alexandria, Egypt, and eventually, Haifa. The ship had been hired by the Jewish Agency, and was filled with Holocaust survivors and other Jews making *aliyah* to the Promise Land. On disembarking from the ship, Harry, his sister Ruth, and his mother were placed in Atlit. Back then it was an internment camp for incoming refugees, but today it is a national park. After years of horror and waiting, a family was reunited...father, mother, son, and daughter.

Although Europe's Holocaust was behind, new enemies greeted them. The vacuum in Harry's development gave place to a rage when he discovered how far behind he was from his contemporaries in normal schoolwork. Added to this, was the requirement to adapt to a new language...Hebrew. The long separation incurred as husband

and wife left a deep chasm between them which became filled with anger and resentment. Rosa Klausner felt betrayed by her husband and left alone to the hands of the Nazis, while he lived in Palestine, free of the horrors of World War II.

Wolf Klausner was now a 52-year old man who had been separated from his family for over seven years by circumstances beyond his control. His wife Rosa had arrived with two emotionally scarred children, each of whom had been through a diabolical nightmare. The internal wounds of each family member became the soil that spawned more difficulties.

"Who are you to tell me what to do? I was in the War with two kids. Where were you?" Although the shooting had stopped and the gas chambers and ovens had been closed down, another war was being waged in the spirits and souls of already broken people. The bullets of sharp words pierced to the very core of each other's beings, shot from the anger and pain of past experiences, but often hitting the wrong target. Countless Jewish families faced these same difficult circumstances after World War II. Harry's family was no exception.

In addition to these family hardships, there were also difficult economic adjustments to make, and they were now in a land where the same hatred that ruled Hitler was now being expressed through the Arabs. Family life became impossible together. Harry was sent to a kibbutz while his parents tried to iron things out between themselves. Once again, the young boy found himself in the clutches of rejection and desolation. He was alone, frightened, and with very little hope.

In Arieh's own words..."I was miserable. I couldn't eat, and I couldn't sleep."

A kibbutz is a place where there is plenty of fresh air, and usually lots of hard work to keep a person occupied. But the kibbutzim were also filled with Jews who had deep problems of their own. Many were recent newcomers from the Holocaust, trying with great difficulty to re-establish their own lives. There was no energy left over to give the care and love to a young man who was filled with rage and anger and who often vented it in aberrant and rebellious behavior.

As Harry rebelled, he was more and more rejected. This in turn fed his rebellion, and the vicious circle continued. He was asked to leave the kibbutz and go back to a family situation that was not yet under control. The next attempt at solution was to hand Harry over to a *moshav,* another form of collective living. He stayed there for three months, and then returned to his parents who did not know what to do with him.

Although most of his violent outbursts had been curbed, Harry continued to remain uncommunicative. He still had not been in social situations that would have been normal for most young people of the time. He had been denied the love of his own father and mother, and certainly bore all of the uncertainties as to whether or not they were even alive, as he hid away for years in a Dutch farmhouse, fearing even for his own life. This was too big a load for a youngster.

Harry was sent to a home for children near Netanya, Israel. It was a place for orphaned children and those from badly broken homes. It was his "big break." He still wanted to be home with his parents, but he persevered through the rigors of institutional living. It was the first time that he was able to go to school on a regular and disciplined basis. He began to develop emotionally, socially, and academically.

Where there had been a void of learning in the past, Harry filled it by driving himself to limits which far exceeded those of the average young person. He was accustomed to deep pain, and the discipline required to study fervently came easily to him. As he saw glimpses of success, it drove him to work all the harder to excel at whatever he did.

Since his parents had no car, and were unable to visit him very often, he continued to feel the deep hurt of loneliness when the other children had visitors, and Harry had none. Although he was making great headway academically, he was way behind physically. During a time when a child would normally be kicking a soccer ball around with his friends, developing co-ordination, Harry was cooped up in a Dutch farmhouse. He was also small physically, but he made up for it all in academics.

As it came time to enter high school, Harry was chosen to attend the best in Tel Aviv. Many of Israel's leaders graduated from this special school, designed to help the most gifted of students to excel. The school has graduated many military leaders, doctors, scientists, and certainly an excellent pilot.

Harry's mother was taken ill, adding more grief to a life filled with torment. His mother became one of the first people in the world to undergo open-heart surgery to replace a defective valve, with the procedure being accomplished in Holland. The surgery was a success and Mrs. Klausner lived to be over 84 years of age. During these difficult high school years, however, Harry was still very much on his own. Although his father stayed in Israel to care for Arieh while his mother was recuperating from the open heart surgery abroad, Harry had to make many of his own decisions.

As he neared his high school graduation, Harry decided upon a military career, and he shed the name, "Harry", taking on "Arieh". It means "lion" in Hebrew. It was customary for Jews making *aliyah* (immigration) to Israel to take a Hebrew name. Perhaps the seeds that had been planted in his heart from having lived through the injustices under the Nazis, and then again in the wars of Israel, would best be expressed in a new identity of strength in protecting others. He remembers as a young lad in Holland how he had wanted to kill the Nazis, but was bound in the frustration of being a young boy, and helpless to fight against such an enemy. A military life would allow for his sense of justice to be expressed, and to help bring to reality an often-expressed Jewish sentiment..... "Never again!"

Arieh joined the Israeli military and began to endure some of the most stressful time of his life. He became literally terrified. It was not from the training, but from all of the unresolved inner conflicts of his life. It seemed that life had no meaning. Arieh had been denied all of the God-ordained supports of life. He had had no parents, no friends, no schooling, and no normal socialization at some of the most critical times in his formative life. When the opportunities came to begin filling these needs, parents, friends, and institutions had their own problems and were unable to make up for what had been lacking for years.

Where there has been little emotional support, and where a person has met so much defeat, and has had to overcome mountainous obstacles, the fear of failure can easily take root and magnify itself as each new obstacle is met. Successes of the past seem to make little difference, because each new mountain to overcome can seem larger than the previous one.

Arieh remarked jokingly, that today in the military there are more counselors than there are teachers and instructors. It is humor born out of the tragedy of fact. The wounds of Israel are deep indeed....going back generation after generation. The institutions have failed, many families have failed, and certainly the nations have failed to encourage and love Israel. They have in fact been most instrumental in inflicting these wounds.

At the time, there were no counselors or psychiatrists on which to pour out one's feelings and receive guidance in resolving the conflicts of life. Arieh simply had to bear the load...whatever that load was that he carried through the gates of flight school.

Military flight training is at best a pressure cooker, designed to cull out the weak. Often, the most normally adjusted men do not meet the standards. Even after a weeding out process in this author's cadet life at the university, my U.S. Air Force pilot training class began with 56 candidates, and only 34 graduated a year later.

As Arieh carried around the baggage of his past life, he was met with the challenge of the tremendous pressure that meticulous performance demanded of any good military pilot. Flight maneuvers had to be performed with precision. There was no room for failure. His psychological knees were beginning to buckle under the strain, much of it self-imposed.

At the time, he had been flying North American Harvards, designated as the AT-6, an old American trainer which demanded a lot of attention on the part of any pilot. It was a single-engine propeller driven airplane with a tail wheel, which could cause the downfall of any prospective pilot if he became the slightest bit complacent while handling the controls.

A biblical proverb states, "Death and life are in the power of the tongue." Few ever realize the importance of our spoken words as they effect others. For Arieh, he gave all that he had to perform well under a tremendous psychological load, as he put his AT-6 through its paces with a check pilot on board. He landed, taxied the squirmy flying machine to its resting-place, and waited fearfully to hear the words of his wise instructor.

"Arieh...you know...you are going to make a tremendous aviator!"

Only a few words...but they shattered the pile of baggage that Arieh had been toting for so long. The world and all its tragedies and disappointments had been lifted from his shoulders. He would succeed. Someone who knew what he was talking about had just said so.

Arieh continued his flying and graduated from pilot training. It was a proud moment for him as with all pilots, and equally so for Arieh's father, Wolf. It would be one of the last milestones that Wolf Klausner would witness in Arieh's life. He died not long after Arieh pinned on his wings.

Arieh, as was the case with many Jews who came to Israel, not only changed his first name, but his last. He took on the surname of Oz...meaning "strength." He had received the confidence to succeed.

Arieh went on and served the military for 13 years, becoming at one time the youngest squadron commander in the Israeli Air Force. Although there were some good times and some victories to celebrate, the battles were not over for this son of Zion.

Arieh joined El Al Airlines early in 1967. As he was training to fly the Boeing 707, the Six Day War broke out, and he was called back into active service with the Israeli Air Force. The miraculous victory for Israel in the war that was finished in only six days boosted the confidence of not only Arieh himself, but the entire nation of Israel.

Arieh returned to his training with El Al. It was back to normal life again. He had to learn the complexities of a large jetliner, and perform all maneuvers and oral exams with precision and accuracy. The lull would not last long however.

Israel has lost more of her sons and daughters BETWEEN her wars than the United States has lost DURING her wars on a proportional basis. Terrorists have made their presence known all too often in the five decades since Israel's re-birth. There have been bombs set off in crowded supermarkets, and explosions at the Western Wall of the Temple, one of the most sacred places in Israel. Terrorists have indiscriminately machine-gunned innocent passengers in Ben Gurion Airport's terminal building, not to mention a similar attack in

Rome. Most people who are old enough, remember the attack against the Israeli athletes at the 1972 Munich Olympics, where eleven of the team were murdered by Arab terrorists.

Arieh is no stranger to such surprise attacks. Early in September of 1970, he sat in the co-pilot's seat of an El Al Boeing 707 at Amsterdam's international airport. He was only miles from where he had hidden with the Dutch family during the dark days of Nazi Germany. He read the checklist and the cockpit crew made their jet-liner ready for the remainder of the trip to New York. In the cabin, last minute preparations were underway. The stewards and flight attendants counted the meals, checked the pressure bottles on the inflatable escape slides, prepared their demonstration life vests and oxygen masks, and seated the last of the boarding passengers.

There were 148 passengers on board, and two of them were ene-mies of Israel. The 707 taxied out uneventfully, the *Magen David* (six-pointed star) painted near the top of the aircraft's tail. The words, "Cleared for takeoff," were uttered from the tower, and El Al's 707 began its takeoff roll.

The jetliner lifted off and Arieh tugged on the large lever which pulled up the landing gear. The flaps were retracted and the plane continued to gather speed even as it climbed. The critical moments of the takeoff were past, and Arieh as well as the captain and flight engineer began to relax as they prepared for seven hours of flying, setting course for New York.

In the cabin, a young couple, two of the last passengers to board the flight leaped from their seats and ran up the aisle past the first class dividing curtain. The young woman carried three hand grenades and the man, a pistol. They began screaming as the man beat on the cockpit door, in hopes of entering the cockpit. A male steward who was close enough to the hijacker received a devastat-ing blow to the head, knocking him almost unconscious. An Israeli security agent, disguised as a flight steward entered the fracas, and the horrifying "pow-pow-pow" of gunshots rang out, bullets whizzing throughout the pressurized cabin. The short but furious gun duel ended quickly. The Israeli security agent, blood spattered and wounded, walked down the cabin aisle. The hijacker slumped to the floor...dead.

Several passengers had jumped his female companion and wrested the grenades from her hands before she was able to pull the arming pins. She was thrown to the floor, tied up with neckties and belts, and sat upon by several passengers. She was Leila Khaled; a 20-year old Arab who had 13 months earlier hijacked a TWA jet.

She had studied at American University in Beirut, Lebanon and was active in the PFLP, the Popular Front for the Liberation of Palestine. She had been a "star" of the terrorist cause and was sometimes paraded in her olive-drab fatigues, toting a Russian Kalachnikov sub-machine gun, as she ran young Arab women through the training of becoming terrorists. She was a rather attractive woman, and when interviewed about her private life as to whether she was engaged, she answered, "I'm engaged to the revolution."

As fast as it had begun, the hijacking came to a swift conclusion. Arieh, along with his crew, declared an emergency and they landed their jet, full of grateful passengers at London's Heathrow Airport.

There were three other hijackings on that same day, a TWA 707 bound from Frankfurt to New York; a Swissair DC-8 enroute from Zurich to New York; and a Pan Am 747 from Amsterdam to New York. These other hijackings were successful for the terrorists. Only El Al's crew, on which Arieh flew as the co-pilot, was able to thwart the attempted hijacking.

It was yet another conspiracy by the forces of evil to wipe out innocent lives—especially those of the Jews. Arieh had once more escaped death at the hand of those who are motivated by hate and deception. He would live.

*Yom Kippur* is the holiest day of the year for the Jewish people. The term itself means, "Day of Atonement". Studying the Torah (the first five books of the Old Testament), one would find that the day was instituted under the Law of Moses, and is a day of great significance, falling just before the celebration of *Succoth*, perhaps better known as the Feast of Tabernacles. More than any other holiday on the Jewish calendar, Yom Kippur is a day that in essence shuts down the entire nation of Israel, as families go to synagogues, and where they pray and fast. It is a day of repentance before God, where each Jew is to live in harmony with everyone else. It is a day where forgiveness is to rule over retaliation, and where restitution is to be made to anyone wronged. For most Jews, it is a day of serious reflection.

In 1973, Yom Kippur approached, and all of Israel made preparations for this day. So too did her enemies. The glee of anticipated surprise permeated the minds of Arab commanders as they geared up for this great Holy Day of the Jews. To an Islamic mind, it was a day of contempt, and the perfect time to express *Jihad*...or "Holy War".

As the day approached, there had been suspicious activity along the borders of Egypt and Syria. The activity had not gone unnoticed by Israeli intelligence, and it had all been discussed in the conference rooms of Israeli leaders. When the evidence had been weighed, the conclusion was that there would be no military action against Israel. The conclusion was wrong, and while synagogues were filled with worshipers, Arab tanks and air forces were pressed into action. The Egyptians from the south and the Syrians from the north along the Golan launched a surprise attack on Israel.

As the news broke, men ran from their synagogues, still in unbelief, hoping that there was some mistake and a giant military SNAFU. But is was not to be. The Arab tanks were rolling into Israel, and there was no one to resist them. Israel stumbled and fumbled her way to readiness, and the nation came to grips with unbelievable reality. It was all out war on Israel's most sacred holy day!

Because Israel had been so surprised, she suffered terrible casualties in the first few days. She was running out of ammunition and other supplies, and she pleaded desperately with the United Nations to call off the Arabs. It was to no avail. She pleaded with the United States for help...even for supplies, right from the beginning. Politicians waffled, excused, and sent polite telegrams of diplomatic gobbledygook.

Soviet ships were steaming into the Mediterranean, and they were pouring supplies into the attacking Arab nations like a waterfall. At last, the United States awoke, and began a supply line, which would come to the aid of Israel.

Israel was in desperate need of some tactical cargo planes which could airlift troops and supplies to desert regions. The United States agreed to give Israel sixteen C-130 Hercules aircraft. They are four-engine turbo-props that are workhorses. They can drop a load of paratroopers, a tank, jeeps, guns, or whatever. They are very versatile, but they are also fairly complex to learn and operate. Studying the workings of the propeller alone can take a pilot days to understand.

Sixteen American C-130 crews flew into Ben Gurion Airport with sixteen C-130's. They landed the aircraft, parked them, handed over the aircraft flight manuals, and departed immediately on another plane. Arieh and his contemporaries now had some airplanes, but there were only three aircrews in all of Israel who knew even a little bit about the C-130. To understand the operation of a complex airplane requires weeks of academic study, and then a good practical course in flying before even an experienced pilot can do a reasonably good job of safely flying it. To make matters worse, the Israeli pilots had to learn the airplane in their secondary language, English. The U.S. Air Force does not print flight manuals in Hebrew.

The orders were given. Arieh and his fellow pilots would fly combat missions the following morning. He and his men stayed up most of the night reading the flight manuals, to figure out how to load, start, taxi, fly, and land the aircraft. It was another emergency for Israel, and there would be no time for anything but the essentials. They would fly...no matter what. The next morning, Arieh and his fellow pilots started engines and were off, flying missions all over Israel. It enabled the moving of precious supplies which were key to Israel's victory only days later. American supplied artillery shells and other ammunition were being flown into Israel, and within hours those same shells were leaving the muzzles of Israeli guns both in the south and north of Israel as the IDF (Israeli Defense Forces) slowly pushed back their enemies. Arieh had flown over 180 combat hours in a plane on which he had never been to school!

He later went through an entire training program, and continued to learn the C-130 so that when he climbed on board and flew the aircraft, it felt like an old shoe. He became entirely comfortable with the plane, and could make the aircraft perform to its limits. It would not be without cause, for Arieh's services would again be needed by his nation, a few years later.

The years had passed since he had first signed on with El Al, and Arieh Oz had moved from the co-pilot position to that of being a captain. While out on one of his normal trips with El Al, he was shocked along with the rest of the world, when on June 27, 1976 an Air France A-300 Airbus was hijacked with 102 of its passengers kept as hostages. Most were Israelis, and their captors were from the Gueverra arm of the Popular Front for the Liberation of Palestine (PFLP). It's a nice way of saying...terrorists. The hijacking had been underway for a few days, with demands being made to the Israeli government by these international outlaws.

As Arieh flew his normal El Al trip back from Frankfurt, Germany, he had stayed abreast of the hijacking situation through the media. He eventually returned to his home base at Tel Aviv's Ben Gurion Airport, and like all other Israelis, carried some of the weight of this recent assault against Israel on his shoulders. As he disembarked from his parked aircraft, an Israeli official met him.

"Arieh...as you know, several of our citizens are being held captive in Entebbe, Uganda. Intelligence and our leaders have worked out a plan to rescue them, and we need your services as a pilot. Will you do it?"

It was Friday, and the Sabbath was approaching. Without hesitation Arieh stepped into the military car, which was waiting for him at the airport.

He arrived at the briefing at a military base somewhere in Israel. It was not just a simple intelligence briefing, but there were men from the highest levels of government involved. The Air France jet with 102 hostages, 78 of whom were Israelis, was parked at Entebbe Airport in Uganda. Uganda at the time was under the iron-fisted rule of another demagogue, Idi Amin. The wheels of a plan had already been turning, and the decision to perform a rescue mission was soon to be made. As the details of the plan unfolded, a superior looked at Arieh and said, "You will be number 3," indicating that Arieh would command the third C-130 of the four that would be used to undertake the mission.

Israel's crack commando team is called *HaHevreh*, which translated, simply means "the guys". "The guys" had already been warming up and practicing while Arieh was still flying his El Al sequence of flights. A careful rescue scenario had been drawn up, practiced, timed, and was almost ready for execution, pending only a political decision. It would be a quick, incisive, and daring raid.

Unlike what is often done in the American military, politics and manipulation don't get their way in Israel when it comes to an important job like the raid at Entebbe. Yes, Israel has its political problems, and they occur in the military, but when it comes down to a delicate operation such as the raid on Entebbe, they seek out the very best...no questions...the best in every position. If the Prime Minister happened to be one of the four best C-130 aircraft commanders in the country, he might very well fly the mission. Likewise, if the best man happened to be one of the sharpest thorns in the political side of the ruling party, he would still be chosen to fly the mission.

The Israelis are keen on individuals, not just on a particular military squadron that happens to be recognized as a good unit. The men for this mission were handpicked...every one of them. Had this been done with the American military, perhaps our bungled raid to rescue the Iran hostages would have been victorious. On a positive note, it seems that in recent history America has learned some good lessons along that line, when General Norman Schwarzkopf was chosen to plan and execute the Gulf War extrication of a madman's army from the tiny nation of Kuwait. He and his men did their jobs well, up to the point where they were allowed.

Arieh made up his mind and gave his answer in the affirmative. He would fly. The mission would be Top Secret, and had to stay absolutely under wraps. The "guys" continued their training, studying every nook and cranny of the Entebbe airport layout, and that of the old terminal building where the hostages were being held. The latest intelligence information was made available, and the Israelis knew almost to the man, where Idi Amin's guards were located, and where the hostages were being kept.

The deadline had been set by the terrorists. They would begin executing the hostages at 7:00 AM on the following day. There had been a week of communicating between Israel and France and between France and Uganda. The Israeli hostages had been separated from the non-Jews among them. It would soon be another blood bath.

As some of the terrorists bedded down for yet another night in the mosquito infested and ratty Entebbe terminal building, the hostages did the same. They were completely unaware that Israel's leaders had given the green light, and that "the guys" were already airborne, with one of the C-130's commanded by Arieh Oz. A C-130 is not a very fast aircraft, and so the flight would take several hours, covering a one-way distance of some 2,500 miles, and they would arrive in the black of night. It would be akin to making a takeoff in Bangor, Maine and flying to a dark place on the western edge of Nevada, with all the territory in-between filled with hostility towards Israel and any mission such as this.

Whenever a commercial flight departs for a destination, there is a requirement that there be a legal alternate airport, so that if the original destination airport is closed due to an aircraft mishap or weather, the pilot simply proceeds to the designated alternate. Such was the case on the night of July 3, 1976 as Arieh, his fellow airmen in a small formation of C-130 "Herky-Birds", and "the guys" slipped through the darkened skies of Africa to come to the aid of their brothers and sisters. Entebbe had been designated as the alternate airport for a British Airways flight from London destined to land at Nairobi, Kenya.

A skeleton staff of airport workers at Entebbe Airport waited patiently for the phone call that would come from Nairobi Airport, reporting that the British Airways flight had landed safely, and that Entebbe would no longer be needed as a ready alternate. This call would be the signal to throw the light switches, which would darken the taxi way and runway lights at Entebbe.

As Arieh and his crew concentrated on the low-level flying, slipping around any known radar facility that would have the capability of detecting the flight of C-130's, the cargo of Israeli soldiers rehearsed their plans. The aircraft were flying with all navigation lights off, and maintaining complete radio silence. The four turbo-prop engines whined away, and the beat of the propellers were heard from within the cargo area of the Lockheed workhorses. The "guys" looked at each other, some lost in their private thoughts, each knowing that this was a raid of the impossible. It would take a miracle to pull it off. There were some who trusted to their excellent and relentless commando training, confident in their abilities as soldiers to defeat any enemy of Israel. Others whose training was just as complete, trusted to the hand of Divine Providence to guide them on this raid to secure the freedom of fellow Jews. Each soldier had to wrestle with the ball of fear and anxiety that attacks the core of any soldier or entertainer just before the performance would begin.

Entebbe was in sight. The runway lights were visible. Arieh sent the signal back to the "guys" who were waiting for the jostling of the touchdown, and for the rear ramp of the C-130 to open. All of the pent up emotion would then be put into action. The days of rehearsal and training would be put to use. They would soon find out if their plan was a good one.

Arieh gave the verbal commands to his crew. The little boy who had been crammed into the dark wooden box with his sister in Nazi occupied Holland, continued to emerge as a valiant warrior for his people. The metamorphosis of Harry Klausner becoming Arieh Oz continued. The shaky knees and the undermined confidence of a Jewish youngster who had come through the pain and suffering of a Holocaust-ravaged family, had become a bulwark of determination and steadiness as he made small corrections on the four throttles in his right hand. His left hand deftly maneuvered the aircraft yoke, which moved the ailerons and elevator. His two feet blended small rudder corrections with the movement of the other flight controls.

"Gear down....Landing check," commanded Arieh, as Hezi, his young aspiring and handpicked co-pilot reached for the lever that would lower the wheels for landing. If ever there had to be a precision landing, tonight was the night. Two of the C-130's in the formation preceded Arieh, and had landed with their loads of surprise on the Entebbe runway, which sat right next to Lake Victoria on the northern shore.

Arieh descended his aircraft in a turn to final approach, and he lined up with the runway lights of Entebbe directly in front of him. His highly trained and battle-seasoned mind absorbed the fountain of information that flowed from his instrument panel. His eyes danced over the display in front of him...airspeed, altitude, rate of descent, power setting, another check of the three green lights indicating that the wheels were down and locked. He glanced around the airport in front of him for any sign of trouble.

"Landing Flaps!" His able co-pilot moved the flap lever to its final setting, and large aluminum panels deflected downward on the trailing edge of the wing. He was about a mile or so from touchdown, and his crew continued working together like a well-oiled machine. Everything looked good. They would be on the ground in a matter of seconds.

The "guys" in the number one aircraft were on the ground and were already about their business. They moved swiftly. Bullets whizzed through the air as the Israeli commandos struck hard and fast. The Entebbe tower operator, sensing the danger, reached across his console, and flipped the switches that turned off the runway lights. He was unaware, and certainly did not care that Arieh Oz, with an airplane full of commandos was on short final, seconds from touchdown.

Arieh had only split seconds to process what seemed like a hundred possibilities. His four-engine Hercules was now within 300 feet of the ground, about a mile from touchdown, and all the runway lights went out. He saw NOTHING but a black void in front of him. Although he and his fellow pilots had briefed that should such an eventuality occur, they would turn on their aircraft landing lights, continue the approach, and land. Although this act would certainly aid him in landing, it would ruin the surprise element by precious seconds, perhaps alerting the terrorists who held the Jewish hostages in the old terminal building. If he left the landing lights off, he might miss the runway, and crash the airplane, not only ruining the surprise, but perhaps killing himself and the "guys" who depended totally upon him.

He could execute a missed-approach maneuver by adding the power, but that would leave two planeloads of commandos on the ground without the support of those in his plane. He could risk landing totally blind...by the seat of his pants, holding his heading, rate of descent, power, airspeed, and hope for a darkened glimpse of the runway. All these thoughts roared through his mind as he piloted his C-130 in the pitch-black air over Entebbe. Sixty tons of airplane, jet fuel, and humanity hurled toward the ground at over

200 feet per second! He made his choice. They were all in this together. He was "one" with "the guys," who would soon rush from his aircraft in probably the world's most daring rescue attempt. He was "one" with the little old Jewish ladies, the Jewish children, and the Jewish men who lay on the hard floor of the Entebbe Terminal building, next on the list for extermination at the hand of terrorists.

He would go for it. He continued straight ahead, landing lights OFF, using every measure of skill that he could muster to bring this landing to a safe conclusion. His radio altimeter showed his distance above the ground. Using no outside references, Arieh drank in the information from his aircraft instruments, and continued. The aircraft touched down, and the "guys" in the back had absolutely no knowledge of the split second crisis that had just occurred.

Arieh pulled back on the throttles and lifted them over a detent. Farther back they came. An intricate array of electrical, hydraulic and mechanical circuits responded, and the blades on all four propellers rotated on the prop hub, putting the engines into reverse thrust. The aircraft slowed quickly. They were on the ground, and the airplane was intact, but it was like trying to drive a car without headlights, along a dark country road. The scenery around the C-130 was as dark as the souls of the terrorists who had been the cause of this needed rescue attempt.

An overhead hatch on the airplane flew open, and one of the Israeli crewmen stuck his head out. He had a headset and microphone, which was connected to the cockpit intercom. He could speak directly to Arieh.

Arieh spoke to his crewman first. "What do you see? Tell me quickly!" In the confusion and fright of the circumstances an answer did not come quickly enough. Arieh brought the aircraft to a complete stop. It was none too soon, for he was about to taxi into a large ditch just off the runway. They regained their bearings, and Arieh at high-speed, taxied to the pre-determined spot at Entebbe Airport where the rear ramp of the C-130 was lowered.

The "guys" leaped into action. They moved swiftly across the tarmac with some jeep mounted guns. They joined the other "guys" who landed in the first aircraft, some of whom jammed themselves into a black Mercedes Benz that had been brought with them to look exactly like Idi Amin's limousine, complete with flags on the fenders. Still others ran at full speed for the Entebbe terminal building, where they would execute the plan that they had been studying and rehearsing for days.

It was all over in 53 minutes. The terrorists had been killed, Idi Amin's most available troops had been silenced, and the Israeli hostages were ushered quickly to the waiting C-130's for their trip home to Zion. As insurance, the "guys" ran down the flight line blowing up Uganda's Russian-built Migs, rendering neutral any effort that might be mounted to chase their comparatively slow C-130's back to Israel. A C-130 was no match for a Mig, any more than a Mack truck would be a match for a Masserati.

The "guys" had thought of everything...almost everything. They had even prepared one of the C-130's as a hospital, where they could tend to any wounded on the way back to Israel. There was no way however, to plan for the heartache and disappointment of losing their commanding officer. As the formation of "Herky-Birds" lifted into the black sky of Entebbe, those who had been condemned to a PFLP "death row" only an hour earlier, were celebrating almost in unbelief that they were free. In another airplane flying only a few hundred yards away, Lt. Col. Yoni Netanyahu, commander of "the guys", fought for his life. He had been a most important part of planning the mission, and he had driven his men hard in the days of training that lay behind.

He had been tough on them, because he loved them, and because he loved Zion and the people of Zion. His love extended even more to those who were held captive by cowardly butchers in an abandoned terminal building 2,500 miles away. This same love would provoke him to risk his own life and even lay it down so that others might live.

As the turboprops of the C-130 carved the night air just outside the aircraft hull, the bullet that had sliced its way into Yoni's body, did its job. Yoni, whose brother Benjamin served as the Israeli ambassador to the United Nations for several years, and who later became Israel's Prime Minister, breathed his last. His "guys" fell silent inside the cramped fuselage, tangled in a web of emotion that wanted to celebrate the victory of the rescue, and wanting to weep for their fallen leader. It was a perfect example of the bittersweet that so surrounds the people of Zion.

Radio silence was broken. The simple message was sent by code to waiting receivers back in Israel. In essence, "Mission complete...Hostages rescued...We're comin' home!"

The news was greeted with great joy. Military officers, Israeli cabinet members, the Prime Minister, all rejoiced. They could not break the news yet to the public, for the C-130's were not yet at a place where they could be considered safely out of danger. They had not the fuel to make it back to Israel, and were on their way to Nairobi where they would refuel.

Although the mission had been successful, and a mighty blow had been struck for freedom and justice, Israeli airplanes full of their soldiers and rescued hostages were "hot potatoes" for most of the world. No one would touch them. Even in Nairobi, they were not welcome. The word was given..."Refuel and get out of here!" It mattered little about the wounded and the grieving.... the age old message to the Jews was once again being sounded. "We don't want you. You make things inconvenient for us...Leave!"

Arieh, along with his precious cargo of "the guys" pushed up the power levers and headed back for Zion. The mission had been a success, but it was not without the cost of lives and money. Even in victory the words of the Psalmist ring out:

> How long shall the wicked, O Lord, how long shall the wicked exult? They pour forth words, they speak arrogantly; All who do wickedness vaunt themselves. They crush Thy people, O Lord, and afflict Thy heritage. They slay the widow and the stranger, and murder the orphans. And they have said, "The Lord does not see, nor does the God of Jacob pay heed.
>
> (NAS—Psalm 94:3-7)

In growing revelation, the psalmist continues as he sees the faithfulness of the God of Abraham, Isaac, and Jacob as He provides promise and hope, but also asks the question which provokes an answer in the affirmative from any man who would claim to be a follower of His:

> For the Lord will not abandon His people, nor will He forsake His inheritance. For judgment will again be righteous; and all the upright in heart will follow it. Who will stand up for me against evildoers? Who will take his stand for me against those who do wickedness?"
>
> (NAS—Psalm 94:14-16)

The answer to these last questions of the psalmist seems to be, "not very many". Although there were messages of congratulations sent to the Israeli government, and statements made to the press, they were very guarded and restrained. Other statements were louder, such as that of France's ambassador to Kenya, Olivier Beleau, in an attempt to distance himself and his nation from the Israelis: "We did not know anything about it, the Israelis did everything themselves." In other words...please be sure that you don't blame us or hook us up with anything that Israel has done...even if it was totally right before God and man.

In general, the nations are more afraid of world opinion and any threat of violence or loss of business to themselves, than in taking a firm stand against those who would invoke terror to accomplish their goals. Momentary safety is more easily found by disassociating from the people of Zion, and withdrawing support, even it be only verbal.

The long flight back to Israel ended as the hostages, including non-Jews, and the Air France flight crew who had been held by the terrorists disembarked to a jubilant crowd at Tel Aviv's Ben Gurion Airport. Once it had been established that the C-130 aircraft were on their way home with the precious human cargo and were out of danger of Arab air forces, the news went through Israel faster than a space shuttle. People poured into the streets, and engulfed Ben Gurion Airport with Israeli flags waving, champagne bottles held high, and tears of joy running down their faces as they greeted their loved ones. Those who were considered dead only yesterday, were alive and well today! It was July 4, 1976, and this raid to Entebbe struck a mighty blow for freedom against the dark and evil forces of the day. It was a special gift to the world, and especially to America as she celebrated her 200th birthday. The forces of democracy and justice had prevailed over those of tyranny and evil!

Today, in the lobby of Ben Gurion Airport, there is a small bronze statue, which because of its location, can go almost unnoticed to busy passers-by. It was crafted and its accompanying statement authored by P. Braslow. The statue is of a helmeted Israeli soldier with a gun slung over his shoulder, wrapping his arms around and huddling over two civilians in protective fashion. The inscription next to it infers a heretofore unacknowledged ignorance of what it is to be fully a Jew, living in Israel. It was entitled, "Operation Yonatan-Entebbe."

> A closeness, an interdependence
> a faith, a trust, "my people."
> I did not know
>     in America
> If it was true
>     if it really existed
> So I came to look
>     and listen
>     and feel
> And I still did not know
>     until Entebbe.

For Arieh, it was simply another day in his life. He is hardly aware of his personal contributions to his people and his nation. He is too humble, and in some ways I believe, too restrained to allow himself to exult in the victories of life. Though decorated by the Israeli government and promoted in rank for his conduct on this rescue mission to Entebbe, he is reluctant to gloat over it. As he lives in hope for himself and his people, he is all too aware that the world is not yet free of the Leila Kahleds, Idi Amins, Sadaam Husseins and their likenesses. He, like most of his fellow citizens of Zion, continue with great hope but with even greater vigilance.

Where there has been great pain in one's life, there is usually equal reluctance to dig around in one's memory bank to relive the feelings. Painful events that have been buried deep in our souls, often have the perceived threat of a junkyard dog. When one goes too near, they bite. The normal defense for all of us is to avoid the junkyard, and thereby, the dog.

For years, Arieh too, left the past behind, trying to forget the terrible childhood years of Harry. As he raised his own family, new birthdays, and bar-mitzvahs were celebrated. It was one such event, with the urging of his faithful wife, which prompted Arieh to dig into the past. In a Jewish family, there is probably no more important event in a young man's life, than that of the Bar Mitzvah, the celebration which marks the step from boyhood into manhood. This significant rite of passage is celebrated by the young man's first public reading of the Torah. Indeed, to become a man of accountability is to publicly acknowledge the Word of God. The Bar Mitzvah can probably be best paralleled with the Christian Confirmation, or age of full accountability, however from this author's observations; the Bar Mitzvah is celebrated with far more fervor and enthusiasm than any Christian Confirmation that I have attended.

As this important event in Arieh's son's life drew closer, and since it was tradition to invite family and friends to witness and celebrate, at his wife's urging, Arieh went back to Holland to those who had nurtured and protected him. He met with the Christians from the Dutch farmhouse in Zeist, Holland near Utrecht, "Uncle" Oepke and family. For these many years it had been impossible, but now it would be faced, and the Haitsma family would have the added joy of seeing Arieh's own child, born in Israel, and Bar-Mitzvahed, another child of Zion, brought to manhood.

What he had for so long been unable to face, became healing salve, as he was able to embrace Oepke and Jitske for what they had done for him as a youth. For the Haitsmas, it was an answer to prayer to know that they had a part in keeping alive one of Israel's sons.

Arieh went further for his dear friends from the past. He documented his story, and the Haitsma family has had a tree planted with an appropriate plaque along the Avenue of the Righteous Gentiles which leads up to the *Yad Vashem* Holocaust memorial in Jerusalem. He personally flew them aboard El Al, and brought them from Holland to Israel when they were so honored.

It was the right thing to do, for it was not long after, that instead of the Haitsmas coming to Israel, Arieh went back to Holland, and watched the casket of his surrogate father lowered into the ground. "Uncle" Oepke had finished his work in this realm, and one of the fruits of his labors stood at his graveside in the figure of Captain Arieh Oz, a son of Abraham, and a son of Zion.

A faithful Jew or a faithful Christian knows that the battle for Zion is not over, but it has already been won. In spite of the question that rings from the Psalmist and even through the heart of Israel..."How long O Lord? How long?"...the time is close at hand. Arieh's own children stand today as added evidence to God's promise that Israel will live!

As I left Arieh's home in Ramat-Hasharon, I did not yet know it but I would soon meet another child of the promise. As with almost every Israeli male, he too was enlisted in the Israeli Defense Forces.

# 5

# SHIMON

I was enjoying the warmth and the sunshine of a Jerusalem day just outside the Dung Gate of the Old City. Sitting on the edge of a wall, my eyes feasted on the array of humanity around me. Bearded orthodox Jews scurried in and out through the gate on their way to the *Kotel* (Western Wall) of the Temple to pray. Arab street vendors sold fresh rings of Sesame bread that still stimulates my digestive juices when I recall the aroma and taste. There were also the standard cans of Coca-Cola for sale, and young Arab would-be merchants pursued their customers as their fathers oversaw them.

People from all over the world were bumping into each other as they came and went from this holy site. Europeans, Americans, and the ever more present Japanese and their video cameras added to the scene. Some Arab teenagers from the local area looked on, some with zest and life in their eyes, but if I read the expression on one young face correctly, it was one of disdain, under girded by a wish that all the foreigners bustling about before him, would go home, and take the Jews with them.

I was only meters away from the site of a military ceremony, which had been held only a few nights before. Israeli soldiers who had completed their training had received their awards and certificates as their parents and friends looked on. It was a time of celebration for all. Some members of the PLO (Palestine Liberation Organization) thought differently about the ceremony.

Two of them had sneaked quietly close to the ceremony and lobbed a couple of grenades into the crowd. The target did not matter to these terrorists, as long as damage was done, blood spilled, and great pain inflicted, especially if the targeted people were tourists or Jews. And if they were Jews...all the better to these deceived souls. As the grenades exploded, sending shards of metal tearing into the flesh of the soldier's families, the terrorists were already running at full speed down the road over a rock wall, into a parking lot, and down into the Kidron Valley where they hid themselves among the local Arab populace.

Above them, mothers and fathers of the newly sworn-in Israeli soldiers lay on the pavement, wounded and bleeding. Some lay dead, victims of yet another surprise of **Jihad**, or "holy" war. Their *Allah* would be pleased. The tragedy had occurred only a few nights before, but life went on with a vigor as I watched. Busloads of tourists were dropped off at the curbside as Israeli soldiers continued to vigilantly patrol the area. They were determined to stave off a repeat of another cruel and senseless attack.

I have traveled extensively, and have spent some time in communist countries, even before the walls came down. When I see gun-toting soldiers in such places, I know that they're not on my side. They are there to keep me under the thumb of their government. In Israel, when I see an Israeli soldier, I know that he's on my side, and instead of being a threat, he is a protector.

One of the soldiers walked up to me. He was **Sephardic** (a Jew whose heritage is from Mediterranean countries such as Morocco, Tunisia, Libya, Spain, etc.) dark complected, dark eyed, and a black-haired young man of 20. He looked at my open shirt collar and noted a small gold chain from which was suspended a small Jewish Star of David, interwoven with a Christian cross.

He smiled, pointed at the curious symbol, and spoke in heavily accented English, "That means that you believe in Jesus...Right?"

"Well...yes...But it also means that I love and stand with Israel and the Jewish people."

That's how our conversation began, and it lasted for some 45 minutes. I learned that his name was Shimon, and that he was soon to be released from the army. He had been involved with Operation Peace for Galilee. This was an effort in 1982 on the part of the Israelis to exorcise the deeply rooted PLO operation in Southern Lebanon, so that the residents of Northern Israel would not have to be victims of the continual shelling and rocket attacks which assaulted them from just over the border in Lebanon.

As our conversation went on, Shimon told me about some friends of his who were believers in Jesus or Yeshua (His Hebrew name). He asked me many questions. I did my best simply to answer them, and I asked a few of my own about his family and some details of his life. He was very friendly and kind, financially broke, and looking for a job. He was scheduled to leave active military service in but a few days. We exchanged addresses, and made a commitment to meet again. He also asked me to write to him. I agreed to try, although I was afraid that other priorities in my busy life might override this good intention.

Although our initial conversation was rather brief, I sensed something special about Shimon...perhaps a need, loneliness, or simply the warmth of his friendship. I liked him very much and purposed to write him a letter when I returned to America.

Keeping my promise, I wrote to him, and in his answer to me I learned that things were not easy for him. He was having difficulty finding a job, and there were some family needs that were unmet. These facts were casually mentioned and I did not sense that the news was being offered to me to provoke a pity that would blossom into a monetary donation. He sent a picture of himself in uniform, and generally gave me some news on his whereabouts. I sensed that I would meet with him again on some future visit to Israel.

Some months passed and I was preparing to make another trip to Israel, to interview some of the people of Zion for the purposes of completing the research for this book. A week or two before my proposed departure, a tall rugged good-looking Yugoslavian man came to my house. He had become a Christian several months before, and my wife and I had ministered to him on a few occasions. Back in his Gentile days, he had been a womanizer and a chaser of money. In the months since he had given his life to the Lord, he continued to seek God's will for his life.

As he and I sat together on my living room couch, he told me a story about how he was sitting in his back yard on a beach chair, reading the Bible and praying, and he was convicted to give his all for the kingdom of God. He had a small collection of gold coins in a safety deposit box, each worth about $400 in cash. He handed me one of those coins, and said, "This is to go to you and your wife to help Israel."

Yugo was hardly a man of means. He worked as a painter and general handy man, and his small collection of gold coins represented his life's savings. He insisted that the coin be used to help Israel. As I sat on my couch, I immediately knew of a young man who was in need, an Israeli soldier named Shimon.

This act of love on the part of Yugo reminded me of the New Testament story where Jesus observed a woman who dropped a couple of copper coins into the Temple treasury. He called His disciples to Himself saying, "Truly I say to you, this poor widow put in more than all the contributors to the treasury; for they all put in out of their surplus, but she, out of her poverty, put in all she owned, all she had to live on." (NAS—Mark 12:43-44)

The coin was in a plastic case, and I kept it in my pocket as I went to Israel. I believed that this coin was to be for Shimon, if and when I made contact with him.

It must be stated, that for years, the religious Jews have fought hard to keep Christians from "buying" converts. I am sad to say that there have been such attempts, either to take advantage of a need, or to create an economic dependence on a person or a ministry with the ultimate goal of converting. There are laws enacted in Israel, which can cause a person to be thrown out of the country if he or she partakes in such activity. I personally think that any such practice of trying to "buy" a convert is an abomination before God as well as man, and I would stand shoulder to shoulder with any Jew in condemning such a practice. Equally, however, it is just as despicable when a Christian makes a genuine effort to help a Jew, and is then accused by religious zealots of trying to convert or buy him away from his people. I was aware that if my little effort of giving was to be discovered by the wrong people, I could easily be accused of trying to "buy" a convert by giving this coin to Shimon, but I knew my heart before the Lord, and I knew Yugo's genuine desire to bless Israel. I proceeded to represent Yugo as the carrier of his gift to one of God's people.

On arriving in Israel, I was able to contact Shimon to arrange a meeting where he could share his life story with me. We met in a lovely apartment in the artist's colony of Jerusalem, *Yemin Moshe*. The apartment was owned by some generous American Christians who offered its use to Hellen and me when we visited Israel.

I turned on my small tape recorder, and Shimon began to tell me his story.

His family came to Israel in 1948, his mother, Miriam from Italy, and Joseph his father, from Tunis. He was born on a *moshav* in Israel in 1966 as the 10th child of 13. (A *moshav* is a form of collective living similar to a kibbutz, except that there is more private ownership of homes, cars, and other properties. The members of the *moshav* are, however, covenanted together in the collective ownership of land, or if the land were privately owned, its produce would be dedicated to the economic good of the *moshav*.)

The work on the *moshav* was long and hard, as is the case with any farm work. There are seasons of extremely intense activity to plant or to harvest, and there are times when the work can proceed on a more moderate basis, but it is never easy. It was after a few years of barely scraping out a living on the *moshav* that Joseph and Miriam left the community and moved to the town of Nahariya, in northern Israel.

Although many if not most Israeli families have endured great difficulties, there are often tales of victory as each family emerges from tragic events of the past. This was not the case with Shimon's family. His home life was one that was surrounded with much trauma. His was a family with too many children, and parents who were unable to properly provide for them. Shimon, who was not looked upon so much as a son, but another mouth to feed, was sent away to a school that generally served as an orphanage, or a refuge for children from severely broken or incapable families.

He was there with his brother Michael, and although they were together, they both felt abandoned. From the point of view of a child, they had both been rejected by their parents. Shimon was afraid, insecure, and cried often from the heartache of not being part of a secure family. While he was in the orphanage, his mother and father continued to struggle with the other kids at home. They were parents whose own lives were not in order, and who had not the ability to discipline themselves or to love each other enough to cope with life. They were forever tired and could barely put food on the table for their large brood.

As Shimon grew in the orphanage, he more and more became "out of sight, out of mind."

Parental visits to the orphanage became less and less frequent, and his visits home became less of a joy, although he always loved to see his other brothers and sisters.

Shimon learned how to survive in his environment, but was filled with agitation, anger, and fear. He was a problem in the classroom, and did not have the ability to sit still long enough to absorb a lesson. Whenever there was a problem at the school, the teachers and even his fellow students would automatically look to Shimon as the culprit. By his own admission, his teachers and students were usually correct in their assumptions, and he became one of the greatest disciplinary challenges in the orphanage. Shimon was looking for fun and laughter in a life that had only sadness and pain. School pranks and rebellion proved to be a good way to get attention, but it was that same attention that usually rejected his behavior, and rejected him as well.

As Shimon continued to tell his story, it became apparent that he did not know who his real father was. His mother had lived with at least two men. It no longer mattered, because both men were dead, one having died from cancer, and the other from a severe automobile accident. On Shimon's passport, his father's name is shown as Eliezer, and was the one who died in the car accident. He loved both men, but now both were gone from his life.

As Shimon came to that important age of 13, he and several of his classmates prepared for his all-important step from boyhood to manhood. Several boys in his orphanage would celebrate their **Bar-Mitzvah**. As the days grew closer, the boys practiced the reading of the Torah, and became more and more excited as the event drew near.

The big day finally arrived, and as Shimon surveyed the crowd of mothers, fathers, sisters, and brothers of the many broken families, he discovered that he was the only one who had no one to take part in this ceremony with him. No family member had come to see him go through his Bar-Mitzvah ceremony. He read the Torah, sat down, and wept. As the ceremony was over, some of the boys, who had fathers, were hoisted onto their dad's shoulders and given a ride of rejoicing. Others were hugged, encouraged, and loved....even by those who had trouble doing it on a regular basis in a stable home. Shimon, in the midst of the joy and celebration of others, never felt more alone.

Miriam, Shimon's mother, had long run out of patience in life. The demands of her many children, and the fact that the men in her life were dead, left her cold and heartless. Even when Shimon would reach out to hug or kiss her, she would often push him away. Her worries centered around the lack of money, and her fantasies of a "good life" which had always eluded her, caused her to blame her children for the things that she did not have.

Things were no easier for his brother, Michael, but at least he had a girl friend. He had the warmth of a woman who cared enough about him to give him all of herself. It was not long before his girlfriend was with child, and Michael, also a soldier, decided to marry. There was a problem, however, because she was non-Jewish. Some of his very religious countrymen became involved in the matter, and fought against Michael's decision to take his pregnant girlfriend as his wife.

One of the greatest perceived threats on the part of the Jewish community is that of assimilation—the intermarrying of their sons and daughters with non-Jews of the world. It is taken by some to be as serious a threat as the Holocaust. Sometimes in the tunnel vision of the moment, the fear can elicit bad advice. This is not an exclusive of the Jewish community, because similar advice has been injected into young couples' lives by Protestant ministers and by Catholic priests. Shimon's brother, Michael, was counseled and severely pressured to have his girl friend abort the child.

"What? ....... You call yourself religious men, and you want to kill a baby? You are teachers and counselors and you want to kill !!!?" Michael pounded his fist on the table of discussion and walked out. A renegade of the Jewish tradition married him and his girlfriend, a woman who legally performs civil ceremonies, and who is hated by the religious establishment in Israel.

The health system is so set up however, that because of their marriage under the given circumstances, they did not qualify for hospital care for the birth of their baby. Because they were financially strapped, it became another burden, which they had to shoulder themselves.

Shimon too, felt the burden of his brother Michael and his wife. The couple had become worshipping believers in Jesus, and they prayed. Their prayers were answered through some people brought into their lives and who helped them with some funds. It enabled them to have a little honeymoon together, and to finance some of the baby's expenses.

One of the helpers happened to be a priest, and gave the couple his blessing along with $300. Michael later paid him back with $600. The overly religious had succeeded in hurting this young couple to the point that they joined the **yordim**, those Jews who have left Israel to live among the Gentiles in the nations. It is a term in Hebrew that literally means, "to go down," and is often looked upon as a turning away from being a real Jew, by those who choose to live in Israel. Although Shimon was now happy for his brother, he would miss him very much. They had been through so much together as youngsters, and he would lose his companionship.

Everyone in Israel has to serve in the army. When a young man comes "of age", he usually receives his papers, and he is expected to serve. Each man has to serve on active duty for a few years, and then periodically throughout his adulthood as a reservist. Without such a system, Israel would have been annihilated years ago by her many enemies.

It was Shimon's turn to don the uniform of a member of the IDF (Israeli Defense Forces). He was selected to train as a paratrooper, where unknowingly, his boyhood conflicts would be disciplined severely by tough Israeli drill sergeants. There would be no pranks or rebellion in the army. This was not an orphanage, although some of Shimon's buddies were also orphans or products of deeply divided families. During army training, it was not uncommon to see Shimon with his shirt off, hands tied behind his back, and sitting in the hot desert sun as discipline for his many infractions and rebellious ways. He admitted that it was this discipline, at the hand of caring but tough father figures that caused him to grow up.

The training was as tough as could be found in any army in the world. Shimon learned all the basics of soldiering and more, to use and to care for his weapons and equipment, and to jump from airplanes. He and his unit were combat ready, should the need arise.

As has been the case throughout history, Israel's enemies are unrelenting. Lebanon, Israel's northern neighbor, had become a land of anarchy. What was once the playground of the Middle East, had become a briar patch of war, with numerous factions fighting the world outside, and each other. Beirut was the capital, and had become a target range for small time militiamen and their causes. Where there was factional fighting, it was diffused by a stronger catalyst....the mutual hatred of Israel and the Jewish people. PLO chief, Yasser Arafat, sat in the midst of the destruction and confusion, orchestrating much of the bloodshed and terror.

In the south of Lebanon, a small group of Lebanese Christians held out for seven years in the hills, trying to stem the tide of the Soviet financed efforts of the PLO to completely take over Lebanon and eventually annihilate Israel. Major Saad Hadad, a man of deep faith and prayer, led his men to frustrate the PLO time after time, with no support from the outside. I sat in Jerusalem at a meeting where Major Hadad spoke after the Israelis had gone into Lebanon.

In his heavily accented English, but coming from his heart, he continued to ask the question, "where was the support from the nations for him and his men?" He had watched in dismay to see the Soviet weapons and equipment flow like water into the hands of the PLO, which used these resources to terrorize the Lebanese into submission. There was not even a gallon of gasoline offered by the hands of the nations to help Major Hadad fight for his own country.

He recalled the many hardships endured by his men as well as the many prayers that he had offered heavenward for help. He continued with a resonant, slow speaking, heavily-accented and deeply sincere voice..."And God sent Israel to liberate us!"

One of the sons of Israel that God sent to liberate Lebanon, was Shimon, along with his unit of newly trained and exuberant paratroopers. All the discipline of his military training would be put to the test, and when the word came down that they would be proceeding to Lebanon, the young troops were eager and ready to meet their adversaries.

For years, the PLO had been shelling the kibbutzim from inside Lebanon. They often would send in a terrorist squad, purposefully killing women and children, inflicting as much pain and damage as possible. Israel would retaliate against known PLO positions with an air strike, but the PLO had been given virtual immunity from their actions by a politically paralyzed world and by the patience and long-suffering of the Israelis.

The day finally came that Israel would mount an offensive that would neutralize this growing cobra, which continued to spit its venom south into Israel. Young and freshly trained Israeli troops were anxious to do battle against their enemy. "Let's go guys...we'll give 'em hell!" The boasts of the young but unseasoned encouraged one another as plans were prepared for Lebanon's liberation.

As with any military operation, surprise and fast action can be one of the best weapons to insure victory. Israel had often used this as part of her strategy in battling her foes. It would be the same for "Operation Peace for Galilee." Israel moved quickly, and began to meet some fierce opposition by the numerous and well-fortified PLO troops. The Israelis were not meeting a mere band of hooligans, but an entire army, dedicated to the annihilation of Israel. Fighting was fierce and casualties mounted. The surprised PLO continued to fall back and to move as far underground as they were able.

Shimon and his unit were in the midst of it. As the fighting began, fear gripped the young Israeli troops. Many were not seasoned vets, but had been in the artificial and relatively safe environment of the training schools. They had not faced the confusion and the hurricane winds of war. Although they were led by the experienced and well-seasoned, the first dose of combat was yet to be tasted.

The shelling started, and the PLO artillery shells began to pound the Israeli positions. Shimon remembers the fear that gripped him and his pals. At one point, he lay in a foxhole, and he and his friends just hugged each other, unable to move, as the shells continued to explode around them. This was not a movie set for Rambo, or for a John Wayne thriller. This was the real thing, and young men were dying. The exuberant boasts of the previous days were silenced and replaced by words undergirded more with humility and reality. The glory of war envisioned by young minds soon became the tragedy of bleeding and dying friends.

The determined Israelis continued to advance, and as they cleaned the terrorist army out of a Lebanese village, the local populace greeted them with applause and cheers. It must be remembered that the Lebanese people had been occupied and held captive by fanatic men from different parts of the Middle East, who had invaded their country were well financed, supported, and trained by Soviet Russia. The Israeli leaders were astounded at the weapons caches that were uncovered as they drove back the PLO armies. Even their best intelligence information had severely underestimated the size and scope of the effort, which was being mounted to destroy Israel. The move into Lebanon had come none too soon.

As the battles raged day after day, the Israeli forces moved quickly, taking territory at an astounding rate, but it was not without losses. The PLO is a defiant foe, and they use tactics that are unlike most armies of the world. Their fanaticism is bolstered by beliefs that to die for Allah, or the holy war, results in instant martyrdom, and a special place in Allah's kingdom. This delusion has cost the lives of untold hundreds of thousands in Iran, Iraq, Libya, and other Middle East nations, where belligerent leaders continue to exact a toll of spilled blood that reaches even into the ranks of their own 14-year old soldiers.

As Shimon proceeded with his unit northward, he was riding in an armored personnel carrier, or APC. It's a vehicle with treads like a tank, but has an open top, which allows soldiers to sit inside and to move along roads or fields safe from small arms fire. Long time residents of the villages, who were grateful that their towns had been flushed of the PLO invaders who had taken over with brute force and terror, had greeted the Israelis. There were however, other "greetings" from fanatic members of the PLO, who stubbornly refused to quit, or who were determined to sacrifice themselves to Allah.

As Shimon and his buddies rode slowly through the town in their APC's, they came to a couple of dead PLO members, whose bodies lay in the middle of the street. A couple of Shimon's buddies were about to jump out of their vehicle and move the corpses aside. An order crackled over the radio from their commander, who had smelled the trap. "You move one of those bodies and you're dead meat!"

The commander and some others had seen other members of the PLO perched on some rooftops, waiting for an unwary Israeli soldier to leave the relative safety of his armor protected vehicle to move the lifeless bodies aside. At that point they would kill the exposed Israelis. Their plan had worked before. It did not work this time.

The slow forward movement continued. The Israelis had been stalled for almost four days while their explosive experts cleared the area of mines. While that was occurring, the PLO made a few plans of its own. With the area considered safe from mines, the orders came to move ahead. The APC's engine roared and the squeaking and clanking of its treads continued to give evidence of their movement. Eighteen, nineteen, and twenty-year old Israelis who had been seasoned in battle were watching carefully as they wove their way through a village street.

The shout came......"GRENADE!......GRENADE!" Shimon's buddy saw their enemy first. He lifted his M-16 and shot the young Palestinian as he ran toward their vehicle, and lobbed the grenade into the midst of seated Israeli soldiers. The grenade clunked and rattled about the floor for only a second or two, out of the immediate reach of Shimon and his buddies. The young Israelis scrambled to leap out of the vehicle. It all happened in seconds.

As Shimon leaped, the grenade exploded. Shrapnel tore into his legs and stomach, as he was airborne on the way over the side. He landed outside the APC on the ground, stunned, and badly wounded. His buddies, who were not able to move as quickly, were killed. Drov, the radioman who was unable to strip himself of the radio gear and leap, collapsed into a pool of blood. In the macabre descriptions that are peculiar to fighting men, Shimon's one word..."Salad"...articulated the horrifying mess that was left inside the vehicle. Those who were filled with life and future only moments ago, were reduced to a heap of twisted corpses. An idle conversation about home had just been interrupted by the intrusion of a baseball-sized mass of metal. The ears on which this conversation had fallen no longer functioned, and the lips from which the words were created were forever silenced.

A young PLO fanatic lay dead only a few feet from Shimon. Shimon's buddy, who shot him, was part of the carnage that lay inside the now motionless APC. Israeli mothers and fathers would soon receive the news that their 19 or 20 year old sons no longer lived, and wounds from that one lobbed grenade would be inflicted in hearts all over Israel, crippling agony that would last for weeks and pain that would last a lifetime.

Shimon continued to speak, and as he described this experience, he lifted his shirt, and the leg of his pants to show me the scars left from that day in Lebanon. He spent a couple of weeks in the hospital, his flesh healing and recuperating, but his mind still ravaged by the sudden loss of his buddies.

After his physical wounds healed, he went back into Lebanon to continue the long job of combating those who desired the complete destruction of Israel. Things were generally more quiet, with an occasional attack or encounter with the now-splintered PLO and its factions. During one spell of boredom, Shimon and his buddies went to their commander. They needed some work to do. Sitting around and waiting was too much of a burden.

Their commander gave them a job. It was not easy work, but it would make an impact which would be remembered for life. Shimon and his buddies were taken to the mouth of a tunnel that had been cleverly burrowed into the hills of South Lebanon. It was one of many such underground caverns, cleverly crafted with thousands of hours of manual labor. As he entered the tunnel it led to a maze of others, about 4 kilometers worth! More than TWO MILES, the tunnels were large and stuffed with Russian supplied weapons...grenade launchers, rockets, Kalachnikov rifles, thousands of boxes of ammunition, PLO propaganda literature, posters of Yasser Arafat, heroin, hashish, sex magazines, phony identification cards, and copies of the Koran. Shimon and dozens of his fellow soldiers worked for two weeks straight, hand-carrying these supplies from the depths of the tunnels and loading them onto Israeli trucks. This was but one maze of tunnels among many that held the ammunition and supplies to destroy the Jewish people, the people of Zion.

Operation Peace for Galilee would continue, and there would be more skirmishes with the enemy. Each encounter with the enemy would bring with it more victories but also defeats. Shimon would lose yet more of his friends. He would make the trip to Mount Herzl in Jerusalem four times to serve as part of the honor guard for fallen buddies. Mount Herzl is Israel's Arlington Cemetery. To be on an honor guard or a pallbearer for a soldier's burial, it usually meant that the fallen son of Israel was more than a passing acquaintance, but a real friend.

On one of the repeat trips to Mt. Herzl, Shimon stood with his rifle. As his friend was laid to rest, the sobs of his parents and family friends pierced to his very core. He knew what it was to cry. He knew the sadness of rejection and loss, of loneliness and despair. This was another painful event that would have to be overcome. Despite his resolve to hang tough, the tears rolled from his black Sephardic eyes, coursing down tanned cheeks. His insides felt as liquid as his tears.

Shimon, along with other members of the honor guard, was to shoot his rifle eight times. The number eight happens to be a biblical number representing new beginnings. The tears were unrelenting, wetting Shimon's face as he contemplated the finality of the ceremony. It was all too much. This was another brick of pain added to the wagon load that he was already carrying. A colonel in charge of the ceremony, perhaps feeling the pain himself, ordered Shimon, in soft but tough tones, "You must be tough. You must shoot. You must be strong. You must not cry. You must shoot...eight times!"

And once again, stifled emotion was shoved back into the recesses of Shimon's tormented soul. The vipers of tragedy had bitten again, and the locusts of the soul continued to gnaw away. The shame of past family life, and the rocket of inferred shame fired at a young man because he was crying for his friend begs for Heaven's answer.

> Then will I make up to you for the years that the swarming locust has eaten, the creeping locust, the stripping locust, and the gnawing locust, My great army which I sent among you. And you shall have plenty to eat and be satisfied, and praise the name of the Lord your God, who has dealt wondrously with you; Then My people will never be put to shame. Thus you will know that I am in the midst of Israel, and that I am the Lord your God and there is no other; And My people will never be put to shame.
>
> (NAS—Joel 2:25-27)

While waiting for these words to be fulfilled, Shimon, in addition to making four trips to Mt. Herzl in Jerusalem, made two others like it to Tel Aviv, and one to a *moshav* cemetery. All buddies...all close...all gone!

Shimon continued to speak as we faced each other during the interview. He spoke of the more than three years that he spent in Lebanon, the wounds, the deaths, and the burials. As he spoke of the final order for his unit to leave Lebanon, he came home to Israel where his fellow soldiers fell into the arms of their mothers and fathers and families. The hugs and kisses of gladness permeated the reunion, but once again, Shimon had no one who either could or would come to meet him.

As we sat in the kitchen of the Jerusalem apartment, Shimon, a son of Zion, began to weep. He was reliving the pain of years of dashed hopes. I momentarily felt guilty, for I had been the "can-opener" which had pried the lid from his memories. The word to perhaps better describe my feelings, is "privileged", for I was being entrusted with the secrets of a man's soul, and yes...even again touching the apple of God's eye through one of His people.

Shimon felt safe with me. He could tell me those private incidents of life, which were snarled in a tangle, which seemed to have no attribute that could be described as good. Even if I had wanted to, I could not hold back my own tears, as I felt, even if only slightly, this Israeli soldier's pain. We hugged each other and we both wept.

At the conclusion of the interview, I reviewed with Shimon the story of King David, who as a shepherd boy had been rejected in many ways by even his own brothers. I reminded him of how he had been relegated to doing some of the most mundane and thankless jobs available at the time. I tried to encourage him in reminding him how God still chose David, one who had suffered and been rejected, and who had faced many fears and trials in the loneliness of the night while shepherding sheep. I told him about God's faithfulness and His provision in the darkest of times.

It was now time to speak to him about a man named Yugo, who only a few days before my travel to Israel, had come to my Florida home and had given me a gold coin...for Israel. I pulled it from my pocket and handed it to Shimon, playing the role of messenger, from a loving heart living in America, to a broken heart living in Israel. I explained to Shimon that this was his...no strings attached...just a gift of love to him to use as he saw fit.

There is no amount of gold, silver, real estate, or possessions that can take the place of love, security, and acceptance. Yet a small gift, which will meet an earthly need, can be an expression of love. Words from the New Testament confirm this truth:

> "But whoever has this world's goods, and beholds his brother in need and closes his heart against him, how does the love of God abide in him? Little children, let us not love with word or with tongue, but in deed and truth."
>
> (NAS—1 John 3:17-18)

It was not the love of money that put the smile of hope on Shimon's face. It was gratefulness and the fact that a stranger, who had never met him, had been the vehicle that God had used to express His love, and His provision for Shimon in a time of need. It was a need foreseen, and not a provision of reaction, and it was there....right on time.

In his experiences throughout Israel, Shimon had met many people. Some of those folks were Christians, and someone along the way had given him a Bible, containing the Old and New Testaments written in Hebrew. Shimon had been reading it and had been praying heartily for a relationship with God, a relationship that I am sure he has, and which is growing to new heights with the passing of each day.

Along with his other meager belongings, Shimon kept and read his Bible almost daily. Basically homeless, he was at present staying with his sister in Jerusalem. She had married an ultra-orthodox religious man who practiced his Jewish religion and tradition to the fullest. Within a couple of days of our interview, his brother-in-law discovered Shimon's Bible. He took it outside, poured gasoline on it, set it afire, and threw Shimon out of his house. To this severely religious man, the presence of what he perceived to be as counterfeit or unholy writing had to be destroyed. He also had to remove the offender from his midst, even if the offender was a relative.

Certainly not exclusive to the Jewish community, but also present among those who would claim themselves to be Christians, is the zeal that takes the form of ritual, liturgy, intellectual one-upsmanship, and even condemnation of those around who do not see things their way. Yet in the words of the Old Testament prophet, Isaiah, we hear the Lord saying:

> Because this people draw near with their words and honor Me with their lip service, but they remove their hearts far from Me, and their reverence for Me consists of tradition learned by rote, therefore behold, I will once again deal marvelously with this people, wondrously marvelous; and the wisdom of their wise men shall perish, and the discernment of their discerning men shall be concealed.
>
> (NAS—Isaiah 29:13-14)

The very same persons (both in the Jewish and Christian communities) who walk the life of "religion" and who pray and fast regularly as "works" to please God, are confronted with very powerful words from the same prophet:

> "Is this not the fast which I chose.....is it not to divide your bread with the hungry, and bring the homeless poor into the house; when you see the naked, to cover him; and not to hide yourself from your own flesh?"
> (NAS—Isaiah 58:6-7)

Once again, the missiles of rejection had thundered to the center of Shimon's being. His world had been torn asunder by the horrors of a broken home, the bullets and grenades of the PLO, and even the gasoline fire set by his own brother-in-law which burned the only book that Shimon owned.

Shimon continues to live. His life is anything but easy. Though great blessing is coming upon Israel, it will not be without a struggle. There are thousands of Shimons sprinkled throughout the land. They are young, wounded, and often despaired, but springing through the infection is *hatikvah*...Hope......

> But Zion said, "The Lord has forsaken me, and the Lord has forgotten me." "Can a woman forget her nursing child and have no compassion on the son of her womb? Even these may forget, but I will not forget you." Behold, I have inscribed you on the palms of My hands; your walls are continually before Me."
> (NAS—Isaiah 49:14-16)

> Thus says the Lord God, "Behold I will lift up My hand to the nations, and set My standard to the peoples, and they will bring your sons in their bosom, and your daughters will be carried on their shoulders. And kings will be your guardians and their princesses your nurses. They will bow down to you with their faces to the earth and lick the dust of your feet, and you will know that I

am the Lord. Those who hopefully wait for Me will not be put to shame.

(NAS—Isaiah 49:22-23)

"For I will turn their mourning into joy, and will comfort them, and give them joy for their sorrow. And I will fill the soul of the priests with abundance, and My people shall be satisfied with My goodness, declares the Lord."

(NAS—Jeremiah 31:13-14)

# 6

# NICHOLE

To the cynic, (and in the earlier days of my life, I was chief among them), it seems preposterous to believe that God intervenes daily in the lives of men. Many believe that God, Whoever He is or might be, CAN or possibly MIGHT walk hand in hand with people, but for most, to sign on to the statement that He DOES, would be too much to admit in light of the world's physical evidence of war, disease, poverty, and pain. Though in the depths of our souls we would LIKE to believe in a kind merciful Father Who loves us, because of the miseries of the world, we often consign what seems to be clear evidence of His handiwork, to the realm of coincidence, a catch-all called fate, or just plain "luck"...be it good or bad.

In an earlier chapter, I provided some background as to how I began this book project, and some of the events, which were involved in putting "wings" to its completion. One of the events placed me in a hotel room in New York with an Israeli businessman who had a Jewish orthodox-believing brother-in-law in Israel.

Although Israel (the businessman) and I had exchanged addresses and phone numbers with good intentions of getting together again, I was also aware that in the busyness of our lives, the odds of it really happening were probably against us.

Nevertheless, it was not an overwhelming surprise when I received a phone call in Jerusalem. I answered, and on the other end of the line I heard Israeli-accented English:

"Hello...ah...This is Moshe! You will come to a Bar Mitzvah this Saturday.... Yes?" It was more of a command than a request. "You met the husband of my sister on the airplane the other day."

"Oh Yes...Yes...I remember. You are Israel's brother-in-law. He told me about you."

Our conversation continued, I looked on my calendar of appointments, and sure enough, the coming Saturday was free. I was being invited to a Bar-Mitzvah celebration, not of Moshe's son, but of the son of a friend. Talk about a stranger being welcomed in the land.... This was a perfect example! I had never even met the man on the other end of the phone, and I was being invited not to a Bar-Mitzvah in his family, but one being hosted by a friend.

The Bar-Mitzvah would be held on the Sabbath at a small community called, Ohr-Akiva, north of Tel Aviv, and very near Caesarea, the location of the old amphitheater where Saul of Tarsus, who later became known as Paul, preached many a sermon. The Sabbath arrived, and I was up before daylight. I cranked up my rented Suzuki and zipped down the mountains around Jerusalem. The little car hummed past Ben Gurion Airport and I turned north on the road to Haifa. Proceeding up the coastal highway, it was a pleasant drive. After two hours of driving I found myself sitting at the entrance of Ohr-Akiva, waiting for a man named Moshe who would lead me the rest of the way through the day.

Moshe, who is a businessman, is also an orthodox Jew. He will not drive a car on the Sabbath, wears his *kippah* (a small round cap that Jewish men wear on the crown of their head) daily, follows the dietary laws, and his wife and children do the same. As I rested my head back against the driver's seat in my parked Suzuki, I closed my eyes to await my rendezvous with this man. I heard the tapping on my side window, and there was my new friend, standing with his family. Being the Sabbath, they had walked from a neighborhood nearby to Ohr-Akiva where we would all attend the Bar-Mitzvah of his friend's son.

I walked with this beautiful Sephardic family of Zion through the quiet streets of the community. Moshe's wife, Sarah, is an English teacher, and speaks English perfectly. Moshe handles the language well, as does their son, Avshalom. We spent the short walk to Ohr-Akiva's synagogue learning about each other. I was still somewhat overwhelmed at the fact that I was where I was...invited to a family event, by a complete stranger who was a brother-in-law to a man that I had met in a Manhattan hotel lobby. When I perceive or sense that the Lord is leading me however, I try simply to accept and not try to figure it all out.

It was a warm and sunny morning as we approached the entrance to the small synagogue. In size, it could be compared to a small chapel serving Christians in an American rural community. It was a day of joy for the 50-60 guests who were standing around the entrance laughing and enjoying each other's company. The dark eyes, dark hair, and tanned complexions of these Jews revealed well their Sephardic origins from countries like Libya, Tunis, and Egypt. Hebrew permeated the air around me, and I was welcomed into their celebration, Moshe translating any conversation for me. As the ceremony was about to start, a man gently placed a *tallit* (prayer shawl) over my shoulders. I would place it over my head as certain prayers were recited. Although there are other symbolic meanings, to be enfolded by the tallit is regarded as being enveloped by the holiness of the commandments of the Torah, denoting a subjection to the Divine Will. I was seated in the front row with my new friend, Moshe. He quietly translated the Hebrew and explained the ceremony to me.

I can only think of the word "privileged" as I once again marveled at the goodness of God in allowing me to experience such a touching, intimate, and beautiful ceremony among His people. The Sephardic Jews are very warm and expressive people. I suppose one could call them the "charismatics" of the Jews. They freely sing, laugh, cry, hug, and are just as uninhibited in expressing their some-times-hot tempers. They're not afraid to let it all hang out.

As the ceremony concluded, the entire congregation exited the quaint synagogue, and began marching back to the apartment of the Bar-Mitzvah boy. I was among them, rejoicing inwardly as the crowd sang and clapped in unison enjoying the day and celebrating the fact that another Jewish boy was becoming a man.

During this march through the streets of Ohr-Akiva, a short conversation took place, which I was to learn about later. The father of the Bar-Mitzvah candidate, who was hosting the coming dinner, was asked by one of the guests, "Aaron...how are you going to get all of these people into your little apartment?"

Without batting an eye, Aaron answered, "If there's room in my heart for them, there will be room in my home for them."

He was right. Had I known the dimensions of Aaron's apartment before arriving, and surveying the crowd that was about to enter in.....I too would have declared, "No way!" Aaron's home proved to be as big as his heart, and we all crowded in, sat down, and ate.

Every kind of Middle East food imaginable was waiting for us. Pizza-sized pieces of pita bread were torn and passed among the guests. Wine, grapes, cheeses, fruits, vegetables, hummus, meats, and rice were lavishly shared by all. Little babies were passed around among the guests to waiting kisses and hugs. Spontaneous songs and hand clapping erupted in celebration as we continued to eat and enjoy. Even America visited this joyous day in the form of a plastic liter of Coca-Cola, snuggled amongst the trays of lavish food.

The door to the apartment was opened, and we heard the songs of celebration from the stairwell. Another Bar Mitzvah had taken place and guests of this celebration were climbing the stairs to another apartment. These were Jews who had made *aliyah* (a return to Israel. Literally in the Hebrew, "to go up") from India. The guests from each party began to intermingle, and I was rushed upstairs to try the Indian-Jewish food that had been prepared. I was welcomed and treated as an honored guest.

I returned to the original party, and at one point during the afternoon, I leaned against the wall of the room while men joined hands and danced. They hopped and kicked with the songs of Zion joyfully streaming from their mouths. *Kippot* popped up and down on black-haired men, hanging on to their spot by a bobbi-pin or hair clip. Choruses of "lai-lai-lai-" added the frosting to the cake of previously sung verses.

It is very difficult to explain to those who have not experienced the presence of the **Ruach ha Kodesh** (Holy Spirit) in their lives. It may even seem arrogant to seemingly infer that, "I have...and you haven't," but in that moment of time, as I observed from the side, I felt bathed in love, and knew that God Himself was enjoying this as much or more than the people in the room. I felt His loving Presence towards His people just as surely as I knew that I was alive. These were some of the "first fruits" of His call to bring His people back to the land.

> And I will take you one from a city and two from a family, and I will bring you to Zion. Then I will give you shepherds after My own heart, who will feed you on knowledge and understanding.
> (NAS—Jeremiah 3:14-15)

As the Bar-Mitzvah celebration concluded, I said good-bye to the Bar-Mitzvah boy turned man, to his parents, and with Moshe, his wife Sarah, and their three children, Avshalom, Liel, and Meir, walked to the gate of Ohr-Akiva where I'd left my car. This had been my first meeting with Moshe. It would not be my last.

Moshe and his family lived on a *moshav* near Pardes Hannah, a small farming community well north of Tel Aviv. It was only a week later, after my wife, Hellen, had joined me in Israel, that we sat with them as their guests for Sabbath dinner. Israel (Moshe's brother-in-law businessman whom I'd met in New York) with his wife, Shoshanna, and children, Shamir, Sagi, and Shir joined us, and we had the opportunity to experience their friendship and love, as well as share my project with them, as a Christian who loved Zion.

It was through Moshe that I discovered another daughter of Zion. He brought me a news story, printed in Hebrew, about a young French girl who had come to Israel under the most trying of circumstances. She has been and continues to be an inspiration to all of Israel. She is as pretty as she is young, and though modest and humble, is a veritable dynamo of energy.

On learning of her whereabouts, I placed a call to the kibbutz where she resided. I heard her voice at the other end of the phone, introduced myself and told her about the project on which I was working. I wanted to interview her, and hear her story on how she came to Israel.

With wisdom beyond her years, she replied, "I am a very young person, and I have not really done anything. I have been interviewed by TV and newspapers.....and I really don't think that I want to do another. I just want to live quietly."

Although I was disappointed, I understood. I asked her if she would perhaps at a later date, reconsider, and I would send her a letter giving more details about my work and myself. We agreed to that and said, "Shalom."

While back in the States, I wrote to Nichole, announcing that I would again be coming to Israel, and that I would call her again upon arriving. I also spent some time before the Lord asking Him for His will in this matter. Returning to Israel, I dialed the number of her kibbutz, and was soon speaking to her. As I look back, it was hardly a "coincidence" that I reached her. There are but two phones on her kibbutz, and she just "happened" to be near the phone for which I had the number.

Although I deeply wanted to meet with Nichole, I vowed that I would simply ask for the interview, and not try to persuade or pressure her. As we talked, she was amenable to my meeting with her and we agreed to a date and time.

Once again, I was nudging the gear lever of a rent-a-car through its shift patterns, and my miniature chariot hummed through the Israeli countryside, powered it seemed, by a little engine no larger than a sewing machine. I drove from Karkur and navigated my way to Afula. I continued on the road toward Tiberias passing Mt. Tabor. I descended into the valley that held the Sea of Galilee, hundreds of feet below sea level, and wound my way around the southern shore of the large lake. I proceeded northward along the Eastern Shore of the infamous body of water, and began the long climb up the Golan on the East Side. I continued to shift to lower gears, as I followed the twisting road toward the summit. Higher and higher I ascended, and the Kinneret (Sea of Galilee) and its surroundings slowly withdrew, becoming a scene of eloquent beauty. There is no view in Yellowstone or Yosemite Parks in the American West that can over-shadow the beauty of this parcel of God's creation as observed from the Golan.

I arrived at my turn, and carefully compared the Hebrew letters on my map, with those on the road sign in front of me. I turned into Kibbutz Geshur, parked my car, and began to look for Nichole.

I was led to her cottage and finally faced the young lady who I had been trying to meet for many months. She invited me in to her cottage and offered me a seat. I felt a little awkward, for though I had been through a few of life's battles myself, I was sitting face to face with a girl less than half my age, who had overcome great obstacles. Daniel, a friend of hers from the kibbutz, and a former Israeli soldier, joined us.

Nichole was born in a small town in the western part of France. The year was 1967, the same year that Israel's borders were enlarged as a result of soundly defeating Syria, Jordan, and Egypt, after they had planned a co-ordinated attack against Israel. It was the year that Jerusalem became a free city, united again, and opened to the world. As Nichole and I spoke, I was very conscious that Kibbutz Geshur rested on land that was not repossessed by Israel until after the bloody battles of the Yom Kippur War of 1973, six years after the liberation of Jerusalem.

While Nichole was learning to walk and talk in France, Syrian mortars and artillery would often spew their deathblows upon the children of Israel in the kibbutzim around the Sea of Galilee. The guns were perched on the high ground of the Golan, on the land where Nichole and I were sitting, for all practical purposes immune from effective retaliation by Israel.

It was a comfortable position for a Syrian artilleryman to be hundreds of meters above the flat land of the kibbutz farms. He was able to roll in a large gun, fire a few rounds into the settlements below, and disappear before Israel could retaliate with an air strike. The Syrians also had many permanent gun emplacements, which were well fortified, and difficult to neutralize. The concrete bunkers can still be seen today. Many of the lobbed shells from these guns hit their mark, and Israelis who were plowing fields, or picking fruit, heard the terrible whistling scream of the warhead just before it exploded near them. All too often, it was the last sound that they would ever hear. Even their children who were asleep in the beds of the children's house, while perhaps dreaming whatever little children dream, never awoke. Their little bodies, as well as their dreams were shattered by the surprise of a shell fired in the black of night from the high ground of the Golan. This was some of the recent legacy of the land on which I was sitting and speaking with a young daughter of Zion.

Nichole's father was Jewish and her mother a Catholic. Although her mother was faithful and practiced her religion, her father was not religious at all. Without realizing it, Nichole's father gave her the Jewish values that she now holds....even though he did not practice the religion. She does not remember celebrating the holidays at home in France, but remembers her father's strength and perseverance as well as his honesty, values which she clings to with vigor.

Nichole grew up within a completely non-Jewish community. The only Jew that she knew was her dad. As she became a teenager, the questions that might gnaw away at any young person prodded her intensely. "Who am I?" "What is life all about?" She had the added question however..."What is it to be a Jew?"

Nichole began to read about Jewish life, and listened to Jewish radio programs. Her friends were not anti-Semitic, and she did not undergo any persecution, but sensed a constant tickle that there was something a little different about her. As she continued to listen to the radio about Jewishness and read various articles in newspapers and magazines, her heritage began to take on some meaning.

Her first experience with anti-Semitism occurred in the classroom when during a discussion, one of her classmates began to speak against the Jews.

"All the Jews are rich.... And they're no good."

"Where did you learn that.... and what do you know about it?"

Her appetite already whetted, and having searched for answers about her Jewishness, Nichole possessed the ammunition and the confidence to answer her bigoted classmate. Her teacher who was moderating the discussion, discovered that Nichole was Jewish.

The sword had been thrust and Nichole tasted the revulsion rising within her toward her bigoted and naive classmate. The pain and rejection were but a small taste of what so many of her people had endured throughout the ages. Her classmate was dangerous. He would inflict a wound for no reason. He was an enemy to the Jewish people, and she began to understand what it was to be a Jew.

Nichole continued to seek answers to her Jewishness and even enrolled in Hebrew class. As she studied and continued to seek answers to the question of "what or who is a Jew?" the fires of desire grew in her heart to visit Israel. Hers was a solo search, in that there was little to no Jewish influence in her community in France. She belonged to no Jewish organizations, and the few that were available were very small and attended only by the few Jews who were already living a traditional and conservative religious life, something that Nichole's personality would not fit.

"I felt that I must go to Israel, and the best way to do that was to go as a volunteer in the army. The army is the people, and I knew that I would meet people from all over Israel in the army." Her idea became reality, and Nichole departed France in July 1984 to **be** in Israel, not just read or talk about it.

She was assigned to a military base in southern Israel, and along with others like her, did many of the mundane but necessary chores of army life. The labors of volunteers like herself allowed some of the regulars of the Israeli army to either take leave, or to devote their energies to more critical matters. As with any army, even though we tend to view only the front line operation where soldiers and tanks maneuver in battle, there are other operations behind the scenes which are vital and in need of manpower. It is in these "behind-the-scenes" operations that many volunteers are put to work, sorting and stacking uniforms, equipment, cleaning and oiling weaponry, even peeling the potatoes that would feed Israel's soldiers. Nichole was one of these volunteers.

She was drawn to Israel by something that she could not explain, but unlike many of her Jewish brothers and sisters in the world, was not afraid of what she might find. She knew before going, that she might like it, and want to stay, in spite of the imagined and real hardships. While many of her fellow volunteers oiled the mechanical devices of a modern army, the oil of Zion had anointed her and drew her to the land and her people. She joyfully did her volunteer service in the Israeli army, and knew that she would be back. She began making plans for *aliyah*, or going "UP" to the land.

Her plans continued to take shape as she studied during her last year of high school in France. On finishing her schooling, she would rejoin her friends in Israel, and become a full-fledged citizen. It was something that did not rest well with her mother and father, who were comfortable with their lives in France.

"Nichole...Think! There is so much going for you here. It's dangerous in Israel!"

"But Mama, I have been there. I want to do this. I must do this."

No parent wants his or her son or daughter to move to another country, especially when they see the possible dangers and trials that are usually quite obscure to their offspring. Israel was a place where such a young person would face trials.

Time continued to pass, and on a cold winter day in the beginning of 1985, Nichole was standing on the station platform in Chambly, France, a little town just north of Paris. She would soon board the train, which would take her to school. As the last passengers jumped aboard the train that was now starting to pull out of the station, Nichole did the same. She had boarded this train perhaps hundreds of times before. It was routine.... the train started to roll, only this time she lost her grip on the railing.

In a moment which would last a lifetime, she slipped rapidly below the steel train steps and the slow rolling wheels of the train continued their motion, totally unhindered by Nichole's two legs which lay in their path along the cold steel rails. There was no one who could see the occurring calamity from the engineer's station of the train in time to stop or undo the damage done. She lay there helpless, a victim of a small mistake, perhaps of arriving at the station too late, or of trying to board a moving train, or of misplacing her foot on the steel step. The moment could not be undone.

As Nichole lay in her hospital bed, now without her legs, the news made its way back to Israel. General Davidi, commander of the crack Israeli paratroopers, had met and remembered Nichole as she worked as an army volunteer on her first visit to Israel. He made a personal visit to her in the hospital in France. He was a man who had seen many wounded soldiers, and to him Nichole was one of his "men."

In war, soldiers are often killed or wounded by the most extraordinary of circumstances, but sometimes in the most ordinary of ways, like a jeep accident, or falling off a ladder. To General Davidi, Nichole had been wounded on the battlefield of life, but she was still part of his unit, loved, respected, and not now to be discarded.

"Nichole, you are one of us. If you still want to come to Israel, you will be welcome."

Davidi's words reassured her that she still belonged to Israel, and that if she wanted to make aliyah, she was welcome. Nichole would be of value to Israel in spite of her handicap. General Davidi had just said so.

Although high-ranking men in other countries have been known to reach to those of ordinary social status, this kind of outreach is commonplace in Israel. At first glance it might seem quite extraordinary for an army general to leave his country to visit the bedside of a now-crippled young lady, thousands of kilometers away. On the international scale, it probably is extraordinary. For an Israeli who serves his people, it is the ordinary and the right thing to do.

His words were life to Nichole. They were the bellows to stoke the fires of hope for her, that even without legs she was wanted, and would be accepted. In Nichole's own words, "This was very important to me."

Contrary to the acceptance that a crippled Jewish girl, Nichole, was receiving in Israel, a few years ago a young handicapped child in Germany, was brutally beaten to death by a rowdy gang of neo-Nazis. In the twisted minds of these brutes, the child was of no value to anyone and needed to be eliminated.

Six months after her accident, Nichole made plans to return to Israel as a volunteer. Her parents and the doctors all voiced their opposition. Their opinions were no doubt formed from having viewed the averages and probabilities of life. They did not view the circumstances through the eyes of faith and hope, those immeasurable fuels that when tapped can overpower all obstacles. For Nichole, her tanks were overflowing, mixed perhaps with the octane of youthful innocence or naiveté.

Her parents offered to find an appropriate apartment in France for her. They continued to try to dissuade her from her plans. It was no use. Nichole would return to Israel.

For Nichole, there were still questions:

"Can I really do it? Can I work as a volunteer and be a help rather than a hindrance to Israel? I will never know until I try," she recalled her thoughts.

She phoned General Davidi and said that she would be coming, and wanted to be assigned to the same army base where she had previously done duty. She would arrive within a week.

Davidi took care of the details, and in July 1985, Nichole boarded a plane in Paris without fanfare. Her parents, along with one of Davidi's officers on embassy duty in Paris, bid her farewell. The blue and white El Al jet lifted from Orly's runway leaving behind disappointed and admiring parents, but bringing another of the daughters of Zion to the Promise Land. Though she lacked legs, shortening her physical stature, she was to become a fire hydrant of love and encouragement to all of Israel.

It was enough of a struggle to overcome her permanent physical handicap. As part of her reasoning for returning to Israel as soon as she did, she felt that it would not be possible for her to rebuild her life twice....once in France, and again in Israel. She had to go "all the way"...NOW...to know if she could make it. Nichole was greeted by General and Mrs. Davidi when she arrived at Ben Gurion Airport, and she was assigned to her former base.

> "Behold, I am bringing them from the north country,
> and I will gather them from the remote parts of the
> earth, among them the blind and the lame...together; a
> great company, they shall return here."
>
> (NAS—Jeremiah 31:8)

This would be Nichole's real test. She would not commit to *aliyah*, that of permanently living in the land and becoming an Israeli citizen, until she was satisfied that she could endure and overcome her handicap, rather than her handicap overcome her.

On her first visit to Israel, Nichole could be seen climbing all over tanks, performing light maintenance. This time she would have to adjust to other jobs. She now had to overcome the obstacle of not knowing the Hebrew language. She had a little background, but no fluency. In her office assignment she was unable to do very much but began to learn. She also worked in maintenance areas, sorting tools, and small parts, nuts and bolts, and added her efforts to the continued building of Zion. The important thing for her was that she was in Israel, and she was able to contribute!

She continued her service in the army, more and more reassured that she was able. She would make it. She would survive and become a viable, living, contributing citizen of Zion.

As part of the formalities of becoming a citizen of Israel, she had to undergo a religious conversion. Under ***halachah,*** (a generic term for the legal system of Judaism, which embraces all the detailed laws and observances), if a person's mother is Jewish, it suffices in order to consider the person Jewish. In Nichole's case, her father was Jewish, which disqualified her from automatically being considered a Jew in the eyes of those in control of the immigration doors to Israel.

Although her heart was much toward Israel, she along with many others like her had to go through the formalities of "becoming a Jew." She had to study religious rules, and go through certain rituals which satisfied the religious authorities as to her "Jewishness." It seemed to Nichole that these motions had nothing to do with the heart, but to those who granted her citizenship, those behaviors were important.

Just as in certain Christian circles, the rigid walls of legalism often stand in the way of God's Spirit as He moves among His special and loved people...Israel. I can remember a certain Christian pastor insisting that I be baptized again, because the full immersion that I had undergone as an adult had not been done by his particular denomination. I stood my ground, knowing in my heart that God had accepted my baptism. I would not succumb to the pressures of undergoing another, simply to please a "religious" minister. However, if it had meant my being refused as a citizen to the land where I was destined to live, I most probably would have accomplished again what God had accepted the first time.

Nichole has known the pain of despair and discouragement of not being able to physically move about as she wants. To be without legs in Israel is to endure many more discomforts and obstacles than would be the case in America. For the past decade or two, America has been relatively sensitive to the physically handicapped, building ramps and oversized restrooms to accommodate wheel chairs for example, but these added expenditures have not yet become the rule in Israel.

Despite the lack of convenience, Nichole continued her studies at the university in Haifa, where she studied psychology and economics. In addition, she is a dynamo of encouragement to the many Israeli soldiers who have come back from battles without arms and legs, and with the myriad of other wounds that keep them from living life like normal people. Nichole teaches swimming, and spends much time encouraging those who are even less handicapped than she. To the soldiers, she is a refreshing slice of life when she visits and encourages them to live and hope.

As though this were not enough, she has been back to France where she has written newspaper articles, done radio interviews, appeared on TV, and spoken to groups all over the country, in an effort to portray accurately what it is to live in Israel.

" The media would have us believe that Israel is nothing but one constant street fight. Nothing could be further from the truth," exclaims Nichole as she speaks out on Israel. She holds back nothing and is not afraid to tell of the difficulties as well as the hope and abundance.

When asked about her religious views, Nichole states that for now she is interested in living as a secular Jew. "I am not atheistic. I am thinking. I feel it, but I cannot define it."

One of her greatest frustrations is that after having spoken so often to her fellow Jews in the **Diaspora** (dispersion, or those Jews living outside of Israel) so many still consider Israel as "too dangerous." She challenges Jews everywhere to not listen just to the words of others, but "to come and see for yourselves. If they SEE Israel, they will understand."

As a Christian, I can echo those words whole-heartedly. I also believe the promises of the *Torah* and *Tenach* (Old Testament) which are coming to pass before our very eyes. God IS building up Zion, but in the process, there are still obstacles to overcome. To spread the vision of Israel as seen on the travel posters, is simply not to tell it all. Israel is not yet a utopia, although she is destined to be that and more.

As God builds up His land and His people, there will be those who will try to frustrate the process. In that frustration, there will no doubt be more Nicholes who will be confined to wheel chairs, and there will be those who will reach Zion broken in heart as well as body.

> "With weeping they shall come, and by supplication I will lead them;.
> (NAS—Jeremiah 31:9)

> "Again I will build you, and you shall be rebuilt, O virgin of Israel.....And there shall be a day when watchmen on the hills of Ephraim shall call out, 'Arise, and let us go up to Zion, to the Lord our God."
> (NAS—Jeremiah 31:4,6)

Nichole accompanied me to my car. She patiently wheeled her own chair up the narrow walk from her kibbutz cottage to where my little Fiat was parked. I was walking with a daughter of Zion, one who has chosen to live on the cutting edge of life. She has chosen the difficult, but in my opinion, the right way for her. She has forsaken the relative comforts of France for the call of Zion on her life. Her life is anything but easy, and she has had periods of despair, loneliness, and frustration. She has left home and family, come to a land where she did not speak the language. She has begun again...all while confined to a wheelchair.

We were but a short distance away from the Syrian border, where there are those who would kill her in a moment, given the opportunity. In the collective eyes of this neighbor of Israel, the only good Jew is a dead one. The land on which we were walking would be the first sought for in any attack by that nation which has time and time again sworn to annihilate Israel, and has time and again tried unsuccessfully to carry out this threat.

As we parted, I knew that I had been with someone significant and important to Israel. I had once again seen and felt another facet of Israel's pain, but equally, I experienced in Nichole, another fact of Israel's eternal hope. By God's grace, by His Spirit, and by the spirit of those like Nichole, Israel will live!

# 7

# CALEB BEN JOSEF

In one of my earlier visits to Israel, I had arisen early in the morning to prepare for another day in Jerusalem. The sky was a crystal blue, and the sun reflected brightly off the light colored stone of the buildings across from my open hotel window. I squinted as I surveyed the neighborhood. My small hotel in Jerusalem was located in an area owned and inhabited predominantly by Arabs. I was only a few blocks from Damascus Gate of the Old City.

My itinerary for this particular day would begin with a visit to the Garden Tomb, where Jesus is believed to have been buried, and three days later, resurrected. The site was but a few blocks walk from my hotel. I arrived right at opening time, early in the morning, ahead of the anticipated crowds. I wanted to enjoy the garden setting in solitude, and to contemplate in quietness, the earth-shaking event that occurred here 2,000 years ago.

My plan was a good one. I was ahead of the tour bus crowd and found the Garden Tomb area to be in almost complete solitude. I walked quietly through the well-kept garden enjoying the sunshine, the immaculate greenery, and flowers. I made my way to the tomb itself. There is a small sign on the door of the tomb, quoting the Scripture from Matthew 28, "He is not here, He is risen...."

As I walked to the entrance of the tomb, another couple joined me. They were from New Jersey, and I would guess in their late 40's or early 50's. The woman held her husband and led him carefully over the stone walk. He was totally blind, but had come to "see" Israel, and on this day to experience the setting of the Garden Tomb. The couple were born-again Christians.

We introduced ourselves, and in moments crossed the stone channel, which would have been used to roll a stone in place over the opening of the tomb. We entered, and together we began to pray. I do not believe that to pray at the Western Wall of the Temple, or to pray in the tomb where Jesus is believed to have been laid to rest, has any more significance in Heaven than the prayer that is uttered by a middle-America housewife as she tackles a sink full of dishes. I did however, experience awe as I contemplated the resurrection, one of the basic tenets of my Christian faith.

My blind friend from New Jersey experienced more emotion than I. I could see the joy on his face, and even faith of great antic-ipation, as he too reflected upon thoughts of eternity, knowing in his own heart that he would one day see again. This man was viewing Israel through the eyes of faith, and had as much joy as any man that I had ever met. We shook hands, went our ways, and I never thought that I would see him again.

Several years later, I was visiting in the office of Johann Lückhoff, the Director of the International Christian Embassy, Jerusalem. After our visit together, Johann said, "There's someone out in the lobby that I'd like you to meet." He led the way, and I was introduced to Johann's friend.

It would be more correct to say, RE-introduced. I stood face to face with the blind man with whom I had prayed several years earlier in the Garden Tomb in Jerusalem. We greeted each other, and I said,

"My brother...we've already met. Do you remember our visit to the Garden Tomb one early morning several years ago?"

"Oh yes...yes, of course!" We hugged each other like long lost brothers. How sweet was our fellowship, simply from having been brought together for but a few moments at the place where Jesus is believed to have been resurrected from the grave.

As we shared with each other about our reasons for being in Jerusalem, I told him about my desire to meet and learn about the sufferings of the Jewish people, and that I was in the process of conducting interviews throughout Israel.

"You must meet Caleb Ben Josef! He has a story that is incredible! Write down this number, and tell him that I told you to call."

We continued a short conversation, and once again we parted to go our separate ways. I called Caleb Ben Josef a couple of days later, identified myself, and explained my interest in meeting him. Caleb was very agreeable to getting together with me, and we set a date for an interview.

As I sat face to face with Caleb, I saw a balding man of short stature, with large kind eyes. He proved to be as kind as his eyes revealed, humble, and soft-spoken.

Caleb was born on November 11, 1928 in a village that was as small as its name is large. Its entire population numbered barely 1,000. Szilvasveved was nestled in the mountains of northern Hungary and served as a summer vacation spot for the more well to do of the time. Almost the entire village was devoted to serving Baron Palavecicini, a man of nobility who owned most of the mountain and the land around the village.

It was a place of peace and solitude, but held inhabitants who had known hardship and sorrow in their lives. Caleb's own mother, Pola, was one of those who had lost her father in World War I. A plaque in the village square testified to that fact. She later lost a brother to sickness.

The village was inhabited by those in the Christian culture, primarily Catholics, but also a few evangelical Protestants. Caleb's family was one of five Jewish families in Szilvasveved. As a result of these demographics, there was no synagogue, and hardly enough Jewish culture among the five families to keep from being completely assimilated.

Caleb was strong as a child, and very athletic. Though short in stature, he had a quickness and speed that enabled him to outrun and compete with those who were much taller. He was always one of the first to be chosen to enhance a pick-up game of football (American soccer). He had the added advantage of being born of a father who did well in business. Though Caleb's father was not rich, he was comfortable by village standards, and was able to provide a few surprises to his family that were out of economic reach for most.

Caleb's father, Josef, owned and operated two small candy shops in Szilvasveved and Caleb made good use of the special privilege of being the owner's son. He would often visit the shop with his friends, help himself generously to the varieties of sweets on display, and then proceed to distribute these delights to his companions. It was good to have Caleb as a school chum. He had almost immediate and unlimited access to the counters of candy that would delight any young child.

When Caleb received a new bicycle as a gift from his father, he became the envy of the neighborhood, with all his friends seeking a ride. The early 30's were comfortable for the little village of Szilvasveved. Though there was little material wealth for most of the working people who inhabited this paradise in the mountains, there was peace, and good fellowship among neighbors.

Caleb's parents were typical of most Jews in the Eastern European **Diaspora** at the time. They placed a high value upon work and education. Lacking a synagogue or **schule** (school), and because of the known discipline contained in the curriculum, Caleb was sent to the local Catholic school in the village. It was here that Caleb learned his ABC's and became much a part of the culture around him...much to the dismay of his parents.

Caleb recalls sitting in the large Catholic Chapel, built by Baron Palavecicini. He enjoyed going into the church, and being with his friends. Because the village was small and everyone know each other, Caleb and his parents were often guests or mourners at any wedding or funeral, all conducted in Catholic tradition. Young Caleb also developed a taste for Gentile foods, many of which were forbidden by Jewish Law. For his parents, who had solid Jewish upbringing, this was a source of increasing discouragement. Caleb was going too much in the Catholic way, and something had to be done about it.

Arrangements were made to have Caleb leave the peaceful village in the mountains, and to spend some time in Budapest with his uncle, who was very much a part of the Jewish community. He was a man who lived hand to mouth; working long hours at the menial task of delivering kosher meat by bicycle from the packing plant to customers. It would be while living with his uncle that Caleb would be immersed in the Jewish way.

Many of the lessons were hard for Caleb. There were no longer any counters full of candy and easy-to-come-by bicycles. Life with his uncle consisted of living in one small room for the entire family, and being grateful for the basics of a loaf of bread and a bed in which to sleep. The room had a sink with cold running water, a stove, and the toilet facilities were outside.

No longer would he be celebrating Christmas as he did back in Szilvasveved, but would learn about Pesach, Shavuot, Rosh Ha Shanna, Yom Kippur, Succoth, and Channukah, all in fine Jewish tradition. He would no longer be confused by the Gentile teachings, and would be nurtured in the teachings of Torah, and the worship of the God of Abraham, Isaac, and Jacob.

In 1936, although Caleb missed his parents and the village of Szilvasveved in many ways, he also had built a new life among the Jews of Budapest, and he was at peace. In the afternoons he attended a Jewish school and remembers being a classroom favorite, often taught from the privileged position of being nestled on his teacher's lap, as the shepherd taught his fledgling flock the ways of a good Jew.

As he continued to grow, it was decided to place Caleb under the tutelage of a good rabbi. He moved in with one who was teaching a small group of six young followers. It was a place where Caleb was very happy under the kindness and wisdom of the learned Rabbi Shuck, who became the chief rabbi of the Hungarian Jews during World War II.

Caleb's mother and father closed shop in their small mountain village and moved to Budapest where they opened up three new shops, one which sold meat, another which sold drinks, and one which sold his favorite...candy. Although the Nazi Party in Hungary was growing in strength, it was not a worry of young Caleb, who loved to walk along the Danube River which flowed between the cities of Buda and Pest. Little did he know that there would soon come a time when the beautiful river would become the conveyor belt which would carry away the evidence of atrocity as the bodies of hundreds of Jewish men, women, and children drifted lifeless, their floating corpses torn open by the bullets of Hungarian Nazis who used their fellow citizens as targets to test their marksmanship. The Jews would be lined up along the riverbank, and fired upon, much as a farmer's son in rural America might plink tin cans from the top rail of a wooden fence.

The winds of war began to blow with more strength as Caleb finished his stint with the popular Rabbi Shuck. Caleb was now at the age where a young man would enter high school. He went on to learn the trade of being an ironworker, where he learned to shape and work with metals. As Caleb learned, Hungary also learned. They were now under the full blown influence of the Nazi doctrines, and in official alliance with Hitler. One of Nazism's strongest advocates came on the scene in 1943, when Caleb was a teenager of 15. His name was Adolf Eichmann.

What had been the subject of stories in the Hungarian newspapers became living reality as Hitler exported his philosophies through human vessels who were only too glad to do his bidding. To Jewish dismay, there were all too many Hungarians who would join his diabolical scheme. Up until this time the only live evidence that Caleb had seen which confirmed the war in Europe, was the large numbers of Jews that had escaped Poland and Germany and had come to Hungary for refuge. It was short-lived respite however, for with Eichmann's presence, Jewish lives were not only threatened, but were now being eliminated on a daily basis. Although the family move from the mountain village of Szilvasveved to the city of Budapest initially brought a new prosperity, it was only temporary. It was a move that brought Caleb and his parents into the snare of darkness, a snare which would devour Jewish lives by the hundreds of thousands in Hungary.

Caleb had six uncles, all brothers of his father. Four would be forced into fighting the Russian army where they were used as cannon fodder and made to charge the advancing Russians without weapons. A fifth uncle was lost somewhere else in the confusion and horror that overcame Europe at the time.

When Eichmann came into Hungary, all the Jewish men above the age of 18 were conscripted and made to work as slaves in work camps all over the nation. Although Caleb was only 15 years of age, he passed himself off as 18, so that he could be near his father. The two of them were hauled away and brought to a camp where they worked as lumberjacks. The work was brutally difficult, and the Hungarian Nazis who oversaw the camp did little to comfort the Jewish prisoners.

They had undergone the humiliation of being stripped of their dignity and uprooted from their livelihood, all to work for the "new order" brought to bear upon them. The ultimate plan would be to use their labor to bring the Nazi philosophy into societal reality, and then when the labor was no longer needed, Caleb, his father, and all the Jews would be "liquidated." Unknown to Caleb at the time, while he and his father labored in the forests of Hungary, his mother, grandmother, a brother and sister were packed into trains and sent to Auschwitz, Poland.

Without communication, and having to work to exhaustion day after day, Caleb could only hold on to hope about the destiny of family members who were left behind. Even though the physical labor of logging could build his strength and endurance, without food, the opposite occurred. It broke down his body and weakened his endurance. Added to it was the humiliation of laboring at gunpoint and the cocoon of death had begun to enfold him.

The Russian army was bearing down on them. It was manned by ill-trained and ill-equipped soldiers, whose love for their homeland and desire to survive was enough to unify them. The conglomeration of misfits found enough strength to drive a weak Hungarian army back to where it had come from. The Russians received their training in the actual battles. As they enjoyed a victory here and there, their resolve and their battle wisdom increased, and they grew continually more formidable. The distant booming of artillery gave the clues that the war was moving in the direction of Caleb's lumber camp.

Waves of humanity were beginning to move westward, away from the advancing Russians. Their very unsophisticated army was soundly defeating the Hungarians who had allied with Hitler. There was no love for Hitler's accomplices, and the Russians stormed through the little nation, burning and destroying everything in their path. Prisoners who were held by the Nazis, like Caleb and his father, began to move westward, first under the control of Hungarian Nazis, but then under the control of the Germans. Their initial part of the journey was in the back of a truck, loaded with large swine. There were nine Jewish men, including Caleb and his father, accompanying the pigs.

Out of a perverse desire to humiliate the Jews, the Nazis loaded Caleb, his father, and the seven other Jewish prisoners into this mobile pigpen. For an observant Jew, a pig is considered an unclean animal. Pork is forbidden to eat according to the *Torah* (Jewish Law in the first five books of the Old Testament). To be treated as part of a herd of pigs was to add further insult to injury.

The pigs were large animals, and they were not tied or caged to limit their movement. As the truck went around corners and over bumps, the bulky and cumbersome animals would fall and roll all over the truck bed, snorting and squealing. Caleb and his father often found themselves pinned against the side of the truck, or slammed against by animals that weighed 400-500 pounds each. The Jewish prisoners, Caleb and his father included, almost did not survive. They were exhausted and bruised all over from struggling against the massive forms of out-of-control swine that battered them the entire way.

The truck finally stopped and was opened. Nine tired and bruised Jews climbed slowly down from the vehicle, sullen and humiliated. The pigs they had ridden with were infinitely more kind than their captors. The city was Pressburg. They were marched into a prison where all nine men were placed together in a long narrow cell. The men were broken. They were tired, battered, hungry, and the flood-gates of inner fears burst with weeping. Caleb doubled over in a corner of the cell, tears of fear and terror pouring from his heart. He wondered about his destiny and the safety of his mother, brother, and sister who were left behind in Budapest.

His life had become a nightmare beyond belief...but the reality of his condition continued to stare back at him. He really WAS sitting in a prison cell, hungry, exhausted, and there really WERE Germans who would kill him anytime. His fellow prisoners were real. It was not a dream, and the tentacles of impending doom tightened their grip around his soul.

After sitting in this cell for four days, the clump-clump-clump of soldier's footsteps broke the silence of the night. Three German guards came to them, opened the cell door, and called out the prisoners. Caleb sat up. Talons of fear clawed at his insides. Perhaps they would now be shot and the nightmare would be over.

They were marched outside into the street where they joined a river of humanity, which was flowing through the streets of Pressburg. Everyone was moving westward toward Austria. The Russians were on the move from the east, and were moving fast. The Germans and what was left of the Hungarian army were racing against time to fall back enough to regroup and stave off the charged-up Russians. There was disorder and confusion among the Germans and the refugees that were running and being herded along the dark road.

So far, however, the bullets remained unfired from the Nazi guard's guns. Unbelievably, Caleb and his father were still alive and walking. Though their fate was yet unknown, they possessed life, which gave them hope. They joined hundreds of others trudging along the road, adding to the human river which swept westward.

As Caleb surveyed the confusion among the Germans and the darkness of the night, he began to think about a possible escape. There might not ever be another chance, and there was no way of knowing what lay ahead for him and his father when they crossed the border into Austria.

Caleb remained alert, watching for a chance to break out of the stream of people who stumbled along the road. He looked for the German guards who had been assigned to watch him. They were still close by, but there was constant movement and distraction caused by a tidal wave of humanity...walking, limping; men, women, children, Nazis, captors and prisoners, all in distress, all trying to survive.

Caleb and his father, Josef, along with the seven other Jewish men were herded out of the crowd and they stopped. Would the German guards now shoot them? Miraculously, it did not happen.

They were allowed to rest, but the Germans remained loyal to their given task, and they kept a careful eye on their charges.

It was springtime of 1944, and though the night was cold, Caleb was able to lie upon the ground and sleep. As the sun rose there were still people walking along next to them, and they again joined the retreating thousands. Their Nazi guards continued to watch them as they marched on for an entire day and on into the next night.

They crossed the border into Austria and continued walking. As they continued, Caleb noted that one of the three Nazi guards had gone ahead to the next village for something. There were only two watching them now. As he walked he noted a wooden bridge which was constructed over some railroad tracks. They would have to walk across the bridge.

Unlike most bridges, this one had a bend in the middle. It jogged to the left about halfway across, and the two remaining German guards who had dropped many meters behind them in the crowd would not be able to see Caleb once he turned the corner on the bridge. He was walking next to his father. It was night.

"Papa...This is the time! We'll make a break for it!"

"No! It's too dangerous. We'll be shot!"

"If we stay with these Germans they'll kill us anyway. If you aren't coming, I'm going to make my escape."

The fast and crucial whispered conversation continued as they turned the corner on the bridge. Caleb gave the command..."Let's go!"

As he said it he moved quickly to the edge of the crowd, his father following. They came to the end of the bridge and the escape was on. They jumped down onto the bank over which the bridge crossed. They fell, stumbled, and clawed their way through the thick brush that scratched them viciously as their actions pleaded for their lives. There was no turning back now, and every calorie of energy that could be mustered was being ordered from their exhausted minds and bodies. It was a full throttle exercise, which would not be slowed for anything but a bullet in the back.

Father and son continued to crash through the thick bushes, half expecting to hear the shots that would end their lives. The shots did not come, and they found themselves scrambling out of the bushes next to the railroad tracks beneath the bridge from which they had jumped. Either the Nazi guards were not immediately aware of their escape, or were too tired and forlorn themselves to pursue them. Whatever the case, Caleb and his father were free...for the time being.

The railroad tracks headed in the direction of their ravaged country, Hungary. They made the decision to use them as a guide back home. Exhausted, they moved eastward, putting as much distance as possible between them and the former captors who might be pursuing them. They finally crawled into the adjoining woods that lined the railbed and found a place to lie down.

The orange glow of many fires lit up the dark eastern sky, testifying that the war was coming toward them. The Russians were advancing in a fury, and they were burning and destroying everything in their path which had even the smallest taint of Nazism associated with it. The booming of artillery and gunfire punctuated the crackling and the glow of raging fires, but it mattered not. Exhausted and in pain, father and son fell asleep near the edge of the woods, at a vantage point that overlooked a field and farmhouse.

They knew that the advancing Russians would soon overtake the territory on which they stood, but they would at least be free of the Germans. As morning broke, the pangs of hunger continued to surge through their tired bodies, and the decision was made to approach the farmhouse that they had been observing from the woods. They would ask for help...perhaps a little food. They walked quietly up to the front door and knocked.

The Austrian farmer answered the door, and his eyes widened as he looked at the two wretched humans before him. Signaling with his eyes, and with a low but firm voice, he announced, "You must not come here...Germans! Get out of here...quickly!"

Caleb and his dad scrambled back to the woods where they had slept the night before. Unknown to them, the farmhouse was full of German officers, and was being used as a headquarters for the local area. As Caleb and his father watched from the woods, about five minutes after they had stood at the front door of the house, a small band of German officers walked up to the house and entered. It had been a close call. Further down the edge of the woods, other eyes observed the farmhouse.

The fires and explosions of war got closer, and Caleb and his father lay in a shallow hole. The Russians were coming full gallop into the area. German officers ran from the farmhouse. The horizon erupted in war. Shells passed overhead. Explosions ripped the ground around them. They soon heard the voice of a Russian soldier who stood over the hole in which they huddled. With his gun pointed at them, the Russian soldier called Caleb and his father out of the hole.

Caleb was overjoyed to see the Russian. To him, at the time, this soldier was his savior. He jumped from the hole, and grabbed hold of the Russian's feet and held on, thanking him for being there.

The Russian was unimpressed. He pushed Caleb and his father away, and began to take any belongings from them, including a watch that was still in their possession. As the Russian was about to add Caleb's wristwatch to a collection that ran up and down his arm, a bullet whizzed through the air and pierced the Russian in the leg. It was as though an immediate justice was administered to this man who enjoyed the looting which war had allowed him.

Caleb and his father helped the Russian. They had observed the Germans running from the farmhouse, and decided that it would be safe to bring the wounded Russian there. As they brought the wounded soldier to the farmhouse, other Russians began to appear in the area. They too, had observed the farmhouse and had seen the Germans vacate the place.

The Austrian farmer stood in his own cellar before a Russian officer and was asked the question, "Why did you allow those Germans to use your home to do their work?"

"What could I do? I am only a farmer. They had guns and took over my house! What could I do?"

His answer did not impress the Russian. The Bolshevik pulled a revolver from his holster, held it up, and shot the Austrian farmer in the head. Caleb and his father looked on helplessly. Perhaps the farmer was a collaborator in some way...but he did give Caleb and his father a warning about the Germans, thereby saving their lives.

The Russian officer barked another order, and motioned to Caleb and his father. The father and son team grabbed the arms and legs of the fallen farmer, and carried his bleeding and lifeless body up the cellar stairs and out the front door of the house where they threw it on a garbage heap that lay nearby. It was the same door that Caleb had knocked on only a few hours ago, and where the farmer had quietly but firmly sent them away.

As they completed their gruesome task, other Germans were being rounded up by the Russians and marched into the farmyard. The Russians felt no mercy toward their enemies. They callously lifted their weapons and started firing. German soldiers collapsed to the ground and lay strewn around the farmyard.

Caleb and his father were summoned to do some more of the dirty work for which they already had experience. "Move the bodies and pile them up over here," came the order.

"Yes Sir," Caleb responded.

The father and son team did the job, lifting the dead soldiers and placing them in a pile. Though these Germans had been agents of one of the most evil empires of history, each one of them was a human being. Each had a family, friends, perhaps sons and daughters. There was a sadness in Caleb's heart as he lifted each body and carried it to the growing pile of dead humanity. How many of these Germans might themselves have been victims of the evil regime that overtook their nation? How many may have been too weak to say no to a system that would destroy anything and kill anyone that resisted it? Perhaps they were not ALL evil killers. Nevertheless, they were dead, and perhaps some had reaped a just reward for past actions.

The farmhouse was converted into a temporary hospital, and more Russians arrived, bringing their wounded to be tended to. The Russian soldier, who had been helped out of the woods by Caleb and his father, testified to his officer of their action, and they were allowed to go free.

It had been another nightmare of war. In but a few hours, Caleb had seen enough killing to last any man a hundred lifetimes. He had seen cold and ugly humanity, depraved from the time that Adam and Eve first sinned. He wrestled with a hundred thoughts as he and his father continued on their journey to the east, crossing the border back into Hungary.

They arrived back in the city of Pressburg, where they and some of their fellow Jews had been held in a prison cell for four nights. The Russians had taken the city, and they were solidly in control. Caleb and his father were swept up in the arms of another empire whose root was no more noble and no less life threatening than that of Nazi Germany. They were thrown into an internment camp with German, Hungarian, and Austrian soldiers.

When questioned, Caleb and his father told their story. "We are Jews! We have suffered for more than a year in forced service to Hitler in one of his camps! We escaped from them!"

"You served Hitler for a year...you can serve Stalin for a year." Their interrogator was not joking.

Of the approximately 5,000 soldiers in the camp, Caleb and his father, as far as they were able to ascertain, were the only two Jews. They were held in the camp for about six weeks with all the other prisoners of war. It was more squalor and more hunger. Men died from their wounds and diseases. No one cared that Caleb and Josef were innocent victims of the whole mess called World War II. The great Russian "liberators" replaced the German Nazis and became just another breed of captor.

Little by little the internment camp in Pressburg was liquidated. Captured soldiers were boarded onto trains and sent into Russia where they would be slaves of Stalin. In their desperation for freedom, many of them escaped from the trains by tearing up the floor boards of the freight cars and leaping from the train whenever it slowed down or stopped. The Russians were not as thorough as the Germans in dealing with their prisoners, and they did not take corrective action to this loss of labor until they had lost hundreds of prisoners.

By the time that Caleb and his father were hustled aboard such a train, a cadre of observant and brutal guards had been selected. They would shoot any escaping prisoner on sight. There would be no escape from this train ride. The Russians were learning more about hanging on to their prisoners.

The prisoners rode to the eastern end of Hungary where they were held in another detention facility for several days. Another train was made ready and the special team of father and son were boarded for another ride, which would take them into Russia.

There were about 100 men crammed into each car. There was not room to sit or lie down. Men slept standing up, lying on top of one another, and relieved themselves through a small hole that had been cut in the floor for that purpose. They were getting weaker by the hour, and they would have to endure two weeks of living like this...in a boxcar...with 100 other men...without any substantial food...and without an ounce of compassion from their captors. Men collapsed and died. The smell of human excrement and death permeated the air. Almost all became deathly sick from diseases and infection that attacked their frail bodies. Caleb's father, Josef, was one of them.

Josef was attacked with a bad case of diarrhea. He was one of many. This further drained his already low reservoir of energy, and it contributed to the increasing squalor of the freight cars filled with broken, diseased, and dying men. They were treated as the spoils of war. A dagger or a helmet picked up as a battlefield souvenir was considered to have had more value than this trainload of human beings.

The train eventually stopped, and Caleb helped his weakened father along. His condition worsened. He was a skeleton with skin, barely able to walk, much less work. They were in Tula, Russia, about 130 miles south of Moscow, when they were placed in yet another camp.

The Russians began to examine the prisoners. As medical technicians and doctors looked at Caleb's father, they concluded that he was not fit for work, and made a decision to send him back to Hungary. At least he was not gassed in some chamber and burned in an oven, as would have been the case in Germany or Poland under the Nazis. It would be another long train ride of living like an animal, jammed together with other prisoners considered too weak to do the heavy labor being required in Russia.

Since their capture in Budapest, Caleb and his father had endured long hours as lumberjacks, forced marches that had lasted for days, prisons and internment camps, not to mention watching fellow prisoners dying, and a farmer being shot to death in his own home. They had watched the mass execution of German prisoners and lifted each dead body to a temporary resting-place. They had endured all of this. They had been a team, each lending support to the other through the horrors that each had to walk. Caleb was now without his father and his best friend. Josef was on his way back to Hungary, and Caleb feared that his father would not live to complete the trip. It would be more than a year before he knew the answer.

Caleb was the only Jew among German and Bulgarian prisoners. There were other nationalities represented among the prisoners, but most were Germans. Even the prison doctor was a captured German, and he hated Jews. Until the end of his stay at the work camp, Caleb was not given a day off. When he was sick and appealed to the doctor, he was always considered well enough to work, and the work was not easy. It was heavy manual labor in a brick foundry.

During the winter, the temperature would drop to more than 30 degrees below zero, and Caleb worked...seven days a week...rain or shine...sick or not. He continued to weaken, and there was never enough food. Whenever he was able to get near one, he would rummage through a garbage can, and would eat anything that had food value. He was determined to live. He ate rotten potatoes, rotten cabbage...rotten anything, always with the hope that it would be less harmful than eating nothing.

He survived the Winter of 1944-45, and Spring brought with it a warming trend. Caleb's morbid "hobby" was to count his bones. Every one of them showed through the thin veil of flesh that covered them. He had lost all hope. He hated everything around him. He even hated God, the God that he had tried so hard to please, and to learn about through his Jewish studies. It had to have all been a lie. There could be no God, and if there was, He was cruel and heartless. Caleb had lost all faith. Indeed he was a broken man...broken in body, and now in spirit. Death lurked close by.

It was April 1945, and Caleb was working late in the evening. The freezing cold of the past Winter was giving way to the more temperate Spring, although there was still some snow on the ground just off the loading platform where he labored. He was alone, trudging through the motions of the slave labor that he had so often repeated over the past year. His weak frame carried a broken inner man. He no longer cared if he lived or died. He pushed his heavy cart, filled with the ingredients that would later become bricks. He came near to the industrial elevator, which would take him and his cart up a level to where he would empty it. He did not see the loose electrical wire hanging in his path. He brushed against it.

The massive voltage in the wire blasted him off the platform and into a snow bank...unconscious. He lay there for hours at his best estimate. He awoke and heard the "thup-thup, thup-thup" of his own heart beating. He was alive, totally stunned, and barely able to remember what had happened to him. He staggered to his feet and as he did so, he sensed the presence of something or someone standing right before him. There was no one physically present, but Caleb "knew" that something was standing before him, and he heard the words spoken to the depths of his heart......

"How long shall you disobey the commandment of God?"

Caleb answered the question, speaking softly but aloud, "Lord...I have tried to keep the commandments. I have tried. In Budapest, I tried, but I could not keep them."

The encounter was finished, and Caleb picked up where he had left off with his work, still stunned, still weak, but strong enough to complete some more work before going back to his cell. He had not seen anything unusual, but the spiritual encounter continued to weigh on his mind. It was as real as life itself. God had somehow spoken to him, and His voice was VERY clear.

Caleb went through his nightly routine of getting ready to sleep. He was exhausted, drained of all energy, and slept as soon as he lay down. As he slept, he experienced the most powerful dream of his life. Caleb described it to me this way.

"I was lying on a bed in the middle of a fair-sized room. Around the room there were several windows, and through the windows came many men wielding what looked like long curved sickles, similar to those that are used on the logo of the former communist-Russian flag. Together, the men ran around my bed and wanted to kill me. As they gathered around and tried to thrust their sharp sickles at me, a power came upon me or rose up in me, and lifted me above the bed, through a hole in the ceiling, and pulled me from the room altogether."

"Upon leaving the room, I began to fall rapidly. I knew in this dream that I was falling toward Hell. I even experienced heat, and a tremendous terror and fear. There was a point in my falling which would be a point of no return. Beyond that, I would fall completely into Hell. At the point of this realization in the dream, I heard a voice calling, to 'worship God'."

Caleb heard the voice in his mind and heart. The voice continued. "But if you believe in Jesus, your Messiah, your life shall be changed."

"At that point in the dream, the feeling of help was there and the same power that lifted me from the bed in the room began to draw me away from the terror of Hell and lift me toward Heaven. I soared in the dream...higher and higher until I knew that I was in Heaven."

Again, in Caleb's own words, "I saw the gates...and then I saw God. I knew that it was God from the holiness and the glory around Him, and I saw the difference between Him and me. I was afraid to go to Him. I was afraid, and tried to draw back. That same power that lifted me in the dream, took me to Him. I "flowed" to Him. He took me in His arms, and filled me with love. He was full of love, and I was full of love. I didn't know how long I was in His arms, but I did not want to leave. After a while, He let me go, and He said to me, 'Here is your Messiah. Worship Him as your Savior.' I looked to His right hand and I saw Jesus...Y'shua (Hebrew name for Jesus). When I saw Him, I knew that He was the Jewish Messiah. The Father said to me, 'Fall before Him and worship Him as your Savior.' As I did so, I felt that I was totally cleansed, and that I was free from all burden and problems. I worshipped and praised Him."

Before meeting Caleb, I knew only his name, and nothing else. As we sat in an apartment in Jerusalem, I was awed as this small humble man was pouring his heart out to me and telling me that he, a Jew, a prisoner of the Germans, a witness to overflowing savagery, who became a prisoner of the Russians in the closing years of World War II, had received a revelation of Messiah as a sovereign act of God. I was listening to a rational, sincere, and polite Jewish man, who was as Jewish as he could be, but who had been granted a revelation that could only have come from God's Spirit. He continued:

"I did not know how long I was there (in Heaven), but the next thing that I heard was the siren from the factory. It was just midnight. I was awake, and I felt all new. I felt I must write all of this down, all that I heard and saw, and bring it back to Hungary some day, so that when I am there, I can ask Rabbi Shuck the meaning of all this."

Caleb went to a small table in his cell, and on the table was a small Hungarian New Testament. A prisoner who was a Seventh Day Adventist had given it to him and had told him to read it. Caleb had glanced at it at an earlier time, but the few things that he read made little or no sense. He had begun in the book of Matthew, finding a long list of names, and it was no more appealing to him than the food that he rummaged from garbage cans. He never read any further.

As he reached for the book this time, he opened it and began to read chapter 9 of the Book of Acts. It is the story of Paul on the road to Damascus when he, a Jew of Jews, educated in the school of Gamaliel, received the revelation of his Messiah. He was knocked to the ground and blinded. The circumstances and geography this time were different, but Caleb knew that this time the scales had fallen from his own eyes. Everything was clear! Caleb wanted to leap and scream for joy. He had found his Messiah. He paced his cell, praising the Lord.

He began to read with fervor. He read all night and into the morning until it was time to go to work again in the dismal brick foundry. This time, Caleb went to work as a new person inside. The hate and bitterness that he had been carrying had dissolved, and the fear was gone. He began to tell his fellow prisoners about Messiah, and they rejected him, looking upon him as though he were crazy. No one could accept Caleb's message.

Work was now a happy place for Caleb. He had in one night received a heart cleansing and the realization that he could rejoice in ALL things, and that he could abase or abound and it made no difference to his relationship with God. Even in a Russian slave labor camp, he could experience joy!

It was not long after this life-shaking event, that the first Russian doctors appeared at the work camp, and Caleb was summoned to undergo a physical examination. All the prisoners were made to walk through the snow fully naked to meet the new medical staff, who would examine each one. There were six men and one woman on the medical team. Caleb had become a replica of his father who had been separated from him a year earlier. He was but a skeleton covered with skin, but filled with hope and a new love that could conquer all circumstances.

As the doctors looked at him, they stepped aside and began to talk to one another in Russian. Caleb had learned more than a few Russian words. As he stood naked and shivering, he overheard the conversation of the mini-conclave, which would decide his fate. He heard a word that stood out..."Rehabilitation". The decision was made. He would be relieved of his workload, and would get some rest and food to rehabilitate his emaciated body. The Nazi doctor had been replaced by medical authorities with at least a degree of compassion. It was a thread of silver lining in the dark cloud that had thus far surrounded his life.

He was placed in a rehabilitation clinic. It was like a dream. There were clean sheets, a real bed, and food. The horrors, which had surrounded Caleb for so long, continued to haunt him even as he viewed this new reality. It was not to be believed. His life for the past few years had been one of severe deprivation. For him, there were no such things as clean sheets, palatable food, and real beds. His diet had been watered down solutions that were presented as soup, a slice of dried or moldy bread here and there, and the few rotten cabbage leaves or potato skins that he might rummage from a garbage pail at the camp.

Caleb's body was in a state of deep malnutrition, and even the normal processes of digestion were almost shut down. He was able to take a small portion of food, and he had to eat carefully. The food was there in enough quantity to be considered a healthy diet, but Caleb's metabolic processes were in shambles. As he ate, everything that went down burned with a fury. He was even given meat, something that he had not seen in what seemed like a lifetime. Meat seemed like something from out of a past life, a distant memory, but here it was on a plate in front of him. Although every cell in his body cried out for nourishment, it was almost torture to eat. He gradually overcame the pain and discomfort, and strength began to re-enter his severely weakened body.

The Russians were eager to rehabilitate Caleb. A weak laborer was not able to do very much work. A strong one was. He began to understand the purpose of this sudden benevolence; at least he was being spared from a firing squad or a gas chamber.

His near electrocution and powerful dream had taken place on May 2, 1946 and it was now well into the summer as he recovered at the medical clinic. He had already met and become good friends with Father Sabo, a Hungarian Catholic priest who was a patient in the same clinic. In their discussions, the priest would ask Caleb for any cigarettes that might be allowed him, and in return for the cigarettes, he would teach him the catechism. Caleb became convinced that the Catholic way was the true way.

In September, Caleb was brought before another committee of doctors to be examined. He had been through this routine before...standing around naked while people looked, probed, listened, and discussed. In a way, it seemed bizarre, a committee of doctors concerned about his health, so that he could be placed back in slavery as a laborer with little or no food. From the front, Caleb looked quite healthy. He had gained weight, his face had filled out, and he was beginning to look like a man again, the bones of his skeleton were now covered with muscle as well as skin.

"Turn around," came the command. Caleb began a medical pirouette that would satisfy the doctor's order. One of the doctors came up to Caleb and looked with great concern at his buttocks. It so happened that this part of the anatomy weighed heavily in the Russian medical mind as to whether a person was healthy or not. If a patient had a good set of "cheeks" it was assumed that this was a valid barometer for the rest of a patient's health.

The curious but serious doctor pinched Caleb's buttocks, and found little flesh. This part of him had not filled out in the months of rehabilitation. Caleb prayed silently. He did not know the meaning of all this concern. Another deliberation took place. Russian words were spoken softly from one medical man to another. The discussion continued. A few nods, a few shakes of the head, a gesture of the hand, revealed that the discussion was more of a debate. Caleb continued to stand naked, praying silently.

The discussion went on. Was it going to be another labor camp?

A firing squad? More time in the clinic? After more minutes, Caleb heard another Russian word which he understood..."HOME!" The Russian doctor had said, "HOME!" He was going home! No more labor camp! No firing squad! He was going back to Hungary! Could it be true? It was.

In only a few days, Caleb had his meager belongings and was boarding a train heading west. This time there was a seat. He did not have to stand with 100 others in a small cattle car as he did for his trip into Russia. He sat with others who were being repatriated.

Mental anguish now took over. In the past, so much of his energy had been taken up meeting his own needs and planning his own survival in the camps. The heavy physical labor extracted a tremendous toll so that there was little or no ability to think about home. He was now heading for the Hungarian border on a train, and what lay beyond that border might yet be the greatest disappointment and test of his life. He would learn whether his father, mother, and other family members survived the war. Would he see his father again...the guy with whom he had been through so much? Had he survived the trip home? Did disease or a bullet claim him? How would he face the disappointing news if his father and mother were no longer alive? In spite of the joy of going home, the questions gnawed at him, making the trip anything but peaceful.

He arrived at the Hungarian border and changed trains. Steel wheels continued to roll toward Budapest, where Caleb disembarked. He made his way to his parent's home, and his worst fears were allayed. He looked into his father's eyes and hugged him. His mother was there, alive and well. They, however, were the only ones. Caleb had lost over 100 relatives to the Nazis, including his brother and sister. Ironically, only he and his father and mother were spared. Every uncle, aunt, and cousin had become mere memories. Of the 825,000 Jews in Hungary during the years 1941-1945, 565,000 were murdered!

He had not even known it until this reunion, but his mother had been taken to Auschwitz and miraculously had survived that hell of Hitler. When his father had returned to Hungary, he had gone back to the little village of Szilvasveved, and people barely recognized him.

"Have you come home to die, Josef?" Questions like this greeted him as he shuffled up the street in the little village that he had called home for so many years. He grieved the knowledge that his wife had been taken to Auschwitz, and he had no idea about her condition. Slowly, he was rehabilitated, and it was not long before his wife stood at his side. They were left to wonder about their children. A welcome answer had come. At least Caleb was alive.

The reunion was joyful but it did not last long. Caleb began to share his new understanding with his family that he had discovered Jesus as the Jewish Messiah. It was not welcome information in his parent's home, because to them, Hitler was a Christian. He had accused the Jews of being Christ-killers, and was even photographed in speeches in front of a crucifix. His officers wore a black cross on their uniforms, as did the aircraft of his *Luftwaffe*.

Perhaps their son had lost his mind. At first they tolerated his belief, but the walls continued to grow between them, and in short order he heard his mother's words. "Caleb, we cannot go on like this. You must choose. Either you must choose your father and me, or you must choose this Jesus that you profess."

It was one more layer of disappointment and rejection piled upon that of the past. Caleb went to his room devastated. It was now his own parents who wanted him out. They were the only family members alive....his own father and mother and they were saying...LEAVE!

Caleb groped for an answer. He was asking the question, "Lord, what shall I do?" He continued to pray, and he picked up his Bible. His eyes fell upon the passage from Luke 14:26. "If anyone comes to Me, and does not hate his own father and mother and wife and children and brothers and sisters, yes, and even his own life, he cannot be My disciple." The word "hate" in the original Greek language of the New Testament, is a word which describes a relativity of devotion. It is not a word that requires a person to literally hate his parents, but is a word that requires him to love God more than his parents, therefore "hating" them in relation to the devotion toward Jesus.

Of the thousands of passages that Caleb could have opened to, this was his answer. He knew it in his heart, and as painful as his decision would be, he had come too far with his Lord to forsake Him now. He would walk through the coming days leaning on

God's Word from the Tenach (Old Testament) to "Trust in the Lord with all your heart, and lean not to your own understanding." (NAS—Proverbs 3:5)

Caleb gathered the few things that were his, and left his parent's home. He was tormented in his soul, the sword of rejecting words piercing his broken heart. He went to a monastery not far from Budapest. He began to discuss his experience with one of the monks in authority who lived there. Caleb at first entertained becoming a missionary to China. Part of him wanted to get as far away from everything and everybody as possible, a misguided but not an uncommon motivation for many who have become missionaries.

As the priest listened to Caleb's story he was fascinated, and when Caleb told of the incident where he and his own parents had to part company, the Catholic monk began to laugh and self-righteously exclaimed, "Those silly Jews!...Those silly Jews!"

The sword, which had been piercing Caleb's heart, had just been twisted, and the pain sent him away stunned. He had to speak with a rabbi. Caleb went to visit one not far from the monastery. Together, the learned rabbi and Caleb sat up the entire night, the rabbi listening to Caleb's story, and each of them studying the Scriptures. After all the discussion, and all of the Scripture lessons, the rabbi's conclusion was that Caleb's experience was untrue, and that this Jesus was for the **goyim** (Gentiles) only, and not for a Jew.

The agony went on. The Germans had persecuted him, and his own Hungarian countrymen helped. The Russians took him captive and almost killed him. He came home to his parents and they had rejected him. A Catholic priest laughed at those "silly Jews," and now his own rabbi told him that his experience was a false one. Caleb walked the streets of Budapest, as devastated as Joseph, the favored son of Jacob when his own brothers sold him into slavery.

As he walked, he ran into an old friend. "What are you doing, Caleb? Where are you staying now?"

"Nothing...Nowhere," came the answer.

"Come with me." His friend took him to a place where he worked with a young group of Zionists. Caleb stayed with them for about a year, and established ties with his Jewish brothers and sisters, and also with other Hebrew Christians in Budapest. It was while he was with other Jewish friends who had the same understanding as Caleb that he decided to undergo water baptism, a Christian ritual which is derived from the Jewish **mikveh,** a bath of cleansing. However, Christian baptism is an outward sign of something which should have already taken place inwardly, and is the very picture of being buried with Messiah, and coming out of the water, being raised in resurrection to walk in the newness of life.

In March of 1948, the Zionists asked Caleb if he was ready to go to Palestine. Caleb brought the question to fellow believers. They listened, and the answers came.

"Caleb, it is a tough place. You should wait a while. You're too young."

"Things are difficult in Palestine, Caleb. Don't go. You're too young."

There was no one in the Zionist organization that believed as Caleb did, although he continued to tell them about his experience and understanding of Messiah. Though they did not agree with him, they did not reject him.

He still had a dilemma. The advice of his fellow believers grated away at him. He did not have peace. Again, he walked in solitude and prayed. "Lord...give me a good answer...YOUR answer!" He was carrying his Bible with him. He stopped, opened its pages, and began to read something that he had never read before.

> "But the Lord said to me, 'Do not say, I am a youth' because everywhere I send you, you shall go, and all that I command you, you shall speak. Do not be afraid of them, for I am with you to deliver you,' declares the Lord."
>
> (NAS—Jeremiah 1:7-8)

The words spoken by God to Jeremiah, were just as appropriate for Caleb on this day of searching. He had his answer.

Caleb had sought, and in his heart had received heavenly guidance. With this guidance he was filled with joy. He headed back to his friends at the Zionist organization. He spoke with certainty. "I'm ready."

On March 24, 1948, Caleb boarded a bus with a group of young people like himself, and headed for the border of Austria, where a few years earlier he had been under the tentacles of the Nazis. He crossed the border and headed for Vienna where he enrolled in a school where he began to study Hebrew, learn about Palestine, and even learn Zionist songs.

This was not the first time that Jews had sung songs about Zion. This phenomenon is clearly recorded in the Scriptures, especially when the Jews were sent into Babylonian exile. But in Babylon, the song was being required by their captors. They were not songs of celebration but of lament.

> "By the rivers of Babylon, there we sat down and wept, when we remembered Zion. Upon the willows in the midst of it we hung our harps. For there our captors demanded of us songs, and our tormentors mirth, saying, 'Sing us one of the songs of Zion.' How can we sing the Lord's song in a foreign land? If I forget you, O Jerusalem, may my right hand forget her skill, may my tongue cleave to the roof of my mouth, if I do not remember you, if I do not exalt Jerusalem above my chief joy."
>
> (NAS—Psalm 137:1-6)

This time the Jews were heading home and there was celebration in their singing. Caleb was part of the beginning of another and final return from exile which had begun, and which has yet to see complete fulfillment.

> "Therefore behold, days are coming," declares the Lord, "when it will no longer be said, 'As the Lord lives, who brought up the sons of Israel out of the land of Egypt,' but, 'As the Lord lives, who brought up the sons of Israel from the <u>land of the north and from all the countries where he had banished them.</u>' for I will restore them to **their own land which I gave to their fathers.** Behold, I am going to send for many fishers,"

declares the Lord, "and they will fish for them; and afterwards I shall send for many hunters, and they will hunt them from every mountain and every hill, and from the clefts of the rocks.

(NAS—Jeremiah 16:14-16)

The indications in Scripture are that even the original exodus from Egypt under the leadership of Moses, will be eclipsed by a final call of God. A massive **aliyah** will take place where the world will see the Jewish people return to Zion in great numbers, especially from Russia, but from all the other nations as well.

Caleb continued to share his belief with fellow Zionists. Most were not interested and began to shun him. A close friend, although not sharing Caleb's belief, stood firm with him in defending his right to believe. His friend later became the head of the Bank of Israel.

Caleb moved from Vienna to Marseilles, France where he continued his training. He exercised to build up his physical stamina, and became more acquainted with the hardships which would face him when he arrived on the soil the land the Romans had named Palestine, but within days would be re-born as the nation of Israel. ( May 14, 1948.)

The news echoed throughout the world. The Jews, after almost 2,000 years of exile saw the rebirth of their homeland. Caleb looked forward to arriving in Zion as he boarded a small boat built to accommodate about 100 people. The name of the boat was the *Fabio,* and he would be packed aboard like a sardine with about 1,000 Jews on their way to *Eretz Israel.* This time the crowded conditions were endured with joy. No one was forcing this trip, as was the case in the Nazi trains. It was probably just as crowded, but here it was by choice, out of a desire to live in his homeland.

The boat disembarked on May 15, 1948, one day after Israel was declared to be a state. It was also the same day that five Arab nations attacked little Israel, who had no standing army, only a very limited supply of small arms, and no allies in the world who would come to her aid.

The sailing was not without severe problems. It was another trial in Caleb's life of suffering. The ship had run out of water and people began to drink seawater, making matters worse. There was severe sickness among the people, and after two weeks of living like sardines, tempers flared, and broken and devastated people who had only a short time ago been plucked from the concentration camps began to lose hope again.

It would not be for long. After two weeks of slow sailing through the Mediterranean, the coast of Israel came into view. The news spread in seconds throughout the ship. People scrambled to the railings to get a view. They were glued there, staring and dreaming, until they were finally in port and able to set foot upon the soil of their new homeland. People fell to their knees kissing the ground of Israel. They were home...but what kind of home was it?

Caleb was immediately sent to an army camp where he received a uniform. Troops from Egypt, Iraq, Transjordan, Syria, and Lebanon had attacked and were at war with Israel. These nations also had volunteers helping them from Saudi Arabia, Libya, and Yemen...ALL of them together, against little Israel.

Caleb walked the ground of the encampment, and looked at the starlit sky. It was pleasantly cool on this night, and every star was in view. It was easy to understand the exasperation and joy that comingled in Abraham's heart when God offered him offspring as numerous as the stars. Now, almost 4,000 years later, Caleb stared at the same infinite stars, shining above the land of Israel. It was the land that God had promised to his forefather Abraham, and he was called and chosen to set foot on it!

He prayed, "Lord...what is your plan? I thought that You were sending me a new solution, and here I am in a new soldier's uniform."

He felt peace in his heart. In a few days he was walking the infamous Burma Road, a road carved out by the Jews to keep communication and supplies flowing to besieged Jerusalem. Moving along this road was not accomplished in an air-conditioned bus, but in scarce and often poorly operating vehicles. Much of the movement was done on foot. Such was the case with Caleb on this night. He and his fellow Jews were carrying weapons and other supplies, desperately needed in surrounded Jerusalem. Along the route, Arab soldiers waited to ambush any Jews who were attempting to lend a hand to their brothers and sisters in Jerusalem. The trek began in the foothills, and it was an all night climb...uphill all the way to the City of David. Each night courageous Jews would pack upon their back everything that they could carry and make the climb to Jerusalem.

Caleb became a medic, and he spent much of his time on hot battlefields, ministering first aid to wounded comrades while bullets whizzed around him and overhead. His weapons were not rifles or pistols, but a medical kit, his Bible, and a love in his heart for his people and his land, which flowed toward each wounded soldier to whom he ministered.

As a medic, he became the brunt of jokes, much as the field goal kicker is on an American football team. He is not the guy that goes head to head with the soldiers from the other army, each trying to kill the other. When the chips are down, he is called in to make the point that counts, the kicked ball sailing through the uprights at the opposing end of the field. In Caleb's case, his job was the last effort which would save a life that was shattered on the battlefield. He was loved and respected in his role.

He fought in northern Galilee where the war was extremely fiery. He was sent to Kiryat Gat, about 25 miles southwest of Jerusalem where he was faced by a formidable and strong Egyptian army. It was here that he lost many of his friends...men who had survived the concentration camps and the war in Europe, and who had braved the British blockades in the Mediterranean. Some of them had been in the internment camps in Cyprus, only to be required to give their lives on the soil of Israel. Nevertheless...they bravely died at home.

Caleb remembers that no matter where he was or under what circumstance, he would always find a place to pray...and pray he did, for his men and for Israel. Even when there was great scarcity of food for the Israeli soldiers, Caleb would take a walk and pray. He said, "God would lead me to places where I would find fresh fruit, nuts, and other refreshing foods. I would load up as much as I was able to carry, and bring the special provisions back to my comrades."

The Egyptians were fierce fighters, and they were known for committing terrible atrocities on the battlefield. When a Jew was captured or wounded, it was not uncommon to find him completely dismembered after having been painfully tortured to death. Caleb had the ugly duty of discovering and caring for the remains in such events. He remembers that there was never enough help on the battlefield. Where he had only two hands he needed ten.

There was never enough of anything for Israel's fighters. They were always short on weapons, ammunition, gasoline, food, medical supplies and everything needed to defend themselves from onslaughts that kept coming from their Arab neighbors. Because of the myriad of shortages and impossible odds that Israel has had to face, time after time in her recent history of 50-plus years, one can only conclude that Israel is re-born not out of a clever plan of man, or as a political accident, but by the hand of a covenant keeping God who will not forsake His people.

No formal introductions were needed when a man was severely wounded or dying. As Caleb answered the screams of bleeding soldiers, he would minister what solace he could from his medical kit and his heart. On several occasions he felt the shock wave of a bullet that sped past his head only a millimeter or two away, as he crawled and sprinted among the dying.

Caleb continued to do his work as a medic in war after war after war. He bandaged and comforted his wounded and dying brothers in the War of Independence in 1948. He faced the fires of combat again in 1956.

As if this were not enough, the Egyptians, Syrians, and Jordanians attacked Israel in 1967, and Caleb was again on the battlefield. Six years later in 1973, on the highest holy day of the Jewish year, Yom Kippur (Day of Atonement), Israel was attacked again. Once again Caleb was in combat array racing around in the midst of battle, patching up the torn bodies of his Jewish brothers. It was this war that took its greatest toll on him. He saw young boys who had battled in the Sinai so terrorized in their minds that they lost everything...their ability to think, reason, or function. It was another blow to his own senses. It was just after this war and its fierce battles that Caleb, too, suffered from nervous exhaustion and had to be hospitalized. Except for a few childhood years in Szilvasveved, Hungary, his entire life had been war and rejection. The words of King David in Psalm 35 reflect the deep longing of

Jewish souls today, and a cry that more than once has flooded through Caleb's soul:

> Contend, O Lord, with those who contend with me;
> Fight against those who fight against me. Take hold of
> buckler and shield, and rise up for my help. Draw also
> the spear and the battle-ax to meet those who pursue
> me; Say to my soul, "I am your salvation." Let those be
> ashamed and dishonored who seek my life; Let those
> be turned back and humiliated who devise evil against
> me. Let them be like chaff before the wind, with the
> angel of the Lord driving them on. Let their way be
> dark and slippery, with the angel of the Lord pursuing
> them. For without cause they hid their net for me; with-
> out cause they dug a pit for my soul. Let destruction
> come upon him unawares; and let the net which he hid
> catch himself; into that very destruction let him fall.
>                                       (NAS—Psalm 35:1-8)

While the prayer of King David has been answered in specific corners of Jewish history, its ultimate and final answer is yet to come when ALL of Israel's enemies shall be judged and once and for all neutralized.

Just before leaving Hungary with the Zionist organization, Caleb had reconciliation with his parents, and as a parting gift they presented him with a small accordion. He used this little instrument to sing with his fellow soldiers, and by his own account, always played the first song to his Messiah, and sang a song that exalted Him. He was never questioned in this practice, and always appreciated.

As the war raged, it would become necessary to move out at a moment's notice. Caleb often lost both his accordion and his Bible. In some cases they would be missing for weeks. But he always got them back...the accordion and the Bible. He still has his accordion today.

Between the wars, Caleb continued to serve, and to draw closer to God. He spent nine months ministering to some of the sickest and neediest people in Israel, such as lepers in Hunson Hospital. With all of the suffering and pain in his own life, Caleb was fully able to empathize with those who were suffering from the dread disease of leprosy. It is a disease that manifests itself in livid swellings and distortions of the hands and feet. Ulcers often form on the soles of the feet or on the ball of the heel, which extend to the bones. As the ulcerations spread, it cripples the patient. Tubercles are often formed on the face, and fever sets in and eventually kills the patient after a long and miserable life.

It was after serving in this hospital for almost a year in 1951, that Caleb took a reprieve, and began to pray for God's leading in his life. Caleb descended into the "Valley of the Cross" just opposite the site where the Knesset Building stands today in Jerusalem. At that time it was uninhabited land. He walked and prayed and by faith believed that God would lead him.

He wound up in Tiberias, a city on the western shore of the Sea of Galilee. It was there in the German Colony that he met some more Christians. They were from a variety of countries, and they formed a mini-United Nations of prayer. They did have one thing in common however. They loved Israel, and they believed in Y'shua (Jesus) as the Messiah of Israel and all mankind.

It was here that Caleb met a Norwegian woman who helped him. She was a lady who along with others in the group, had experienced a new dimension in God. After one of the meetings, she and another lady came over to the sofa where Caleb was sitting and asked if they could pray for him. Caleb, who was at a low point in his life, tired from war, tired from the long and desperate hours in the hospital for lepers, and seeking a closer relationship with God, consented.

He knelt down next to the sofa, and the ladies began to pray for him. Elizabeth, who would later become Caleb's wife, was one of them. As they prayed, Caleb felt a power come upon him. As he knelt and the ladies prayed, he noticed the shadow of Elizabeth's hand cast upon the wall next to him. As her hand came closer to his head, he felt a tremendous power coming upon him. After about 5 minutes of this prayer, he received the baptism in the Holy Spirit, manifested in the speaking of tongues. It is one of the gifts of the Holy Spirit listed in the book of First Corinthians in the New Testament. Caleb spent the rest of the night until the hour of 5:00 AM praising God in his new language.

Caleb had another problem. He was able to speak Hungarian, a little Russian, some German, and Hebrew, but he was unable to speak Norwegian or English, the two languages that Elizabeth spoke. She began to help him with English and he grasped it within approximately seven days. It was a new prayer language in 5 minutes, and English in one week!

The New Testament is filled with examples of those who spoke in tongues, as fulfillment of a prophecy mentioned even in the book of Isaiah. "Indeed, He will speak to this people through stammering lips and a foreign tongue..." (NAS—Isaiah 28:11). Caleb was merely receiving and enjoying the promises of God's word which thousands upon thousands of His children enjoy today.

Caleb and Elizabeth were married in Tiberias in 1953. Some years later, in 1958, they went to Norway to minister to Christians there. Caleb was totally unprepared for what he would experience on this trip. Once he was in Norway, he needed the Norwegian language to round out his vocabulary. He attended a tent conference of Pentecostals who numbered about 1,000. Caleb was asked to speak.

He began to tell his dynamic story, speaking in English, a language that most Norwegians understand. In the middle of the talk, Caleb made the following statement to the crowd. "If you believe in the Lord Jesus Christ, your life shall be changed!"

Suddenly, his tongue became "thick" and he was unable to utter another word. A lady in the audience, who had only the day before received the baptism of the Holy Spirit, stood up and began to speak in tongues. When she was finished, a Norwegian from the Congo stood up with the interpretation. It was as follows:

"My people of Norway...you have been faithful to Me for all these years, in all the fields of the Gentiles, to bring the good news to them, to work for them, and to proclaim My name to them. But now, I turn to My people...ISRAEL!"

As Caleb stood on the speaker's platform, still unable to speak, the normally conservative and stayed Norwegians broke into spontaneous praise and worship. They jumped, and praised, and the tent billowed and swayed. After a few minutes, Caleb began to resume his talk......in Norwegian! His tongue loosened, and he spoke to the audience in their native language. He had been in Norway for just three weeks until this time.

Caleb and Elizabeth were then called to Sweden, and Caleb spoke to the Swedes in his newly found language, Norwegian. The Swedes heard him in Swedish. It was merely another miracle that God was performing through one of his tested and faithful servants. They went on to Denmark, and the same phenomenon happened there as well, and why not? It was a promise of God in His Word for His people!

Caleb was able to reunite with his parents when they made *aliyah* to Israel. They moved to Kiryat Gat, not far from Jerusalem where Caleb had spent terrorized hours fighting the Egyptians. Josef, who had gone through so many of the trials and tribulations with his son, began to love Israel more and more and read his own Bible daily. He was unable, however, to come to the same conclusion as his son about Jesus.

As Josef aged, he had a vision one night. An angel spoke to him and said, "Josef, if you go the way that you are going, you shall never come to the goal." In the morning, Josef asked his son the meaning of the vision. Caleb explained to his father what he had been trying to explain for years.

Josef was now an old man, and he had not much more time to live. He lay on his bed and as Caleb continued to tenderly explain things to his father, Elizabeth knelt down outside the room and prayed earnestly...

"Lord...I will not let you go until you reveal Yourself and save Josef."

She continued to pray, beseeching the God of Israel in the throne room of heaven. Inside the hospital room, Caleb continued his explanation to his father, and according to Caleb, God's Spirit fell into the room over father and son.

Outside the door, Elizabeth continued to pray, and as the burden lifted from her heart she became aware of the sounds of two men crying and praising God with joy. Her father-in-law had seen. He received. Elizabeth came into the room. Josef then closed his eyes for the last time, filled with peace, knowing in Whom he had believed. Caleb, his beloved son, partner in many tribulations, stood with him at his bedside, sad at the passing of his father, but knowing that he would have eternal fellowship with him in the ages to come.

Caleb and his wife, Elizabeth, continue to live in Jerusalem. There are no more precious people on this earth than these two. Caleb has lived the life of a suffering servant. He is one more of many others in the land of Israel, who has paid a price in his own life, that has touched depths of pain and disappointment that most could barely imagine. He is one of God's chosen, too. He is a natural branch to the olive tree. (Romans 11:24 & Jeremiah 11:16). To him and others like him, we who are the wild branches (Gentiles), grafted in, owe a deep debt of gratitude. May we as Christians begin to pay this debt by bringing into live expression, love and support for the Jewish people everywhere.

# 8

# YAKOV

It was in September 1985 that I sat in the bustling lobby of a modernized hotel in Basel, Switzerland. The walls were covered with angled tongue-in-groove teakwood, accented with plenty of track lighting and built in mirrors. Some potted plants added just enough greenery to bring some life and Swiss *Gemütlichkeit* (atmosphere or coziness) to the squeaky-clean surroundings. Outside the hotel, electric trolley cars breezed by the hotel on slick steel rails imbedded in impeccable streets.

My wife and I had taken part in the first day of the Christian Zionist Congress, held in a meeting hall only a few blocks away. It was the very same hall in which some 88 years earlier, in 1897, Theodore Herzl, a Jew, chaired a similar meeting, planting some of the seeds that would become the roots for modern day Zionism. It was in this same spirit, that hundreds of Christians from several continents came to reaffirm Herzl's vision, not as a political movement, but as the fulfillment of biblical promise, recorded by Spirit-inspired Jewish prophets more than 1,000 years B.C. The promise was for a scattering of the Jewish people, but it was also for their re-gathering to their homeland.

> "Moreover, the Lord will scatter you among all peoples, from one end of the earth to the other end of the earth; and there you shall serve other gods, wood and stone, which you or your fathers have not known."
> (NAS—Deuteronomy 28:64)

> ...then the Lord your God will restore you from captivity, and have compassion on you, and will gather you again from all the peoples where the Lord your God has scattered you. If your outcasts are at the ends of the earth, from there the Lord your God will gather you, and from there He will bring you back. And the Lord your God will bring you into the land which your fathers possessed, and you shall possess it; and He will prosper you and multiply you more than your fathers.
> (NAS—Deuteronomy 30:3-5)

It was in the spirit of these ancient words that the noises and motions that competed for my attention in the Swiss hotel lobby, grew strangely distant as I sat face to face with Yakov, a son come back to possess Zion.

I had heard him speak...once in Jerusalem, and once in Miami. He was an imposing and proud man, pink-cheeked, with a receding hair-line, the silver-gray of his beard testifying to his maturity. A hand-cro-cheted **kippah** accented his appearance and announced his Jewishness. His eyes were deep and serious, shining like the twinkling of a Christmas tree bulb when his humor was provoked, but piercing as lasers when he spoke against injustice and tyranny. His slow and deliberate gait revealed a man who had suffered deeply. It was aided with a cane, which he used as support for his one good leg, and the other which was artificial. If one were to call his name from behind, Yakov would stop and turn his attention slowly to the one who called, almost as if he had to make a conscious decision as to whether to expend the energy to turn around. He was never in a hurry.

As I sat with him, he would sometimes lean forward with both hands on the top of his cane, perhaps to support his tired torso, or to create an on-the-spot podium as he shared his life and ideas. Yakov's accented English revealed his Russian background, and added clout to anything that he said. He would pronounce a word like "sure" with a slow and inflective " shooo-ehrrrr," the R's rolling off the end of his tongue like coins from a beaten slot machine. "Going" would come out as "Goh-ingk." Whatever the accent, it was only the surface color to Yakov, much as paint is to an automobile.

I counted it a great privilege to have this short private encounter with him. He had lived in Israel since 1970, when he immigrated to Israel from Russia. He was a decorated soldier and an official in the Russian legal justice system. However, when his stand for truth and freedom began to shine and expose the corruption of the Soviet bureaucracy, he became an enemy of the State, and spent 14 years of his life in more Russian prisons than he could remember.

When Yakov heard my Polish surname, "Kosak", he frowned strongly. It was a name that would provoke many Jews to recoil. The name is obviously derived from the "Cossacks", who were peasant-soldiers in the Russian empire, who received special privileges in return for their military service. Even though they later fought against the communists, they had a history of aggressive anti-Semitism driven by the czars in the era of pogroms against the Jews.

However, I did learn from a Jewish friend that many Jews in Poland also had the surname "Kosak". I also discovered on my visit to the Auschwitz death camp that there were several Kosaks (with a variety of spellings) who had perished there and whose names were recorded in the archives.

I had met other Jews who had cringed upon hearing my name. As I have announced my name while being introduced to older Jews, I have invariably been greeted with some slowly nodding heads, a half-smile, and some words which in effect said, "Boy...if you only knew what that name means to us Jews."

Such was the case as I spoke with Yakov. There were nods, accompanied by the half-smile as he digested my name and its meaning. I sat with him, totally fascinated with who he was, what he had experienced, and frustrated about the fact that I had only about 15 or 20 minutes to spend with him. His life experience could no doubt fill several volumes. I found myself painfully torn, as I excused myself from our conversation, wondering in my heart if I would ever meet him again.

A year later, as I finished my introductory conversation with Shimon, the young Israeli soldier already introduced in these pages, I saw Yakov maneuvering his car through the crunch of traffic near Jerusalem's **Kotel** (Western Wall). I immediately caught his attention and told him of my desire to meet with him to record his story. He graciously accepted and invited my wife and me to his home in Zikron Yakov, a lovely and peaceful town high on a hill just inland of the coastal site of Caesarea, about a two hour drive from Jerusalem.

I arrived at Yakov's home. He and his wife fed us a sumptuous lunch. We then made ourselves comfortable in his living room, Yakov leaning on his cane. I pushed the red "record" button on my tape recorder and began to listen.

One of his earlier but very significant memories in Russia, was the day that his father was arrested. Yakov was only 13 years old. Life up to that time had been a deep struggle for his entire family. It was during the mid 30's where the Bolshevik revolution had been growing for almost 20 years, and had tightened its grip on the Russian people. Life in the Soviet Union at that time made the American Depression look like a banquet. It is futile to list the scarcities that existed, for the only thing that was in abundance was misery. It was a misery that has continued for decades even through **peristroika** ("new thinking" that has been made popular through the efforts of Mikael Gorbachev and passed on to the leadership of Boris Yeltsin and now Mr. Putin).

A joke that circulated in Russia for a long time went like this: An old Jewish man and his wife were standing in one of the long lines that form daily just to purchase some of life's necessities. As the old man continued to wait he spoke out..."After 50 years of this great and wonderful communist system, we still have no bread!" In a few moments, a KGB man stepped out of the same line, showed the dissenting Jew his ID card, and warned him that his statements were very inflammatory against the great Soviet State. He reminded the old Jew that "in the Stalin era, you would have been shot for such a statement, but now we are more merciful." As the KGB agent walked away, the elderly Jew turned to his wife and whispered, "Not only do they no longer have bread here, but they must also be out of bullets."

The ideology of Marx and Lenin had become the computer chip that had programmed rigid conformity to the new economic ideal which Russians believed would save all mankind. The Russian people were continually promised that if they co-operated, the ideal society would soon come into full bloom with abundance for all. So the lie would be spoken...again and again. It could never succeed because it was a system that negated God.

Yakov's father was not impressed with the Bolshevik rhetoric. He remained cynical towards the new ideal, because he saw the reality. His concern was in merely obtaining enough food to keep his family alive. He was not afraid to voice his opinion about the revolution either, often through humor. One day, one of his jokes fell on the wrong ears. The KGB agent that overheard his humorous blasphemy against the State eagerly "proved" that Yakov's father was an enemy of the people. His father was sent to prison for "maligning the State".

Always needing secret informers to control the populace, the communist bureaucracy knew from where to draw them. Shortly after Yakov's father was incarcerated, agents came to speak with his mother. "If you will co-operate with us, perhaps we can work something out for your husband. If you will not, we will kill him in prison."

She stood her ground. "I will not be a part of such a system."

The KGB kept their promise. Yakov's father died in prison some 10 years after first being sentenced. It was a slow agonizing death. The system stripped him of his physical strength through the hard labor and lack of food. Slowly, measured in moments, days, months, and years, a man's spirit, soul, and body were carved away by the whittling knives of loneliness, despair, starvation and disease. When there was but a sliver left, death came to pluck the remaining toothpick.

Yakov was then in his late teens and was drafted into the Soviet

Army. He was considered no more than a "hooligan." With a father who had been an enemy of the great new State, and a mother who would not co-operate, how could the son of such a marriage be any better? Yakov donned his uniform in 1939 while the German Nazis were rolling through Poland and into Russia. He was assigned to a penal battalion, filled with the criminals and rejects of the Soviet system. As Yakov tells it:

"I was an innocent boy...about 18 years old. I felt that I was being punished, but I did not commit any crime. When I was put in this battalion, we were given about 10 rifles for more than 200 men, and they were not even real rifles. They did not shoot. When we asked how we were supposed to fight with them, the Russian commanders would say, 'your weapons are in the hands of the Germans. Go get them!' We were sent barehanded against the German troops! We were but children! We had no guns and we were only teenagers!"

There was a special rule for the penal battalion...one that few were able to obey. If a man was wounded four times, he was considered brave and loyal enough to be transferred to a regular battalion of soldiers where he might receive a real rifle with which to fight.

Yakov received his first wound, a bullet in the leg. He was decorated and given the little medical attention that was available. When he had sufficiently recovered, he rejoined his penal battalion. He had accomplished the first step of four, which would qualify him for graduation from his rag-tag group of Soviet "misfits" to a normal battalion. Once again on the front lines without a gun, and facing the determined and well-equipped German troops, an enemy bullet found its mark, and Yakov fell wounded. He was sent back for medical attention, and was again decorated. He was halfway to graduation.

He continued his story, smiling. "I knew that this was not the way to grow old gracefully. I knew that I would soon be sent back to the front lines, so I changed my identity."

At the time, record keeping had not become the bureaucratic art that it is today. And during wartime, the added confusion made matters all the worse. This was a terrible disadvantage for someone trying to find out about a missing son or husband, but it was a great advantage for someone like Yakov.

As he was being shuffled through the paperwork process for further medical care, he filled out his forms with some new information. He disguised himself with a different first name, birth date, place of birth, and a variety of other details. He was smart enough to keep his last name intact. For the time being it would serve to outsmart any investigators trying to track him down. The basic assumption of any investigator was that no one would keep his actual last name if trying to pull a fast one against the Soviet system. Yakov's plan worked, and he was shuffled off to new duties, disappearing from the eyes of the KGB and the commanders of the penal battalion.

Yakov was transferred to another unit where he became an excellent soldier and ultimately an officer. He was decorated many times, was well thought of, and survived the war. Although he had pulled his little coup against the system, and had favor among those who were its mentors, he had not succumbed to it. He remembered too well what the system had done to his father. He was determined to outsmart his adversaries.

As Yakov continued to live his life in Russia, other events took place in the world. The most significant for him was Israel's rebirth to Statehood in 1948. Israel was declared a State, and the War of Independence had taken place with Israel prevailing. Up to that time, Yakov knew only that he was a Jew, but had no religious or cultural training in Judaism. According to him, "my whole Soviet education was without God, and without Israel." He had some Jewish friends who had equal curiosities about their Jewishness. Together they went to a library, the biggest in Moscow, and found some poetry and articles about the Promise Land, along with a map.

The information they found was in very old books. Maps in general, especially of Israel, were very hard to obtain, but Yakov and his friends sat together examining the yellowed pages of an antiquated book, staring at the ink that diagrammed the land that his forefather, Abraham from Ur of Chaldees, would one day call home. At the time, he could not even imagine such a reality.

His military officer status gave him the calling card to rub elbows with some of the bureaucrats and Communist Party officials.

Already having watched the system kill his father, destroy his mother, almost take his own life, and oppress the millions of other people, Yakov was determined to change it. His love for truth and justice had been constantly violated, and he detested those who had pledged their lives to the perpetuation of the Bolshevik lie, yet served themselves through bribes and favors.

One such man was a procurator, a chief prosecutor in Moscow. Yakov jokingly described him as a man with real class, because he didn't drink his vodka straight from the bottle, but used a glass. Yakov had established a friendship with an authority in a local liquor plant, and was able to obtain all the "spirits" that he needed to feed his new "buddy" in the Moscow prosecutor's office. It was the system. Sought after and hard to obtain alcohol was the price of admission to this man's willingness to dispense a favor.

"Yakov, maybe you would like to work for us...in this office. I could arrange it."

Yakov squirmed a bit. He knew that he had no formal credentials that would qualify him, but appearing confident he said, "Why not?"

The two walked over to a map. His boozing friend gestured and asked, "What do you prefer? Are you from around Moscow? Would you like to work here?" He was enjoying the moment of being in charge. His gestures were dramatic, as if to impress Yakov that, "if you want anything, I can grant it."

Yakov surveyed the map and answered the questions. "Well...ah...I have fought very hard in Moscow winters. My wounds are many and sensitive to the harsh cold. Perhaps you could send me somewhere in the South."

The truth was that Yakov was afraid of Moscow. If ever there was a place that might find him out, it would be Moscow, and to be located a couple of thousand kilometers or more south of the city would offer some safety.

"I'll take care of it." The bureaucratic weasel smiled through the vodka fog that misted over his brain. The few snorts of spirits had given him a mellow heart, and he was only too willing to help his new friend.

Yakov was sent to an area adjacent to the Black Sea. It was

carved up into about 96 districts with large farms. He was 22 years old and was appointed the chief criminal investigator with 300 investigators in his charge. It was an area noted for some of the highest crime in the country. As Yakov marched into his new position with his written orders and recommendations, the whole office was afraid of him, because he had the favor of those whom they feared in Moscow. They, too, knew the system, and how to survive.

The Black Sea area was like the Florida of the United States, where many thieves and criminals who were on the run would head in an effort to stay hidden. Thieves and criminals from all over the country disappeared there when they were avoiding legitimate prosecution. This influx of lawbreakers added to the normal crime committed by the residents of the Black Sea district.

Yakov wanted to uproot the real corruption in the system. Every time he prosecuted a petty criminal the charges would stick. However, when he would take on the corrupt official or the crimes of the justice system itself, bribes and favors of others in higher positions than his own would frustrate his efforts. Even when Yakov prosecuted legitimate cases, he would soon see that the long arm of bribery would reach to the offices in Moscow, and he would be ordered to close the books on a particular case or bend its direction toward acquittal.

He was gradually pulled into the mire of the system himself. Instead of changing it...it was beginning to change him. As he continued his investigations, it was clear that millions of rubles were changing hands through the cleverly masked systems of bribery. The corruption reached all the way to the Kremlin.

Idealistically, but naively, Yakov thought, "I must put them ALL in prison!"

As he began to tackle these issues with some of his own prosecutors and department heads, his fame grew with the people. Instead of being crushed by the system, this Jewish hot potato was given a promotion. He was moved out of the Black Sea district, and brought to Moscow, where he would be closer to the top of the pyramid of influence peddling and bribery schemes. He would also be more visible, and therefore more closely watched.

After several rounds of sparring with the system, there came a day when he was paid a visit at his home. His visitor was a very important man in the Soviet investigative system. He sat down, took out a gold whisky flask with two gold shot glasses, poured each of them a drink, and toasted to the "good life", but with an added admonishment, "young man, don't ever do such things again." Yakov's investigations and his efforts in exposing dishonesty were not being met with approval. Behind the toast to the "good life" was a veiled threat to shut up.

"Keep digging up dirt with your shovel, and we will bury you with a bulldozer," and "you have seen the prisons and you know what they are like...just keep doing what you're doing and we can arrange for you to spend some time there too." A decision was made to move Yakov with his zeal to a War Industry Department.

He could not have been more delighted. Now he would be able to learn yet more about the system and how it REALLY worked. Because he was so exasperated with Soviet Russia, he thought that he would be able to glean some information that he could use to get out of the country and go to the West. He had come to that point of realizing that his efforts to change things were futile. As Yakov explained:

"I was very anti-Soviet from even before 1930 and I was like a caged wolf in this system. I wanted to fix it, and bring the REAL criminals to justice, but it was more and more becoming apparent that I was not able to change it. I must also say, that I never told ANYONE my true sentiments. I had no friend that I could say these things to, and in fact I did not even tell my wife. Under such a system, you must be suspicious of everyone!"

This statement coincides with the same sentiments expressed by Lt. Victor Belenko, a Russian fighter pilot who had been filled to his eyebrows with the propaganda and failure of communism. After mentally blueprinting his escape for months and sharing his ideas with no one, not even his wife, the day finally came when he would execute the plan. He was up before dawn, kissed his sleeping infant son, went out to the air base, and took to the skies in his MIG-25, purportedly to take part in a military exercise. He departed Chuguyevka in southeast Russia, pointed his fighter southeast, and streaked across open ocean for Japan, where he landed his state-of

-the-art war machine at Hakodate Airport, a small civilian field. When he shut down the engine, he had 30 seconds of fuel remaining. To succeed with this plan, he was forced to keep his feelings and frustrations to himself for years, unable to share them even with his own family out of fear of being turned in as mentally ill or an enemy of the State.

Since the walls have fallen between East and West, and during the time that I lived in Germany, it was an incredible revelation to see how many escape attempts from the former communist East Germany were foiled by parents or relatives who exposed the plan of a prospective escapee. They had become so loyal to the system that kept them in bondage that they were convinced that anyone who would want to seek his freedom, was either sick or an enemy. To be free with one's own thoughts, even among family members, was often a terrible mistake.

Yakov kept his secrets to himself. By accident, he met a very high official from the War Ministry, and he was appointed to be the legal advisor to one of the largest military plants in the country. The plant had some 45,000 workers and was located in the town of Tula, not far from Moscow. It was there that he learned how manufacturing under the Socialist system operated. Production quotas were rarely met, but always appeared to be in excellent order on paper. He also discovered first hand that when the State owns everything, even its people, then NOTHING works well. Lies and thievery become the building stones for almost everything that is accomplished.

Some of the most obvious evidence was found in Russia's aviation program. It was not built on solid scientific experiment and ingenuity which resulted in legitimate discovery, but was built largely on the stolen efforts of others from other nations. Russian aircraft and space vehicles became close copies of the originals which were designed, built, and tested in the West. To make any claim to the contrary would be no more truthful than their official statements that claim the communist system to be supportive of human rights.

This is not to say that there are not bright capable scientists in Russia. There are. And there have been many discoveries and innovations made on a legitimate basis. In fact, the Russians are probably the most advanced in the world if one considers strictly aerodynamics. In that area, they have few peers. Nevertheless, it is obvious that much of what was touted as original, was simply the application of stolen ideas and discoveries.

While he was working in the War Industry factory, Yakov learned some more lessons about international politics. In 1947 during very tense voting sessions in the United Nations, the Russians had cast their vote in FAVOR of partitioning part of Palestine in order to create the modern State of Israel as a homeland for the Jews. This was another one of those dichotomies of life, because the treatment of the Jews inside Russia was abominable in many places.

According to Yakov, there was also political naiveté within the newly formed government of Israel. Golda Meir had been dispatched to Moscow to a government which based on its vote in the United Nations, would have caused anyone to believe that the national leaders were pro-Israel. She arrived in Russia and began asking for Jews who wanted to emigrate to Israel. She spoke to various Jewish groups, and in a matter of days had long lists of volunteers who were ready to leave Mother Russia to go to Israel. They were ready to leave in a moment. They had been social outcasts for too long. Yakov was still insulated in his position at the Tula War Industry plant, but he was watching...and learning.

The lists of Jews wanting to immigrate to Israel were made known to Soviet officialdom, which served only to help the regime further harass and pressure the Jews. The Jews were made to be social outcasts on a greater scale than before. They were stripped of jobs, apartments, and were generally designated as the scum of society. After all, how could any grateful and loyal Soviet citizen ever want to leave the motherland with all its greatness? Many Jews did, and they paid the price for saying so. As Yakov observed all of this, his appetite for more knowledge about Israel was whetted.

Yakov knew the dangers of sharing his deep feelings with anyone. Because the Soviet system gave lip service to the ideals of honesty and integrity, he was in the position of being academically correct in trying to change it through his efforts. The stark reality, however, was that his efforts stepped on too many toes and embarrassed too many bureaucrats. His deepest feelings, known only to himself, were that he absolutely hated the entire corrupt structure of fear and tyranny. He had known nothing else, but yet knew that there was a better way.

In spite of his playing the "spoiler" to the system, he continued to survive in its web. He moved from the War Industry plant back to Moscow, where he became a chief legal advisor. It would equate to having an influential position under the United States Attorney General in Washington. Yakov continued his rise to power, but in the process, his goal of changing the system was always frustrated.

His efforts stirred things up, like a noisy visitor to a barn full of chickens. He flailed his arms, and made noise as he walked through the hen house. The chickens squawked, flapped their wings, went airborne for a few feet, but they always came right back down to roost where they had been all along. It was as if his hands were greased with liquid Teflon and every foul thing that he would try to lay hold of and tear from its foundations, would simply teeter for a moment, slip from his grip, and remain as it was.

True to the system's trait of being ever suspicious, someone in the bureaucracy decided to do a more thorough background check on Yakov. Much to the delight of the KGB, the information revealed that they were not dealing with Yakov, the courageous Russian officer who had become a legal investigator. They now had Yakov, the hooligan rebel who avoided being sent back to the penal battalion to fight one of the world's most formidable armies without a gun. He was Yakov, son of a State enemy who had been thrown into prison to die. He was the son of a woman who would not co-operate in becoming an informer for the system...worst of all, he was a Jew!

The bureaucrats of the corrupt Russian legal system had finally uncovered Yakov's secret. He was immediately tried and convicted by the State and sent to prison. Yakov knew that he was forever ruined, as far as any career was concerned in the Soviet Union. Even if he could look beyond his upcoming years in prison, he knew that once released he would always be a marked man. He would have to go through a period of exile, living in a "house arrest" situation where he would have little to no opportunity to succeed professionally. The unearthed discovery of his past, even though his life was not filled with actual criminal activity, meant that his life was ruined in the USSR.

Yakov was a deeply spiritual man, and looked at his suffering not from the myopic "woe is me" view, but from a cosmic point of view. Even during his years in prison, he was convinced that the suffering through which he passed would ultimately make him a better person. While not absolutely certain, he wondered whether he was being punished for a past life, a concept that is not of Jewish religious tradition, but more in harmony with Far East religions.

As a convict under the Soviet system, a man loses everything. He loses his job, apartment, and his friends. No good Russian dares associate himself with criminals. To do so puts the person at great risk. Fear is a powerful weapon to control its victims.

With nothing to look forward to, and knowing that to dwell in the past would be futile and disheartening, Yakov spent his prison years training himself to live for the moment. He learned to live in the present moment where both enjoyment and suffering could be experienced with meaning.

There was no question in Yakov's mind that God was the Master of all things, and that He ultimately ruled over man's destiny. Therefore he could always leave even his own miserable circumstances in His hands. As Yakov entered the prison, he would not see freedom for 14 years. The Soviet prisons have no work-release programs, weekend visitations to the family, televisions or game rooms. They are designed to punish and denigrate the human being. They are very successful in doing so.

In those moments when Yakov would think ahead, he imagined that perhaps he might be allowed to become a forest ranger, and in the isolation of that job, at least be free to roam the thousands of acres of woodland in Russia. He learned later that such jobs were reserved strictly for the KGB. Because of the Soviet paranoia of believing that enemy agents would be parachuted into forest lands, KGB agents were always on the lookout for unusual activity and consequently even controlled the forests.

Yakov continued his life of oppression in many prisons, always trying to learn his lesson from suffering. He continually asked himself and God, what it was that he was supposed to learn through it all. He was certain that there is ultimate purpose for each moment, and that the purpose is ultimately good. Yakov spent hours each day probing the depths of reason, going beyond that which could be observed in the physical, always asking "why?" Why was he in prison? The surface answer was that he did not comply with the expectations of the State, but he was in search of the deeper significance.

His mind delved deeply into mysticism, looking for the ultimate answers. In this path of suffering, he met many of the worst elements of Soviet society, but he also met the best. They were not considered the best by the Kremlin rulers, but he met the ones with loving hearts and compassionate souls, people who would not succumb to the Bolshevik vice-grips. He met the oppressed, the ones who might have stolen a loaf of bread to feed their families, or the ones who looked at reality and voiced an opinion or accusation openly, behavior which was not tolerated under communism. According to Yakov, the majority of the thieves that he met as a prosecutor or as a prisoner, were thieves because of hunger. It was not the desire for more or better things. It was the matter of simple survival.

Yakov met a Jehovah Witness in prison. "They are strong people," he added. "The Jehovah Witness was a religious man who would read a Bible which was allowed him and walk around with a smile of contentment."

"Why are you smiling?" Yakov asked.

"I'm so happy, because God is punishing me in this life."

Yakov was amazed at how this man went through the days in prison on such a "high." This man also would taunt the guards with a perverse sense of humor. He would literally take a needle and thread, obtained from who knows where, and would run the needle and thread right through his lips, and would sew his mouth shut.

When the Soviet authorities would ask why he was doing it, he would reply, "Why do I need a mouth when you do not allow me anything to eat?" It was his way of hitting back at the tyranny of the system.

The Russian guards would find no humor in his actions. Most were hardened and cruel beyond imagination. Their consciences were seared. To decide to kill a man was no more difficult for them than for a normal man to decide to tie his shoes. They would beat and curse the misguided Jehovah Witness, and he would be convinced that the punishment received in this life would be that much less than he would receive in the next.

Although Anti-Semitism is rampant throughout the former Soviet Union (now the C.I.S. Commonwealth of Independent States), it is probably worse in the prisons. Yakov received his worst encounters from the Ukrainians who were held in the camps.

Yakov loved the young people—the teenagers who were political prisoners. They also were in the camps, laboring, and being punished for being outspoken. They often spoke up for Yakov. A guard might yell, "Get away from that Jew...that Kike...." His young friends would defend him. "He's not a kike! He is Israel!" Only days before that answer, Yakov had taught them about Israel, what it was, where it was, and any morsel of knowledge about the Promise Land that he understood.

Yakov was shifted from one labor camp to another. There were "transportation prisons," ones that would be used as prisoners were being moved from place to place. They might stop and be incarcerated for only a few days, and then move on to another camp. There were times that he was made to stand in the below zero cold in the snow, his feet so frozen that they were as white as the snow in which he stood, the last vestiges of any circulation totally unseen. There would be another price exacted from Yakov as a result of this physical brutality inflicted upon him that would come much later in his life.

At last estimate, there were more than 2,500 labor camps and prisons in the former Soviet Union. The State lived up to the movie, "Prisonland", the inspiration for it coming from Yakov's life experience.

Yakov spent time in literally dozens of prisons. He was transferred here, transferred there, and his love for freedom was reflected in his seven escape attempts. He was never successful, and each time he was caught he was sent on to another prison, each one more strict than the previous one. As he stated, "...so I came into the deepest pits of the prisons in the Soviet system."

Even in his escape attempts, there was little hope of succeeding. "You don't understand," said Yakov, "HERE (meaning Israel) you might be able to escape from a prison, but Russia is a land of barbed wire and watch towers. There is always more barbed wire and more guards. The whole nation was one big prison!"

The escape attempt that brought him closest to success found him just outside the camp, hiding in a small hole. The Soviet Union is not a land of bathrooms and running water. As Yakov described it, "it was not my 'karma' when, as he hid in the hole, a Soviet guard dropped his trousers and began squatting over top of Yakov. When the Russian guard looked down to take aim, he saw Yakov's face looking back at him. It frightened the guard enough to cause him to scream and leap forward, snared at the ankles by his own trousers. Though Yakov was caught and punished, it is a memory that causes him to shake with laughter as he tells the story.

Yakov continued to ponder the answer given him by the Jehovah Witness, "I am happy because God is punishing me in this life." This statement would be with him for years, and Yakov's conclusion is that the answer was deep. He concluded that its meaning was that if one were punished in this life, he would not be punished in the next one. This conclusion added fuel to Yakov's belief that there are many lives that a man must go through until perfected. He is not the only Russian Jew that I have met who believes along these lines.

As Yakov plodded through the years in the camps, he met many fellow Jews. Many of them were in the camps because they signed the lists for volunteers that Golda Meir had requested when visiting Russia. As these Jews would meet each other, it added a boost for each man's thirst for Zion. All of the suffering and deprivation became the fuel for these Jewish souls to seek Israel.

Yakov spent 14 years of his life in baking hot summers, and Arctic-like winters. There was little if any heat in most camps. Men froze, starved, and were buried with no more attention paid to them than to the garbage pails that Americans place on their tree belts twice a week for pick-up. Death was as common in the camps and no more significant than putting out the trash.

Fourteen years of a man's life is a long time. It was 14 years of freezing cold, physical beatings, sickness, starvation, and death. These conditions preyed upon Yakov's war wounds; and where gangrene started its work on Yakov's twice-wounded leg.

The day finally arrived however, when his sentence had been

satisfactorily served. His original sentence, plus that which had been added due to his escape attempts, all came to an end. He was free to leave the camps, but not free to leave Russia or to travel within it. The barbed wire of the camp gave way to the barbed wire of the borders. The entire country was a prison, and he was being given the right only to sit in one of its corners. He was now in exile, in Kazakhstan, some 5,000 kilometers from Moscow.

When various Jews completed their sentences and were released, the seeds of Zionism that had been germinating in the prisons began to grow all the more as they met with each other in various cities in Russia. Their meetings had to be quiet and secret, nevertheless they met.

Yakov continued to try to make me understand what this was like. To be caught meeting meant more time in the prisons. He related a story of a drunken Russian man who he saw converse with a foreigner in the street to ask directions or some other innocent question. Within three minutes of the encounter, he was scooped up by the KGB, and sent off to a long sentence in prison. It was not his drunkenness that earned him the sentence, but it was his conversation with a foreigner. Yakov met another man in the camps who had been given a 25-year sentence for speaking with a foreigner.

While in the prisons, someone had slipped Yakov a copy of Leon Uris' book, EXODUS. Yakov translated it, and it made the rounds to different Jews. Yakov brought the book out of the prison with him. It had to serve as his "Bible" for Zionism. He met with another Jewish friend who was an ardent Zionist, always trying to figure out a way to leave Russia and go to Israel. He encouraged Yakov to circulate Uris' book.

The system hadn't changed much in 14 years, and Yakov knew how to work it well. He found a man who had supervision over a copy machine. A large bottle or two of vodka would purchase plenty of paper and a couple of hours at the machine. The one tattered copy of "Exodus" soon became twenty-four, and they were sent to other Jews throughout the Soviet Union. Each of those copies was multiplied into hundreds more, most often by hand or typewriter. One book became a catalyst among thousands of Jews to seek their homeland, Israel! From Yakov's point of view, Leon Uris birthed Zionism in the Soviet Union.

After his exile in Kazakhstan, Yakov made a decision to relocate. He contacted his Zionist friends, and asked their advice. Mikael was a leader who ardently desired to immigrate to Israel. He suggested that Yakov go to Odessa where almost 400,000 Jews lived. Odessa is a port city on the northern coast of the Black Sea. His assignment..."Go there, and organize them."

One could not go freely from one place to another in the Soviet Union. There had to be papers and stamps that gave Mother Russia's permission to travel, visit, or live in a given locale. Yakov made a trip to Odessa, and met a man who managed a woodworking plant. The manager was searching for a man with woodworking talent and supervisory abilities. Yakov had been working with wood for years as a hobby and was made for the job. As he shared his abilities with the plant manager, the man said, "God sent you to me. Only the other day I was punished for not having a man with your skills to administer a department like you are suggesting."

This factory manager had only about 2 slots per year that he could use to apply to the Central Communist Party division to allow someone to move to Odessa. He would see to it that Yakov would have proper papers. This pleasant surprise meant that he would live in close proximity to the many Jews in Odessa. It was a miracle!

After receiving his papers with the proper stamps, there were those who wanted to revoke them. However, the Soviet bureaucracy was inflexible. Once something was done...it was irrevocable. To retract or cancel the papers would be to admit that someone had made a mistake, and very little changed in Russia without a lot of upheaval. Yakov's papers were a done deal. He kept them, and moved to Odessa.

Yakov became the head of the Zionist movement in Odessa. He continued to have fellowship with perhaps 15-20 of his fellow Jews who had the vision. They remained a close and dedicated group. There were other groups in cities and towns all over the Soviet Union...15 here, 25 there, and they shared all the information that became available on Israel. In addition, through their grapevine of communication they kept each other informed about any in their fold who might find a way to leave Russia. Yakov was aware of perhaps

150 Zionists all over Russia at the time (1968).

Although he remained faithful to his group and they continued to be supportive of each other, Yakov never thought that he would ever see Israel. Significant events kept occurring which continued to bring attention to the plight of the Jews. He still wonders why he was not one of the many arrested when a couple of his close friends tried to hijack a plane and fly out of Russia. It was an unsuccessful attempt, and though they were known to be friends of Yakov, he was never questioned about it.

Mass arrests were made, and the heat was turned upon the Jewish community as a result of this hijacking attempt. It was a time where other things were being planned also. In January 1969, the Zionists were preparing tents and other gear that would be used for an encampment that they were organizing for the coming summer.

His good friend Mikael was desperate to leave Russia and go to Israel. He was willing to risk all for the chance. Unknown to anybody, Mikael made his way to Moscow and stood with some of his fellow Jews as Arthur Goldberg, America's ambassador to the United Nations, made a visit to the Jews at Moscow's synagogue. KGB agents surrounded Goldberg's car. To get near him was impossible.

As Goldberg got into his car to leave, he rolled down his window, and began shouting, "Shalom...Shalom," and waving. The KGB agents had dropped their guard only momentarily. That's when Mikael dashed from the crowd and made a suicidal dive into the open window of Goldberg's car. It was an all or nothing decision that he had just executed. He would either be released from Russia, or he would spend the rest of his life in prison. His whole upper torso was inside the car, and his legs were outside kicking as KGB agents tried to pull him out and away.

He had already prepared a letter which he thrust into Goldberg's hand, and with his head in the window and practically on Goldberg's lap, he begged him to intercede for him before Leonid Breshnev, the Soviet leader at the time. "Tell that thug that he must open the gates for me! I want to go to Israel!"

Goldberg, who later met with Breshnev, obviously talked about Mikael's desire to leave. The command was given, papers were issued, and Mikael was gone...to Israel! He was out of Prisonland.

Yakov and his Zionist friends were astounded. It was too good to be true, and yet they knew that there would be few visiting Arthur Goldbergs and open windows through which to jump. They were delighted for their friend, but they still had to live out the reality of their own situations.

Little by little, Yakov and his fellow Jews, who had now earned the title, *"Refuseniks,"* pressed the Soviets harder. Yakov began to wear a **kippah** all the time. It was not his religious convictions that caused him to do it, but it was a gesture that acknowledged his Jewishness. He and his friends also began to wear stars of David where they could be seen, as another way to keep reminding the Soviets of what they were doing to the Jews. It also brought the attention of an occasional reporter of the West. It was all done little by little, a step here, and a step there.

His next move was to continue organizing the summer encampment for Jewish Zionists. There had been a number of glitches but it was important not to fold up under the heat being applied. There would be some more pain however. Yakov, who had been nursing his leg since the time he was shot by the Germans, during World War II, kept limping along all these years, in prison and out, fighting infections, poor circulation, and often excruciating pain. The battle would soon be over.

He was informed that the leg had to be amputated. He knew it, and made the decision to go into the hospital to have it done. As he was recovering, one of his friends visited him, and said, "Yakov...we need you for this encampment. You must help us make this a success." Yakov knew that he would be unable to do very much physically, but instead of lying around for days waiting for a full and proper recovery, he forced himself out of bed, onto crutches, and left the hospital prematurely. He headed back to Odessa.

Invitations had been sent out to the Zionist community all over the country. At first, Yakov and his friends were looking at the possibility of perhaps 50 or 60 people showing up. But interest was developing and it looked as though they were going to need more tents.

There were other problems besides obtaining tents. Permission had to be obtained from the State to have such an assembly. In Russia, one did not simply go to a local hotel and tell them you would like to have a convention for Zionists. This would require a few State signatures. Yakov, although he knew that there was no guarantee of receiving the required permission, knew how to handle the bureaucrats whose endorsements would be required. He started with a colonel in charge of such affairs.

Yakov went to the colonel's office in Odessa, sporting his new wooden leg, a painful reminder of all that the Soviet Union had done for him. It was the perfect metaphor for what life under the communism had done.

He began the meeting with a little small talk. The colonel then brought up the real reason for the meeting. "You want to go to Israel...I know." He continued on with some chatter that seemed to make little sense. It was Yakov's turn to speak.

"Colonel...you know my biography."

"Yes, Yes...we know all about you," came the gruff and impatient reply.

"And if you know my biography, you know that I do not throw my words around lightly. If I do not get permission to have this encampment and to go to Israel, one day I will go to Red Square in Moscow. I will have a big sign written on my chest, with your name in big letters, that YOU...YOU personally are to blame for my plight. And I will throw some gasoline on my wooden leg, and I will burn it. I will burn my wooden leg. But I will burn only my leg...because I will not die for you. And when the flames are on my leg, and when there will be all the foreign correspondents around me, and the news photos with your name on my chest...your epaulets will be torn from your shoulders!" Yakov made his statement in a low, firm voice, with his piercing eyes aimed like bullets at the core of the squirming colonel. Permission was granted for the Zionist encampment.

However, the KGB continued to put great pressure on the Jews. There was talk among the Zionists about canceling the encampment, but it was too late. People were already on the way. As the word spread it became like an injection of courage for others and more Jews began to show up in Odessa. This show of support by Jews from outside of Odessa challenged those who lived there. Many more dropped other plans and appeared alongside their brothers and sisters.

They continued to arrive, and the encampment would take place. They had pulled out all the stops, and threw themselves into this gathering with whole hearts. They sang **Hatikvah** (the national anthem of Israel, which translated means, HOPE!). They danced the Horah and delighted in each other, laughing and enjoying themselves, knowing that there was the specter of mass arrests any moment. The arrests did not materialize.

Three days after the encampment was over, Yakov was summoned to appear before the KGB. He complied with their invitation. As he sat before a team of investigators, he heard the words,

"You must leave Russia in three days!"

The encampment had gotten to them. They were throwing Yakov out of the country. He saw the victory that he and his fellow Zionists had won, and was both astonished and delighted. It was like telling a six-year old boy that he MUST have a hot fudge sundae!

Yakov was also well seasoned by now, and was not about to give his captors a hint of his delight by dancing around like a child who had just been given his first bicycle. Although his entire being was rejoicing inside, he looked calmly at the KGB puppets, and in a manner of a hard-line Jewish negotiator asked with an incredulous look on his face, "Three days!!? I only need ONE! Why not tomorrow?"

The blazing red in the KGB agent's face gave evidence that Yakov's barb had found its mark. The anger of the investigation team was barely contained, as they looked at this resilient man with one leg now making fun of them. They were so angry that instead of writing up a paper that said three days, it was dated for seven days away. It was their attempt to have the last word.

Yakov had realized that many a bureaucrat was losing his head in Russia over Zionist activities. They seemed unable to cope with the encampments and the hunger strikes that he organized, and because he had stood his ground, the decision was made to throw this Jewish "hooligan" out of the country. In fact, within three months of this encampment, everyone who had attended received their exit visas.

The Soviets were certain that they were cutting off the head of the Zionist movement when they did this. By sending the more courageous ones out, the remaining 2.5 million Jews would stay and give little trouble. Opening the gates to these "enemies" of the

Motherland was done with little fanfare, but with enough publicity to let the populace know that these Jews were traitors and a shame to the great Russian society.

Yakov began his free life in Israel in 1970, and remained on a steady campaign to bring the truth to the Western world about life in the Soviet Union. Probably more painful than the death of his father and many of his fellow prison inmates, the loss of 14 years of his life, his wounds, his amputated leg, and the constant tyranny and fear which hovered over him for all those years in communist Russia, was the callous and unbelieving attitude of those in the West. The Soviets were winning the propaganda war.

Yakov continued to speak out and expose the system. He made a film called, "Prisonland" which documents much of what he says. He has spoken in many Western nations of the world, and in Israel. He has received some acclaim but not as much as the famous Alexander Solzhenitsyn. Both have lived with the same pain however. The pain is that their voices have gone much unheeded by the West.

People have nodded their heads, shaken his hand, patted him on the back, but have gone on about their business, joyfully swallowing the new "Glasnost." Western World leaders have tried to encourage new Russian premiers, giving space in periodicals and news editorials for "Peristroika," the new thinking. The glitzy new image of Russian leadership has been bought from American public relations firms and gullible and godless media people.

According to Yakov, this has caused more pain than an amputated leg and 14 years in the gulags of Prisonland. Even politicians in Israel, intent on getting the Jewish people home, have wanted Yakov's message to be silenced. Some Israeli politicians have been too intent on cuddling up to the Russian bear. Many believe if given even the slightest opening, the Bear will devour not only Israel, but also the world.

As the facts have been laid bare on the table, they expose the fact that Russia has trained and armed the archenemies of Israel like the PLO (Palestine Liberation Organization), and the PFLP (Popular Front for the Liberation of Palestine). When the Israelis launched "Operation Peace for Galilee into Lebanon in 1982, the underground weapons caches were filled with Russian equipment. Russia armed the Syrians with the latest Migs and missiles. Russian tanks and half-tracks were pulled off the Sinai Desert as the spoils of Israeli victory.

Facts like these give the Yakovs of the world an incessant case of heartburn. Here was a man who has been in constant communication with the realities of Soviet life. The prisons are still there. The Jews are still persecuted heavily in many places by bands of anti-Semites through neo-Nazi organizations like the Pam-Yat. The Pentecostals and the Baptists were held captive in prisons because they believed in God. Men who exhibited compassion and made decisions to stand against the communist lies were branded as insane and thrown into psychiatric prisons. Now that there are a few "politically correct" statements and overtures made by the heads of State, many of those who have suffered the most, have been forgotten.

There is no question that in recent days, some of the pressure has been lifted within Russia. I am convinced that this is not because the Russian leadership suddenly got religion, but because the lie on which the entire system was built finally caved in. Because this has happened, doors have opened, so that some of the Jews have been able to immigrate to Israel, and Russian Christians can begin to practice their faith openly. Church doors are opening again, and people who have been told all of their life that there is no God, are suddenly begging for Bibles.

As they have seen the reality that the yellowed wax-like idol that lies in state next to the Kremlin is really dead, as is Lenin's attempt to bring a utopia without God to the world, thousands of Russians have clamored for gifted preachers and teachers. Lenin, who himself may have had the best of intentions, had been elevated over Russia as an idol, along with his communist philosophy. Eventually, idols bite and they crumble. We are witnesses to that fact today.

As a Christian I feel I owe men like Yakov a debt of gratitude and constant prayers before God for the sake of his family. He was a significant force in battering the traverse rods of the iron curtain until it finally came down. I believe all of us owe it to ourselves and to fellow Christians who are only beginning to breathe freely to continue to raise our voices against any new tyranny that would try to choke off this blood-bought freedom. We must hold our leaders accountable when they are tempted by political expediency, selfish business interests, or out of sheer ignorance sally up to tyrannical and despotic leaders that would squeeze the life out of anyone or anything that gets in their way.

Jews also owe Yakov and those like him their undivided attention and the intellectual honesty to look not at what Russian leadership SAYS, but what it DOES! It is important to look beyond the leading newspapers to get accurate information on what life was really like in Prisonland. It is crucial to support your people, many of whom are still waiting to immigrate to Israel. A united effort of all Jewish groups would help to support those who remain under the thumb of discrimination and any form of tyranny.

It is ever beyond me, how a man like Yakov, with all of his life experience to display before us, can be relegated to the closet shelf. Meanwhile, the latest statements from slick propaganda machines from illicit regimes all over the world find their way to the front pages of newspapers and news magazines of the increasingly gullible and all too often godless West.

This has been Yakov's pain. Truth is ever being exchanged for lies and deception. Both Jews and Christians owe a love debt. He is yet another son of Zion who has paid his dues. It is with sadness that as I close out this chapter, I have learned of Yakov's death. He died at home...in Zion.

# 9

# YOSSI

It was Saturday night and the sun had gone down. We had just finished another Sabbath meal in the home of Moshe and Sarah, in Kfar Pines, (K'far pea´nez) Israel. The doors and windows to the house had been flung open and the guests meandered outside into the enclosed courtyard at the front of the house, where it was a perfect evening. As the children frolicked with one another, the men began to sing some of the songs of Zion. As the only Christian there, I joined in the hand clapping but was unable to sing along to the Hebrew lyrics, even though I sensed in my spirit the general meaning of the songs as they conveyed joy and celebration.

Stories were swapped with one another, and a half dozen conversations took place among the guests all at the same time. Children ran in and out from the scene with little interruptions, along with the family dog that begged the guests for a good scratch. As the evening continued, the children challenged a then 62-year old man to demonstrate his skill with the family broom. Yossi stepped up to the moment and obliged.

As he stood on one foot, his arms stretched out like the wings of an airplane; he lifted his other foot about 6 inches from the ground. In delicate concentration, he made all the right motions to keep the broom balanced on the tip of its handle from his raised foot. Every time the broom would begin to lean, he would deftly move his raised foot to counter the movement, and the balancing act provided entertainment for all.

Yossi handed me the broom and challenged me to do likewise. It didn't look all that difficult, so I gave it a try, only to find myself falling dismally short of Yossi's performance. While Yossi had perfected this balancing act of fun and entertainment, he had also endured the balancing act of staying alive during some of the most painful and cruel years of history. His is a story not unlike others, where small seemingly insignificant movements could have severe consequences. His was a balancing act where to be wrong even once, resulted not just in a broom falling to the pavement, but perhaps a firing squad, a hangman's noose, or a gas chamber.

❦

In 1925, Yossi was born in the city of Lodz, Poland, about 80 miles southwest of Warsaw, at a time of great suffering. The Poles were still rebuilding after the devastation inflicted upon them by the Germans during World War I. Most of Lodz had been destroyed, and along with the city, thousands of businesses. Lodz was where raw textiles were manufactured and sent all over the country and other parts of Europe. It was a place where almost unprecedented growth had occurred among the Jewish population over the previous century. In 1820, there were only 260 Jews in the city. When Yossi entered the world, there were about 170,000 Jews in the city of Lodz. By the outbreak of World War II, Lodz had some 230,000 Jews, or about one third of the city's population.

Anti-Semitism was alive and well among the Polish population in the 1930's. With a third of the city populated by Jews, and with their hard work and creativity engaged in all aspects of business, jealousy began to fuel their competitors. There were many organized murderous attacks on the Jews, and in the municipal elections of 1934, anti-Jewish parties won power within Lodz, campaigning on a platform to rid the city of the Jews. Fortunately these municipal leaders held power for only about two years and were overthrown by the Polish and Jewish Socialist Parties.

The overthrow made little difference, for in these same years, the Nazis of Germany were sending Anti-Semitic literature to the small German population, which inhabited Lodz. These local Germans helped to keep the pressure upon Lodz's Jewish population. In only a few more years, on September 8, 1939, Yossi was watching the German army pouring troops through his hometown moving eastward. As they arrived, many of the Jews left. Some departed for Warsaw and others to the Russian occupied territories east of Poland. Memories were still fresh from the forerunner of the latest Nazi assault. Only 21 years had passed since the last German invasion.

The Germans re-named Lodz to Litzmannstadt. They brutalized and removed the leaders of the Jewish community, sending them away to God knows where. In November 1939, the Nazi tyrants burned down the great synagogue and publicly hanged two Poles and a Jew. These were some of the early signals that demanded a teenage Jewish boy to grow up quickly. They spurred his survival instincts to the forefront of his thoughts.

The purveyors of the Third Reich showed little to no mercy, and they wasted no time in accomplishing their mission. Anything or anybody that stood in their way was cut down immediately. Yossi walked to the marketplace one day and saw the corpses of four Jews hanging by the neck. Signs were hung around their necks. One said, "Thief" and other signs were derogatory accusations toward the persons that hung motionless above the frightened populace which tried to go about their business. Yossi had seen a dead person for the first time.

As Yossi stood emotionally paralyzed at the sight of four of his fellow Jews who had been murdered by the Germans, an army truck rolled into the area filled with German soldiers. They began rounding up Jewish men to put them to work. Yossi quickly darted away from the area and ran to his home. As he ran he heard shots being fired. To this day he does not know if they were aimed at him, or whether those bullets found their mark in the bodies of other Jews who happened to be in the marketplace at the time.

Home was a very small apartment in what would become part of the Lodz Ghetto. Although other Jews were rounded up from around Lodz and sent to the ghetto, Yossi did not have to move. He already lived in the low-rent district of Lodz. The Germans moved quickly, commandeering properties in the better part of the Jewish area, and herding the people into the already crowded ghetto, called "Baluty," the poorest section of Lodz. Hundreds of families could be seen carrying their belongings on their backs, and wheeling them on carts with the look of terror in their eyes. Many of the families already living in "Baluty" had to receive two or three other families into their tiny apartments. In many apartments, there were 12-16 people living in only two or three rooms. The families often did not even know each other, but were forced into these situations by the Germans.

There were now about 200,000 Jews compressed into this small and dilapidated collection of apartment buildings, all in an area of about two square miles. Lodz became a gathering point for other Jews who had been captured by the Germans in other countries such as Czechoslovakia, Greece, and even Germany. When more Jews would arrive, they would be forced into the bulging ghetto. Those already there had no choice but to make room for the newcomers.

Yossi was one of the "lucky" ones. He was already trained as a locksmith and metal smith. Small in stature, he was nevertheless strong, wiry, and able. The Germans put him to work making and repairing wheels for their tanks and wagons. The pittance that he made allowed him to purchase whatever might be available in a local market.

Food was extremely scarce, and it became a currency of its own. It was better than money, because even if someone had a few *zlotys* or food coupons, he still had to find someone with food to sell or trade. Starvation was reality. Disease was rampant. During the winter there was no fuel to heat the apartments. There was no privacy of any kind. Sewer systems were few, and those that were in place did not work. People would leave their apartments during the winter and relieve themselves in the snow. It wasn't so bad in the winter when the temperatures were below freezing, but in the spring thaw, the stench and filth were overwhelming.

During the first winter, people were able to find a few sticks of wood here and there and build small fires in their apartments to provide heat for warmth and cooking, if they were able to obtain some food. When the wood from the outside was exhausted, furniture was burned...board by board, table leg by table leg. When the furniture was gone, the doors were taken from their hinges, broken up and burned. Then it came time for the floorboards, and even some of the structural framing.

Entire families lay on whatever was left of the floors in their apartments. While one member might find some work which would allow for the purchase of scarce food, others were sick and dying in freezing apartments. There was no medicine and no doctors to call.

The Germans instituted more **Aktions**, ("Actions" which were merely the rounding up of people for the purpose of liquidation). From about 1943 to 1945, Yossi did not see a child or an elderly person in the ghetto or in the other places where the Germans sent him. The very young and the very old were rounded up and murdered. They were of no value to the German machine. They could not work and so were deemed worthless.

As Yossi went to work each day from the Lodz Ghetto, he had to step over the dead in the streets. The Jewish bodies had been dragged or carried by their family members out of their apartments where they had breathed their last. Other Jews were forced to pick up the bodies and dispose of them. The streets would be clean for just a few hours. The process would be repeated, day after day. Yossi would stuff his emotions, and his heart became hardened as he endured his walk through death each day. In his own words, "After a while, I had no feelings...I simply went to my work and came home, always hoping for the ability to live." Could this have been a living out of Jeremiah's words, scripted around 600 B.C.?

"Death has climbed in through our windows and has entered our fortresses; It has cut off the children from the streets and the young men from the public squares."
(NIV—Jeremiah 9:21)

The orders came, *"Alle Kinder"* (all the children) to be rounded up. Children would be placed into trucks and hauled off, while parents wept in terror. The children were never seen again. Other orders would be barked from time to time. *"Alle raus!"* (Everybody out!) or *"Alle unter!"* (Everybody come down [from their upstairs apartments]). The youngsters and the oldsters would be picked out of the crowd and away they would go in the back of German trucks...never to be seen again.

Yossi lived in an apartment building that could at best house about 150 people. There were over 600 crushed into the old building. When the entire ordeal of the Holocaust was over, he and one other woman out of the 600 survived.

Up to this time, Yossi had managed to keep his distance from the Germans. He observed them from afar. Where he worked as a locksmith and metal smith, he took his orders from other Jews and Poles, who interacted with the Germans. It was better this way. However, things would soon change.

As he made his way back and forth from his job, and as he learned where he could observe the Germans safely, he was able to see first hand how these harsh invaders handled another group of people. They were Gypsies. Many had been hauled in from all over Europe. For some reason they were brought to Lodz, and many of them murdered right there.

Yossi described his family life as strained but all right. It was worse in many of the other Jewish families. Where there were not close-knit and loving relationships, the agonies of war and persecution brought out the worst in people. Jamming three and four families into a small apartment, starving from lack of food, wasting away from disease and lacking medicine...all contributed to strained relationships.

The Germans had experienced great opposition in the attempted liquidation of the Warsaw Ghetto. The Jews there, under the worst of handicaps, fought a heroic battle, which is still a hallmark of their veracity. Not only did they stand against the Germans in battle, they stood against them by recording meticulously an entire history of the ghetto and its people. Through the efforts of many, but with the leadership of Dr. Emanuel Ringelbaum, the Warsaw Ghetto and its people would not be forgotten. The code name for his effort was

"Oneg Shabbat", which means the "joy of the Sabbath". The Germans overseeing the Lodz Ghetto did not as yet know about Ringelbaum's history, which was accumulated and preserved in the bowels of the Warsaw Ghetto in boxes and milk cans. His incredible work would later be exhumed as a testimony of truth for all humankind. They did, however, know about the fight put up by the Jews in the process of the ghetto liquidation.

The Nazis overseeing Lodz decided that it would be best not to have a repeat uprising. They began to ease up on the Jews in the Lodz Ghetto. Food became available and for the first time in over a year, Yossi saw a whole loaf of bread. There was even some meat! At first, the new availability of food took its toll on emaciated people. Their feeble bodies had so shut down, that the consumption of these new foodstuffs, brought agonizing death. Those that lived began to regain some semblance of health.

The food would act as a lure to bring the Jews out of their ghetto buildings. They were being prepared for the "final solution" as the call came to board trains *"für einen besseren Platz"* (for a better place). Warnings were also issued that those who stayed behind, trying to hide, would be shot. There seemed to be little choice. The bait worked, and most of the ghetto inhabitants complied with the Nazi orders. There was no ghetto uprising as had occurred in Warsaw. They boarded the trains, hoping against hope...that perhaps there truly would be a "better place" at the next stop.

Because Yossi's father, Leon, had been put in charge of managing the entire building in which his family lived, he could officially hold out to the end. However, with most of the inhabitants gone, the ghetto economy dried up. The work stopped for Yossi. There was now no money, no ration coupons, and the rumors traveled like a windblown prairie fire. The train rides were not bringing them to better quarters. They knew that on the other end of those railroad tracks lay their graves...and the remaining Jews began to hide in the ghetto in any way they could.

"I fought with my family...especially with my sister, Lior. She wanted to go...to be with our parents, who were convinced that this was the best choice. They were very weak and frail at this point. I did not want to go. I knew what lay ahead of us."

"Please, Yossi...come! We are all sick. Our parents are weak. We cannot stay here," Lior would plead.

Yossi continued. "I was not fooled. I had already had experience with the Germans. I had the experience of living through this hell from 1939 and it was now moving into 1944. I knew that there was no rainbow at the end of that train ride...and yet for most of the ghetto inhabitants, life was so miserable, that it was difficult to imagine that it could be any worse somewhere else. Perhaps it was the adventure or the willingness to TRY...at least TRY...ANY-THING else...but what we had! Finally, after all the pleading and crying of my family...I gave up. We decided to leave the ghetto. I would later find out that about 95% of the very few who chose to stay behind and gut it out in the ghetto...survived. My common sense was right, and yet I gave in to the pressures of my family."

Yossi reluctantly spoke of the bad relations that he had with his father. His father verbally attacked Yossi about his plan to stay in the ghetto. His mother defended 19-year old Yossi, creating a further rift between the parents. It was a bitter time for him. The emotional wounds were deep. As he poured his soul out to me, he said, "But I forgive them. I forgive them."

The decision to go to the trains became action. They left as a family of four. The trip would not be a distant one...only about 180 miles from Lodz to Oswiecim (the Polish name for Auschwitz). However, the journey took two days and nights.

Suitcases were packed. Each family had its own ideas as to what was important to bring. The obvious things were there and common to all...some clothes, shaving brush, perhaps some dishes or a pot, some keepsakes or pictures...all the same, yet different for each individual.

As I listened to Yossi, my memory took me back to 1986 when I was able to obtain a special visa to visit Poland. I went alone. Communism was still the order of the day. My contacts inside Poland had been arrested only two days before I entered the country. Their "crime" was that they belonged to the "*Solidarnosc*" (the Solidarity movement), a grass roots effort by the Polish people which contributed mightily to the toppling of communism in Poland. I nevertheless flew to Poland and I visited Auschwitz, preserved as a museum of horror. I saw the thousands of suitcases that had been collected and piled up as a monument of reminder of the atrocities that had taken place within meters of where I was standing. In another display, thousands of shaving brushes, and still another pile of thousands upon thousands of eyeglasses lay motionless...all material vestiges of the people that would never wear them again. I was overwhelmed with sorrow and tears ran from my eyes. A woman but a few meters from me burst into deep emotional sobs as she viewed the pile of children's shoes. I had visited the Auschwitz museum in 1986. Yossi was about to arrive there in 1944 as a slave of the Third Reich.

The journey was miserable. The Jews were jammed in the cars like cattle. Yossi's trip to Auschwitz was a "luxury journey" by his words. "Jews from other European cities endured eight and nine days in those cattle cars. There was no room to even sit. There were no toilets. We were like standing sardines and we could barely breathe."

When these trains arrived at Auschwitz and the doors were slid open, dead people fell out. Some walked out, and some were carried. It was the same with all of the train arrivals, it's just that the percentages were higher...or lower, depending on whether you were counting the dead or the living. For those who survived the journey, they were driven along the station platform by modern-day pharaohs; Nazi guards cracking whips, and beating those who moved too slowly.

This was to be a final *aktion.* Most of the Jewish leaders of the Lodz Ghetto were on this train. They arrived at Birkenau, the adjoining camp to Auschwitz. The rumors were already doing their damage. It was said that if you stayed at Birkenau, you would last perhaps two weeks...and then you were finished.

Meeting the arriving trains was a favorite duty for a German doctor by the name of Josef Mengele. It was no different on this night. Yossi stood in line with his father and continued to move forward a step at a time toward the notorious German medical man. Mengele gave a once-over look at each incoming Jew, and then pointed with one of his hands. One direction would lead to "Kanada" the dark-humored name for the gas chambers. It was the slang of the camp, or the cruel joke of the Nazis, that would send a prisoner to "freedom" in "Kanada". Wherever the gas chambers received this nickname....it did not matter, for in truth...no one escaped once they traveled down the road to "Kanada."

If Mengele saw potential as a slave laborer, he would point with the other hand, and the new arrival would be spared his life, at least for the moment. Yossi walked up to Dr. Mengele. The savage man, acting as a god, pointed quickly with his right arm. Yossi obeyed the silent command and walked to Mengele's right. Leon, Yossi's father was next.

Mengele looked straight at Leon. "*Wie alt sind Sie?*" (How old are you?)

"*Seben und fünfzig, mein Herr.*" (Fifty-seven, Sir.)

Mengele's left arm did the pointing as he looked past Leon. "*Nächster?*" (Next?)

Although Yossi wasn't sure at that moment, Leon was on his way to freedom...."Kanada". It was that quick, that callous, that hideous, as father and son looked at each other for the last time and walked their respective paths, dictated by a human being turned monster.

Yossi continued to tell his story to me, and with a look of pain on his face spoke. "I stood there watching the man that had given me life on this earth, the man whom I had argued with vehemently, the man that I sometimes hated, but also loved.....and Dr. Mengele, with a motion of his hand, sent him on to eternity." Yossi was numb with a thousand fears and question marks as he watched the silhouette of his father disappear into the crowd headed for "Kanada".

Yossi continued his in-processing at Birkenau. Part of the administrative procedure was the humiliation of being tattooed, labeling the person as a slave of the Third Reich. The brand on Yossi's arm is still very readable after all these years. The number "B 8056" was a permanent reminder that daily spoke of man's inhumanity to man. The "B" stands for Birkenau.

When the tattooing procedure was over, prisoners stood in another line and had their heads shaved. It made no difference whether they were men, women, or children. The purported reason was that they were protecting the prisoners from lice and disease, but the fact was simply that it was another way to humiliate and degrade. The Nazis would also use the hair to stuff pillows, upholstery, or perhaps for tailor's lining. Prison clothing was handed out and it was almost always several sizes too large, adding further fuel to the process of degradation.

Thousands of Jews from all over the European continent arrived. Despots of the Third Reich categorized the prisoners according to their abilities in order to please themselves. If a person appeared strong and in decent health, he was used for labor. If pretty, taken in to be used for Nazi sexual pleasures. Even young children were used for perversions that are unmentionable. Lack of co-operation meant immediate death. If a prisoner was able to play a musical instrument, he might be allowed to entertain the officers. If a Jew had nothing to contribute that was of value to the Nazis, he was put to death.

In the confusion of all the trains and groups arriving at Birkenau, young Yossi spotted a group of young people that were herded together. He was able to speak to one of the group. It seemed that they were being processed to be moved somewhere else besides Birkenau. Yossi invited himself along, and joined the group. It was a decision that may have saved his life.

Because he was small in stature, he was able to slip in and out of crowds of prisoners and in so doing found his cousin, Avi, on the night that he arrived. They stuck together like glue; Avi followed Yossi at every opportunity. In their new group, he was assigned to Auschwitz, the adjoining camp to Birkenau.

Yossi was assigned as a carpenter to make repairs around the two adjoining concentration camps. He often did his repair work in and around "Kanada". He saw everything......the gas chambers....the dead bodies....the assembly line of fellow Jews who were forced to extract the gold from the teeth of the dead before the bodies would be sent to the crematorium. The reality of what happened to his father became more and more clear, and the pent up rage pressed its heat down into the hard rock of Yossi's wounded soul. The internal lava continued to bubble as he watched trainloads of his fellow Jews march the road to "Kanada" under the evil eyes of human beings gone mad.

Because the women and the children were put into one group on arrival by train, and the men in another group, Yossi was not able to see what had happened to his mother and sister on that fateful night. It soon became apparent however, that they, like his father, had not survived the selection process. He wept uncontrollably in a place where there was no comfort.

In a testimony given at the 1961 trial of the notorious Nazi Officer, Adolf Eichmann, Yehiel Di-Noor spoke. "This is actually the history of the Auschwitz planet—the chronicles of Auschwitz. I, myself, was at the Auschwitz camp for two years. The time there is not a concept as it is here in our planet. Every fraction of a second that passed there was at a different rate of time. And the inhabitants of that planet had no names. They had no parents, and they had no children. They were not clothed as we are clothed here. They were not born there and they did not conceive there. They breathed and lived according to different laws of nature. They did not live according to the laws of this world of ours, and they did not die (according to those laws). Their name was a number, Y. Di-Noor, number so-and-so....."

It was a madness that has wounded even new generations of Jews as children of the Holocaust survivors grew up under parents whose inner beings had been torn to shreds. Parents, who would normally have loved their children in healthy ways, often shrank back into the nightmares of the past, reliving the horrors that never went away. The fears and terror, even if unspoken and repressed into the subconscious, often were passed on to the children.

Yossi continued to instruct his cousin, Avi. "Whenever they split us up in groups, if you feel as though one of the groups is destined for the gas chambers or the firing squad, do your best to get into the other group. Play your cards right!" Numbers of times, Yossi and Avi took the risk. They jumped from one line into another....or one group to another when it looked as though they were in the group being sent to death. There was no room for a mistake in this game.

One night in the middle of this "Auschwitz Planet" where life was a nightmare, and where everything was surreal and upside down, the Nazis handed out blankets, some bread, and some sausage. Yossi thought that he and his cousin were dreaming.....but this was a good dream. After a little more contemplation, they were convinced that they were awake and alive. The Germans were giving them a little nourishment so that they would survive their trip to the next destination...Sachsenhausen, another camp near Berlin.

"If they were feeding us....they must be planning on keeping us alive," thought Yossi. But there had been so many aberrations of German logic and reason thus far, that drawing such a conclusion would be premature. Their captors were demonically cruel and deceptive, and this might be just another ploy that would be used to dash hope or purchase a little co-operation for a short period of time until the Germans would inflict an even greater pain.

White steam puffed from the sides of the black locomotive and the hushed roar of the fire in the boiler could be heard as a background for the orders being shouted at the Jewish prisoners.

Guards with German Shepherds moved quickly up and down the station platform as Yossi and hundreds of his fellow Jews stood still and silent. Their starved emaciated bodies did not begin to fill their over-sized prison uniforms. Thousands of eyes once filled with life and hope revealed the pit of exhausted despair that reigned in each soul. The countenance of sadness and defeat was registered on a thousand faces. Each prisoner was lost in his own thoughts, some thinking of the past and still pondering the "why?" of this ghoulish insanity, others enduring the vacuum and numbness of the now, robotic in appearance, and waiting for the next order to obey. A few anticipated the future, and those with any spiritual and psychological strength began looking for a possible way to escape, once the train got moving.

Orders were given to board the trains. They climbed into the freight cars for another ride. Again, Jewish men and women were stuffed into the cars like upright rolls of carpet. The clacking sound of metal latches banging against the solid wood of the freight car doors and the un-oiled squeaks of steel slide bars rotating to the locked position confirmed that there would be no escape. The chuffs of the steam engine and a quick toot on the dissonant train whistle began the journey northward.

It was days and nights of standing. People vomited, urinated, and eliminated their human waste. There were those with fever, and there were those who drew their last breath while on the torturous ride. Some of them fell from the freight cars when the doors were opened. Others who had been shoved to the back or rear of the cars simply slumped to the floor in death, and were carried away when the train arrived at its new destination.

Sachsenhausen concentration camp, which was located right near Berlin, had been opened in 1936. By 1943 the camp held a prison population of 26,000, one of the largest concentration camps in the German system. It was here that a Nazi-run counterfeiting operation existed. Many of the Jewish prisoners sat at large tables and made phony passports, stamps, and many other documents and credentials, under the direction of SS man Bernard Krueger.

For Yossi and Avi, arrival at Sachsenhausen was a new place. For a number of other prisoners, it was a return from where they had started a few years earlier. They had survived Auschwitz and were returned to Sachsenhausen, where these Jews were now mingled among many Russian prisoners.

Another selection process took place. Avi hung onto Yossi like a magnet. During the questioning, Yossi elaborated his work experience with metal and locks. His cousin tried to mimic Yossi's routine, but could not come up with the right answers to difficult questions and he was not believed. Avi remained at Sachsenhausen, and Yossi was sent to the Heinkl factory where the Germans built aircraft.

Strict orders had been given to the ordinary German factory workers that they were not to speak with the prisoners. When working in close proximity for days and weeks at a time, however, communication occurs, regardless of someone else's orders. The haggard looks on the Jews that had been brought to the factory, provoked a lot of questions from the workers. Yossi saw first hand that although he had been the victim of a perverse and evil system, that many Germans were not aware of the atrocities that were taking place at the hands of Hitler and his followers.

It was January 1945 and the crumbling walls and cracked foundation stones of the Third Reich were becoming more visible. German morale was breaking down, and work went on in the Heinkl factory with little enthusiasm. The dreaded *Schutzstaffeln* (Protection squads) or S.S. men still controlled the factory.

Yossi was working with an acetylene torch. There was a hose of oxygen and a hose of acetylene that were hooked to his torch. These two gases fed the hot flame which he applied to metal tubing, bending it to conform to templates. The bent piping would form fuel or hydraulic lines for Heinkl aircraft. While Yossi does not remember how it happened, on one day he somehow burned through the oxygen hose that fed his own torch. This started a quick out-of-control fire that was consuming the oxygen hose and spraying flame in all directions. Yossi knew the penalty for sabotaging the work of the aircraft factory, and knew that he would be charged with this act of criminality. He would be shot.

A quick thinking German foreman, the *Fabrikmeister*, stepped in, shut off the supply line of oxygen, and quickly put out the fire. While Yossi anticipated the firing squad, the German factory foreman turned on his heel and went on to other duties. Thankfully, no S.S. men would discover what had happened.

It was not uncommon to hear the air raid warnings on an almost daily basis. The allies were penetrating deeply into the heart of Germany with aircraft bombings both day and night. The distant explosions of bombs hitting their marks provided more evidence that the Third Reich was tumbling down. Germany's war machine was coming apart everywhere. Communication was breaking down, transportation, production, and those that had been committing war crime after war crime were coming to the realization that a day of reckoning was on the horizon.

Some of the Nazi officers and men began to disappear from their military duties if they were in Germany. Some headed back to their villages in an attempt to disavow their connection with Hitler's Reich. Others who were loyal to the Führer would remain on duty to the end. Each would at some point, however, try to save his own skin whether by disassociating himself from the crimes, or doing away with the evidence.

Much of the evidence lay in the memories of thousands of Jewish prisoners who remained alive in a myriad of concentration camps throughout Germany and Poland. They needed only the forum, and if the evidence of the German war crimes were transferred to paper, it would fill a dozen warehouses. Harried orders were now being given to a broken-down military machine, and the orders were to destroy the evidence before it could be spoken in words or written on paper. The attempts to accelerate the murder of the Jews failed. The gas chambers and the ovens were over-capacity, and German soldiers were fast losing their enthusiasm for continuing their allegiance to Hitler.

Yossi was now weak and sick with typhus and was among thousands of prisoners that were herded into large groups and forced to march away, even from the Heinkl factory. Again, he did not know the destination, but there was probably a place that had been chosen where this group would have been gunned down and buried in a pit by bulldozers. Yossi did not know. He just marched with the others.

It was now a matter of just putting one foot in front of the other. Each step was another lifetime. He spoke to himself, "just one more....just one more....just one more." The memories of a thousand nightmares glared at him from within. Yossi would not see the results of the shots that he heard behind him. But he saw the results of the shots that he heard in front of him as he continued his march. The bodies of the weak were strewn along the roadside with bullets in their heads. The fever and nausea kept ordering him to just "sit or lie down for a little while." This assault on his body, coupled with exhaustion, was trying to steal the last sparks of life. To sit down now would bring a bullet to the brain.

"Maybe it would be best...to just let them kill me." ... "I must make another step. I cannot sit or fall. I must make another step," the argument of self-talk continued as more shots rang out both in front and behind.

Some of those shots were coming came from the guns of allied British and Russian soldiers who were killing the cobra of Nazism. As suddenly as the march began, it ended. The SS troops and the Nazi guards just walked off the job in an attempt to hide themselves from the assaulting British and Russian armies. Yossi was free but he did not yet know it. He had nothing but his life, and that was being stolen by disease.

He had come to the end of everything and was taken to a British field hospital. He collapsed and lay semi-conscious for two weeks, not knowing where he was or what doctors ministered to him. He would awaken for a few moments, and then drift back into unconsciousness. After several weeks he was moved to Bergen-Belsen, which was also the site of another Nazi concentration camp. Fortunately, he went to another British hospital, where he continued to recover, along with wounded German soldiers.

While Yossi battled for his life, his cousin, Avi, fought his own battle for life back in Sachsenhausen. Avi survived, but had to have a lung removed. He eventually recovered and went on to marry, raise a family, and lives in the United States.

Yossi continued his story. "I stood before a mirror for the first time in years. I could not believe what I saw. I was always a strong athletic person with a decent physique. I was now looking at something that I could not recognize. But slowly...very slowly...I...we...began to realize that it was over, and we were free...and we began to make love with each other...not the kind that you see in American movies...but making love with each other in the joy of life. It was brotherly-sisterly love...of knowing that we have survived...that the ordeal was over...and that we were 'born-again'. We had some parties, where we sang and danced and celebrated."

"Romance.....the right kind, began to bloom. People began to hope again and make plans. We were from different places, and different concentration camps, but we were 'born-again'. It really is as if I have lived two lives. Most human beings live a life with a continuity, where things continue and evolve......but I lived two lives.....with a break of five years. It was like I was on another planet. I lived a nightmare and woke up in the morning to find a new life."

Yossi continued to gain strength while staying at the Bergen-Belsen rehabilitation camp. Several of the survivors, Yossi included, had read about and began to believe in the philosophy of communism. They formed a group, and made a pact to become a commune, and to share equally with each other. While they remained at the rehabilitation camp, Yossi began to enlist others, preaching communism, and preaching against Zionism, that of going to the Jewish homeland.

Yossi and his fellow cohorts were espousing a New Testament

concept, however, not communism as it had become known in the 20th century. The New Testament espouses *communalism,* which at its root says, "What's mine is yours!" *Communism* says, "What's yours is mine!" In these two simple statements is a universe of difference.

Most of the former prisoners who were being nursed back to health at the British rehabilitation camp at Bergen-Belsen were becoming ardent supporters of going to the Jewish homeland.... a homeland yet to be officially created in the eyes of the world. There were many Zionist organizations coming to life even with the rehab camp. Yossi, with his friends decided to join the 'real revolution' and head back to Poland to be part of the communist dream. Yossi's eyes would be opened shortly.

Yossi and his group of new "communists," gathered what few belongings they had and headed back for Lodz, Poland. The return to his city of origin was not without tears. Gone was the old Jewish neighborhood as it once was known. Worse yet, the people had disappeared....dead because of disease, starvation, and the mass murders at the hands of the German war machine. Of the 233,000 Jews who lived in Lodz before the Germans invaded, there were only 870 remaining when the Russians took over at the end of World War II. Another 50,000 eventually made it back there within the two years following the war, but most left as soon as they were able.

As Yossi walked the streets of Lodz, the hammer of reality continued to strike. For him and for most others, there would be no more family gatherings....no family squabbles....no family anything....period. He would look ahead, plan for the future, be a proponent and supporter of the Russian revolution. He and other young people like him, began their own commune near Lodz. They were filled with the idealism that man could create a society on earth where everyone would have their needs met, and that there would be co-operation and peace. Yossi stayed on this course for about a year and a half, speaking up for the Russian revolution, communism, and speaking out against Zionism.

One day, Yossi saw first hand, hundreds of Jews who were at long last released from Russia. Perhaps he'd seen the same train that returned Zelda from her tour of Stalin's utopia. They had been held in slave labor camps that were no better than those of Hitler. His fellow Jews had run eastward away from the onslaught of the Germans, only to be captured and accused of being spies. Those that expressed their desires to return from whence they had come, confirmed to Russian minds that they definitely were spies. Instead of being returned to Poland or Germany, they were placed on trains and sent as far as Siberia. To express a desire to leave "Mother Russia" at the time, was as good as committing a crime.

Yossi had been arguing for a system that he had not seen in action. As he continued to observe the trainloads of Jews returning from Russia, and as he had opportunity to speak to them, the picture became clearer. "I had been preaching communism from the textbook....the theory, and now I was confronted with a bunch of Jews who had just spent most of the war under its system. "

More stories came in. According to Yossi, "I was hearing the stories about the massacre of Polish officers, and the Katyn Forest Massacre where thousands of Poles were murdered and buried in mass graves. Some were Jews, but most were not. The communist system, however, was being exposed to my own eyes as well as others."

More news came in almost daily. The work that Hitler did not finish, was being continued in places all over Poland. Small *pogroms* took place where the Poles were killing Jews. Battered Jews had come back from the torturous years of the slave labor camps in Germany, Poland, and Russia, only to find that they were not welcome in their villages and towns. In some cases the local populace had seized their property. When the Jews tried to lay claim to what was rightfully theirs, they were murdered.

As with many Jews in the Western world, Yossi equates Gentile and Christian as being one and the same. In Poland, a "Christian" culture enfolded the entire nation in Roman Catholicism. The unfortunate misunderstanding is that all Roman Catholics are Christians. This same misunderstanding occurs all over the West, even in Protestant Christianity, where to be a Baptist or a Presbyterian, is to be a Christian. The misunderstanding is so great that to a Jew, Hitler was a Christian. To the Jews of Poland, those that continued to persecute them and even murder them after the war, were Christians.

Yossi had seen enough. The Germans had murdered his family

and had almost killed him. The Russians had enslaved and killed thousands upon thousands of Jews who were only running away from Hitler. Now that the war was over, the Poles continued in a smaller way what the Germans and Russians were unable to complete. Yossi joined up with the very people against whom he had been preaching......the Workers of Zion! He joined up with "Ha Kibbutz ha-Me'uhad" (The United Kibbutz Movement).

One of Yossi's friends had been called into the Polish army after the war. He endured almost as much hatred as he had in the concentration camps. Yossi's own draft notice came in the mail, and became the final prod that caused him to finally commit to a move to Zion. In what seemed like moments, Yossi found himself near the Polish border waiting for his girlfriend, Deborah. When they rendezvoused with each other, they crossed the border into Czechoslovakia. They, with other Jews, were leaving ALL behind, seeking a place of freedom, where they would be wanted and welcomed, even if only by other Jews. Zion seemed to offer the best possibility.

The Jewish "underground" helped them through Czechoslovakia into Austria where he and Deborah trudged through the rugged Alps. Bribes were used on occasion to entice a guard to look the other way while a border was crossed. It was on to Italy where he and Deborah waited their turn for passage to their British-controlled homeland. They boarded the ship *Patria* and began another agonizing journey, this time, across the Mediterranean Sea.

As they approached the coast of Palestine, the British navy intercepted them, 30 miles from their destination. The British led this tub of sick and broken people to port in Haifa. The people were each given a new suit of clothes.....that of a prison uniform. The British put these Jews back on a ship and deported them to the island of Cyprus, and placed them in an internment camp. The suffering continued.

It was now 1947. Yossi had watched the Germans march into his city in 1939. He lived through the crowdedness, disease, and starvation of the Lodz Ghetto, the murders and starvation of Auschwitz, the deprivation of Sachsenhausen and work in the Heinkl factory. He survived the death march away from Sachsenhausen, lived in a Bergen-Belsen rehabilitation hospital, and made his way back to

Poland where he endured more rejection and brutality from some of the Poles. He lived under the deception of communism and under great danger, escaped Poland through Czechoslovakia, Austria, and on to Italy. He and Deborah were now prisoners in Cyprus.

The captivity would continue for another 7 months, and Yossi and his wife would experience a blessing in the midst of deprivation. Their new baby daughter, Yael, was born, in a Famagusta, Cyprus military hospital.

Although the physical conditions in their internment camp were horrible, at least no one was forcing them into hard labor. There were no gas chambers or firing squads, and the people of Zion continued to have hope that they would soon have their turn to be released and allowed to continue to their homeland. They were almost in Israel.....not quite....but almost!

That day finally arrived, and the little family, Yossi, Deborah, and baby Yael, boarded a ship for the short 200 mile journey to Haifa. At long last, they disembarked. They were home!

Awaiting them now was another war, that of surviving and building up a land that had been nothing short of a wasteland for centuries. There were no tract homes or condominiums to buy. There were no trailer parks. If a home was needed, it had to be built. There were no Home Depots or lumber yards down at the next traffic light, and no hardware stores on the next street. It would require more sacrifice and deprivation.

Deborah and Yael stayed in Netanya at an encampment for the women and children of the new kibbutz, and Yossi and 10 other men headed south into the Negev Desert where they set up a little outpost. They would be the foundation stones of the new kibbutz. The men had gathered a few chickens, a tractor or two, some tents and other provisions. They worked day and night, gathering more provisions, building another cabin, and then bringing in a few more members to the kibbutz. Little by little the conclave of God's people grew like a new embryo going through mitosis in the womb. It was now time to bring the wives and children. When Yael finally saw her daddy, she cried. It had been that long since she'd seen him, and she did not know him.

The process of building the kibbutz was not as easy as pitching a camp, building up some cabins, planting crops, and raising some livestock. In addition to these heavy chores, there was the nightly guard duty necessary to maintain security from the Egyptians who resented the presence of the Jews. Attacks were not uncommon, and their fragile kibbutz organization could not afford a moment of non-vigilant slumber.

As the kibbutz grew, Yossi also experienced a new sense of accomplishment and gladness to be in a land that was his. His grasp of the new Hebrew language grew in leaps and bounds. He seemed far ahead of Deborah in making yet another adjustment in life. She had difficulty with the language, and the strains of primitive living in a desert climate took their toll. As with so many other Jews, the wounds of the past that had scorched the souls of the *kibbutzniks*, were not yet healed. In spite of strenuous human effort to continue the ideal of sharing and co-operation, frayed nerves and inner cauldrons of emotional lava often made their way to the surface, and relationships between wives and husbands and other families often were strained.

Yossi kept changing jobs on the kibbutz, trying to find just the right place for himself and his talents. "I had so much conflict within myself, and words were often exchanged between other *kibbutzniks* that were harsh and unloving. I could not adapt. I was going through so much psychologically." It was the case with everyone.

The deep unhealed spiritual and psychological wounds continued to create a rift between him and Deborah. Eventually, like so many other things around Yossi's life, his marriage died. Deborah left Yossi's side for another man, and another part of Yossi's inner man bled. He left the kibbutz in 1952, never to return.

Yossi, as much as any Israeli that I have met, exudes a zeal for life. He can be seen working with the mentally retarded and handicapped children of Israel. He is an accomplished ceramic artist, and a catalyst for joy for children who have entered life without the full measure of mental and physical abilities.

A doctor of psychology once asked him if his work with ceramic ovens was not connected in some way to the ovens of Auschwitz. Was he in some way within himself, creating beauty out of ashes?

"I don't think there is any connection between these things...the ceramics and the Holocaust...and the fact that I help these helpless little ones. That's just the way I am. I just happen to have the ability to relate to these kids and others."

Indeed, reader, he does. He is a precious man molded by the crucible of a very harsh life as a Jew, but out of him flows a stream of human love, unknown even to himself. It is not forced, but natural. It is seen and felt however, by the people around him.

"I don't believe in life after death. I don't believe that the creation of Israel is a miracle of God. I don't believe in religion, but I respect people who do. To depend on the Lord?!......I just can't! We just have to do it ourselves."

Yossi continued, "Hitler was an accident in the human nature. I am pessimistic about human nature in so many ways, but I am still optimistic about the future."

His advice to Christians: "Struggle against Anti-Semitism in all of its forms, shapes, or in whatever ways that it would appear. Struggle without compromise. Struggle tenaciously against this evil. This has been a sickness of the European nations, and even in America. This is a struggle for all humanity."

# 10

# YONI

Yakov, the Israeli mechanic who ran the garage at the end of my street in Miami, handed me an elegant envelope. I opened it and read the invitation to his son's wedding. It would be held in Miami Beach, and was only a month or so away. My wife and I were deeply honored.

We had been steady customers of Yakov for some years and watched him struggle to make a very successful business out of pumping gas and fixing cars. Yakov worked day and night, along with his sons, and was able to fix just about anything, and he did it for a very fair price. We had often talked about Israel when he had a spare moment around his busy garage. Yakov is one of many Israelis whose heart and roots are imbedded deeply in Zion, but who for one reason or another, found life to be impossible in the homeland. He had joined the many Jews in the *Diaspora*. Almost all who venture out away from Israel have the intention of staying only a few years, and then returning to the land. Most, however, stay beyond the initial intention of "a few years". Although their lives may be economically better in America, they are a torn people, their bodies placed among the nations, but their hearts still longing for Zion.

My wife, Hellen, and I were often invited to Jewish functions in the Miami area. Many of our friends are Jewish, and it was always our pleasure and desire to give support to the people involved in the causes that affected the Jewish community. We knew that we would have opportunity to meet more Israelis at the coming wedding, and we very much looked forward to it.

The violin music, the *hors d' oeuvres*, and the decorations were magnificent. No expense was spared for the wedding guests. It was elegance overflowing, however, in typical Israeli fashion, there were very few guests who would fit the Anglo-Saxon description of "upper class". Most were down-to-earth, feet-on-the-ground people who worked hard and loved life. One such wedding guest was Daniel, who worked in construction. He was much more comfortable in his work-a-day open collars than he was in the suit that Americans required for such a festive occasion. Our friendship grew quickly and the next day Hellen and I were guests at his home in Hollywood, Florida.

Daniel's friend, Yoni, was there also, and the three of us headed out the back door to launch out in a 25-foot boat that Daniel was considering as a purchase. The boat was tied to the dock behind Daniel's canal home. Swarthy and short of stature, Yoni took the controls, fired up the engines, and we cruised out for a little test run. During that afternoon, I learned enough about Yoni to know that I wanted to know more. He was a walking Encyclopedia Judaica, and not only knew a lot of things, but had lived out in his own life, a remarkable adventure that needs to be told. We met at his apartment some days later. We sat down, and once again I pressed the "record" button on my tape recorder.

Baia Mare, Hungary was smack-dab in the middle of Transylvania, an area that throughout history had its borders moved hither and yon as a result of many wars. Today, Baia Mare lies in the country of Romania, but when Yoni was born in 1934, the small city was part of Hungary. It was a fine city, served by the Somes River, and quite in touch with the latest that the world had to offer, but not rivaling the intensity of the larger cities of the time, like Budapest. There was a significant Jewish population there, whose roots went back to the early 1800's. After the Hungarian revolution in 1848 the Jews were allowed to go into the cities, form their own businesses, own their own stores, and pursue education. They did so with a passion, and became the leaders of the local culture as accountants, doctors, lawyers, bankers, and businessmen.

The Jewish community was very united. There were 6 or 7 synagogues, a rabbinical school, and roughly 10,000 Jews represented by a little over 2,500 families. Jewish schools taught Hebrew, Torah and Tenach (Old Testament), Mishnah (Jewish Oral Law and Commentary), and a full array of religious studies.

Little baby Yoni, crawled around on a deep blue and red flowered carpet. It is one of his first memories. His house was located in the mainstream of Baia Mare's activities. Yoni's grandfather lived his Jewishness from inside out. He was as orthodox as a Jew could be, gentle, wise, and believing that God was supreme. Their mutual visits to one another's home were pleasant bookmarks in the pages of Yoni's life.

Yoni's father, Ilushka and mother, Elizabeth, had let go of the orthodoxy in which they were brought up. They felt that it was important to identify more with their neighbors around them. The strict keeping of the Sabbath, the dietary laws, dress codes, and the many Jewish rules had become a burden, and the importance of getting along with the neighbors seemed more important. Their new religion became art, music, and culture.

A Gentile family lived behind Yoni's home. One day he heard a loud screeching and squealing coming from their neighbor's back yard. Yoni hurried out of the house to observe his Gentile neighbors chasing down the pig that they had fattened up for the kill. The pig knew that something wasn't quite normal, and had become terrorized as the man of the house came at him with a large knife. Yoni observed the whole thing. The pig eventually became the center of a feast for the family and neighbors, Yoni's family included. Yoni was given strict orders not to tell this to his grandparents, on either side of the family, for eating pork was forbidden under Jewish law, and each set of his grandparents followed the Jewish tradition explicitly.

Yoni's grandfather on his father's side, had been a businessman. He had made quite a fortune through logging, and owned rights to cut the trees from thousands of acres of woodland around Baia Mare. A small river provided the transportation for the logs to be brought to market. Life was good......until the river dried up for a season. Granddad decided to build a small railroad into the forest that would supplant the need for the river. The railbed was cut through the forest and most of the tracks were laid when he ran out of money and had to declare bankruptcy. In those days it meant losing everything including his house. He had made a bad business decision.

Yoni's grandfather was down but not out. Using his entrepreneurial skills, he went through all of the necessary paperwork for permission from the local government, procured the needed parts, and installed the first gasoline pump in the city of Baia Mare. Young Yoni loved the challenge of trying to turn the big crank, which provided the power to move the gasoline from the tank to the customer's container. The year was 1942, and motor vehicles were fast replacing the horse and buggy, even in Baia Mare. In a few short months, life got better again, but it would not remain so.

The tentacles of Nazism were reaching into Hungary. Although the Germans themselves had not marched into Baia Mare, the local Hungarians had already formed their own movement, which sympathized with the Nazis. They had formed the Nyilas (Nee-lasch) Party, whose own logo was a black cross. On the end of each "arm" of the cross was an arrowhead. It was their *swastika*. The movement gained support from much of the populace, and was as anti-Jewish as the German Nazis.

One day, Yoni's father, Ilushka, came home from work for the last time. As a certified public accountant who had worked faithfully for years, he had been fired.

"I'm sorry, Sir, but you know the difficulties today. We have to let you go."

The reason was not given, but Jews no longer had a place within the economy of Baia Mare. Despite his attempts to co-operate with the Gentiles and get along with his neighbors, Yoni's father was still betrayed. After all, "he was one of those Jews!"

The little village of Felsobanya lay about 5 miles from Baia Mare. It was there that Yoni loved to visit with his great-grandfather, a deeply Orthodox Jew who made a decent living from his farm and buying and selling produce. Next door to great-grandfather's house the first headquarters of the Hungarian Nyilas Party opened its doors. Yoni looked through the "store" window and saw the uniforms, banners, flags, posters and other regalia. He was fascinated, but in his boyhood naiveté, he did not understand the evil that the paraphernalia represented.

In Yoni's own words, "My great-grandfather was about 85 years old at the time. I would often go to the synagogue with him on Fridays. He would have his *tallit* (prayer shawl) over his shoulder, and I would walk next to him. He would wrap his *tallit* around me as he held me close to himself, as we would walk together. He loved me so much.....and I loved him. I was his first great-grandson. To get to the synagogue, we would have to walk right past this Nyilas Party headquarters. I remember going past one day, and hearing the shouts, 'Bidush...Bidush...( Hungarian for smelly or dirty). You dirty Jews! We are going to kill you!' They threw stones at us. "

"My great-grandfather just tucked me close to him and said, 'do not pay attention to them. Do not even look at them.....not to the left...not to the right....just straight ahead.....and do not talk to any of them.' I felt very safe with my great-grandfather, but this was also the first time that I felt and understood what it meant to be a Jew. I was only about 6 years old at the time. It must also be said that there were sometimes other voices that would be heard, 'leave them alone'.....or 'he is our neighbor'. There were two forces at work."

Because Yoni's father, Ilushka, lost his job, he decided to take his family and move them to Budapest. Little did he know that this decision probably saved his family's lives. Unknown to Yoni at the time, he had seen his great-grandfather and his grandparents for the last time. It was now 1943.

Yoni's father officially changed his last name from one that was Jewish, to a very Gentile sounding name. He thought that he would be able to fit in to the Gentile community in Budapest far more easily, and would be able to provide for his family. Budapest was full of excitement for Yoni. There was so much culture...theater, museums, trains and trolleys. There were even traffic lights. There were also 200,000 Jews in the city at the time, and in general, as a community, they were comfortable. For the Hungarian Jews, Budapest was their Jerusalem.

Yoni was an only-child. The new apartment in Budapest was very large. It was built in a quadrangle, with the best apartments looking outward from the quadrangle, over the street. The inside apartments that looked over the courtyard of the quadrangle, were the lesser apartments. Yoni's family had one that looked out over the street. It was a large apartment, and with the new job that his father had procured, they could even afford a maid. Yoni took his new Gentile name-change in stride. He was only a child, and such things did not matter.

It was a Saturday. His father had taken Yoni to the transportation museum in Budapest. It was an exciting day for a young boy and his dad. Trucks, trolleys, cars, and airplanes were all on display. It was a fantasyland for the young boy, and also for his father who was young at heart. It was a beautiful walk for him and his father along Andrasch Boulevard on the way home to their apartment address at Chengaeroota 51.

A drunk staggered along the street coming toward them. His slurred speech did not obscure his message. "The end of Hungary! The Germans are in Budapest already....the end of Hungary!" He continued to repeat himself, staggering his way to his own destination.

Yoni saw the painful look on his father's face. He asked, "Daddy....what does it mean....Germans in Budapest? What does it mean?"

"Don't listen to him, son.....He's drunk. He doesn't know what he's talking about." The words were spoken to calm his young son, but Ilushka's face could not hide his own concern.

Father and son arrived at their beautiful apartment, and there were Yoni's mother and grandmother waiting at the main gate. "Do you know what's happening, Ilushka? The Germans have come into Budapest!" The staggering man had been drunk, but he was not wrong.

Ilushka's name change had meant little. Although it might give greater favor with the rank and file citizenry, Hungary's officialdom still knew of the Jewishness of Yoni's family. In two weeks, Yoni's father received his orders to report to a work camp, supervised by the Hungarian Nyilas Party. He was given a yellow armband to wear, and because of his penchant towards obedience, complied with all of the orders. During those times in Hungary, if either of a person's parents were Jewish, the child was considered Jewish. Husbands and fathers were being arrested all over Budapest now, and sent to labor camps, some in Hungary, and some in Poland.

The shock of all this change among the Jewish community could not be immediately absorbed. "This was Budapest! We have leadership positions all over the city.......Budapest is modern. It has culture......... We have a thriving economy......We are part of the aristocracy of Hungary...... This 'thing' must soon pass...... This will only be temporary. Someone will intervene and clear all of this up." Jewish conversations continued to deny the reality. The unbelievable had become fact.

Yoni and his mother, Elizabeth, accompanied his father to the train station. Ilushka was 38 years old at the time, and was sent to a Hungarian labor camp. Yoni felt lost and confused.

School time reinforced the new reality. As Russians and the allied armies continued to blunt the Germans on many fronts, bombing raids occasionally came to Budapest, and school children had to be trained to evacuate to the cellars when such raids occurred. Yoni's Jewishness began to rise to greater profile in his life.

"All the Jews to the wall!" came the command of a teacher. The Jewish children lined up against the wall of the school corridor, and the Gentile kids were ushered quickly to the basement bomb shelter. If there was enough room remaining after all the other children were in the shelter, the Jewish children would then be allowed to enter, and then find a place to settle in among their Gentile classmates.

Yoni continued his narrative, "It made me afraid and scared, and I did not understand. We were not stupid at this point, although we were very young. We knew that bombs killed people. We knew what death could be. Why were we being singled out in the school so as to allow the Gentile kids to head for the shelter while we had to wait against the wall? I kept asking my mother for answers. Why had they taken daddy away? Why do they call me a dirty Jew? I was beginning to understand that I was different."

The manager of the apartment building where Yoni lived was German-born. The winds of circumstance favored the releasing of her own hostilities towards the Jews in the building. She was nick-named, "Nametnay", which meant "German-lady". She and her son lived a couple of doors down from Yoni and his family. It was her job to open and close the main gate to the apartment quadrangle. The closings were done promptly at 10:00 PM each night. If an apartment resident would come home later than that, Nametnay would come with her large key and open the gate. She would be rewarded with an appropriate "tip" for her after-hour service.

Generally silent and restrained in the past, "Nametnay" would now harshly complain if a Jew were to come back to the apartment after the 10:00 PM closing. She forbade her young son to play with Yoni. At this point in time, the Gentiles in the building and neighborhood more and more took the politically correct stance. While many of them did not take active part in ridiculing and persecuting their Jewish neighbors, neither did they stand with them. They simply turned their heads and shrugged their shoulders in the face of any persecution that came.

The pincers of the local Hungarian Nyilas Party continued to close on the Jews. Orders came that required the wearing of yellow Jewish stars on the exterior of their clothing. Small local businesses began to spring up. People made these stars in different qualities, which could be purchased. Yoni had been given a very nice one. He pinned it on, and as a young boy, was very proud of his new badge of honor. He touched it and stroked it, as an American kid might do to a toy sheriff's badge that came with a new cowboy outfit. The first time Yoni went public with his new badge, the finger pointing started, and verbal abuse followed. "Look....a Jewish kid!"...... "Go away dirty Jew!" The laughs and taunts would continue, and Yoni would head for his apartment dejected and confused.

This humiliation was not enough for the Nyilas. They followed lock-step with the Nazi plans which had been implemented in neighboring Germany and Poland. The time had come to confiscate the property of the Jews.

Certain apartments were soon designated as "Jewish houses" and "negotiations" would occur in the process of these exchanges. Gentiles would come and insist to the Jews that they had to exchange their apartments with them. Yoni his mother Elizabeth, and grandmother, lived in a lovely and spacious apartment. This however, did not appear on the list of "Jewish houses". Regulations now required that it be exchanged for a one-bedroom apartment. Yoni and his family moved from Chengaeroota 51 to Chengaeroota 61. The required Star of David was hung on the door of their new "*Jidohaden*" (Hungarian for 'Jewish house'). The Gentile "negotiator" promised that after the war, he would return the apartment and the furniture to little Yoni's family.

In Yoni's own words: "He was nice to me. He even helped me with my homework and would draw pictures for me before this "exchange" took place. He never kept his word however, and we never received our belongings back".

The *Nyilas* continued to gain more and more control over the Jewish lives. It now became safer for the apartment manager, Nametnay, to release the floodgates of her own rage against the Jews. She would scream at them, "You Jews.....you Jews.....You will see!......We were your servants, and now you will serve us!"

The Jews still had a very limited "freedom". They were allowed to leave their houses for about two to three hours per day, but a curfew required that they be off the streets and in their houses at precisely 6:00 PM. Yoni and his mother had made a trip to the outskirts of Budapest to try to make a connection with a Gentile family who had been recommended to them as someone who would be willing to hide them......for a price. The connection was made, but Yoni's mother did not have the price. It was too high and the return trip by trolley to their house began. Yoni and his mother stepped off the train at 6:05 PM.

"Well....what have we here? You know you're breaking the curfew. We will now have to arrest you." Two Hungarian Nazis arrested them. Immediately, they were taken to the local Nazi headquarters and brought to the basement.

Many Jews were already there, leaning against the wall face-first with their hands held high. People were crying and screaming. The Nazis took the people one or two at a time, and brought them down the hall to another room. From there the shouts and screaming could be heard, and then the shots......and silence! Yoni and his mother moved up in the line against the wall. They would soon have their private meeting with the Nazis.

"Mommy....I don't want to die. I want to live!" The Nazis would then come to another and say......"Next." The line kept moving a little at a time. Some more shouts, agonizing screams, and more shots rang out only a wall's width away, followed by silence.

"I don't want to die, Mommy....I don't want to die. I am too young. You are old already....I don't want to die. I am scared!" Thirty-year old Elizabeth held her son tightly, and tried in her own panic to comfort Yoni.

A Nazi guard came over to Yoni and yelled, "Shut your mouth," and began to beat him. Suddenly, Yoni's mother, Elizabeth, fell to the floor and began moan with labor pains. She was five months pregnant, but barely showed that fact physically. She pushed out her stomach, to try to make herself look further along than she was. Her acting job touched the feelings of one of the Nazi captors. He came over and asked about her problem.

"I am in a terrible state! I am going to have my baby!

"If it is true, you are safe, but if it is not, we will kill you." He started to drag her away to a nearby hospital.

"My son......my son!" she screamed holding on to little Yoni. She would not let go. The Nazi allowed Yoni to accompany them to the hospital.

On arriving at the hospital with two guards, Yoni and his mother were brought to the doctor. She did all that she could to communicate with her eyes to the doctor, that something was radically wrong. He got the message, looked at the two guards and spoke, "You cannot come in. You must wait here."

In the safety of the doctor's private office she leveled with the doctor. "I am not really having my baby right now. I'm only in my 5th month. We were in the Nazi headquarters, and they were killing the people......I am trying to save my life and the life of my son. If you tell them all this, they will kill us." The Hungarian doctor listened and nodded with understanding and compassion. In about 10 minutes he left the examining room and spoke to the Nazi guards.

"I'm sorry, the woman has to stay here in the hospital."

The guards left. When it became dark, Yoni and his mother left as well, carefully making their way back to their "Jewish house". They had been spared.

Time dragged on. The broken little family waited for some word about Dad. Yoni continued his story. "We were always hearing stories about this one or that one being killed or dying from some disease in the camps. We just wanted to hear something from my father. Up to this time there was no word whatsoever."

Tears flowed regularly from little Yoni and the unanswered questions, "What about my father? Where is he? What have they done with him? Why is all of this happening?" tormented his young mind. To add to this pain, the local Nazis would raid the Jewish apartments and confiscate anything of value. They would come on the pretense of looking for radios, which were forbidden and also scarce, but in the process would take gold jewelry and watches. They periodically looted the Jews, until all semblance of wealth had been extracted from each family. There was nothing left now. There was no money for heat. There was nothing with which to buy food. Hunger and starvation were daily realities.

Yoni continued his story to my wife and me. We sat in his apartment in Miami, and he had become speechless. The words would not come, and tears filled his eyes as the resurrected memories of his childhood stabbed at his soul. We offered to stop the interview, but Yoni felt that he must go on and he did.....just as he has gone on throughout life. Little Yoni, the boy, had been forced by evil circumstance to become a "man" back in that little apartment in Budapest. He had also endured more terror at the age of six, than most men experience in a lifetime.

The order came to leave the "Jewish houses" and to move to the ghetto, which had been designated for the Jews. Months had passed. There was no word from or about Yoni's father, Ilushka. Elizabeth was pregnant, and little Yoni felt the burden of his grandmother and mother. From the new ghetto, the people were almost daily loaded aboard trains to be taken to the prisons and gas chambers of Poland, a process that had already occurred in hundreds of small communities throughout Hungary.

The ghetto's population was thinning out little by little. No longer were there three and four families per tiny apartment, but perhaps only two. The time had come for Yoni and his family to join a line that would put them next on a freight train to Poland.

An interruption occurred. An announcement came by radio from the Hungarian authorities, that Germany was losing the war and that the Hungarians would be disassociating themselves from the Nazi machine. It was a political attempt for the local Hungarians who had so brutally collaborated with the German Nazis, to save their own skins, and to look like great leaders and saviors of the Hungarian society. The speaker whose voice was heard by radio all over Hungary was the Minister of Justice. This same man, although he had no way of knowing it then, would, decades later, stand before Yoni's desk in Argentina, hat in hand, begging for a job.

This announcement brought hope to those in the ghetto, and it had the effect of keeping Yoni and his mother and grandmother off the train to Poland. However, the pain did not stop.

The little three-some went back into the ghetto and hid themselves, hoping for respite from the terror that still surrounded them. Daily, the Hungarian Nazis patrolled the ghetto and lived up to their German counterparts in brutality and cruelty.

Yoni heard the stern voice of his mother, insisting that he come back to their little hovel in the ghetto. He had been in the street with his friends playing and celebrating the news of the announcement from the Hungarian authorities.

"Yoni.....come here! Yoni....I said come in the house.....NOW!" Elizabeth's voice was insistent, as never before. She meant business and came into the street to drag Yoni by the hand into their little refuge.

Yoni looked out the window of their ghetto apartment, still smarting from his mother's decisive action that dragged him away from his friends. He continued watching and saw two cars from the local Nazi party drive down the street where he had been playing with his friends. Shooting started, and Yoni watched in terror as his friends dropped to the pavement, dead victims of the local Nazis. Only minutes before, he had been playing with them.... six, seven, and eight-year-old kids, now robbed of their lives by the monsters that had pulled the triggers in the name of National Socialism.

The promises of the Hungarian Minister of Justice were only words, perhaps to assuage his own guilt and the guilt of the Hungarian system, which had married itself to Hitler's Nazism. Perhaps they were words spoken to disarm Jewish vigilance. The local Nazis, however, would continue their goal of exterminating the Jews.

Days later, the Jews were ordered out of the ghetto. They lined up...thousands of them, mostly women, children and old men. They marched. Yoni struggled along with his grandmother and pregnant mother, exhausted and weary. Their frail bodies, weak from starvation, were barely able to obey the commands of their own minds. Yoni was weak and covered with a rash and some kind of fungus. He could hardly move his arms or legs.

For two hours they marched through the streets of Budapest. As they marched, jeers from the local populace came like darts.

"You will learn who's boss!" "You'll get yours...you Jews!"

They lined up on the riverbank of the Danube River. The river whose beauty inspired the writing of famous classical music would that day be become a defiled stream, carrying the carnage of Nazi misdeeds. The tired, starved, emaciated Jews were made to stretch out the line, single-file, along the riverbank, like sitting ducks in a shooting gallery. That's what they were to become in only minutes. In this gallery, however, there was no rangemaster who could pull a rope and raise the targets once they were hit.

Hungarian Nazi soldiers lined up with their rifles as a massive firing squad. They needed target practice. The shooting began. The little man, Yoni, held his mother's hand and the hand of his grandmother. Bullets, which had missed their human targets, whizzed overhead. Others smacked the ground around them. Still others found their mark.

The river had a fairly swift current. As the Jews each fell after a volley of rifle fire, some tumbled into the river. The bodies of others were thrown into the river. Some were only wounded, but they were thrown into the icy waters anyway, their heavy winter clothing acting as weights that would cause them to drown in a frigid liquid grave. If the bullet that struck them did not kill, the icy waters would.

More volleys of rifle fire burst forth and Yoni watched as multitudes of bodies floated past him, surrounded by blotches of crimson which oozed from the bullet holes in their bodies. They turned and twisted, banging up against the river bank, and continued their lifeless journey to wherever the historic river would take them.

The terror of these moments stayed locked in the minds and hearts of Yoni and others who watched. Although untouched by the lead bullets of the Nazi riflemen, they were permanently wounded by the bullets fired into their souls, tearing their hearts while watching the maniacal behavior of perverted humanity. There was shouting and screaming, but most of the Jews stood in silent acquiescence, helpless victims being slaughtered as sheep.

As suddenly as the shooting had started, orders were barked, and the guns stopped. The little boy was still being held by both hands. Yoni's mother and his grandmother had survived, and he was also alive.

The survivors of the massacre were marched back to the ghetto. The scenes of the previous moments were engraving their memories. As they silently marched, they were filled with a deep grief that had punctured their souls for a lifetime.

Back in the ghetto, many of the rooms and apartments were empty. Their previous inhabitants who had scrounged a meager breakfast that morning, now floated and twirled as corpses in the currents and eddies of the Danube River. Previously crowded families might even have their own room or apartment now, but it was no solace for the survivors who looked for a place to lay their heads back in the ghetto.

Yoni, his mother, and grandmother, found that they now had an apartment to themselves.

They looked around and opened the oven. There was a cake prepared to be baked. It was a small kitchen project that had been interrupted when the orders came to march. The previous tenants, who were probably drifting down the Danube were no longer there. Yoni, his mother and grandmother, all wondered where the previous occupants had gotten the ingredients to make a cake. The wondering soon stopped. There was no time to question or mourn. Life must go on whatever minutes or days remained. They got the stove going, baked the cake, and ate it.

While Yoni and his mother and grandmother continued to survive in Budapest, another drama was taking place, which began in his great-grandfather's village of Felsobanya. The local Nyilas Party (Hungarian Nazis) "cleansed" the village of Felsobanya of all the "dirty Jews."

Yoni's great-grandfather, who was a massive six feet three inches tall, accompanied his petite little wife to the trains. She had stood with her husband for all these years, had lived a life of faith, and had enjoyed the blessing of great-grandchildren. They had marched next to each other, still lovebirds, a contrast of opposites, he a tall and imposing man of gentleness, she a petite little great grandmother who could influence her giant husband with a mere look. Physically, they were Mutt and Jeff caricatures living life in a traumatic chapter of human history.

Great-grandfather had done most of the talking in the family, and great-grandmother most of the listening. In very traditional fashion, he took care of all the business outside the home, and she ran the inside, spending most of her waking hours right around the kitchen, maintaining the home fires of her nest for her husband and children. She was a typical "*Yiddishe* Mama".

The elderly couple was jammed aboard one of Hitler's cattle cars, where there was standing room only, and worse than the worst crowded subway during a Manhattan rush hour. The trip to Auschwitz took three days and three nights. Once again, from another country, cattle cars filled with the living dead were being transported to the infamous death camps of Poland.

Another train had arrived, filled with living and dead. Those who had the strength, climbed over bodies to meet their captors face to face. Yoni's precious petite great-grandmother had not survived the journey. Suffocation had spared her the humiliation that awaited her. Other Jews dragged her body along the floor of the cattle car, and dropped it on the station platform of Auschwitz.

"What happened to my wife? What happened to my wife?", the old great grandfather screamed as he bent over his wife's lifeless body. "God! What are you doing to me? I have been so loyal to you." Great-grandfather had gone to *Schul* every Friday. He had always been a loyal faithful Jew, a protector of his family. "God, I served you all my life.....what did you do to my wife? Where are You?" He prayed in Yiddish, crying out to his God, whom he felt must have abandoned him at that moment.

"Shut up, old man!.....Shut up!" roared the voice of a camp guard.

"*Sh'ma Yisrael, Adonai Elohenu........,*" the old man prayed with one of his hands raised to heaven.

"Are you going to shut your mouth or not, old man?"

"*Sh'ma, Yisrael...*what is happening, O God of Jacob?" He continued to hold up his arm. His face looked straight to heaven, in great agony, while he expressed undying faith to his God, Who in that precise moment he did not understand.

A shot rang out from the pistol aimed right at great-grandfather's head. The old man fell right on top of his already sleeping wife. They had lived together through terror and triumph all throughout their earthly lives. Now they would nobly die together.

(Yoni related this story in all its detail, because an Auschwitz survivor who had witnessed the entire scene had related it to him. An additional comment from Yoni bespeaks his penchant for seeing life with an optimism. "My great-grandfather was very lucky because he avoided the gas chambers.")

In the same train with Yoni's great-grandfather and grandmother, were his uncle and two older cousins, Sheini, and Urche. They had survived Nazi doctor Josef Mengele's greeting and sifting of the prisoners. They had been deemed "fit to work". The arrogant flicks of Mengele's finger sent them in a direction away from the gas chambers to their work stations where at least they would stay alive. The father and his two sons stuck together through everything. Their loyalty as a family was as complete as it could be. They, along with their father had lasted for many months through the ordeals of Auschwitz.

There were rigid rules at Auschwitz. and its adjoining camp Birkenau. No one was "allowed" to become weak or sick. This "crime" would invariably send a prisoner to the gas chambers. Even after having survived the degradations and inhumanities of the camp for many months, Yoni's uncle became sick. It occurred only days before the Russian army liberated the camp. So near...but eternally far. His diarrhea and fever stole all of his energy, and he could not work. This was a serious offense on the "Auschwitz Planet". The sentence, death!

Sheini and Urche knew that their father was on his way to the gas chambers, but they hung on to him. They would not let him go. They had been through much together, and they loved their father intensely. The Nazis told them to leave their father and go back to work. They refused. Their honor, and the dignity of their father was more important to them than mere existence in the hands of Nazi demagogues. Sheini and Urche carried their father into the "showers" where German-manufactured and German ministered Zyklon-B gas canisters poured forth their fumes of death. All evaporated into a memory along with most of the rest of Yoni's extended family—all exterminated.

Back in the Budapest ghetto, Yoni, his mother and grandmother, continued their struggle for survival. The ghetto grapevine had received the word that the ghetto was destined to be totally liquidated. It no longer mattered whether it was a rumor or true. Desperation as never before erupted among the ghetto Jews.

In the insanity and hypocrisies of war, situations arise that seem to be total aberrations of what the nature of the war is about. It is like imagining Adolf Hitler applying salve to a wounded British soldier, or Josef Stalin bending his knee to give a cup of water to a beggar. This was the case in Budapest. There, in the middle of a philosophical and shooting war, small oases existed, perhaps as false fronts to hide the atrocities that were being perpetrated, or even as acts of courageous dissenters.

In the midst of Budapest, there were "safe houses" set up by outside governments, which allowed for some protection, and sometimes-safe passage, out of the hell that was engulfing the Jewish people. There was a Swedish protection house, as well as one from Switzerland, the Vatican, and a few others. Protection papers could be obtained through the various embassies that maintained these "safe houses", perhaps for a price, or if there was a political connection, or if someone was just plain lucky. It was in such a place that the famous Raol Wallenburg did a great work in finding and even creating papers that would allow Jews to escape Hungary. Although a Swedish diplomat, Wallenburg far exceeded the quotas that had been set up to receive Jewish families.

Yoni, his mother, and grand-mother were some of the fortunate ones who received a set of forged "protection papers" which allowed them to exit the gate of the Jewish ghetto. They walked through the streets in search of their "safe house". On arriving, they found themselves among hundreds who had also done the same thing. The walls of the safe house were almost bursting from those who had legitimate papers, along with those who had forged papers. All however, were desperate human beings in search of true refuge.

People were sitting on the stairs, in the hallways, and every square foot of space that would contain a human being. A large house that might have accommodated 100 people in a crowded condition, was the scene of 400 laying claim to the space. Yoni and his mother and grandmother were accommodated on a stairway. They sat there and they slept there.

This Swedish "safe house" existed, but it was not safe. There were no diplomats, guards, or soldiers present, only an address with a roof, which was glutted with frantic people seeking to save their lives. The "safe house" was not off limits to the local Nazis. They came in periodically, knowing that desperate people, perhaps on their way out of the country, would have their most valuable possessions. The "safe house" became a literal slot machine of stolen wealth, as the Nazi thieves garnished all that they could from the Jews. Watches, jewelry, money.....it was all taken. Only some of the lives were spared.

Sometimes the Nazis would come and take eight or ten of the healthier in the crowd, and send them about the neighborhood to sweep and clean streets and to do other mundane chores. Sometimes 10 were taken, and only 8 returned, the fate of the missing 2 unknown. It was 1943 and right in the middle of the great World War.

"All women under the age of 40.....front and center". The command came from a Nazi woman, sold out to the new socialist movement, which had been birthed in Germany.

"Every woman.......if you are under 40, line up and do it now!"

Yoni's mother obeyed the order.

Yoni ran up to the Nazi. "No....don't take my mother away! She is going to have a baby! Please....please.....don't take my mother away!"

Little Yoni's pleadings had as much effect on the female Nazi as a child's popgun against a tank. He watched the brutish woman snatch his mother away. Yoni would never forget this female robot of the Third Reich. His mother was taken away by truck to the other side of the city, to a brick factory that served as a holding point for Jews to be shipped by train to the death camps in Poland.

Elizabeth sat shivering in the cold. There were dozens of others around her within the factory gates. Most were women, and their faces reflected the hopelessness and despair that permeated the Hungarian Jewish community. Elizabeth, however continued to look for a way out of her predicament.

There seemed to be little security, so she decided to take a risk. It was now, or not at all. The choice was possible death now, or certain death later. She began walking toward the factory gate as though she knew what she was doing, and had the authority to do so. She walked, looking straight ahead. The gate was open. She walked through the gate and continued walking along the street. Nobody stopped her. She walked for seven hours through the city, stopping often to rest or to duck into the shadows of the ice-cold night, avoiding any moving vehicle or person. She arrived back at the "safe house" and was re-united with her own mother and son. Once again, her life was spared.

The tragedy of the Jews took its worst form in Hungary toward the end of the war. As desperation mounted on the part of the Germans and their Hungarian collaborators, they stepped up the pace of rounding up, shipping, and executing the Jews. Their strategy was to capture the Jews from the far off rural villages and towns and send them to their deaths. When that was accomplished, the plan was to take the Jews from the cities, leaving Budapest, apparently until last. It was this plan that worked in Yoni's favor. Although his father had already been shipped to a Hungarian labor camp, his mother, and grandmother and Yoni continued to survive in Budapest.

Back door negotiations took place, especially at the end of the war between various governments and Hitler's Third Reich. The Germans were even using some Jews as bargaining chips to obtain desperately needed money from foreign governments. Some of these governments began offering the Germans and their accomplices money and other needed items for Jewish lives. The Germans even tried to obtain American trucks in exchange for Jewish lives in some of their negotiations.

Times could not be more desperate. The Jews were simply trying to survive. The German and Hungarian Nazis knew that their time was short, and the truth of their barbarism was beginning to come to light for all to see. In those final days and hours of countdown, the barbarians participated in a desperate orgy of depravity, killing or maiming almost anybody that came into view. Yoni would be one of about 35,000 Jews out of 600,000 in Hungary that would survive the entire World War II ordeal.

There were efforts by the International body of the Red Cross to salvage Jewish children from the ongoing Holocaust throughout Europe. In one case, an entire "safe house" of Jewish children had been established. Some of them were orphans, and some had been entrusted to this system by Jewish parents who wanted to ensure their children's survival. The Germans and the Hungarian Nazis had other ideas. In one of their final pushes to liquidate the Jews, they walked into the children's "safe house" and murdered the entire contingent of children. Many were Yoni's friends and acquaintances. Elizabeth, however, would not agree to separate herself from her Yoni. If they were to die, they would all die together.

Still in the Swedish "safe house" on Nederland Street, Yoni and his mother and grandmother continued their lives. It was winter of 1944-45. The Nazis raided the place again, looting the inhabitants of any jewelry, watches, and valuables that had not been taken before. They took over a large room in the top of the building, and brought all belongings there. Furniture and even food was taken to the top floor and locked in that room behind a heavily padlocked door. All of the other rooms had been stripped of anything of material value, leaving only the further weakened and harassed Jews without even a chair to sit on, or a morsel of food to eat.

There were mostly women and children, and a few older men

that comprised the population of the "safe house". They needed to get into the top floor room but had no tools with which to work. Yoni, who was small and wiry was chosen to be the human ferret who would break into the room. In spite of the heavy door with several locks, there was a small window in the door, about five feet above the floor. The glass was broken, and Yoni lifted to the window. He just barely was able to squeeze himself through the opening with the help of the adults outside the door.

Inside, Yoni found some food and began handing it out through the miniature opening. Clothing came next. Little Yoni became a combination shovel and conveyor belt as he moved as much as he could in a short span of time. He was in forbidden territory, and to be caught there would be certain death.

Word came up the stairwell. "Nazis!.....Nazis are here!" Sharp pangs of panic stabbed at everyone present. The little crowd of Jews headed down the stairs with the exception of Elizabeth and Yoni's grandmother who remained just outside the door. Little Yoni stood on a chair on the inside of the door, and tried to help himself through the window opening. His mother pulled from the outside. Moments passed like hours. The faster they tried to work, the more mistakes they made, and Yoni remained stuck inside, unable to get high enough to move through the window opening on his own. Some more effort from Yoni on the inside and from his mother on the outside, and Yoni's little frame began to edge its way through the tiny opening. Shards of glass that were still lodged in the window's framework, dug like shark's teeth into his little body as his mother pulled and yanked her little treasure back to safety. Yoni's arms, body, and legs were all cut and bleeding, but there was no time to cry. He was hidden in one of the downstairs rooms until their enemies left. His escapade went undiscovered, and he and his guardians lived another day.

Several days passed, and the shooting war was coming closer. The Russians had made their way into the city, and were storming building after building. Street fighting was vicious and cruel. The Russians showed no mercy to the Germans nor to the collaborating Hungarian army. There was chaos everywhere. Shop windows had been smashed, buildings burned and soldiers died in the streets. In the confusion, people went any and everywhere in search of food. The Jewish contingent of the "safe house" carefully made their way among the confusion, picking up a can of food here, a jar of jam there. The streets were strewn with the rubble of blown up buildings, dead bodies of soldiers and civilians, and dead horses that had given their all in battle.

Yoni scoured through the disorder. He lifted up his new treasure. "Look Mama, I found it!" It was a large can of tomato sauce. This was more valuable than gold right now. It meant that they could eat, even if only for a few more days. These were times when even a barrel of gold was of little value. There was no food to purchase, and this large can of tomato sauce gave them life for several days.

Death and confusion were the realities of each day. Fighting continued in the streets as the Russians devoured any resistance in their path. Explosions that destroyed buildings and shook everything else around them, continued around the clock. Bodies of men, women, children, and horses lay strewn in the streets. In the midst of the chaos and death, the iron grip of the Nazis had been broken over the Hungarian Jews, and those who remained in Budapest in the ghetto and in "safe houses" began to head back to the homes and apartments that were once their own. These decisions were very risky, because no one knew what they would face when arriving at their former households, nor did they know what would happen in the streets, since the gunfire continued with a fervor.

Yoni and his mother and grandmother were relocated within the Swedish "safe house". Evidently, the Swedish government did not own the building, and perhaps had stopped paying the rent on the building. Other families who apparently were the previous owners of apartments within the "safe house" began to come into the building and demand that the Jews being housed there, get out. Yoni and his lady guardians headed for the basement of the same building and took shelter there in its darkness. The days of the war continued, with vicious fighting continuing in the streets.

It was night, and the basement was divided into boarded off enclosures, with a corridor that ran down the middle. The boarded enclosures had been designed to provide private storage facilities for the apartment dwellers in the building. The corridor gave access to these enclosures. Yoni sat in the darkness, a boy of eight, with a pregnant mother and an aging grandmother. His mind tried to process the events of his past. He thought of his grandparents, great-grandparents, and his father whom he had not seen for months. The terrors of seeing his young friends machine-gunned in the streets of the ghetto caused him to shake within. Questions and other thoughts raced through his little mind. "Would I die too? What has happened to my father? What about grandfather and grandmother? My mother is pregnant. She is weak. What's going to happen to us?"

The silence of the night was abruptly ended in a quick burst of machine gun bullets shot the length of the basement corridor. Russian voices at the other end of the cellar shouted and gave commands. The Jews hiding in the cellar knew only that the words were Russian, but they did not understand. Yoni's grandmother stepped out of hiding and began to speak. "Don't kill us. We are Jewish people.....we have been through so much!"

Although the Russians did not understand the meaning of the words, there nevertheless was understanding from the inflection and the tone of what she said, and as an older matronly woman, she presented no threat to the battle hardened Bolsheviks. The Russians lowered their guns and treated the hiding Jews with kindness.

Yoni's grandmother was able to speak Romanian. One of the Russian soldiers also had command of the same language, and communication was now possible between the new liberation army and those who had been the victims of their mutual enemy. The Russians surveyed the condition of the Jews hiding in the basement, and soon brought some food to them. It was a small gesture, but it gave life to the devastated Jews.

Slightly restored from the food that had been given them by the Russians, Yoni and his mother and grandmother decided that they would try to leave the cellar of the "safe house" and head back to their original neighborhood and apartment. The threesome gathered up what few belongings they had left, and headed out into the streets to walk home.

In Yoni's own words, "I remember seeing the whole city burning. It seemed that everything was on fire. I saw the beautiful major train station in the city center engulfed in flames. We had to cross the bridge by the train station. I remember a Russian soldier saying something to warn us.....something like.....'You cannot be in the streets...you will be killed!' We continued to walk, pushing a little cart with our belongings. We walked between burning neighborhoods. We walked as soldiers shot each other and died. We eventually made it back to our apartment."

Yoni, his mother, and grandmother, stood outside the door of the apartment that they owned. Many months earlier, the Hungarian Nazis had ordered them out. They had come to reclaim what was theirs. They hammered on the door. No one answered. The door was locked tightly. Inside, the inhabitants cowered in fear, not knowing whether it was a neighbor or a Russian soldier that hammered on the door.

The threesome were not able to force their way into their own apartment, and so they headed for the small apartment in the same building that had been their refuge after having their own apartment confiscated. The apartment was empty, and it became refuge for them. It was January 1945 in the dead of winter. The temperature was well below freezing. Survival would still be a problem.

Yoni and his female entourage had been moved from their apartment, to one of the small *Jidohaden* (Jewish houses), from there to the Jewish ghetto, on to the Swedish "safe house", and were now almost back to their own apartment. Shots and explosions continued in the streets. No one knew who was winning the war. Rumors were as common as bullets. "The Germans are mounting a powerful counter-offensive and are taking the city back." The next one might be, "the Russians have won and we are soon to be living in great freedom again." In the midst of all this, they had to survive.

The occupying German army had been crushed by the advancing Russians. It soon became apparent to all. The shooting had died down. The raging fires had consumed their buildings and were reduced to smoldering embers. People began to come out of hiding and venture into the streets in search of friends, neighbors, and food.

It was now January 26, 1945. Yoni, his mother, and grandmother were huddled together in the one room apartment that served as shelter. There was no heat. The three of them were trying to sleep, depending upon each other's bodies to provide a mutual warmth that would keep them from freezing.

It was now the fullness of time. Yoni's mother felt the contractions that indicated that she would soon be giving birth to her baby. Ilushka, the baby's father was either dead or alive, but none of his family knew which. He had not been heard from for many months. Yoni continued to be the "man" in the family at age eight.

Elizabeth began to breathe heavily and cry out in pain. She gasped out her request between contractions and heavy breathing.

"Yoni......go.....go and find Bronchia. Bring her here.....quickly Yoni......hurry!"

Bronchia was a mid-wife of sorts. It was not known if she was even alive, much less still living in the neighborhood just up the block and around the corner.

Yoni, the little man, ran down into the courtyard of the apartment complex. He yelled for help from the apartment manager to open the locked door so that Yoni could get to the street. The manager was not in the mood to help. Yoni picked up a rock in the courtyard and smashed the only window pane that was unbroken in the door, just to let the manager know that he meant business. He needed that door open. The manager slapped little Yoni, sprawling him on the floor, but opened the door.

Yoni ran into the dark January night sliding and slipping on the ice and snow that covered the streets and sidewalks, tearing the flesh on his bare feet. He dodged between the dead bodies of men and horses lying in the streets. He scurried to Bronchia's house, screaming and yelling.

"Please....please come and help. My mother is having her baby! Please....come and help."

"Yes....yes....I will go with you," Bronchia responded to little Yoni as she saw the pleading in his face and eyes.

The midwife walked quickly, following Yoni as he tried to hurry her even more. They arrived at the little apartment to discover that Yoni's new baby sister, Miriam, had been born. Yoni stood outside in the cold while Bronchia aided in the clean-up of the new infant and exhausted mother. The whole matter lasted only a few more minutes. Bronchia went back to her apartment. Grandmother went back to sleep, and Yoni lay on one side of his mother, and his new baby sister, Miriam, lay on the other side. All slept, layered in blankets and coats, their breath visible in the unheated apartment.

Unlike the Jews in the Lodz Ghetto in Poland, Yoni and his family still had a fair supply of furniture in the apartment. The decision was made to use it for fuel to heat the freezing household. They broke up the chairs, tables, picture frames, and anything that would burn. They used it in the fireplace and the wood stove. It would keep them alive in the coming freezing weeks.

The freezing weather was a blessing in disguise, for although it became a problem to stay warm and nurture a new baby, the below freezing temperatures and snow preserved the dead bodies of men and horses in the streets. Yoni kept one horse covered in snow, spreading aside only enough snow to cut into the carcass and take meat a little at a time as it was needed. When he had cut into the carcass and taken a kilo or so, he would cover up his meat supply with white snow, much as a surgeon might cover his patient with a sheet. The dead horse was their food supply, and the furniture provided the fuel with which to cook and heat the apartment.

The words still ring happily in Yoni's thoughts. "Yoni....Yoni....your father is here! Your father is home!!" The truck delivered Ilushka to the front of the apartment building. He was weak and sick, but he was home. In Yoni's own words, "My FATHER was home! My FATHER! I was alive! My grandmother was alive! My mother was alive! My newborn sister was alive......and now my FATHER was home! I saw him in his glory. He walked from that truck. He was alive. We were all alive!"

The news would come all too soon, that Yoni had lost the rest of his extended family. The Germans had executed all his grandparents, uncles, aunts, and cousins. Yoni's family was one of the more fortunate, for although their extended family had been cruelly annihilated, their immediate family was totally intact. Few Jewish families of the time were able to say the same.

Almost immediately, the fortunes of Yoni's family began to change. Ilushka was given a new job as a Deputy-Secretary in the new Hungarian government. Although still weak and sick from the mistreatment of the labor camp, Ilushka was able to provide for his little family. They returned to their street-view apartment. The Gentile family that had moved in and taken over the apartment and possessions, were dispossessed of what had been wrongly confiscated.

Yoni, with his school friends, began to collect small amounts of change, and the beautiful artistic bridges that spanned the Danube River, connecting Buda and Pest, were in the process of being restored from the damage done during the shooting war. The theater started again. Schools were opened, and the city began to thrive, little by little, but still in deep deprivation.

Yoni's room was on the ground level floor of their newly restored apartment. His window overlooked the street. It was here that he studied, read, and sometimes watched the passers-by. On one afternoon, as he looked out the window, she appeared. There she was as real as could be.....the Nazi woman who had snatched Yoni's mother from him and sent her to a brick factory to be held for deportation to the death camps. Despite Yoni's pleadings at the time, the female monster obeyed her orders and sent Yoni's mother towards death. The memory was from only months before, and here she was walking along the street as though she had no care in the world.

The bottled-up rage within little Yoni exploded faster than he could contain it. He leaped out the window right on top of the surprised woman. He kicked, screamed, and even bit the Nazi clone, as others came to the scene and pulled Yoni off the woman. As Yoni poured out the story of his personal encounter with this woman to the onlookers, she was held, arrested, and taken away to jail. It was a small satisfaction for all the pain that had been inflicted against so many Jews. Yoni later walked from his house with other friends and family, and witnessed the public hanging of the leader of the Hungarian Nazi Party. The hanging took place in what is now known as Freedom Square.

It was 1947 and the war had been over for two years. Budapest's economy and infrastructure were still being repaired. The deprivation and forced hard labor of the logging camp had taken its toll on Ilushka, however. His body never fully recovered, and he died just after Yoni's Bar Mitzvah.

Yoni had been a man since he was eight years old. He had shouldered pain and suffering that weighed far more than his capacity to carry it. He nevertheless persevered, carrying more than most men have endured in a lifetime. Now it became official. He entered manhood, at age thirteen, according to Jewish tradition.

The past decade had been beyond words to describe for the European Jewish community. They had experienced a taste of hell perhaps rivaled by no other time in history. World War II was over, but the Jewish struggle was not. Local populations in Germany, Poland, and Hungary continued to persecute the Jews even as they staggered home after years in concentration camps. As they tried to knit their lives together with whatever remained of their families and community, in great weakness and vulnerability they continued to endure the hostility of the Gentiles.

Life for Yoni however, became special. He tried out for the Hungarian Theater Company and surprisingly strummed the cords of many a heart. In his youth, he was a natural on stage, and his older mentors of the theater loved and coached him in the parts that he played. He became a celebrity around Budapest. His life fast became one of special attention and bouquets of flowers. He was picked up at home, driven to the theater for rehearsals and performances, and delivered back to his door when his work was finished. He was paid well. Yoni's life had turned the corner from searing pain to growing comfort and success. As he continued his schooling and his work in the theater, he nevertheless stayed connected to the Jewish community and one of their Zionist organizations.

Many of the Jews became active in Zionist organizations that sprang up all over war-torn Europe. There was always the question as to whether the war was really over or not, and whether it would be but a few months or years before something even worse than Hitler would begin again, and the Jews would be completely eradicated as a people. The Zionist organizations were focused on saving young Jews and bringing them to their God-given homeland. Sadly, some of their effort was a zeal without wisdom.

The Jews in leadership would teach the young teenage Jews about Zion and a Jewish homeland. They would bring the youngsters on outings, teaching them camping, survival techniques, farming, weaponry, and the need to be ever vigilant in a world that was out to kill them. It was a needed education, and it was good for bringing the Jewish youth together in community. There was however, in some organizations, a cleverness that bordered on deceit. They were preparing the kids to be shipped to Israel, unbeknownst to their parents.

After the youngsters had been sufficiently trained and instructed, they were brought on an outing that was to have lasted for a weekend. When they got there, they were taken to the Czechoslovakian border. They were told that they had a decision to make. To cross the border would mean that they would continue on to Zion, to become part of a new nation that would be birthed there as a Jewish homeland. Each youngster could do as he wished. If he went on, there would be no return, and his parents would be told after they left Hungary. If they chose to stay and return to their parents, they would not be able to go with their peers to Israel.

Yoni was convinced that he would go to Zion. He arose at 4:00 AM. He'd not told anyone in his remaining family that he was even contemplating an adventure to the Promise Land. Carrying a small bag of personal items, he slipped out through the familiar apartment door in the darkness of early morning. Even he did not know that upon closing the door, it would be the beginning of ten years of separation from his remaining family.

The chatter of his many friends could be heard as he joined them at the local train station. Most of his friends had absolutely no idea as to the decision that would confront them later in the day. Yoni had been let in on the secret by one of the Zionist organizers and at least carried a few personal items. His lips remained sealed regarding the decision that would confront each member of the group that day.

The outing began by boarding a train and heading north for the border of Czechoslovakia. There was the usual excitement and continued chatter of teenage youngsters as they watched the countryside roll by. They were glad to be together, and were enjoying the present. They disembarked close to Hungary's northern border. They hiked into the woods as they had so often done on other outings. Their leaders brought them to a secure and quiet resting-place. One of them spoke:

"Listen up, everybody. We are doing something different today.

You've all been on many outings before. You have continued in your training and have understood the necessity for a Jewish home-land.....a place where we can be secure with each other." The young-sters sat in the woods cross-legged, some leaned against a nearby tree, but all were paying full attention to the speech.

"Today you will all have your opportunity to commit fully to the Zionist vision. Right now, you can make your decision. Either you are committed to Zion, or you're not. Today you can vote with your feet. If you walk with us....we will soon cross the border into Czechoslovakia and will continue our "outing" all the way, and make *aliyah* to the Promise Land. If you make this choice, your parents will be informed once you are on your way. If you choose not to go with your fellow Jews, you may leave now, and go back to your parents. It will not be held against you, but neither will you have the opportunity to go to Israel. Think about it...make your decision, and we will proceed."

The choice hit everyone like a fist to the stomach. In one sense it awakened them fully to the seriousness of life and choice, and of continuing to walk out the vision for Zion. In another sense, it took their breath away and gave a sick queasy feeling as they pondered the separation from their families. "What would mama think?" "What about my friends at school?" "Should I really do this?" Hundreds more personal questions poured through the minds of the Jewish teenagers. While they were idealists, and had been taught about the glories of Zion, they were also realists. They had endured a real war in their young lives. Some were parentless. Some had only one. All had lost significant numbers of their families to the Nazis. All knew that it could happen again, perhaps any day.

Yoni still had a few questions. "Is there theater in Zion? Will I be able to continue in the theater?"

"Of course there is, Yoni. You can be what you want to be," one of the Zionist leaders answered.

One by one the youngsters committed. Of the almost 100 teenagers in the group, all but one girl who had a very sick mother, answered in the affirmative. They would be real Zionists. They would go to the land and build a place where they and their children would be safe, and where they would no longer be persecuted. They hugged each other nervously and continued their "outing" through the woods. They did not look back with their eyes, however none were completely and totally committed from the core. If such a thing can be quantified, the percentages probably would vary from 51%, just enough to make the decision to go, to perhaps an 80% commitment, for those who had nothing to leave behind, but who nevertheless feared what Zion really had to offer.

Days passed, and the word did not reach some of the parents and others in the lives of the new young Zionists. The Budapest theater was desperately looking for their child star, Yoni. His picture was in the paper, and Hungarian theater-goers were looking for him. His own mother could not give any answers. She did not have any. The fear of having lost her Yoni to some accident or whatever, began to consume her.

Yoni had made his way through Czechoslovakia with his peers. The Zionists were fairly well organized and led their new charges on into Austria and to Vienna. Yoni contacted an aunt who lived in Vienna. She insisted and got a call through to Budapest.

"Yoni....Yoni.....it's you! Where are you? When are you coming home? We have all been worried about you! The theater has been calling!"

"Mother.....I'm OK. I am going to Israel." He was safe. He explained his decision to a tearful and distraught mother. He was not coming back. He would go to Zion, in his teenage mind, a land of proverbial milk and honey.

Yoni stepped off the ship and onto the Land of Promise. His young mind and the fame that he had already experienced in Budapest had twisted reality for him. He was expecting flowers and a reception. It was not to be.

"Sorry kid....we don't have much theater here. We don't need actors. We need workers and soldiers."

Yoni had been taken in by another's interpretation of a dream, which began to turn nightmarish for him and many others. He had set foot onto a land that was surrounded by hostile Arab nations, bent on the destruction of the Jewish people. It was a land that had lain dormant for centuries, dry desert, hard rocky mountains, with mosquito infested swamps. There was little infrastructure and many of the Jewish organizations fought against each other as to how best to build the land and protect their interests. Yoni looked at his barren surroundings and was taken to a kibbutz where he would begin life in Zion.

The only acting that he did, was in a field. He was to act like a good Zionist, act like a good worker, and act like a good farmer. There was little time for entertainment. There were almost no provisions for the emotionally broken people that came by the boatloads. The only thing that Zion had to offer at this time, was more work, more war, and more isolation and hardship. It was a second holocaust of sorts for 14-year old Yoni.

He left the kibbutz and was put into an institution for young boys without parents. He escaped and headed for the Port of Haifa, where he tried to get aboard a ship as a stowaway. He wanted to go back to Hungary. Yoni was caught, and turned over to yet another Jewish organization, most members of which had come from Hungary.

"Look Yoni.....stick around for about a year. Give it a real try. If you are then dissatisfied, we will get you back to Hungary."

There were thousands of "little problems" like Yoni who lived in the dark corners of Israel's fledgling cities. The individual problems faced by these who were so alone were however, very minor as compared to the survival of a new nation. Thus, there was little aid for the helpless and homeless individual. He either lived or died on his own accord.

Yoni endured his year in the new land, institutionalized with others like him. He was too young to take on large responsibilities in any organization, too young to be a soldier, and lacked any professional training in the trades. He became more and more restless. He knocked on the door of the Hungarian Zionist Organization in Haifa.

"I want to get out of this institution and go back to Hungary."

"The only thing we can do for you, Yoni, is to have a relative sign you out of here and take you home."

Some of the youngsters in the institution were able to find "relatives" who would sign them out of the institution, and once out the door, they were free, but on their own. Yoni found his "relative". He signed his name as Yoni's "uncle" and Yoni was free.

They walked down Herzl Street in Haifa and the two strangers said good-bye to each other. Yoni was out and on the street, but had no place to stay, no food, no relatives, no money....no nothing. At night, he rested his head on the sandbags that people would pile around their doorways as protection against bullets that flew around during street fights against the Arabs who wanted the Jews gone or dead.

Communication by mail had been established back to Budapest. Yoni would receive a letter now and then. He was too embarrassed to write home and tell how things really were in the Promise Land. He also did not want to burden his mother with worry. The news coming back from Budapest was also not good. Immediately after the war, Hungary began a miraculous climb out of the miseries of the previous years. The economy began to rebound, and life took a real turn for the better. It was short-lived however, as the Russian form of communism took over. The economy and the personal freedoms of the Hungarians took a dive, and the advice in letters from his mother, was to stay in Israel. Do not come home.

Yoni and two cohorts were able to secure work in a small bag factory. The factory made and reprocessed burlap bags that were used to transport rice and other similar products. Once the bags were used, they would be re-processed by being cut and sold again as foundational material for the making of furniture. Yoni's days were spent in the hot factory with his buddies, cutting and sewing old burlap bags. Their meager wages were enough to purchase a bowl of soup, perhaps a little hummus, some pita, and to escape to a movie once in a while. The factory owners allowed them to sleep among the stacks of rat-infested burlap at night. This was now home for Yoni and his two friends. As they were able to save a little of their meager salary, together they were able to rent a small room of their own in the Arab-occupied section of Haifa. Their stake in life had begun to grow.

Yoni has continued to live and grow as an international businessman. Today, although he spends most of his time outside of Israel, his heart is still in Israel. A self-educated man, he has held down important jobs in the Israeli government, and has endured the rigors of combat in Israel's many wars.

He further speaks, "I think that the pain in Israel is worse now than ever before. I think that the people have changed. You still have to see a future for your children, but...can you imagine? Every family in Israel is a tragedy...every family! If not the father, then the son, or the cousin, or the brother. Everyone has had the tragedy of having lost someone dear. We have been living in wars all our lives. Everybody wants peace and happiness in their own lifetime. Twenty years in history is a very short time, but in an individual's life, it is a long time. So...this is the reason people are frustrated. They want peace in their lifetime.

I sat in Yoni's apartment, looking directly at him as he continued to tell his story. I asked him if he thought that Israel was really going to survive?

"Yes...I met David Ben Gurion on a few occasions while he was a leader in Israel. I will never forget his words. I had said to him, "Sir...you are always saying that time is working with us. I think that time is working against us."

The white-haired political sage of Israel looked at Yoni and said, "The Jews will survive, and perhaps there is an arrogance in thinking themselves better. The Jews have not seen that their blessing and talents come from God. There is a spiritual truth here that QUALITY will prevail over QUANTITY. There is only ONE God.....and there are billions of humans....and who knows how many angels or demons. He......QUALITY....will prevail over all!"

In the earlier days, there were about 40 million Arabs surrounding about 2 million Jews in Israel. Today there are probably 150 million Arabs surrounding 5 or 6 million Jews. To the natural eye, the odds seem insurmountable. Looking through that same natural eye in 1948, 1956, 1967, 1973, 1982, (Israel's wars) and even now during the so-called "Peace Process", the natural eye would conclude the situation to be impossible for the Jewish people.

David Ben Gurion is right! There is only ONE who will prevail over all. It is this ONE who has given the promises for Israel, that the land and the Jewish people will be restored, survive and prosper, as well as have her enemies subdued.

"I will restore them because I have compassion on
them. They will be as though I had not rejected them,

for I am the Lord their God and I will answer them......I will signal for them and gather them in. Surely I will redeem them; they will be as numerous as before. Though I scatter them among the peoples, yet in distant lands they will remember me. They and their children will survive, and they will return. I will bring them back from Egypt and gather them from Assyria. I will bring them to Gilead and Lebanon, and there will not be room enough for them. They will pass through the sea of trouble; the surging sea will be subdued and all the depths of the Nile will dry up. Assyria's pride will be brought down and Egypt's scepter will pass away. I will strengthen them in the Lord and in his name they will walk," declares the Lord.

(NIV—Zechariah 10:6-12)

Yoni, to this day, is not as sure as David Ben Gurion. He looked at me and said:

"You are a religious person, and you think it is a question of God. This is your feeling, but it is not my feeling....even though I came from a religious family. Unfortunately, the war did not make me more religious. Quite the opposite is true. I still have a very deep conflict with God and believing. I am not an atheist, and I am not secure in my position, but I think that one day when I see God, I will have a very serious fight with Him."

There are a few million "Yonis" in the world of the Jewish people who have suffered immensely, and who have concluded or almost concluded that God doesn't care, or that He might not even be there in the first place. As part of a community of Christians in America, it is all too easy to see the dozens of hopeful promises of the Scriptures toward our Jewish brothers and sisters. However, unless there has been deep suffering in the life of the Christian, the endurance of the "dark night of the soul" over protracted periods of time, the great temptation can be to react with incredulity as to how a man like Yoni might not see the hand of the Almighty working out His purposes in the lives of the Jewish people. It is for men and women like Yoni, that as Christians, we owe our prayers and committed loving support to help them regain their true sense of identity.....that of being faithful Jews, filled with the hope, faith, and the perseverance of their father, Abraham.

# 11

# ELENA

Our appointment had been set, and I followed the meticulous instructions to Elena's home. It was a pleasant drive up the coastal highway between Tel Aviv and Haifa. Passing the towns of Netanya and Hadera, we soon saw the sign to Caesarea, where the ruins of a Roman aqueduct still stood and where the Apostle Paul had preached many a sermon in the old amphitheater that still remains as a tourist site. My wife and I found the exit road to Zikron Yakov. We wound our way to the top of high terrain, on which the beautiful town sat, overlooking the Mediterranean Sea from a distance. Elena's husband, Yakov, met my wife and me at the door and welcomed us into their cozy bungalow.

We began the process of becoming acquainted. How does one enter into the home of someone, meeting her face to face for the first time, and then ask her to bare her soul, revealing deep, intimate, and painful memories of the past? How can a non-Jew expect that a Jewish lady who had been deceived, persecuted, and betrayed by

Gentiles, to be able to trust enough to reveal the pain of her past that was still throbbing in the present? Yet, Elena, as had so many of her Israeli contemporaries, did just that, displaying a courage and willingness to risk herself that defies reason.

Yakov, her husband, told his story earlier, and is the subject of a previous chapter in this book. He sat close-by listening again to the story of his own wife, and also reliving the past that the two of them had endured in "Mother Russia". At the time of their sufferings in communist Russia, they were not husband and wife, and each walked separate paths of travail and torment. Once again, I pressed the red "record" button on my tape recorder, and began to enter yet another Israeli's life.

Elena's father was Colonel Mikael Pletnevsky, chief ophthalmologist of the Red Army Medical Corps in Siberia. He was a man who had almost lost his Jewish identity except for the words annotated in his personnel records, designating him "Jew". Although he knew the word and the sterile fact that his family was Jewish, it had no real meaning.

Dr. Pletnevsky was a man deeply entrenched in the Soviet system. He was no great ideologist, but more a medical man who did his job within the mighty Red Army. He was aware of the many inequities of communist rule within his nation, but life for him was rather stable and predictable, insofar as a military life can be. His own emotional scars were deep and hidden. His own father had been executed during one of the Stalin purges of 1937. Dr. Pletnevsky fought with the Red Army during World War II, was twice wounded, and received several medals for valor.

Dr. Pletnevsky's wife, Leah, was a woman of deep sensitivity and a perfectionist to the core. As a doctor, she was a well-studied electrocardiologist and hematologist. Leah was never satisfied with her abilities and her work. She always strived to learn more and to do better. She was a woman of ideals, so much so that she was absolutely loyal to the Soviet system, and seemed blind to the many realities of its daily workings. In her own striving for perfection, it was as if she could ignore the hypocrisies of the system, and in her own power and dedication, bring the communist ideal into existence, despite what others were doing in opposition to the ideal. It was a heavy burden to bear.

Filled with altruism, Leah Pletnevsky's goal was simply to help people. She was not interested in large salaries, even if such rewards were available in communist Russia, and they were not, unless one was involved with the massive and unrestrained system of bribery. She held rigid belief in the communist system, even though she had to fight it every day, as she attempted to plow through the mounds of bureaucracy to accomplish even routine medical procedures for her patients. She fought for those in her charge and merely accepted all of the needless stress and bureaucratic battle as part of the system, which she continued to idealize.

Elena remembers her mother's insistence on always looking for and living by truth. In spite of her vocalized ideal, Leah, earlier in her life was unable to see the truth of the system that held her captive. Even as Elena grew into adolescence and adulthood, she also held the Soviet system in high regard, although she began to see its hypocrisies and deceit. At the age of seventeen, Elena became clearly aware of the great chasm between the words of communism and the facts of communism.

In her own words, "For many of my friends, they might discover that a certain leader was corrupt, or that a certain government program did not work, and little by little they discovered that the communist system was a lie. For me, it was an almost overnight revelation. I just 'knew' that I had idealized a lie, and that I must now spend as much of my energy fighting against this evil system as I had spent in defending it before my eyes were opened."

None of this had anything to do with Elena's Jewishness or Zionism. At this point in her life, she had never even heard of Israel. She wrote in her diary that she felt guilty for her own grandparents' part in the Russian revolution in the early part of the century. They had participated enthusiastically, and Elena now felt that she must try to undo the harm that had been done through this revolution. She still loved her country, but knew that things had to change in order to eliminate the miseries under which so many people suffered.

Despite the fact that Elena's father was a high ranking military doctor, life was not a cakewalk. Although life was better for her family than for the average citizen, it could never be described as one that would rival even a lower middle class family in America.

Elena remembers coming to the end of each month and not having enough money to make ends meet.

In the normal moves of a military officer, the Pletnevsky family was uprooted on a number of occasions when the colonel would change posts. Mrs. Pletnevsky, although profoundly interested in her own service as a physician, would often find it difficult to find a place to work with each move. The bureaucracy did not allow for private practice, and if there was no slot in the system, there was no job, even for the very qualified.

When work was found, Leah Pletnevsky expended herself 110 percent. At age 34 she suffered her first heart attack, and at age 37 suffered another which disabled her from any further work. The system, which demanded so much and gave back so little had taken its toll. The fog through which Leah had been viewing the system was beginning to clear, and side by side with her youngest daughter, Elena, both were coming to the same conclusions without discussing it with each other.

In 1965, young Elena, made her first contacts with Moscow dissidents who were secretly publishing anti-Soviet literature. Almost all of them had family members who had been arrested or persecuted, and simply answered the call for dignity that exists in every human heart. They banded together and began pointing out the hypocrisy and the corruption of the system wherever they were able. Their resistance work was strictly prohibited and any sympathizers were subject to long prison terms if discovered.

In communist Russia, it was not allowed to have any private printing presses or copy machines. These were under the strict control of the government. If someone had something to say to hundreds of people, he could not run to the nearest "Sir Speedy" and have a thousand copies run off for a few rubles. There was no such possibility. Elena, who had procured an old manual typewriter, began her publishing. She would jam as many carbons copies as the machine would allow, and manually type all of the dissident literature to be distributed. The work was long and tedious just to reproduce a few dozen copies of a document or article.

"I thought that I was doing all that I could, and that I was doing what I was supposed to be doing...then I met a Zionist for the first time." Elena began to understand, albeit superficially, what it was to be a Jew. She began to understand the longing in her heart to break out of the Soviet system that did nothing but enslave people. Her original desire to become a doctor like her mother gave way to the creativity of language study and stage direction.

She was able to enroll in a special school, which would train her in these disciplines. It was a university steeped in much tradition, but where every few years there would be bunches of people arrested for anti-Soviet activities. Creativity required a freedom of thought and expression, and in this environment, many of the students began to see more clearly the possibilities of their own humanity when they were not pigeon-holed and restrained by the State bureaucracies. This freedom of thought eventually would be interpreted to be anti-Soviet, and another clamp-down by those in power would try to snuff out the flames of freedom, which were always defined as rebellion by those in charge of maintaining the status quo.

Elena continued her story. "I did not know what it was to be a Jew. It was only a word. I would experience it on the first day of school each year when I would be in the registry for class. We moved around a lot because of my father's military assignments, so I had no contact at all with other Jews. There were none where we were. The teacher would ask for my name, the name of my parents, and my nationality. We always had to answer those questions, and of course I had to answer that I was a Jew. And from that moment on throughout the remainder of the year, I was a "Jew"...and I did not know what it meant. Everyone from that point on was saying that Elena was a Jew, and everyone was looking at me as if something was wrong. I was different. I was an alien. It was not only that I was simply called a Jew...but also I felt different. I could not explain it."

In 1967, the Six-Day War had begun and ended. Elena had barely heard the name "Israel". She certainly was not aware of the war that had just been fought and won by the Israelis. She had no radio to listen to the foreign news stations, and to listen to the Soviet controlled news was to receive only what the system wanted the people to know.

One of her university contemporaries came up to her. "Nice going! You guys won!"

There was another, a noted anti-Semite who said, "Great, you did it!" Others spoke words of congratulations to her, and she did not even understand what it was about. Gradually, she was able to put together enough information to somewhat understand what Israel was, and that her fellow Jews had managed to defeat the Arab armies that surrounded her in six days.

According to Elena, her Russian contemporaries respected power. In past history, they had seen Jews as weak and passive cowards, and they respected the power and the victory that was demonstrated by the Israelis. It was an acknowledgment of strength and courage. She was being acknowledged for what other Jews had accomplished. These congratulatory words and acknowledgments inspired her to feel included as part of Israel. It was at this point that she realized that it had something to do with her personally and that she would now work towards a goal of becoming a part of Israel. She continued her studies.

"By the end of the first year, all of the Jews were expelled from school, including me", Elena explained. She was learning firsthand more lessons about living as a Jew in a Gentile world. Her learning curve accelerated. She had finished her exams before expulsion, but she was involved with life, expending her energies faster than they could be replaced. Her weakened state made her vulnerable to tuberculosis, which confined her to bed for the better part of a year. With her body fighting the disease, her emotions were also low, and study, learning, and seeking out more information on Israel took a back seat in her struggle simply to stay alive. Living in the area of Siberia in a nation that could barely feed itself, left her constantly hungry and the minus 40 degree temperatures of winter, left the household anything but warm and cozy.

After a year of slow, painstaking recovery, Elena immersed herself in working on underground literature, writing, reproducing, and distributing it. She also continued to study.

Elena had reached a point in her development where she was looking at two situations side by side. She had learned more about her Jewishness and Israel. At the same time, she was seeing the evil that existed in communist Russia, how it had destroyed and impoverished its citizenry and enslaved much of the world with its corrupt ideology. She struggled with where to expend her talents and energies...helping Israel or fighting the communist system entrenched in Russia.

Her chance meeting with a Jewish Zionist in Russia continued to plant the seeds of Israel in her heart. This man however was one who always loved an argument. If one person said "black", he'd say "white" and though his Zionist ideology was rigid, his arguments were forceful enough to press these seeds into the soil of Elena's heart.

Elena shared this vision of Israel with her family. Her mother, who had been deeply oppressed by the system, in her fight for the simple privilege of using her skills as a physician to help others, accepted Zionism readily. Elena's older sister, Victoria, an almost perfect replica of her mother, also received the ideas and the hope for Israel.

It was at this time that her father, Dr. Pletnevsky, was receiving the brunt of rejection for simply having the word, "Jew" stamped in his personnel file. After 30 years of military medical service, Elena's father was asked to take a chair of leadership with the University of Novosibirsk. He was recognized by the scientific community as one who had much to offer in an academic setting, however, the anti-Semitic spirit that ruled over much of the Soviet system came against this appointment. Influential bureaucrats in the Health Ministry, although working illegally within their own system, were able to block Dr. Pletnevsky's appointment at the university.

Discouraged by the fact that his own abilities and talents were now being shelved by the system, he too began to think about Israel. His wife, Leah, had already made up her mind to leave Russia. The Pletnevskys together arranged to obtain an "invitation" from someone in Israel to come and live there. This was the preliminary part of the long paper duel that was fought by Russian *refuseniks* to leave the national prison of communist Russia for a better place, usually Israel.

There was another obstacle, however. Leah's parents were very old and in need of care. The Pletnevskys could not leave them behind, and would have to convince them to immigrate to Israel as well. The old couple lived in Kiev and was in need of oversight and care. Even while considering an application for an exit visa, Elena and her family had also to obtain permission from the Soviets even to make an internal move to Kiev where they could care for Leah's aging parents.

Dr. Pletnevsky applied to the military. When he was drafted into the military some 30 years earlier, he was taken into the service from Kiev. He asked to be returned there in order to be with his wife's parents.

"We already have too many Jews there," came the reply. "We will not move you there."

One has to understand, that the Soviet Union had laws and they had regulations. Laws that were on the books clearly stated that Dr. Pletnevsky would be entitled to such a move. Bureaucratic regulations however, often superseded the law in the practice of everyday life. Cumbersome regulations became the roadblocks to allow bureaucrats to frustrate the lives of the average Soviet citizen.

In every large corporation or organization, it has been said that there are "half the people trying to go someplace and get something done, and the other half are there to stop them". If there was ever a nation that epitomized this axiom of the workplace, it was communist Russia. In Russia however, it was not a joke, and it would seem that perhaps only 10-20% of the people there were trying to go someplace. The other 80-90% did the stopping.

To fight against a regulation so that law would work in a person's favor, one would have to battle the bureaucrats and the regulators by filing a lawsuit and have a case heard. The process alone was enough to break a person financially and emotionally. Most Russians resigned themselves to living under the corruption of the system. Another way to accomplish something was to use the everyday business of bribery, something that Dr. Pletnevsky would not do.

Elena eventually finished her education and received her diploma. Her gifts and talents in language made her an excellent interpreter for Russian and English. Despite the fact that there was a deep need in Russia for English speakers, when she interviewed for different positions all would go well for her until it came time to show her identity papers to those who interviewed. The word "Jew" would always be there, and upon reading this word, the interviewers would turn sour.

"Thank you, Miss Pletnevsky. We will call you next week." The calls never materialized.

It was spring of 1972. Elena had managed to land a temporary job at a Musical Academy. While there she organized an English Theater, where she taught her students how to act and also to perform in English. Behind the scenes, she continued to publish underground literature about the Russian political system. She became so involved in her work with her students and the publication of underground literature, that thoughts of Israel had been pushed to the closets of her mind. During this time, Israel was becoming as big as life in the minds and hearts of her father, mother, and sister.

After she developed an English play, taught it to her students, and had it performed in a theater setting, her immediate goal had been accomplished. All of the preoccupation and work had come to a conclusion and in an inner vacuum, thoughts of Israel burst through those closet doors of her mind and became prominent.

"When I finished this play, I came to realize that no matter how I felt...my place was in Israel. Even though I knew little about it, and had no idea whether I could be used there or not, I was prepared to go there. All my friends, who were non-Jewish, would remain in Russia. Everything that I knew and loved would remain in Russia. Regardless of all this...I knew in a moment that my place was in Israel."

Elena continued. "I realized that in Russia...Russia decides what is good for you. The time had come when the Russian people needed to decide for themselves what is good for them, and not to receive instructions and advice even from a Jew like myself. The best thing that I could do for Russia now was to do nothing...and the best that I could do for Israel was simply to get there. I then realized that I had little to no chance of going."

Although on a modest military pension, Dr. Pletnevsky had no work. His wife, Dr. Leah Pletnevsky, cardiologist and hematologist, had no work. Elena's older sister, Victoria had a job, and Elena was just finishing her temporary job as a stage director of her newly created English Theater.

As a family, they made their application to the Russian system for an exit visa. When such a paper is passed across a government desk, it usually becomes the trigger that sets off a volley of persecution and hardship that heretofore had been only tasted by the applicants.

To want to leave Mother Russia was viewed as nothing short of crime and treason. It was believed that such a person was either criminal in his intentions, or going insane. People so indoctrinated and enveloped by the lies and fear in such a system, became the tools in the hands of evil and deceived men. They considered it patriotic to inflict more pain and damage on those who yearned for freedom and the fulfillment of their own destiny.

Elena's sister, Victoria, had to face her co-workers. After having made her application to leave, each of her fellow workers was summoned and they were forced to spew out every bad thing that they knew about her. If such employees did not co-operate in this endeavor, they were subject to losing their own jobs. They became hired accusers, who would dig up the worst in real or imagined character defects, and charge the visa applicant with the terrible attributes of being a "lover of Zion", an "imperialist", or an "enemy of the beautiful mother country of Russia." Even Victoria's best friend at the time, betrayed her and mouthed a stream of invectives and lies that demolished Victoria. The process had begun and each of the family would now endure the winepress of Soviet Russia.

If an exit-visa applicant were to answer his accusers with the idea that he or she was leaving to receive one million dollars from a long lost cousin, or that a beautiful home had been left to him by a distant relative, such a reason would have credibility with the widely taught philosophy of dialectical materialism, a fundamental pillar of communist-atheist thinking. But if someone leaves Russia because of an ideal...the conclusion is that such a person is an evil traitor.

Opening night of Elena's English Theater play had concluded, and Elena had gathered all of her students together to congratulate them and to critique the performance. After a few minutes of running over the technicalities, Elena found herself speaking to her students on a different subject. From theater, the subject turned to Zionism. In that she had made a commitment to leave Russia and emigrate to Israel, and knowing how the system was designed to vilify and defile the personage of anyone making such a decision, Elena wanted to open her own heart to her students. She wanted to express her deep love and respect for them, but also to let them know how her decision was one that was not against them or Russia per se, but more a step in her own destiny which she felt compelled to follow. She did not want them wondering what had happened to her, or to have to answer such questions that might come from the State. Elena wanted them to know the truth, and by stating this in a group setting, put herself at tremendous risk.

She poured out her feelings and reasoning for about an hour. Her students listened intently. She told them everything that she knew about Israel, and how she needed to fulfill the compelling call that seemed to come from the land of the Jews. She also spoke of her love for Russia and its people, and how very much she would miss them. Eleven years later, Elena would find out some of the impact that her little speech had upon her students.

Normally, in such a group, there is usually one who would go to the KGB and inform them about such a speech. It was apparent that no one did so immediately. Perhaps a parent or an official overheard a conversation at a later time, but eventually the KGB got wind of her speech, and began calling in each of the students for an interrogation. Each one of them was highly encouraged and coerced to denounce Elena, and to testify that she was speaking out anti-Soviet propaganda. To Elena's knowledge, none of the students co-operated, and many were expelled from school because of it.

Elena was then accused of spoiling the lives of these students, because of the price that they had to pay to protect her. It was an accusation that was unjust and built on the lie of the communist system. Elena taught her students more than English and more than theater. She taught them values and principles that were never to be betrayed for the sake of a career or position. If anyone should be accused of spoiling lives, it should be the people who were the operables within the communist system...those who insisted upon false confessions and the slandering of innocent people.

Elena's grandmother in Kiev continued to weaken. She was a lady who had been very political in her earlier years, and who had promoted the communist ideal of Soviet Russia. Toward the end of her life, having seen the best that man had to offer in a socio-economic system, she became almost totally apolitical. She was a lady that was at the threshold of death's door.

Elena, who considered her grandmother to be her best friend, sat by her side. Her grandmother had also made the decision to make *aliyah* to Israel, however her weakened state would not allow for this. Elena stayed by her bedside in the last days of her grandmother's life. As she lapsed in and out of consciousness, she would become lucid at times and would say, "Israel is with me!" "Israel is following me."

No one knows what was going on in the soul of this dear woman, but it was obvious that something deep and something beyond the reason and logic of man was touching her in ways that only she could fathom. Perhaps it was the call of God's Spirit moving upon her in the mystery of His own ways. Perhaps this woman was living out a portion of biblical truth penned by King David almost 3,000 years ago when he was crying out to God and panting for Him as the deer pants for water.

> Deep calls to deep in the roar of your waterfalls; all your waves and breakers have swept over me. By day the Lord directs his love, at night his song is with me— a prayer to the God of my life.
>
> (NIV—Psalm 42:7-8)

Elena's grandmother passed away, thinking and speaking about an Israel that she had never seen. Elena was alive and she continued to speak and to think about that same Israel. Her efforts to reform Russia were changed to efforts to encourage and promote Zionism and *aliyah* to the Promise Land.

The entire Pletnevsky family was now in Kiev. With the passing of his wife, Elena's grandfather who was also becoming weak and frail, lived alone and needed the care of his offspring.

Elena continued to publish literature about Israel and the call to

Zion. Unfortunately, the KGB caught some of the people to whom she had given this literature. The plan, in any such event, was for the Jewish dissidents to say that they had received their literature from other Jews who had previously left the country with exit visas. The KGB would know the names, and of course would have no way to call them in for questioning. The problem was that those who were presently being questioned about the Zionist literature had never met the other Zionists who were now in Israel, and they had forgotten their names.

The process was easy for the KGB. They simply told the incarcerated couple that if they did not reveal the name of their source for this literature, that their baby would be taken from them, placed in an asylum and they themselves would be placed in prison. It was a threat that they could back up. The quavering couple gave the KGB Elena's name, and they were soon released from interrogation. The couple immediately came to Dr. Pletnevsky and revealed what they had done, warning him to hide Elena and protect her.

The *refuseniks* were very active in Kiev, and there were lots of them, which helped to provide mutual encouragement. They were participating in demonstrations and communicating with tourists whenever they could. Elena's facility with the English language enabled her to tell of their plight to many Westerners. She would give her phone number to as many as possible. They would call her from the West when they were back in their own countries, and Elena would update them on the latest condition of the *refuseniks*. She also read letters and petitions that were written and signed by large numbers of Jews wanting exit visas for Israel. These same documents that were dictated over the phone were also given in hard-copy to trusted tourists who would bring them back to the West for appropriate distribution and publication. This was a strategy that began first in Moscow, but then began to be employed by the *refuseniks* of Kiev.

These group-signed letters would then be sent to the United Nations, to the President of the United States, to other Jewish groups in the West, and to the State of Israel. These brave *refuseniks* were stirring the cauldron of Soviet wrath. In so doing however, they were also backing their captors into the corner of decision.

Russia, which wanted a better image in the West and which wanted loan guarantees and most favored nation status, had to step carefully in handling a growing number of *refuseniks* who were risking all to make their plight known.

It was summer 1972 and the Olympic games were being held in Munich, Germany. The tragic news that Yasser Arafat's Palestinian Liberation Organization had struck and killed the many Israeli athletes, had reached the ears of the Russian *refuseniks*. They immediately prepared a letter and had it transmitted to the Olympic Committee requesting that the Olympic flag be lowered and the games stopped. On the same afternoon, they headed for Babi-Yar, a place just outside of Kiev.

One hundred thousand Jews were massacred and buried in mass graves during World War II at Babi-Yar. There were also a number of Soviet citizens that were shot there as well. A plaque there memorialized the Soviets, but made no mention of the Jews. It was the only place around Kiev that had a sacredness to the Jews, and so whenever there was to be a demonstration, Babi-Yar became the rallying location for whatever point that the *refuseniks* were trying to make.

The KGB was still looking for Elena. She had not yet answered to the "crime" of distributing Zionist literature. As Elena approached Babi-Yar with her fellow *refuseniks*, it was obvious that the KGB had surrounded the entire area, and was prepared to make arrests. Elena and her sister, Victoria, withdrew from the demonstrating *refuseniks* and hid. They watched from a distance as the KGB rounded up their friends and put them in vans to be taken to their interrogation rooms.

Elena headed for her home immediately, got on the phone and began calling. She had been given a phone number in France that she was told would be of help to her. She placed the call to Paris, and did not know to whom she would be speaking. Miraculously, the call went through and Elena began to speak with the man who answered. She immediately announced that she would be reading a letter signed by a group of Jewish activists in the Soviet Union, who have just been arrested.

"This could be very dangerous for you," stated the male voice.

"If I called you, it is not because I do not know that it is dangerous to do this. I have to convey some information!"

"You do not know with whom you are speaking."

"You're right.... I don't...So tell me.... Who are you?"

"This is the number of the Israeli Embassy in Paris."

"You are just the person I need! Here comes the letter!"

Elena began to read the letter over the phone. She did not realize
it then, but the KGB wanted the names that were on that letter and
so as they monitored the call, they received all the information that
was contained in the dictated letter. Everyone whose name was on
the letter however, was prepared to pay the price that the KGB
would try to compel.

Elena's ordeal was just beginning. She and her sister, Victoria,
were picked up the next day by the KGB. The interrogations began.
The sisters were questioned separately, Victoria was browbeaten,
threatened, and cursed as her interrogator raged against her. Elena's
interrogator took the soft slippery approach.

"Just tell us everything, and no harm will come to you or your
family...We just need to know these things for the record...We know
that you mean no harm to our people, and that there was simply a
mistake made that can be easily rectified...just tell us..."

Elena saw through the approach and revealed only what she
knew would be routine information. When her interrogator spread
out all her personal letters, publications, and documents taken from
her apartment, she was questioned on everything. New documents
were pushed in front of her, all in Russian legal jargon..."We the
undersigned Jews hereby admit...." and on and on the questioning
went. Each question held another trap, each interrogator hoping for
the admission of guilt that would put Elena in prison for a long time.

Elena and Victoria were released. Elena immediately went to her
phone and called a foreign correspondent in Moscow. Before her
call was completed, the KGB was at the door and arrested her again.
Elena was tired and worn down from a day's worth of interrogation
that had been completed just an hour before. Yet she stood against
one of the young KGB agents who arrested her. He tried to intimi-
date and undermine her, but she stood her ground. It was early
evening.

"Did you eat your supper, Miss Pletnevsky?"

"No."

"See...you don't even know how to use your life and your freedom."

"I think we have different views on this," Elena shot back.

Elena began to strike a cord with this somewhat rattled agent. He asked her about her background and what she'd been trained to do.

"I'm an English teacher."

"I too was an English teacher, but I went to work for the KGB because it was impossible to earn enough money as a teacher and raise a family."

He was a man who was apologetic, but who had compromised his own principles and was now being convicted by the strength of character that he saw in his petite but fiery prisoner.

In the hands of yet another interrogator, Elena was exhausted and emotionally weakened. She felt the grips of terror coming upon her and the helplessness of being a victim of a ruthless machine that had no care or compassion for a human being.

The interrogator brought up the young couple with the baby who had first revealed Elena's underground work with forbidden Zionist literature. Elena turned around the plan that had originally been crafted by the *refuseniks*.

"I don't know why she gave my name. She was probably told by somebody to use my name because they thought that I'd already left the country for Israel. It is just a big mistake."

"Miss Pletnevsky," he spoke to his weary prisoner, "you need to confess everything, and this will ease the situation for you."

Elena stood her ground, and in spite of other documents that were found in Elena's apartment, this seemed to satisfy the KGB interrogator. The interrogator allowed her to leave, but she now had to deal with the possibility of a long drawn out legal case being filed against her, with the distinct possibility of going to prison for a long time.

Elena's parents were still committed to leaving the country. They had filed their papers and there was no turning back. Whether they wanted to or not, they had to be activists for their own cause of leaving Russia. If they sat passively waiting for the bureaucracy to produce an exit visa, they would die in the process. The only way to get the process to move was to be an active thorn in the side of a corrupt system that was actively trying to make it look good to a Western world.

The scenario was surreal and bizarre to describe it at its best. Here was a family of people, where the parents were both physicians. The father had spent 30 years of his life serving in the Russian army, rising to the rank of colonel. There were two daughters, each of who were highly educated and capable, and they were being treated as sub-human life in a laboratory of twisted and perverted political demagoguery.

Mikael, Elena's father, was now committed to his role as a *refusenik*. All that he had become and accomplished in Mother Russia was counted as mere rubble. The course on which he had embarked was an all or nothing attempt to reclaim his own life and that of his family where they might live in the freedom that had been ordained and purposed by their Creator.

After the interrogations that were endured by Elena and her sister, Victoria, the KGB took them to the railroad station and told them that they did not have residence permits for Kiev, and that they could no longer stay there. They were ordered back to their hometown of Novosibirsk, where their father was now staying. Their mother, Leah, stayed with her aged father in Kiev. At this point in time, Elena and Victoria knew that the KGB was in the process of building their case against them. Fear began to eat away at them, not enough to paralyze... but enough to motivate.

Doctor and Colonel Mikael Pletnevsky received his answer to his exit visa request. It was "not expedient" for him to leave Russia and the permission was a resounding, "denied". It was not an unexpected answer, but it had the effect of dashing any hope that did exist.

The demonstrators that had shown up at Babi-Yar had been in prison for 15 days. They were being released, and Elena's mother, Leah, went to greet them. She was part of a group of Jewish *refuseniks* that wanted to offer support to their fellow Jews who had committed the "crime" of publicly stating an opinion. In the crowd of supporters, Leah found out that one of the single men had received his exit visa. It was a welcome surprise. Leah went into action.

"Do you really have an exit visa?"

"Yes.... I just got it."

"Are you ready to marry my daughter, Elena?"

"Sure...why not?"

This was matchmaking in its finest hour. A man with an exit visa would have much more influence for his wife to now obtain one. The word was sent to Elena that she had a new "husband"-to-be.

Elena made her way back to Kiev, her grandfather's home, and the city from which she had been expelled. She disguised herself and went through every gyration to distance herself from anyone that might be following her. She was in forbidden territory, and in the application process for marriage, she had to wait one month. It was Soviet law. She hid out for that month in Kiev, unable to go to her grandfather's apartment where her mother, Leah, was caring for the old man.

The marriage ceremony took place, and now Elena could apply for her exit permit under another name. The computer had not made its way into the ordinary bureaucracy of Russia at the time, and the files of papers in the KGB, the marriage office, and any other government department had little or no way of being cross-matched to point to Elena as a semi-fugitive of the KGB.

Elena received her exit permit and could now depart Russia with her new "husband". It was the fall of 1972, and things were happening fast. The timing was right. The Soviets were very anxious to see Richard Nixon elected as president in the United States. They were not looking for any more bad press that would put them in a negative light as they went about their own type of lobbying. If Nixon had to make a public statement against Soviet actions against the Jews before his election, he may have to be held accountable for those words after the election, and this would mean more pressure on the Soviets...pressure that they did not want.

In October and November of 1972, the Soviets gave thousands of exit visas to Jewish *refuseniks*. They did it with a malice however. They seldom granted the permits to entire families, but would break up the families by allowing a daughter or son to leave, and forcing the parents to stay...or vice versa. They wanted to be able to show numbers to the West, that their nation was responding to the requests of their citizenry. Behind the numbers game however, was a deep-seated hostility that would continue to bludgeon the Jewish *refuseniks* and their families.

By dividing the families, they could inflict pain on all. Those that were allowed to leave had to do so without their loved ones. Those that were left behind, were the family members of traitors to the Soviet paradise, and so were treated as traitors themselves. They lost their jobs and were subject to every type of degradation that could be inflicted upon them. During all of this the false front of "numbers" was paraded before the gullible Western press and governments, who bit and swallowed...hook, line, and fishing pole. And the Jews suffered.

In addition to Elena's exit permit, the Soviets also granted an exit visa to her old and ailing grandfather, who was seen as no threat to the Soviet system if living outside of Russia. He was seen more as a burden that they would be happy to have gone. Although reluctant to do so, Elena was able to settle her grandfather with some relatives in Switzerland while she made her way to Zion. She knew that she would have to become extremely active, and that she would be unable to caretake her beloved grandfather while living this role. The best solution was for him to be in the care of extended family while she engaged herself in trying to obtain the release of her father, mother, and sister.

Elena arrived in Israel with her new "husband". She immediately changed her name back to its original and began communicating again as the daughter of Dr. and Mrs. Mikael Pletnevsky. Elena was now the source of invitation from Israel to call her parents to the land. With Elena's invitation in hand the elder Pletnevskys re-applied for exit visas. They were immediately refused with the explanation that "you don't have *enough* close relatives in Israel". From this response, Elena knew that this fight would be long and hard.

Petite and fiery, she mustered all of her energies and prepared for all out war with the Soviets and their system. She had no idea how long it would last and how much it would cost to fight the battle. It would be a battle that would have casualties.

The Soviets were going to make a showcase of the Pletnevsky situation. It must be remembered that Dr. Pletnevsky was a former colonel in the Red Army. He had been one of their chief medical specialists. He was one of the firsts with such a high status who had made application to leave Russia. The Soviets were not about to allow this victory. Dr. Pletnevsky was well known and popular among his contemporaries. His application for an exit-visa sent shock waves among friends, acquaintances, and the Soviet system. If such a person is allowed to leave, it was felt that others would have even a better chance of leaving. This would create an increased flood of new visa applicants. And one does not apply for such a visa unless he believes that there is at least a chance.

It was November 1972, and Richard Nixon had been elected as President of the United States. The Soviets could now go back to some business as usual. The Jewish *refuseniks* came under more pressure. Leah Pletnevsky and her daughter, Victoria, headed for Moscow with other activists to petition the Supreme Court of Russia for the right to leave Russia. Every one in the activist group was arrested, and thrown into prison. It was normal to receive a 15-day prison sentence, simply for demonstrating. Most dissidents knew this, and were prepared to put up with the squalor and horrible conditions of a Soviet jail as well as any tainting of character that would occur as a result of such an arrest. Because of having made application to leave Russia, an applicant was already declared a social outcast. Having a jail sentence on his record made no difference.

Mother and daughter were separated during the imprisonment, and were given additional time that would increase their incarceration for 6 months. It did not go well with Leah. Earlier in her life, she had already experienced two heart attacks, and was diabetic. The prison stay inflicted much pain on both Leah and Victoria, almost completely dousing the fire within them to fight for their freedom.

Elena, now in Israel with her new "husband", continued her fight on as many fronts as she was able. She spoke for days with members of the Israeli government trying to convey to them the way that the Soviet system really worked. Many were interested and compassionate, but did not know quite how to help. As Elena continued her fight for her own family, she became a magnet for many others in Israel who had similar family situations in the Soviet Union. She found herself arguing their cause as well. Her "husband", also a good speaker and one who had good command of the English language, helped her.

Back in Russia, Dr. Pletnevsky was now being accused of experimenting medically on human beings. The Soviets were working hard to bring an accusation against him that would put him away and out of their hair for a long time. If they were successful in doing so, it would also squelch further activity among the Jewish *refuseniks* by sending a strong harsh message of the hammer and sickle government.

These hammer and sickle symbols, criss-crossed as the logo of the Soviet communist system, were meant to epitomize the grass roots of their communist ideal. The hammer and the sickle were tools of work, and in the hands of the masses would be the physical implements that would bring about a new societal order, guaranteeing a good life for all. The "system" however was far from the ideal. The hammer had become a tool of the State, and was used to bludgeon its citizenry into compliance and slavery. The sickle, instead of harvesting abundant fields of grain, was the State apparatus that would cut the legs out from any single citizen or group of citizens that were considered to be in opposition to the Soviet hierarchy.

In their twisted and perverse accusation of Dr. Pletnevsky, the Soviet hammer was being swung with the purpose of smashing any plans that the loyal doctor had of leaving Mother Russia, and smashing any energies or hope that percolated within the doctor's soul. It would also be used to smear his reputation as a military leader and doctor. In the process, it would be made to appear that the KGB was concerned over the welfare of its citizens and basic human rights, playing the part of the "white-hats" who were protecting the citizenry of Russia from criminals and trouble-makers like Dr. Pletnevsky and his family.

As Elena continued speaking out in Israel, she became a veritable dynamo of energy. Her visits to legislators and other Israeli leaders began to have effect. She was delighted when she received an invitation to go to the United States to lecture on the plight of Russian Jewry. The plans were executed as fast as they were made. As she honestly and innocently related the truth about what was happening to her family and many thousands of Russian Jewish *refuseniks*, she soon became a threat to the delicate diplomacies that existed between nations.

At the time, the Jackson Amendment was being considered for passage in the U.S. Senate and Congress. This was an amendment where Senator Henry "Scoop" Jackson had almost single-handedly held up a treaty that would grant trade credits and the commercial status of most-favored-nation to the Soviet Union. If the U.S. President did not certify a communist country as allowing 'unrestricted emigration', then the most-favored-nation status would be denied. It was a sensitive issue at the time, and many diplomats, including Secretary of State Henry Kissinger, felt that such an amendment would be a "step away from détente".

Prior to her briefings, Elena did not even know what the Jackson Amendment was, or who Senator Henry Jackson was. She was told not to mention this pending legislation in her talks. She was briefed and rebriefed by the Israeli Foreign Office on what to do and what to say, much as a young child might receive instruction from his parents when going into a new situation. An innocent child is not concerned with the fineries and sensitivities of diplomacy. If it itches, the child will scratch, wherever that might be. If something hurts, he'll say so, and let it be known to all around.

Elena was a proverbial child, an innocent in the arena of international politics. She had a message to speak. It was a message of truth, and it needed to be heard by those who could do something about the miseries being endured by Russian Jews. Human lives were at stake, and even if she had been educated in the delicacies of political diplomacy, this was not a time to be timid and super-sensitive, but blunt and searingly truthful.

In essence, although not officially appointed as one, Elena was now an ambassador for Israel and of the millions of Soviet Jews.. What she said and the way that she said it in any public forum, could have serious consequences for all of Israel. If she were to offend influential leaders in the United States, it might create relational troubles for Israel. If she was not forceful enough, her message might never be heard.

Elena's "husband" also toured the United States, both of them speaking to influential government people and others. Little by little, the right things were said to the right people, and backroom pressure was exerted all the way to Moscow. Elena's mother, Leah, and her sister, Victoria, had their 6-month prison sentences cut short. It was not soon enough, however. Victoria had contracted a severe case of tuberculosis while in jail, and Leah Pletnevsky had sunk into deep despair and depression.

The occasional phone call that Elena was able to get through to her parents did not reveal the gravity of trouble that was being endured. Although she was talking to her own flesh and blood parents, they had become the representatives of all Russian Jewry desiring to emigrate from Russia to Israel. Conversations that might have been deeply emotional that would have ministered to the depths of each party became superficial and dealt with the mechanics of visas and permits with some hope of getting many Jews out of Russia as well as her family. Leah Pletnevsky, although apparently in a deep depression, did not allow her daughter to hear this in her voice when talking on the phone.

While Elena continued to work diligently in the United States, her elder grandfather sat in Switzerland. He sat for days at a time, hoping to hear the good news that his daughter and son-in-law would be released from Russia, and that they would all, once again, be restored as a family. His 84-year old body had become extremely weak, due partially to the incredible emotional load that he carried. Only months before, he lost his wife. He had left the only country that he'd ever known and was re-located in another country whose language he did not speak. His family was all split up, with him in Switzerland, his daughter and son-in-law in Russia, and his granddaughter in the United States, battling for Soviet Jewry. The load was too much to bear, and this elderly man passed away...alone and forlorn.

Elena flew from the United States to attend his funeral. Her heart was torn all the more as she made contact with her mother and father in Russia. They were at the central post office in their hometown of

Novosibirsk on a hunger strike, demanding an exit visa to attend the old man's funeral in Switzerland. In despair over her grandfather's death, and now with the news that her parents and sister were on a hunger strike in Russia, she somehow found the energy to make an issue of this. If the West was not made aware of the plight of this family, it was certain that the Soviets would not reveal their own sins of tyranny. Elena would have to act fast.

She decided to hold her own hunger strike to join her parent's efforts in Novosibirsk. But where? She was informed that to accomplish a hunger strike in Geneva, would gain her no publicity or support. If she did so in Paris, the Arabs there would beat her up, and the French police would do nothing to help or protect her. This was the advice that she received from those who knew the situations around Europe. She decided to head for London and to begin her supportive hunger strike there. She called her "husband" who was continuing their speaking tour in the United States.

He answered the phone and heard the voice of his "wife". "We must start a hunger strike to support my parents and other Jews. I'll do one in London, and you do one in Washington, D.C. while my parents are conducting theirs in Russia."

"Elena, I don't think that this is such a good idea. I don't think that the Israeli government will appreciate this. It could be a problem in many ways." His reluctance soon turned to support, and the two on opposite sides of an ocean, hastily proceeded to organize their respective hunger strikes.

Elena flew to London, and contacted the Jewish activists there.

"I'm here, and I am going on a hunger strike in front of the Soviet Embassy."

"What? You can't do this without any preparation!"

"I don't need preparation to start fasting! Please write a placard for me. I won't need anything else from you."

The three hunger strikes were on...one in Novosibirsk, Russia, one in London, and another in Washington, D.C. They were timed perfectly, unbeknownst to Elena. Senator Henry Jackson needed such an event to call attention to those in the legislature as to the need and plight of Soviet Jews as they existed under a system of oppression gone mad.

The embassy buildings are in the middle of a park in London, and it is not a good location for pulling off a successful hunger strike. Elena decided upon an appropriate location near the Russian Embassy. She placed a phone call to the Emigration Office in Russia and told them what she was about to do on behalf of her parents and sister.

"If you will allow my parents and sister to leave Russia, I will not conduct this hunger strike."

"Go ahead and have your hunger strike! We don't mind. You can even die there, and we don't care. And remember...no matter what you do, your family will sit and rot here. We will never let them out!" The words stuck like knives in Elena's heart.

It was early March 1973 and the London days were cold and rainy, mixed with snow. Elena had received her answer from the Russians. She now had to follow through with her hunger strike.

Elena in London, and her "husband" in Washington, hunkered down for their fight. Elena sat on her chair in a London street with her placard. The weather was as miserable as it could be and was a living metaphor of what many Jews were enduring behind the Iron Curtain in Russia. Elena was without food, freezing cold, soaking wet, and miserable. The *refuseniks* in Russia, whom she represented, fared no better. The local Jews in London would come by and encourage her, bringing warm clothing and books to read. They fasted for 10 days, and the publicity received was excellent. It resulted in a U.S. State Department request to Moscow, specifically on behalf of Elena's parents. They asked the Russians to release this family.

Since this was so unusual, Elena in London, and her "husband" in Washington reasoned that they should give the Soviets some slack to respond to the State Department request, and not put them in a place where they would be humiliated in the public eye. They mistakenly called off their fast. Nothing happened. The Russians did not respond, and it became doubtful that the U.S. State Department even sent the request in the first place.

In Novosibirsk the situation was extremely serious. Elena's mother, who had had many other health problems, collapsed and fell unconscious in the middle of her hunger strike. Dr. Pletnevsky, striking with her, called for medical aid. The Soviet response was:

"When you stop the hunger strike, you will get help." The ambulance arrived at the scene where Leah Pletnevsky lay unconscious. The medical authorities stood there and watched, demanding that the hunger strike be called off before there would be any medical aid. The system was far more powerful and oppressive than the few who dared resist it. Dr. Pletnevsky called off the Novosibirsk hunger strike, and unconscious Leah received treatment.

Many of the Russian Jewish dissidents had been allowed to leave, and there was less and less support available for those like the Pletnevskys. The terrorizing continued. Dr. Pletnevsky was run down by an anonymous driver, but survived and healed from his injuries. The family dog was killed. Their phone was disconnected. There were constant threats and intimidation made against them. Other *refuseniks* that had already made application to leave Russia were afraid to offer aid to the high-profile Pletnevskys, out of fear that they would never be allowed to leave. Mikael and Leah Pletnevsky, along with their daughter, Victoria, were isolated as never before.

The only way to converse with her parents now, was for Elena to send a cable, letting her parents know at what time she would call them at the Central Post Office in Novosibirsk. When her parents would show up to receive her call, they would be told that no one had called her. Elena would be told that her parents were not at the Post Office facility to receive the call. It was more aggravation and torture to those who simply wanted to be together as a family and enjoy freedom in Israel.

This remained as the status quo for the Pletnevskys. They continued to live in isolation in their small apartment. Any phone conversation that might take place was normally cut off by those monitoring it. Dr. Pletnevsky, his wife Leah, and their daughter Victoria, continued to persevere. But they continued to become more weakened and disillusioned. Any thread of hope for release from their plight was dashed by the strength of the evil system under which they lived.

One of their heroes, a Jewish *refusenik* by the name of Alexander Dobrin continued to defy the Soviet system. He was a simple man with only moderate education, but a man who had a triple portion of courage. He continued to distribute anti-Soviet literature. He demonstrated relentlessly, and eventually was arrested and incarcerated. This inflamed the remainder of the Jewish dissidents who gathered all of their remaining resources and strengths. They began a whole series of letter-writing campaigns and hunger strikes. Their quarterback had been arrested and they would support him. The Pletnevskys, already down to the dregs of any energy remaining, poured out all for their inspiring leader.

Dobrin was released from prison and from the Soviet Union. He was gone, and the remaining *refuseniks*, their energies and resources spent, were without strong leadership. Their organizational fervor continued to flounder, and each of the *refuseniks* became more and more isolated.

The Pletnevskys were worn out physically and emotionally. The months of fighting the system had now turned into years. It was now May 1975. Leah Pletnevsky was now losing her mind. She became more and more controlling of her own husband and daughter, and more suspicious than ever of anything that was happening around them.

They locked themselves into their apartment, and had no dealings with the neighbors. For food, they would lower a small basket from their window, send down a few Russian rubles, and in turn receive some bread or other staples from co-operative passersby. They continued to barricade themselves in their apartment, receiving no visitors. The last letter to Elena, who was now back in Israel, warned her not to do any more demonstrating or hunger strikes, because this would work against them in their quest to get out of Russia. There were many contradictions in Leah's letter, which revealed her confused state of mind. Elena could only despair in the frustration of not being able to help.

Leah had taken control over the family now. Dr. Pletnevsky had lost almost half of his body weight from lack of food. His emotional state, although more logical, was nevertheless weak in the presence of his own disturbed wife. Victoria was going down fast. The Soviets were winning.

This isolation of darkness continued for four more years. The secluded and deluded threesome would continue to lower a basket from the window of their apartment to do their meager shopping with the help of others. They would receive minuscule supplies of bread and a few other foods, which kept them alive but not healthy. Eventually, the money ran out, and they bartered with their belongings in the same manner, never leaving the apartment.

The insanity of a system had now invaded the minds of its subjects. All was now lost. There was no health, no hope, no money, and no possessions...only a tyranny from without, that had now anchored itself within. Victoria was now losing her mind. The small family closed even the curtains of their apartment and lived in total darkness.

Dr. Pletnevsky was now in the clutches of a mentally ill wife and daughter. They were accusing him of being part of the KGB. When he defended himself, the accusations became worse. Attempts to reach the forlorn family were unsuccessful. Elena, upon hearing that someone would be going to Russia, would ask him or her to visit her family to find out the latest about them. Most were unsuccessful in even getting the Pletnevskys to open the door to their apartment. One or two of them had short dialogue, but found themselves facing an impossible situation.

In my interview with Elena, reliving these burning details of her life brought her to agonizing tears as we sat in her home in Zikron Yakov. She, as did so many Jews who had suffered and survived, asked punishing questions of herself. What if I had not left Russia when I did and had remained there to help them? Was there something else that I could have or should have done? Why were they so punished by the system, while some of the others were let out? If I had not made those speeches or stopped my hunger strike, would they have been released? The tormenting questions continued to bombard the mind of a rational and thoughtful woman, but these questions have no answers this side of heaven. She was left to bear the recollections of these events with the hope that the pain would somehow be disarmed. The memories would remain as a testimony to the evil of man's inhumanity to man, but also a hope that men, with God's guidance, could choose to rise above such depravity.

Because many of the Jewish activists had been punished so severely, and courageous leaders either put in prison or released from Russia, their zeal had been disarmed by the power of the Soviet system and their seemingly limitless resources to taunt and berate their own citizenry. Many who had struggled valiantly and many from the West who had lent an empathetic ear to the plight of these Jews began to lose interest when they were faced with a family like the Pletnevskys. They were so damaged by the system that they seemed beyond help from the ordinary person.

Dr. Pletnevsky, his wife, and daughter continued their agonizing existence. Elena, continuing to live in Israel, divorced her "husband" who had agreed to this arrangement simply to get Elena out of Russia. The two had accomplished magnificent things on behalf of suffering Soviet Jewry; however, the battle was still ongoing in the case of Elena's family. When Elena married Yakov, her parents, still in Russia, became convinced that he was a member of the KGB.

Although support from the public had waned in Elena's case, thankfully there were still some courageous and persevering senators and congressmen in the United States who supported her. They were finally able to get the Soviets to grant exit visas to her parents and sisters. It was now February 1979.

But it was too late. The Pletnevskys had been sitting in their darkened apartment for so long, that it was like living in a cave below the foundations of the earth. They had lost touch with reality. Word had reached them that their exit visas had been granted, and Dr. Pletnevsky rose up with all the emotional strength that he had with the goal of getting himself and his mentally deteriorated wife and daughter out of Russia. Arguments raged in the dark apartment. The visas were awaiting them, but Leah was convinced that it was a trick of the KGB.

Elena began to find out more and more about her family's real condition. Up to this point, she only had sketchy details of the condition of her family. Things were really worse than she had originally thought. The system had done its work.

The Soviets apparently felt that they had gotten their mileage out of the Pletnevsky case, and they did not now need a martyr. They began to go to other Jewish activists and solicit their help in getting the Pletnevskys out of their darkened apartment and on their way to Israel. Even when these activists visited and explained the situation to the Pletnevskys, Leah would not believe them, so convinced was she that it was all a trick and seduction on the part of the KGB to get them to leave their apartment so that they could kill them.

Dr. Pletnevsky had reached the end of himself and the situation. He decided that if his wife and daughter would not leave the apartment, he would. He had to physically fight with his own wife in order to open the door to his own apartment. He walked out, headed for the appropriate agency, and had his exit visa processed. He felt that if he could go to Israel, have some photos taken with his daughter Elena and send them back to his wife and daughter, that they would have to believe, and that they would soon follow. He was applying his own sane logical process, assuming that a mentally ill wife would see things through this matrix. It was not to be.

Dr. Pletnevsky made his way to Israel. He rendezvoused with his daughter Elena who had fought for him for so long. They immediately had pictures taken together and sent them back to Leah and Victoria. Instead of receiving the news for what it was, in their own pain and handicap of depression and mental illness, mother and daughter began another hunger strike. Leah died in the middle of a darkened apartment never having seen the freedom for which she had originally longed. The Soviet system had so damaged her that she was incapable of healthy reason and could not even claim the victory that was hers for the asking.

To add even another boulder of pain upon this mountain of tragedy, Victoria, who was also sick and fragile, knocked on a neighbor's door to ask for help when her mother died. Victoria was then hospitalized. The Soviets considered that a hunger strike was a suicide attempt, and were treating her in this manner. After a few days Victoria walked out of the hospital, and none of the staff missed her.

She went back to the neighbor's apartment, got the key to her own apartment, entered the darkened hovel where she had spent so much of her recent years. No one really knows what specific thoughts prevailed in her mind, but they were those of hopelessness and despair. She was now totally alone and for her the only way out of this living hell was suicide. Victoria hung herself.

It was reasonably quick, illogical to those whose minds are

functioning well, but so real and so final. This act became yet another testimony of what an evil system can do to people. There are those who have inner strengths that seem capable of resisting the very worst that man can conjure up. There are however, those whose inner resources are weak, and who need the daily aid of strong functional people to guide them through the miseries that have been inflicted upon them. No such help was available to Leah and Victoria. They became yet two more victims of the communist system that has been responsible for more than 130,000,000 deaths worldwide since its inception.

The official answers of the Soviets to any inquiries about Leah and Victoria were that they were *normal* people who did not want to leave the Russian motherland. Only *abnormal* people leave the Russian paradise, and that Leah and Victoria were forced into their final decision by the pressures from the outside of abnormal people who had agreed to leave the Soviet Union, so the lie would continue.

Doctor and Colonel Mikael Pletnevsky did get to see his daughter, Elena. He lived to see and reside in Zion. He was able also to practice medicine in his own field. He died in 1986 of a heart attack.

Elena and her husband, Yakov, have raised their own family in Israel. Together, they often have spoken out on the plight of Soviet Jews and spent untold energy to help new Russian *olim* (immigrants to Israel) as they made adjustments to their new life in Zion.

Yakov has recently passed away. He lived his life with integrity and honor, and was a bastion of courage under the worst of circumstances. Elena, equally courageous, continues the work of helping Russian immigrants and staying abreast of conditions in the former Soviet Union.

# 12

# ......AND OTHERS.....

Our telephone conversation between Jerusalem and Ramat Aviv was a short one. I insisted that I would drive to meet Avi, while at the same time he insisted that he would come to Jerusalem to meet me. Finally, overcome by his insistence, I gave in and agreed to meet him in Jerusalem at the Windmill Hotel.

I waited in the hotel lobby and Avi arrived on time. He deftly maneuvered his wheelchair and we went to a quiet corner of the hotel lobby where we could get to know each other.

Avi had been born in Poland in 1921. He was 18 at the time the Nazis overran the nation. He had a Zionist vision from the time he could remember. There was something and someplace beyond Poland to which destiny called. His Polish village was very small, and unlike other towns when the Germans came through, they did not bother to put the Jews on trains and send them to labor camps and gas chambers. They simply shot them all there in the village, and buried them in a mass grave.

Avi, however, having felt the first breezes of the winds of war coming through Poland, and having believed that Hitler would try to do what he said he would do, took the message to heart and left Poland before the Germans swept through his boyhood village. Most others stayed behind, and because of these respective decisions, Avi is alive, and the rest of his family and fellow villagers were executed.

The pit of pain and anguish endured by Jewish families is often obscured by glossing over the personal details of an entire community that disappeared at the business end of German firing squads. Behind every callous "here-today-gone-tomorrow" statement about the horrors suffered by the Jewish community, there are rivers of tears and welled-up memories that continually batter the souls of those who survived.

Avi's new life in the Promise Land started with beaching a small ship loaded with refugees. This group of immigrating Jews ran their ship aground on the shoreline of British-held Palestine as their first footprint on the land of Zion in 1939. Avi soon became part of the British Army and served in a variety of historic battles as a soldier in the Jewish Brigade. He endured a year of combat while fighting the Italians in Ethiopia. From there he was in the Western Sahara, taking part in some of the most significant battles of World War II, fighting the Germans at Tobruk, Benghazi, and El Alemain. In these few statements of fact, are bound up a barge-load of painful memories and sufferings that would fill volumes.

An already seasoned combat veteran, he was in on the invasions at Salerno, Albania, fought in Greece, and in Yugoslavia. Right at the end of the war, Avi and his platoon commander were on a routine patrol. After all the battles of North Africa, Southern Italy and the hundreds of combat miles covered on foot, one mis-step changed Avi's life permanently. His foot triggered a land mine, and in a split second he found himself turned upside down and heaved to the ground. His legs had been blown off at the knees. His officer, in shock himself, tried to carry Avi, but finally had to leave him and run for help.

Avi was placed in a hospital in Italy, where surgeons patched him up and where a nurse who would soon become his wife led him through rehabilitation. The two returned to Palestine in November 1947, just after the United Nations had agreed to partition the land so that the Jews would finally have a homeland.

The Arab nations, not receptive to the idea of a Jewish homeland, stepped up their attacks on the Jewish settlers. Wherever the Jews were...they were attacked...Haifa, Jerusalem, Tel Aviv, Tiberias, wherever. Avi, because of his extensive combat and commando training, now without legs, continued to serve his people in training them and preparing them for the inevitable war which would come in 1948.

With the background already set, and with the majority of the nations of the world in agreement, Israel made her declaration of independence on the 14th of May 1948. On the 15th of May, she was attacked by 5 Arab nations, and she fought long and hard during this War of Independence to keep from being annihilated as a new-born who had not yet learned to walk as a nation.

After the Six-Day War of 1967, where the Israelis had totally decimated the Egyptian armies and taken over the entire Sinai Peninsula, Avi became one of the first settlers of the newly acquired land. He had settled in an area called Neu Bar, on the road to Sharm el Sheik. Avi's new war was that of isolation, with few like himself willing to settle on land that was part of the spoils of war. Handicapped as he was without legs, Avi, with his wife and sons, made their choice together to bear the burden of being pioneers.

The years passed and Avi's family grew. His three sons were the pride of his life, possessing the fervor of pioneers, front-line people who were never content with sitting around and letting life pass them by. They were young, vibrant, full of life, and they too took their turn in serving their people. As a proud father, Avi noted their strength and dedication to Israel. They had been taught to appreciate and love their land, and to know that to preserve it from their enemies would take a constant vigilance and willingness to stand strong in the face of enemy opposition. They were now taking their part as human guardians of Israel. They were strong, well trained, and in their army uniforms projected the appearance of youthful invincibility.

It was 1973. The Syrians in the north, and the Egyptians on the southern front had been massing their troops along the borders of

Israel. The Israelis, still confident over their victory in the Six-Day War of 1967 saw the military maneuvers dangerously close to their borders, but concluded that these maneuvers were only "smoke and mirrors", designed to irritate and provoke, but of no real threat to Israel. It was this kind of thinking that enabled Hitler to inflict so much pain on the Jewish people. It was the false optimism or the wishful thinking of the Jews to continue to believe that the next threat would be a false alarm. They believed that their neighbors wouldn't really attack...especially so close to the highest holy day of the year, *Yom Kippur*, the Day of Atonement.

Israeli leaders allowed their military units to be reduced to bare-bone levels, as thousands of soldiers, sailors, and pilots went home for the holidays to be with their families. Synagogues were filled, much as the churches are in America on Christmas and Easter. The Jews were observing this important time, some simply out of tradition, others truly seeking the God of Abraham, Isaac, and Jacob, renewing their trust in Him and calling on Him to forgive their sins. A peace had settled over Israel, but it was not to last.

Arab tank commanders who knew their battle plans waited anxiously for the go-ahead signal to execute those plans. Anwar Sadat, the president of Egypt gave the word, and the attack was on. The Syrians from the north began to roll into and over the Golan Heights. In the south, Egyptian units drove quickly into Israel with ferocity. Frantic calls from the few Israeli troops who were guarding the borders were at first met with disbelief. But it was reality. Front line radiomen screamed into their Comm sets and telephones, to unbelieving ears in Israel's command posts.

"Kaen, kaen, (Yes, yes) I KNOW it is Yom Kippur!"........."Yes, the Arabs are attacking from the north and from the south!"

The call had gone out all over Israel. The Arab attacks were furious, and the outnumbered and unprepared Israelis had to fall back in the face of the oncoming tanks and troops.

Israeli men left their families at home while others ran from their synagogue services. They reached into the backs of their closets for their M-16's and reported to their duty stations. They drove cars, buses, trucks and anything that would speed them to their assigned duty stations. In that the Israelis were totally caught by surprise, the

Syrian tank commanders moved with lightning speed into Israel. They moved so quickly and with such ease that they feared a trap. They stopped their "blitz" and waited.

Although they did not know it, Israel was truly unprepared at the time. There was no Israeli defense plan that had been designed to allow the Syrians to penetrate so deeply into Israeli territory that Israeli forces could outflank them, surround them, and defeat them. The fear within the Syrians at this point in their own attack plan was unfounded, but this basic of human emotions was enough to put on the brakes. The Syrians mistaken decision to slow down and stop gave the Israelis just enough time to mobilize and begin the arduous task of driving their enemies from their land.

During the ensuing battles, Avi received a telegram. All three of his sons were on the front lines. One was in the south facing the Egyptian army, and two were in the north facing the Syrians on the Golan. The telegram was a typical government communiqué. "Dear Sir.....We are sorry to inform you that your son, Asher, has been seriously wounded while fighting in the Sinai. He is at present being tended to at Haddasah Hospital......."

Avi, a son of Israel, having fought many a battle during World War II, having trained many of the soldiers in the Haganah in the early years of Israel's armed forces, and having fought the front line battle of living without legs for so many years, received three such telegrams. The first two inflicted great pain. Both of these sons were officers. One had his eye burned out from the shrapnel of a phosphorus shell. The other was wounded enough to be hospitalized, but eventually made a full recovery.

Avi's pride and joy, Yair, a 22-year old young man at the prime of his life was the subject of the third telegram: "Dear Sir: We are sorry to inform you that your son, Yair, was killed in battle on the Golan. His body will be sent........"

The news totally stunned Avi. It was news that would cause the strongest of men to sit down. Avi however, had been sitting down for years, looking at the stumps that were once legs that had been left to an enemy mine in Italy. Two sons wounded, and now the youngest, killed in action! Rage, anger, despair, fear, and depression all flooded the soul of this already broken Israeli. It felt like two daggers plunged into the belly of an already wounded man, followed by a lance to the heart, but he was still alive and crippled with pain. The emotional gaffs continued to tear the fibers of his soul. If one's soul could bleed, Avi's would have poured forth a tankcar of blood.

I was reminded of the biblical account of the Jewish Patriarch, Jacob. He must have felt completely dejected when his sons lied to him about the fate of their youngest brother, Joseph. The conspiring brothers, who had sold him into slavery, handed Joseph's multi-colored tunic to their father. The coat had been carefully splattered with the blood of a goat that the brothers had killed. They told their father, that some wild beast had no doubt devoured Joseph. The Scriptures tell us that Jacob could not be comforted as he pondered and mourned the death of his favorite son.

Avi was still without legs and in a wheel chair. Two of his sons were seriously wounded, and the third, his youngest, was dead. Yair was buried with full military honors at Mt. Herzl in Jerusalem, and even years later was the focus of Avi's thoughts as he drove his car from Ramat Aviv to Jerusalem to meet me for this interview.

There would be additional bad news for Avi. After the stunned Israelis pulled their forces together, they drove the Egyptians back through the Sinai Desert. The Syrians were driven back from the Golan. It would not be long before the world would side with Israel's enemies and pressure them into giving back the land that they had won with the blood and courage of their own sons, and this after their enemies had initiated a surprise attack against them. The Sinai was being given back yet again, to Israel's enemy, after it had been won in a war of defense. Because Avi had become one of the settlers in the area of the newly won territory, he had to pull up roots once more. Political compromises had been made and treaties had been negotiated. The land on which Avi had settled, was to be given back to Egypt. The price of peace was very high for Israel, yet its reality seemed always elusive.

Avi's life is a proverbial microcosm representing all of Israel. In many ways, Israeli legs have been blasted out from under them, leaving them with little or no support in this world. Over the centuries, they have been deeply wounded by the rejection of the nations. They have lost their sons in the many wars that have been fought against them. They have endured hundreds of terrorist attacks and murders both in Israel and throughout the world, by men whose minds have been filled with beliefs and philosophies born out of evil. Although ravaged in spirit, soul, and body, the Jewish people continue on, a testimony of their own courage and perseverance but a greater testimony to the faithfulness and promises of God.

Today Avi's dream is to develop a resort area for handicapped people. It would be a place where all would be welcome, no matter how severe the handicap. It would be a place of recovery, rejuvenation, and total acceptance, for all who are broken in spirit, soul, or body. May Avi realize his dream.


## LETTER TO MIRIAM

My wife and I stood in the long line at the Frankfurt Airport waiting to board a flight to Tel Aviv. The silver-haired lady who stood behind us lived in Israel, and had just finished a visit to some friends in Germany. She had not been in Germany for a long time, and had been able to escape its troubles during the years of World War II. She did not endure the physical atrocities of the German concentration camps, but endured the horrible losses of family members who did. This "chance" meeting at an airport resulted in an invitation to her home in Haifa, where she shared much of her own life, and introduced us to other Israelis whose stories are in this book.

Probably one of Miriam's most prized possessions, is a letter, written by her mother, Elizabeth, during those terrible years of the war. Her mother was working at various domestic jobs here and there, hoping only to be able to buy some food, and to keep from being picked up by the German officials and sent away. The letter was written by a despairing woman as she awaited her fate at the hands of Nazi murderers. The letter to Miriam was written over a period of several months, her mother adding a few sentences here and there to eventually complete it. She eventually mailed it, and Miriam received it.

Miriam translated it aloud from German to English. To this day, Miriam does not know the full story of how her mother came to her end. She knows only that her mother was taken to a Gestapo cellar, and that was as far as she was able to trace her. Her mother's letter is as follows:

My darling daughter,

For many weeks, on each night I have written long letters to you in my thoughts. To you, in these letters of thought, I write about the dreams that have never come true. But now, it is one minute before midnight. At any moment I may have the same fate as the rest of the Jewish population from our Fatherland (Germany), and this is almost too horrible to contemplate.

I sit with a packed rucksack and my bedding and a little suitcase, but I do not know if I can carry this to the last destination. And I do not know what is awaiting me. I am cowardly in one sense, because maybe the little bit of hope that I have to see you again keeps me from performing the "final solution" on myself. Should it happen that we see each other again, then it will have been worthwhile.... this last and very hard struggle in my life.

Whatever may happen, please don't be sad. I am not alone in this fate. It is always so difficult to write in a few words what is happening, knowing that it may be months before you receive the letter.

We have had very little correspondence, but I can tell you one thing, it has not been so bad until now...only the state of my soul. Now all of my financial reserves are gone, but nothing is important anymore because of this last journey. It takes all of the strength that I can find to overcome my state. Bernard (a cousin) promised me last week, a visa for Ecuador, but I telegraphed him that it is impossible to leave any longer. Should it happen that I am able to leave through some miracle, I will immediately leave.

A few months ago, it would have been possible to leave, but who could know about the development of all that is going on now? Leo (her mother's brother) tried to get a visa to Cuba, but now everything is closed and he cannot leave. Yesterday, I visited with him and his family, and you cannot imagine how the atmosphere was so sad everywhere. The day before yesterday, I visited Kate (mother's cousin). She has been very ill for a long time, but this is not so astonishing. She has been working in a factory very long hours.

(Weeks later the letter continues) Now they have taken Kate away, and her sister Lisa.....and that is it. We don't know where they have gone.

Another week has passed, and I am at least lying in a decent bed, and I am caressing it because of the joy that I can still lie down on it. Many ugly things have happened in this past week. Leo (mother's brother), was almost a part of it, but in the last moment something happened that caused him not to be made to go. In any case, we endured terrible fear and terror.

I don't know how long we will be able to endure this. Every day I have seen people prepare themselves for the last station. These are not nice things to see. I continue to console myself in the thought that this is happening only for an interim, and that better times will come.

Now six months have passed since the beginning of this letter. Leo was taken away four weeks ago and we have not heard from him or about him. Greta (mother's sister) and I should have gone also, but with these people (the ones for whom they did household labor) we still manage to stay here, and it is still a wonder that we can still do it week after week. I work in many households now, because all the people that can still work, are very necessary, and from this point of view, I could continue to live, because, thank God, I know how to work, and especially, I help with the sewing.

It is Pentecost now (an important holiday among Gentile Germany) and I have been with Greta for two days. It has been like a beautiful dream and I do not want to awaken. But I have to go back to go to my place of work. I do not make any money now, but I do receive food for my labor. With great fright I think of when I will not have anything more, perhaps not even food.

You cannot imagine how sorrowful I look at every new day to come, because every hour they can put me out of work and tell me to leave. How happy I am at the end of the day, when I find that the thing that I feared did not come to pass. I don't know how long my nerves will be able to take it. In the winter time, everything seemed easier. Now in the summer, it is not pleasant to go to my work. I have to risk a lot, even when I walk down the street.

My thoughts are always with you and around you, and I have the feeling that you are all right. How different we wish that everything could have been, but all is fate.

Be well my dear one. Everything well for the future, and if this letter comes into your hands, then it is my last sign of life, a last embrace, and a last greeting with many good wishes.

Love, Mom

During all of this time, Miriam, who had moved to Palestine, knew the distant terror of realizing that her father died and her mother was killed by the Germans. Added to this was the additional anguish that many of her cousins, uncles, and aunts also lost their lives at the hands of the Nazis.

Miriam is one of millions of Jewish people, who did not personally experience the cold steel of a Nazi bayonet, the lead of their bullets, or the fumes of their gas chambers, but who have lost almost all that was of earthly importance, their loved ones. They have had to live their lives with these emotional wounds, some of which have never healed, and which daily inflict deep pain.

# ROSE

We boarded the Pan Am plane in Miami, and prepared for the long overnight flight to Frankfurt, Germany. Our final destination was West Berlin, and the infamous Berlin Wall was still in place. West Berlin was an island of freedom surrounded by the tyranny of communist East Germany, but only about forty years earlier Berlin was the headquarters of one of the most evil demagogues of history. My wife, Hellen, and I sat a few seats away from Rose and Charlie. The trip was an adventure for all of us, but for Rose the adventure was also a battle.

Rose had been born a Jew, and was a teenager in World War II Poland. Of her entire immediate and extended family , only an aunt, a sister, and a few cousins survived those hellish years of World War II. Rose had endured the concentration camps of Poland, as well as both Bergen-Belsen and Dachau, Germany. The list of deceased family was a long one. Aunts, uncles, cousins, brothers, mother and father, even her six-year old sister........*all* were murdered, most at the Treblinka death camp in Poland. When Rose was liberated from Dachau, she was able to immigrate to the United States. She was a container of un-shed tears and terror that had not yet been assuaged.

Rose met and married Charlie, and together they raised a family in Philadelphia. Although life in the United States was pure pleasure, compared to that which Rose endured in Poland and Germany, it was pleasure only by comparison, and existed only on the outside. She was still a Jew in a predominantly Gentile world, and after the carnage that she had endured in Germany's death camps, she trusted no one who was not Jewish. The memories of the past continued to torment her, and the question "why?" became the prevailing word regarding any thought about her past. "Why was I chosen to live?" " Why did it have to happen?" "Why couldn't they have killed me too?" "Why did God allow this?" There were no answers....only more questions.

Rose and Charlie continued to raise their family. As their children grew, they were exposed to all of the usual things of the world, new ideas, and new movies, both good and bad. They were also exposed to Christian thought. As Jewish offspring, they were caught between that which the Christians were claiming, and that which the rabbis taught at the synagogue and the traditions of the Jewish home.

One of Rose's daughters came home as a young teenager. She had with her a number of booklets that told about Jesus. She made the statement, "Mama....I think that Jesus is the Messiah." Rose became enraged. She took the literature brought into her home by her offspring, and threw it into the garbage can. To Rose, Adolf Hitler and his followers were Christians. To become one of them, or to even entertain the ideals or thoughts of these Gentiles, was to desecrate her home. It was terrifying that her own daughter could not see the damage that she was inflicting upon the family, and that as a young Jewish girl she was embracing the ideas and thoughts of the Hitlers of the world, and their "Jesus".

After what Hitler's "Christians" had done to Rose and her family, she would embrace a good old fashion atheist any day, rather than a "Christian". Her mind was set. There would be no more bibles and no more Jesus literature brought into the house. As time passed, not only her children believed in Jesus as their Messiah, but her husband, Charlie also came to this conclusion.

Rose's health had been poor. Her emotional wounds had never been healed, and they were taking their toll even in her physical body, resulting in aches, pains, and surgeries. There were people who were brought into her life however, that were praying for her and who continued gently to encourage her to give consideration to the idea that Jesus really is the Jewish Messiah. What Hitler and his followers did had nothing to do with the real Jesus. Jesus was a Jew. He was a Jew in the best of tradition and love. And the world cast Him out too. He could identify with Rose's pain.

Little by little she dared to utter His name in prayer. Little by little, as she read the New Testament, she met a Jewish Jesus, a suffering servant who only did good. As she began to understand, her emotional pain began to subside. The sky started to look blue again, and the colors and sounds around her took on new meaning and intensity as she continued to allow herself to be wooed by the **Ruach Ha Kodesh** (Holy Spirit). As she fell more in love with her Savior, He gave her more revelation of Himself and His ways. The process went on for several years.

Our plane started its descent. We had been flying through the blackness of night and dawn had now broken over Germany. Rose had remembered her vows as a teenager. She had sworn that after being freed from the German death camps that she would never utter a German word again, nor would she ever set foot on German soil. She would be breaking that negative vow today.

She continued to pray, as the plane touched down on the concrete runway of the Frankfurt Flughafen, asking for more grace from her King. She and her husband, Charlie, disembarked and we said good-bye to them for the time being. We would meet again in Berlin.

The Berlin Olympiad stadium was crowded with tens of thousands of European Christians and others like myself who had come from America and other parts of the world. The "Berlin for Jesus" rally was well underway, and there had already been signs that the Almighty was pleased with what He was seeing. The open stadium had been threatened with fairly heavy rain. Prayer went up, and a double rainbow appeared in the distance, visible by all in the stadium. There was rain in every direction, but at the stadium it was dry.

Rose walked to the speaker's platform in the middle of the grassy stadium, and faced the crowd of people from all over the world, the vast majority of whom were Germans. She had been in the land of Germany now for a few days, and had spoken a few German words in light conversation. It was now time to speak to the massive crowd. The little Jewish housewife began her story, speaking in English and being interpreted in German to the crowd.

She spoke of the atrocities perpetrated upon her people and specifically on her family. She told in brief terms, her struggle that lasted for years both physically and spiritually. She told the crowd that she would never be able to stand in Berlin on that day and speak her message were it not for the Jewish Savior who had entered her life and enabled her to speak the words that were yet to come from her mouth.

In summarizing her talk, and realizing that it was one of the highest callings of God, she spoke a message of forgiveness. "Germany...I forgive you! Germany...I forgive you!" Her amplified voice reverberated and echoed around the stadium.

I sat in the crowd and heard the sobs of grown German men and women. Tears welled in my own eyes as I sensed the Presence of God's Spirit working through the words of one of His ordained servants. The little housewife continued to speak to the hearts of Germans who had been bound up in a national guilt that had lasted for decades. While the self-righteousness of other nations of the world had often "rubbed the noses" of the Germans in the stench of their own recent history, Rose, the little Jewish housewife who had literally endured the atrocities that we have only read about, was speaking a message of forgiveness. Tears from thousands of eyes flowed down cheeks into handkerchiefs and dripped from bowed heads to the concrete steps undergirding the stadium seats, as the anointed words penetrated hard and secluded hearts.

More went on after Rose departed the speaker's platform. As she moved about on the grass, six German men came up to her, one at a time. The last one of the six spoke heavily accented English.

"Did you really mean what you said about forgiving the Germans?"

"Yes I did," Rose replied.

"What if you knew that I was a Nazi during World War II?"

"I still forgive you."

A long pause..."What if you knew that I was a guard at Dachau...in charge of punishment?"

Momentarily, questions flooded Rose's mind. "Was this the one who hung me by my wrists and who beat me and ridiculed me? Was this the one who put me in the sewage tank where I had to stand for 24 hours on my toes to keep from drowning in the slime of human waste? Could this be one of those who did the most horrible and unmentionable atrocities to her fellow Jews?"

She gritted her spiritual teeth, and gave no place for the vengeance that these questions invited. She chose with her will, and set her face toward her God. She looked at the elder German and answered,

"I still forgive you.....and I mean it!"

The wrinkled German, a former Nazi and a former guard at Dachau had carried his guilt for all these decades, and God used a little Jewish housewife, with His message of forgiveness, in the middle of the Berlin Olympiad Stadium, to set him free. He fell at Rose's feet, and heaved deep sobs. It was this same man who tracked down Rose at the Frankfurt Flughafen as she was about to board her return flight to America. Tearfully, he told her that he had slept a full night for the first time in over 35 years since he had taken part in the Nazi plan to murder and demean God's people. He had received the forgiveness that Rose had spoken over him.

During another visit to Germany, Rose was invited to visit the saintly evangelical woman, Basilea Schlenk, whose writings and ministry have influenced thousands throughout the world. Basilea presided over the *Marienschwestern,* (Sisters of Mary) in Darmstadt Germany, only a few kilometers south of Frankfurt. All during World War II, Basilea had been a deeply disappointed and God-fearing Christian. She knew that her nation was wrong, and that they were co-operating with evil. She led and ministered bible studies in a private home in Darmstadt throughout the war, and led small groups of like-minded Germans to minister especially to the Jewish people during and after the war.

In the closing days of World War II, Darmstadt had been severely and brutally bombed by the allied powers. It is recorded for all to see, the photo of the house where Basilea Schlenk had held her bible studies and prayer groups during the war. Everything in that particular neighborhood had been absolutely leveled by the bombings. The house where Basilea and her fellow Christians had prayed stood unscathed, alone and tall, mid the rubble of the surrounding houses and buildings which had been reduced to random heaps of bricks, broken beams, and shattered glass. One can draw his own conclusions over this relatively obscure fact of history.

Years after the end of World War II, Basilea Schlenk was celebrating Christmas with the Order of Mary Sisters whom she led. To help them build their own faith, she suggested that each sister write down a request that they would like God to answer. They were to seal this request in an envelope and lay it at the foot of the manger setting that had been assembled for display during the Christmas season. Each sister of the Order did just that. Basilea Schlenk wrote her own request, sealed the envelope, and laid it by the manger scene.

She had sealed the envelope some time in the late 50's. When Rose made her visit to the weakened Basilea Schlenk, the elderly servant of God asked that one of the sisters go to fetch the envelope that she had in safe-keeping all those years. She opened the envelope in the presence of Rose, her honored guest, announcing that Rose was the answer to her request and prayer to the Lord, made more than 20 years earlier.

Basilea had asked the Lord during that Christmas season to someday allow her to meet a Jewish woman who had come to know Jesus as her Messiah, and one who was going about speaking and teaching His Word. Rose became the answer to Basilea Schlenk's prayer.

Since that time, Rose has traveled extensively, bringing the message of reconciliation to Christians and Jews in the United States and other nations throughout the world.

## ANNE

There are always those critics who have listened to the lies of those who are insanely hostile to the Jews, as if for them to admit to the facts of history, would somehow destroy their own personhood. "Theories," however bent and twisted, have been proposed in many varieties of anti-Semitic literature. Some propose that the Holocaust never occurred, and that the whole thing was a plot of the Jews to win sympathy for themselves. Other absurd statements even contend that the mountains of photos, films, documents and testimonies are fabrications of clever Jewish political and media types. Supposedly, all of this was done for some fabricated Jewish plot to overtake and control the world.

To people who have allowed such thinking to infest their minds, no amount of evidence will convince them otherwise. They are self-deceived and focused on hating the very people that God ordained as His own. Only a miracle from above could break the darkness of such bondage. People such as these could stand on the rim of the Grand Canyon, overlooking its vastness of color, stamina and size and still insist that it is all an illusion of laser lights and a movie screen.

Because some of the readers of this book may be deeply cynical and leaning towards the type of thinking that I just described, I felt that it would be important to include the testimonies of a couple of individuals who were brought into my path who are not Jewish, but who saw with their own eyes some of the realities that are discussed in this book. Anne is one such person. We sat together surrounded by the beauty of the Rocky Mountains at a convention facility called Glen Eyrie in Colorado Springs.

Anne, who now lives in Canada, was 12 years old at the time of the German occupation of Holland. The early part of the occupation was not bloody. There had been rumors and stories that floated among the Dutch about the possibility of the Germans coming to their unique little country, but up until then there had only been stories.

But, the day arrived. Anne had gone to bed on the night of May 9th, 1940. She awoke to find German soldiers all throughout her hometown of Assen. They had suddenly appeared. There were no explosions or shootings...just lots of ordinary soldiers of the German *Wehrmacht*. The relative calm would not last long however, as the Germans began sending in their Gestapo and SS troops. Arrests and interrogations became commonplace. Dutch citizens who were not perceived as being co-operative and compliant were taken out of circulation. Hitler's vision of eliminating the Jews also became real, and soon the Jews were required to wear the Star of David on their clothing. Anne saw some of her friends and neighborhood merchants humiliated by the increasing squeeze of the German occupation.

Just before the occupation of Holland, the Dutch government issued statements to the Dutch citizenry that there was more than eight years worth of basic food stored for the nation. The communiqués explained that there was no need to worry, even if perchance the German war machine should come their way. Apparently, The Dutch were not the only ones that heard the announcements. When the Germans occupied, ration cards were issued to everyone, and the raid on the food supply began. Germans were the first that were allowed to shop on any given day. They had no restriction on what or how much could be bought. Afterwards, the local Dutch were allowed in the stores to purchase what was needed for the day. When that was accomplished, the Jewish people were allowed to shop, for a maximum of one hour a day. Over a period of several months, the food supply that had been put away by the Dutch, had been removed and shipped eastward for German consumption.

The black market also flourished in such an atmosphere, and a slogan emerged among the language of the Dutch that gave expression to the realities of life. *"Nicht in der vinkel, alles in der kelder."* (Nothing in the store, but everything in the cellar). It was the Dutch version of an expression I encountered when visiting the communist country of Poland in the mid-80's. Their version of the same reality translated to "Nothing in the shops...everything in the homes." Despite the efforts of a tyrannical government to control the people and economy, the people would find a way to trade and barter.

As a nation, the Dutch did well in resisting the German occupation. They had a well-organized and loyal underground that saved thousands of Jewish lives. But, as with any group of people, there were also some collaborators, willing to co-operate with anyone or anything that would enhance their position. There were also those who seemed to collaborate, but whose very private missions were dedicated to preserving lives.

One such "collaborator" ran a small bar and restaurant in Assen. He worked day and night to keep his business going and serve his customers, many of whom were German soldiers. The local populace began to hate Jan, who owned and operated the bar. He welcomed the Germans, sang songs, listened to their jokes and laughed with them. His theatrical performance earned him the wrath of many of his neighbors as they judged him for serving and collaborating with their enemy. It was only after the war, when charges were to be brought against him, that Jan's real life surfaced. While he entertained and hosted the German soldiers and tolerated their presence, he earned as much money as he could from them. In the stables behind his restaurant, Jan housed and fed an entire Jewish family for the full period of the war, right under the noses of the German occupiers. He had endured the hostility and rejection of many of his own neighbors and friends throughout the wartime period, knowing that to try to explain himself to anyone, might have meant the betrayal of those whom he protected.

The Dutch were extremely loyal to their own people and nation. They had little or no tolerance for those among them that gave any comfort to the German occupation. According to Anne, when Germans would walk down the street, the Dutch would not even look at them, would turn their backs on them until they were past, or would go out of their way to avoid them, not out of fear, but out of disdain. They were very hard on their own. When Dutch girls were caught flirting with or having romantic affairs with German soldiers, the Dutch would often capture the girls, shave their heads, and send them back into their own society, wearing their badge of shame.

As the initial German occupation became more entrenched and the Germans took control of everything, the liquidation of the Jews became a priority. The Dutch underground worked feverishly to hide their Jewish friends and neighbors, however, the Germans were far ahead of them in many instances. The Germans herded the people into holding areas like Westerbork, loaded them on trains, and shipped them to the death camps in Germany and Poland.

In addition to sending the Jews to death camps, the Germans also commandeered the young and healthy males of the non-Jewish Dutch population. Many were sent back to Germany to work in German factories in the war effort. Others were conscripted to work for the Germans within Holland. Anne's father, Willem, was one such man, and was put on a team of inspectors that would inspect the rail yards and the railroad tracks for any bombs that might be planted by the Dutch underground. These bombs would disrupt the flow of military supplies and troops coming west, and stop the flow of the Jews headed east. Willem did his job daily, appearing to be working for the German machine, but in the nighttime hours he went with his fellow Dutchmen in the resistance movement and helped them to set up the explosives that would cut the rails and slow the German war effort. He and his staff would occasionally "discover" a bomb that was planted and report it to the German authorities to help keep their own cover.

It was during his long walks along the railroad tracks that this

Dutch servant would observe the trainloads of Jews rolling along on their way to their death. He could see the anguish on faces that might be pressed against any gap in the wooden slats framing the train cars.

He would come home each night with large quantities of letters and notes that had been tossed out of the rolling trains. These notes and letters were often the last words that would be communicated to friends and family. Some were clipped or tied to fountain pens or other objects that had some weight, causing the letter or note not to be swept under the train and be lost or damaged.

Willem would carefully gather up every note, letter, pen or pencil that he found, bring them home and lovingly sort them all out, and deliver the messages to the families of the Jews who were being herded to their slaughter in the East. Anne remembers reading many of these notes and letters that were to children and other family members that were being hidden by the Dutch underground. Unfortunately, there were also notes that were vindictive in nature. Some of these notes revealed the locations of other Jews who were still in hiding, probably spurred into existence by the jealousies that so often affect human beings. Sadly, it was someone Jewish turning on another Jew. When such a note or letter was discovered, Willem would destroy it.

One such letter was almost like a small parcel, and tied to it was a beautiful fountain pen. It had been hurled from a passing train by desperate parents on their way to German concentration camps. An attached note said, "Whoever finds this, please make sure that this letter gets into the hands of my children, and whoever finds this and sends on the letters, may keep the fountain pen." Through his connections, Willem sent the letters to the rightful people. He also sent along the fountain pen. The two children to whom the letters were addressed, sent the fountain pen back to Willem. The children had gotten their message from their parents whom they would never see again. Willem kept this pen throughout his life as a reminder of those dark and sinister years of World War II.

As the Jews continued to be rounded up in the various neighborhoods around Anne's home, there were as many stories as there were people. Some went compliantly to the gathering points where they were boarded on trains and sent to their deaths. Others, seeing no hope in any of this, would put their children to bed at night, turn on their gas stoves without lighting the burners and commit suicide.

Assen was about six kilometers from the infamous Westerbork, where the Nazis would round up the Jews and board them on trains. Sometimes, due simply to the overcrowding at the Westerbork station, the Jews would be marched from Westerbork to Assen. Anne watched the old, the young, and pregnant mothers, each carrying a small bag or suitcase and wearing their Stars of David as they headed for the trains. She watched as the Germans would stuff more and more Jewish people into the cattle cars to where there was no room to do anything but stand. She listened to the Germans yelling to each other, "There's more room in this car.....We've got space for ten or fifteen more over here". She watched them push and prod more and more people into each of the cattle cars.

Anne watched as her father and many of the Dutch townspeople tried to stop this Nazi nightmare on one particular day. While the Jews were being marched to the railroad station at Assen, the townspeople tried to create a "traffic jam" of people. They waded into the streets near the station, so that the marching Jews would not be able to get through to the trains. There was also the chance that a few of the Jews would get lost in the crowd and could be pulled away from almost certain death and hidden with other Dutch families. The effort was stopped with a few machine gun bursts from the Germans. The soldiers fired above the heads of the people, and it became apparent that without weapons, it would only be another blood bath in the streets. The effort would not spare the Jews from the train rides to the death camps. The Dutch crowd had two choices...disperse and go home, or die from machine gun bullets.

Anne recalled other tragedies in her childhood. One of the teachers in her Christian school made some remarks in his class about the Germans, the occupation, and the handling of the Jewish people. Unfortunately, one of the students was the child of a Dutch collaborator who co-operated dutifully with the Germans, causing the deaths of many Dutch who were doing their best to defy the Third Reich. After the teacher had made his statement, the student who heard it informed his father.

The teacher greeted his family that evening and recounted the things that he had said in the classroom that day, anticipating out loud, "You know...I wouldn't be a bit surprised if they come and arrest me tomorrow." His words spoken to his wife were prophetic. In the school the next day, the Gestapo showed up, arrested the teacher, and he died of a heart attack before he was taken into custody. In deep grief and strain, his wife collapsed and died the next night. The two of them left eight children.

The double funeral took place. Eight orphaned children felt the horror of losing both of their parents at the same time. After the funeral, discussions ensued about what to do with the eight children. The sister of the dead woman, who had twelve of her own children had no question in her own mind. She took on eight more without hesitating.

This same Dutch collaborator continued his work of uncovering his fellow Dutchmen who were involved with fighting the Germans. Karl, one of Anne's neighbors, had a radio receiver and transmitter. He was very instrumental in finding downed Allied pilots and getting them back to England. Just outside of Assen there was a very large motorcycle race track that was well paved and long. It made a perfect clandestine landing strip for small aircraft to pick up downed fliers. Karl was instrumental in setting up many such rescues.

This information about Karl found its way to the same collaborator that had caused the death of the school teacher. The German Gestapo came to Karl's house at noon one day, and literally tore it apart from the inside. They found the radio. They took Karl and his four sons for a quick interrogation. They never returned home. His fifth son had not yet come home. Two days later, Karl and four of his sons were observed by another Dutch member of the underground who hid in the woods. The Germans drove them in a truck to an off-limits forest near Assen. There were nine other male prisoners with them. Karl and his sons were observed to dig their own graves. When they finished this father and four of his sons knelt down, prayed, and the Germans gunned them down along with the nine others and buried them.

Anne continued to share that in spite of the brutal horrors of war, there are often humorous and clever acts of humanity that are worthy of note. One such story regards Mr. Ganz, a Jewish shoe store owner in Assen. The Nazis knew him and his name was on a list to be deported. In anticipation of this possible deportation, Mr. Ganz came to Anne's uncle, and asked if her uncle would be kind enough to take care of his inventory of shoes, so that he might reclaim them when the war was over. Mr. Ganz had the faith that he would somehow survive. Anne's uncle answered in the affirmative and arrangements were made to store Mr. Ganz's shoes.

Mr. Ganz also made arrangements with another friend of Anne and her family, and they too agreed to store an inventory of Mr. Ganz's shoes. At the end of the war, shoes were extremely scarce and people were in great need of such items. No one had seen Mr. Ganz, and assumed that he might have met the same fate as 6,000,000 other Jews.

Anne's uncle went to his storage facility and decided to look through some of the shoes to see if any could be used for friends or family that were in need. As he opened the boxes, he discovered that all the shoes that he had were "left" shoes. A similar scene was being repeated in another storage facility unknown to Anne's uncle. There, the man who had agreed to store Mr. Ganz's shoe inventory discovered that he possessed all "right" shoes. Neither of the men who stored Mr. Ganz's shoes knew each other, but both knew Anne and her family. Loyal Dutch had hidden Mr. Ganz deeply underground, and he showed up one day to reclaim all of his shoes. In his own clever way, he preserved his shoe inventory from possibly being pilfered throughout the war, and used this inventory to get back into business as soon as he was able to make his survival public.

Anne saw with her own eyes the thousands of Jewish people that were paraded through the streets to the trains. She sat in her own home with her father and read and sorted the hundreds of notes and letters tossed from the trains by desperate people, most of whom were on the last journey of their lives. She knew many of the Jews in her own neighborhood who never came home from their forced journey on the train, and some, who in desperation and hopelessness, took their own lives rather than submit to the humiliation and degradation of a Nazi death camp.

While Anne would be the first to acknowledge that not only Jews, but also Dutchmen and other Europeans suffered deeply at the hands of the Germans, it was also apparent that so much of the focus of this war was pointed at the Jews. The Jewish people were singled out and put to death, not for bearing arms against an aggressor nation, or for taking strong stands politically, but for simply being born Jewish. That was their "crime".Anne saw it with her own eyes, and gives trūe testimony that the Jews were singled out, and they were punished and killed as sheep being led to slaughter.

## CARL

I heard about Carl from one of my friends. I made a call to his store in a small town in southern Georgia. He answered the phone personally, invited me to meet with him, and gave me directions. I arrived at the store at closing time. He then led me to his home where I spent some hours with him, learning about his life, in order to bring some of his story to you, the reader. He is another non-Jew whose personal experience gives credence to the hell lived by the children of Zion.

Carl is no ordinary man and was no ordinary soldier. As I viewed his collection of medals and battlefield awards, I knew that this man had "been there". He is mentioned several times in Stephen Ambrose's book, "D-Day June 6, 1944: The Climactic Battle of WWII". Carl was wounded four times in battle, and after each period of recovery, went right back to the front where his expertise as an infantry soldier was needed.

He has four Purple Hearts, several Bronze Stars, and numerous other awards and campaign ribbons. He has also been inducted into the American Order of the French Croix de Guerre. He was a paratrooper and as an infantryman, stood out among his peers. Credible as a leader, he was given a battlefield commission as a 1st Lieutenant. He became the #1 team leader of the Regimental Intelligence and Reconnaissance of the 501st Parachute Infantry Regiment of the 101st Airborne Division.

Carl often found himself way out ahead of the Allied front lines, and in enemy territory. He was often so close to German soldiers at night that he could hear them breathe. He also faced many enemy soldiers eyeball to eyeball and survived the confrontation while his adversary was slain. He saw the blood and the guts of war, lived its terror, and today the memories are still as real as the actual scenes that took place fifty-plus years ago. He is still able to shed tears when reliving the emotion-stirring moments of preparation for battle, as well as the battles themselves. I found him to be a tough loyal soldier that any army would be privileged to have, but still tender-hearted and concerned for his fellow man.

As the battles of World War II raged, Carl, more often than not, found himself on the cutting edge of these battles. His unit fought in the southern regions of Germany, and Carl became one of the first American soldiers to discover Hitler's bunker and underground tunnel system below the infamous "Eagle's Nest". Hitler and his cohorts could see all over Southern Germany from its heights. Although a place of beauty and splendor, it was a haven for demagogues who made evil plans.

Because of its isolation and almost total privacy for Hitler, it was also the storehouse for the riches of art, gold, and silver that were pilfered during the war effort. Hitler had trained, or instilled enough fear in his followers, that they would ensure that these valuables reached the destination of Hitler's treasury. As Carl made his way through the underground array of rooms and tunnels, he came upon a room that had the dimensions of a medium-sized American living room. It was filled from floor to ceiling with only gold—rings, earrings, and various other jewelry, but mixed among these valuables were gold teeth.

While there no doubt was gold in that room that came from non-Jewish sources, the teeth could only have come from the forced assembly lines at places like Auschwitz, Birkenau, Treblinka, and the dozens of other death camps. Jewish prisoners who were allowed to live, were forced to "process" the dead bodies of their recently gassed Jewish brothers and sisters. They removed the gold teeth and crowns, as well as gold fillings. They also checked for any jewelry that may have been on the body and continued this gruesome labor until a Nazi order came down that would put them in the gas chambers as well. Other Jews would then pick up the ghastly chore of extracting the gold from the corpses.

Not only the dead gave up their gold teeth, but even the living. Elie Wiesel, in his book entitled, "Night" describes the removal of one of his own gold teeth.

"Franek, the foreman, one day noticed the gold-crowned tooth in my mouth.

'Give me your crown, kid.'

I told him it was impossible, that I could not eat without it.

'What do they give you to eat, anyway?'

I found another answer; the crown had been put down on a list after the medical inspection. This could bring trouble on us both.

'If you don't give me your crown, you'll pay for it even more.'...

Franek grinned.

'What would you like then? Shall I break your teeth with my fist?'

That same evening, in the lavatory, the dentist from Warsaw pulled out my crowned tooth, with the aid of a rusty spoon."

Carl stood in horror of this incredible testimony of the butchery and brutality that had occurred throughout the years of the war. While the gold was inanimate, it spoke volumes about what happened to the Jewish people, and coupled with all of the mountains of other evidence, the truth of the Holocaust is irrefutable.

Carl, and some of his men had to stand guard over the mountains of treasure that Hitler and his followers had wrenched from their victims. The U.S. Government then sent representatives to collect and decide what to do with these spoils of war. Carl never did get a straight answer from anyone after that, but it was estimated that there were literally billions of 1945 dollars represented in that room and others. It may very well be that much of this gold stolen from the Jews and other victims, was used to finance the rebuilding of Germany after the war. Carl has asked many questions of the United States Government, but has not received any straight answers through the years.

# HAYA

A very recent murder occurred at a Sbarro Pizza restaurant on a bustling street corner in Jerusalem. It is a street corner that I have personally observed during different visits to Jerusalem. It is a place of busy crowds and bustling activity that begins in early morning and continues until late into the night.

Haya Schijveschuurder is one of the survivors of a mini-Holocaust that took place in that restaurant. Her Dutch family had made *aliyah* to Israel, as a family of eight. Only three remain.

Haya is a little girl of eight. She has been the subject of many news stories as she recovers in an Israeli hospital, one of the latest living victims of outrageous, demented, and misplaced rage. Another Arab extremist strapped a bomb to his body, waded into the dense crowd and detonated the device, killing more than a dozen people. Little Haya lost five of her family. Both her parents were murdered, along with three of her siblings. Only Haya and two of her brothers remain. She is courageous and exhibits a faith in God beyond her years.

Haya was interviewed on Israeli television from her hospital bed and I include her words from various press releases. Allow this eight year old to speak to your (the reader's) heart.

She described herself as a "happy girl, and I want to be that way again".

"Suddenly there was an explosion. I saw my brother there, the last time…his name was Avraham Yitzhak, and I said, 'Avraham Yitzhak,' because I knew that we wouldn't be taken to the same hospital. I wanted to tell him goodbye, until we all returned home. He didn't answer; he lay there and didn't do anything."

"Everything that happens here…it's all a miracle, and nothing happens for no reason, and God knows what He's doing. He wants to tell us that we need to behave better, and that soon the Messiah will come, and that then all the dead will rise again."

"My brothers came, and said, 'our parents were dead, and that my 13-year-old sister was dead, and that my little brother and sister were dead.' My little sister…she was two. She was really lively. I didn't cry. I didn't believe them. I didn't believe that this was what would happen to my parents, to my sisters and brother…I especially didn't believe it about my little sister."

Little Haya is only one victim of this particular terrorist attack. There were many others who were killed, whose names we will never know. There are hundreds of living victims who are having to deal with the soul wrenching pain of having lost their family members and friends, all because of unbridled rage and self-styled vengeance.

For whatever personal reasons that are rationalized by the so-called "martyrs" of *Jihad* (holy war), love of man is not one of them. It is a sad commentary that so many Arab young people are being used as pawns and victims by Islamic leadership that continues to choose death as their aspiration; not their own deaths, but the deaths of their youth whom the leaders have deceived. They choose indiscriminate death for the Jewish people. Like sharks in a feeding frenzy these Islamic leaders seek only blood, no matter from whose veins it flows, as long as it is not their own.

The *Torah* gives God's view regarding life and death:

> I call heaven and earth to witness against you today, that I have set before you life and death, the blessing and the curse. So <u>choose life</u> in order that you may live, you and your descendants.
> 
> (NAS—Deuteronomy 30:19)

Choosing life is a foundation stone of Jewish thought. It is seen also in Israel's willingness to help their neighbors. Even during the crisis in Kosovo, Israel dispatched medical teams and sent supplies to help Moslem refugees. Israel was one of the first on the scene when the American embassies in Dar-es-Salam and Nairobi were blown up…again by Islamic terrorists. Israel, which has endured so much terrorism, lent their expertise in finding victims that may have been buried in the rubble. Find a crisis in this world, and it is not uncommon to find little Israel giving of themselves to "choose life" for those who have suffered from natural disaster, war, or terrorists. I am still waiting for some news that would indicate that Islamic leaders and nations are doing likewise.

Once again, the Jews are the victims of world rage and ambivalence. They were made to sit still during the Gulf War as Saddam Hussein launched 39 Scud missiles against them, while other nations, including America, politically tied Israel's hands from even defending themselves. Today little girls like Haya are being violated to the core by hate-filled men while Western leaders demand that Israel "show restraint" in their responses to the Palestinian Authority and its thugs. More and more, I too lament with the psalmist...

> How long shall the wicked, O Lord, how long shall the wicked exult? They pour forth words, they speak arrogantly; all who do wickedness vaunt themselves. They crush Thy people, O Lord, and afflict Thy heritage. They slay the widow and the stranger, and murder the orphans.
>
> (NAS—Psalm 94:3-6)

As this same psalm concludes, there is strong warning for those who have been dealing out terrorist blows against Israel and her people. Although the Lord's solutions may seem slow in coming as we in our humanity measure time, His solutions will come. Hear the concluding words of the same psalm:

> They band themselves together against the life of the righteous, and condemn the innocent to death. But the Lord has been my stronghold, and my God the rock of my refuge. And He has brought back their wickedness upon them, and will destroy them in their evil; the Lord our God will destroy them.
>
> (NAS—Psalm 94:21-23)

I am concerned that there are going to be more Hayas, innocent victims of evil. It is more the reason that Christians double their efforts to bring aid and comfort to Zion.

# 13

# A WORD TO THE JEWISH PEOPLE

Most of my reason for writing this book is to encourage and develop support for the people of Zion. Throughout this chapter I will be speaking directly to my Jewish readers. Wherever you may be living at the moment, my longing is to provoke and exhort you to give greater consideration to what it is to be Jewish, and what your role is to be as a Jew. It may seem presumptuous for a Christian to be defining for a Jew what it is to be one, but I entreat you to allow me some liberty in this matter, as one who is grateful for what the Jewish people have given me.

In speaking to one of Israel's Consul Generals in Miami some years ago, we were enjoying each other's company and some light-hearted conversation. The Consul General spoke. "You know... when you Christians get your act together, then you can tell us Jews how to run ours." At the time there were a number of high profile scandals within the Christian community, and although this statement was made in light-heartedness and humor, there was a tremendous truth in it. Since the time of that light-hearted statement, there have been all too many more failures and scandals within the Christian community. I am tempering my words with this truth in mind, but yet some of my thoughts may seem a bit strong for a particularly sensitive Jewish reader.

I am no theologian. I am not a highly educated man in the sense of having copious amounts of professional training as a historian, but I have spent thousands of hours of my life studying the Jewish people as individuals, as a people, and becoming as intimately acquainted as possible with you. I read the Torah and Tenach very regularly (in English), and I believe that I am in touch with your God. I have made personal effort to travel and to visit the places where you are and where you were, to meet you personally, and to understand your pain.

I have stood for long agonizing moments in the flickering light of the "eternal flame" at the **Yad Vashem** Holocaust memorial in Jerusalem, allowing my eyes to slowly read the plaques in the floor illumined by that flame; Auschwitz— Sobibor— Bergen-Belsen— Majdanek— Buchenwald and many more. I have paced over the stones of Dachau, Germany, contemplating the horrors of the past. I have walked the grasses of Treblinka, Poland and knew that I was on holy ground, almost hearing the blood of your people crying out from the ground. I have stood by the "wall" at Auschwitz, where countless numbers of your people were executed by firing squad. I've seen and walked through the "showers" (gas chambers). I have stood at the oven doors at Buchenwald where the remains of your men, women, and children were barbarously turned to ashes and smoke. I have listened to the testimonies where Nazi soldiers ripped Jewish infants from their mother's arms, held them by the feet and swung them like a club, popping their skulls against brick walls. I have spent time on Mt. Herzl (Israel's equivalent to America's Arlington Cemetery) in Jerusalem, contemplating the stinging pain that has been inflicted upon Israel in the loss of your sons who gave their last in defending your land and people. I heard with my own ears the testimony of an 80-plus year old lady who watched her own pre-school children machine-gunned by the Germans.

In 1986, I met two Jewish-American sisters in a hotel lounge in Warsaw in my solo quest to understand and learn about the Jewish people. They were on a journey with their elderly parents, who had returned to Poland for the first time since World War II. Their dad was a survivor of the Warsaw Ghetto. I was introduced to him, in the lobby of the Intercontinental Hotel. The next day this man and his wife took me on a 6-hour walking tour of the former Warsaw Ghetto, telling me the most intimate and horrifying details of his own life, and showing me the very streets over which he had walked and suffered as a young man. He pointed out the sewer covers that he had used to sneak out of the Warsaw Ghetto at night in order to barter for guns or food. He walked me to a street corner where his own sister was hanged by the Nazis, and where her body was left swinging in the noose for days as a warning to any Jew who would defy the orders of the Third Reich.

I can only speak as a student and an observer, and certainly not as one who has lived the pain of the Jewish people, except through the process of empathy. Yet, I am aware that observers have a vantage point over a situation that is often obscured to those who live out the pain and suffering of brutal histories. I have experienced this in my own life as I have received counsel from others who can see more clearly than I through a situation or problem with which I may be coping. I have been in that same seat as I have counseled others as they have tried to get some sane viewpoint in a life that has been turned upside down and brutalized. I believe that I have at least some degree of credibility that would allow me to speak to you as a community. I hope that you can hear me, and to hear genuine concern and care undergirding my words.

I am a believing man. I believe in the God of Abraham, Isaac, and Jacob, and that as Jews you are not an accident of evolution, or a political phenomenon that just happened out of chance. One has only to superficially dig into history to see that your contributions in medicine, law, art, music and entertainment, engineering, and more are monumental and completely disproportionate to your actual numbers within the world's population. All of mankind has become the richer for these Jewish contributions.

It must be remembered however, that Jewishness is something

created by the Almighty. The first Jew, according to all historical and/or biblical accounts, was Abraham. But Abraham was a Gentile (pagan) until God made him a Jew. Abraham did not make himself Jewish. God made the first move, and Abraham obeyed. Abraham was chosen by God and called out of the world of darkness and idolatry in order to begin a magnificent plan that God had conceived. It was and is a plan of great redemption for the world. We can all be thankful that Abraham answered God's call.

While I have visited with many Israeli Jews and have come to know them intimately, I have also had the opportunity to dialogue with Jews from many other parts of the world. Many have a deep and profound faith in God along with a humble gratitude and a sense of responsibility in their hearts towards their own Jewishness and mankind in general. I have also met hard-hearted unbelievers whose only god seems to be money, power, or prestige.... just like the Gentiles. I have met too many Jews who unbelievably have little or no empathy with Israel nor their own people. The title "Jew" to such as these, might just as well be New Yorker, Californian, or Canadian. Allow this Christian to gently provoke you, that as a Jew, you are called to something much greater.

Your heritage and your legacy call for example-setting and leadership. God has called you to be torchbearers for Him. You are to carry His light to a world of darkness. You are to be bound to His laws and precepts, being faithful to Him at all costs, rather than just "successful" in the eyes of the world and each other. When people of the world look at a Jew, they should see a reflection of the God of Abraham, Isaac, and Jacob. They should see a righteous, humble, and a blessed person. Those of the world should marvel at the wisdom and honor upheld by the Jew. Gentiles should be convicted by the Jew because of your righteous walk with the Almighty, and provoked to seek out your God.

As a Jew, are you satisfied with writing a check to charity once in a while, or doing your duty by showing up for Passover or Yom Kippur services at your synagogue, much as the Gentile Christians do at Easter and Christmas? Do you think that having your name on a new hospital wing or on the doors or windows of a cultural center is the epitome of honorable living? Or, is your idea of greatness having your name announced in front of your local community that you have just donated a large sum of money to the latest cause? My dear elder brothers and sisters, you precious Jewish people...you are called to far greater than that.

I have had wonderful opportunity to meet with and fellowship with you, the Jews of the religious community, both in Israel, and in the **diaspora** (scattering of Jews throughout the world). I have melted with enthusiasm and love for many of you who have a deep love and respect for the God of Israel and who live out that love daily. I have seen many of you in the religious Orthodox community provide abundantly for your families in both the material and the spiritual realms of life. You appear to love God deeply, and seem balanced with your feet on the ground. I have seen thousands of you regularly praying in the synagogue or with your families, but who also have the courage to risk your own lives in war when Israel is threatened by their enemies. Your prayer book and **kippah** goes with you, but you also carry your M-16 or medical bag to perform the real and necessary duties of life.

I have shuddered and been driven away by those of you who wear the garb, but whose eyes and actions do not provoke me towards loving God and my fellow man. I have seen and experienced a few of you at the **Kotel**, (Western Wall of the Temple in Jerusalem) and in **Mea Shearim** (ultra-Orthodox neighborhood in Jerusalem) and **Bene Baraq** (ultra-Orthodox neighborhood near Tel Aviv) who nervously and compulsively go about the rituals of your own brand of Judaism, but who wear the facial expressions of condescension toward your fellow Jews and Gentiles who do not 'measure up' to the religious bondage to which you have succumbed. I have met some of you who have fathered many children, and who burden your wives to work and provide, while you study the Torah all day, and continue studying even when enemy tanks are rolling over Israel's borders. Dear Jewish people, you are called to so much more.

I have been with scores of American Jews, some of you spending your last ounces of energy and much of your money in bringing comfort and aid to Israel. I have met others of you who scream, politicize, complain, and become thorns in the side of Israel, as you clamor with news organizations and politicians of the world to "give up the Golan...give up the West Bank!" while you prop your feet on the hassocks of America. Dear Jewish people, you are called to much higher than this.

When a member of the Jewish community is indicted and convicted of massive monetary indiscretion on Wall Street, or when a high-profile member of your community skates through the cracks in the law making ungodly profits as a slum-lord, it hurts us all. You are not to be as the Gentiles!

The call to the Jew is one that was exemplified not many years ago. His name is Mr. Aaron Feurstein. He was the owner of Malden Mills, a textile manufacturer in Massachusetts. His entire factory burned to the ground. This could have been the end of it all. Mr. Feurstein had insurance. He could have listened to some of his advisors, "Aaron, take the money and run."

Mr. Feurstein would have no part in that. He employed hundreds of people. His factory practically supported the entire community. He stood the gap. He paid the price of servant leadership. He paid his employees for a significant period of time, even while they were not able to work. He rebuilt the factory. He stood by them. He set a righteous example for all of us. He answered the call of the righteous Jew. When the world sees this kind of example-setting and mentoring even in the corporate world, all of our hearts are gladdened and softened.

Dear Jewish people, you are a people greatly blessed of God. Because of your inborn giftings and talents, you are capable of your call, to be torchbearers for the Lord. However, if your giftings are used unwisely, or if they are even inadvertently used in the service of ungodly pursuit, the damage caused can be great.

To those of you who are Jews in the film and entertainment industries, you have so much influence on the societies that view your creations. As a Jew, you are not called to provide pornography and/or decadence for your audiences. As judges and lawyers you are not to twist and turn the truth of the laws of our land, and be a part of legislating the Ten Commandments out of classrooms and government buildings. You are not to take part in calling evil good, and good evil. You are not to be like the Gentiles! Your call is to greatness!

You cannot divorce being a Jew from the roots of the Torah and

Tenach (Old Testament). There is no Jewishness apart from these oracles of God. Your Scriptures are the very essence and foundation of the whole concept of Jewishness. One of the greatest admonitions of the Bible defines a Jew by the heart, and not the flesh. The Torah speaks:

> Yet the Lord set his affection on your forefathers and loved them, and he chose you, their descendants, above all the nations, as it is today. Circumcise your **hearts,** therefore, and do not be stiff-necked any longer.
> (NIV—Deuteronomy 10:15-16)

It is a time for you as Jews to reflect again on your history and on your God. He is calling you to Zion...right now. Begin to answer that call in your hearts, and allow Him the freedom to bring you back to the land where He promised to bring you, Eretz Israel. Make **aliyah** in the heart. The Hebrew word means "to go up". Go *up* to the Lord, dear Jewish people, and then go *up* to Zion. Hear the word of the Lord, written more than 3,000 years ago:

> .....and when you and your children return to the Lord your God and obey Him with all your heart and with all your soul according to everything I command you today, then the Lord your God will restore your fortunes and have compassion on you and *gather you again from all the nations where He scattered you.* Even if you have been banished to the most distant land under the heavens, from there the *Lord your God will gather you and bring you back.* He will bring you to the land that belonged to your fathers, and you will take possession of it. He will make you more prosperous and numerous than your fathers.
> (NIV—Deuteronomy 30:2-5)

My wife and I were on an adjoining hillside of the recently built community of Ephrat, Israel. We strolled with Rabbi Shlomo Riskin, the founder and developer of that community. Rabbi Riskin heard the call of heaven...**Shuvee**...Return to your land. He had been a rabbi and a leader of a synagogue in New York, but the call to Zion was greater. He left all, took many of his congregation with him, and continues to build up Zion. As we overlooked the houses and buildings of Ephrat, Rabbi Riskin told us of the day, several years ago, when he stood in the same spot where we were now standing, and saw an empty hill. He had the vision for Ephrat, and proceeded by faith to see it built. Today it is a town. Rabbi Riskin has answered the call of his Jewishness and of Zion.

Dear Jewish friends, do you see what your God has been doing? Do you think that the rebirth of the State of Israel in 1948 is the result only of political negotiation? Is it simply the generosity or indulgence of the nations? Not at all. It is the answer to God's rhetorical question from the prophet, Isaiah, where he penned the words of the Almighty:

> Who has ever heard of such a thing? Who has ever seen such things? Can a nation be born in a day or a nation be brought forth in a moment? Yet no sooner is Zion in labor than she gives birth to her children.
>
> (NAS—Isaiah 66:8)

Your very existence as Jewish people, and the re-birth of the land of Israel is proof that there is a God, and that He is bringing about His perfect plan and redemptive purposes through you. Nowhere in all of human history, has a people been dispossessed of their land, scattered throughout the world for 1900 years, and not been absorbed and lost as a people. You, the Jewish people, were scattered from your land in 70 A.D. and dispersed among the nations of the world.....*according to the prophecies of your own Scriptures*.....and you are now being regathered to that land.....again *according to your own Scriptures*. You have not lost your identity, and He, the Lord, has not lost His.

More? Listen to some selected words from the prophet Hosea, penned around 785 B.C.

> "When Israel was a child, I loved him, and out of Egypt I called my son. But the more I called Israel, the further

they went from Me...My people are determined to turn from Me...How can I hand you over, Israel?...My heart is changed within me; all my compassion is aroused. I will not carry out my fierce anger nor devastate Ephraim again, for I am God, and not man—the Holy One among you. I will not come in wrath. They will follow the Lord; He will roar like a lion. When He roars, His children will come trembling from the west. They will come trembling like birds from Egypt, like doves from Assyria. I will settle them in their homes," declares the Lord.

(Hosea 11)

Return, O Israel, to the Lord your God. Your sins have been your downfall! Take words with you, and return to the Lord. Say to Him:

> "Forgive all our sins and receive us graciously, that we may offer the fruit of our lips. "I will heal their waywardness and love them freely, for my anger has turned away from them."...Who is wise? He will realize these things. Who is discerning? He will understand them. The ways of the Lord are right; the righteous walk in them, but the rebellious stumble in them.
>
> (NIV—Hosea 14:1, 2, 4, 9)

A word about the land of Israel. Dear Jewish people, as a Christian who has combed through the **Torah** and **Tenach** (Old Testament), it is my strong opinion that in spite of your deep-rooted desire for peace, your land is not negotiable. God gave that land to you as *an everlasting possession* (Genesis 17:8). He dispersed you from it, just as He said He would, but He has now restored the land to you, and you to the land, again just as He said He would. Your land should not be a bargaining chit for a promised peace from the mouths of your avowed enemies.

While the world is against you, Israel, God is for you. The Golan is your land. Judea and Samaria ( today's "West Bank") is your land. Again, it is my opinion as I read your Scriptures, that it is not to be placed "up for grabs" regardless of the pressures that are placed upon you by the United States of America or any other nation or coalition of nations. Dear Jewish people, do not be hood-winked into giving away that which God has given to you. It is your free choice to do so, however, I am convinced that it will not pur-chase you the peace for which you long. Buying a worldly promise with your land will yield only more heart-ache and destruction.

Are you afraid of your enemies? Don't be. It's easy for me to say as a Christian living in America, but not easy for you as a people living in Israel, surrounded by those whose desire is to push you into the sea. However, in these perilous days your foundational hope must be in your God and His word, not in America's loan guaran-tees, its F-16's and Patriot missiles. God will not forsake you. One of my great concerns is that America probably will.

Just a few weeks after Saddam Hussein had finished pummeling Israel with his Scud missiles during the Persian Gulf War, I stood in an empty lot in Ramat Gan, Israel where one of these missiles had destroyed a couple of buildings in a residential area. I was told that no one was killed by that particular missile, in spite of the property damage. My heart leaped with joy when I learned that much of Israel had publicly begun to stand on the word of God. There were printed signs on buses and public places all over Israel, saying, "Tehelim neget Telim." It was a play on words in the Hebrew lan-guage, but its clear meaning was "Psalms against Scuds."

Israel, you have survived some of the worst that Saddam had to offer. You did so with incredible patience and restraint, and with lit-tle loss of life. Could it be that the hand of the Almighty was upon you and protecting you.? Be encouraged with the words of the Lord spoken through the Jewish prophet, Jeremiah:

> "The word of the Lord came to Jeremiah: This is what the Lord says: 'If you can break my covenant with the day and my covenant with the night, so that day and night no longer come at their appointed time, then my covenant with David my servant—and my covenant

with the Levites who are priests ministering before me—can be broken and David will no longer have a descendant to reign on his throne."

(NIV—Jeremiah 33:19-21)

In so many words, Jewish people, if you can stop day and night from happening, then you might give some consideration to the possibility that God might forget His covenant with you. Going back to the book of Judges, written around 1425 B.C. we read:

"The angel (messenger) of the Lord went up from Gilgal to Bokim and said, 'I brought you up out of Egypt and led you into the land that I swore to give to your forefathers. I said, 'I will *never* break my covenant with you......."

(NIV—Judges 2:1)

There are the many promises of the Book...*your* Book...*God's* Book, that are unbreakable simply because He gave *His* word. Living today, we can look back through thousands of years of history, and discover that God has kept His word to the Jewish people, and He will continue to keep His word. To appropriate His promises, however, you must know His word and know Him! As one faithful person has said, "God does not reveal Himself to the casual inquirer." To know Him will require an effort and a search. Again, I go to the Book:

"But if you seek the Lord your God, you will find Him if you look for Him with all your heart and with all your soul."

(NAS—Deuteronomy 4:29)

Searching for Him will require a careful and honest study of His Word, given to you in the Torah and the Tenach. He will reveal Himself to the *honest* searcher who seeks Him with all his heart. He will show the honest searcher the emptiness of living life according to the dictates of this world and its systems.

Tragically, there are those in Israel who periodically try to enact legislation that would limit freedom of religious expression. Such legislation would make it a crime to distribute literature or speak about that which is contrary to current Jewish theology as interpreted by those who are in leadership. If such laws are enacted, Israel will be on the road to becoming just like the Gentile nations that surround her, where to express a political or religious opinion that is contrary to that which is allowed by those in power, can result in prison terms and in some cases, execution.

Where there is true freedom, any arguments or philosophies will rise and fall on the basis of the *truth* of those arguments or philosophies. But where political men have their own agenda to maintain their own position and power, they often cannot tolerate that which challenges the shaky philosophical or spiritual platform on which they stand. That is why there is little to no freedom of speech in Saudi Arabia, Libya, Syria, Sudan, Egypt, Iran, Iraq, and the many countries that surround Israel. Because, Israel, you have been a bastion of freedom in an area where there has been no freedom, it will be a blow to threaten your own existence, and a blow to freedom in general if such a law is ever enacted.

A similar blow was inflicted on at least one other occasion in Jewish history. It was done almost 2,000 years ago, when political and religious leaders incited the populace to crucify the most gentle, kind, and compassionate Jewish miracle worker of all time. They had to shut his mouth, because his words and ideas shook the foundations of the system. With the cooperation of the Gentiles (Romans) Jesus was crucified like an ordinary criminal.

There was a momentary "success" for the time, because the Jewish religious leaders of the time no longer had to face the person of Jesus. However, it was Jesus who lamented over Jerusalem and predicted that "not one stone here (of the Temple in Jerusalem) will be left on another; every one will be thrown down." And so it came to pass in 70 A.D. when the fall of Jerusalem took place along with the destruction of the Second Temple. The leaders of the time had their way, and the people agreed to go along with them...but at what price?

Putting aside any arguments for or against Jesus, Buddha, Mohammed, or Confucius there is one argument that must be made.

There must be freedom to speak about them. There must be freedom for a person to try to convince another of his or her ideas. When that freedom is taken away and free expression is defined as a crime with ensuing punishments, then tyranny has entered the household. The results of that tyranny is visible all around you, Israel. It is my hope that you might not be seduced into buying into such tyranny.

Again, dear Jewish people, return to your God and to your land. Learn who you are in His sight. Be the torchbearers for the world, and point us all to the living God of Israel. Part of doing this requires that you maintain an open culture and not legislate away people's freedom of speech.

I know that the question "Is it good for the Jews?" has to always be considered in deciding for or against a particular course of action. Again I point to your Scriptures. God has given you promises that as you stand with Him and on His Word, your struggles and dilemmas will be brought to victorious conclusion. Hear the heart cry of your God calling out to you:

> "Oh that My people would listen to Me, that Israel would walk in My ways! I would quickly subdue their enemies, and turn My hand against their adversaries."
> (NAS—Psalm 81:13-14)

I will close this chapter with a challenge and conditional promises.....from the Torah:

> "You will lend to many nations but will borrow from none. The Lord will make you the head and not the tail. *If* you pay attention to the commands of the Lord your God that I give you this day and carefully follow them, you will *always* be at the top, *never* at the bottom. Do not turn aside from any of the commands I give you today, to the right or to the left, following other gods and serving them."
> (NIV—Deuteronomy 28:12-14)

May you hear the cry of your God, calling out to you!

# 14

# A WORD TO THE CHRISTIANS

As Christians, we owe a tremendous debt of gratitude to the Jewish people for what they have bequeathed to us. Yet, for centuries our community has done little to express appreciation. We have, on the contrary, been indifferent and even persecuting toward the Jewish people. Soon after the church was born and years later became institutionalized there has been a continuous stream of pressure and bias against the Jewish people. Throughout the ages there have been those Christians who have loved and served the Jewish people, however, by and large our history as a community toward the Jews has been abysmal. Although there are many truly believing and practicing Christians today who would claim that the many anti-Semitic acts perpetrated against the Jews throughout history were not done by *real* Christians, the facts seem to say otherwise.

There has been a great misunderstanding within the Western

world that to be non-Jewish is to almost automatically be a Christian. If Mr. Gallup were to poll 1000 people at random in America or Europe, a large percentage of people would answer "yes" to the question, "Are you a Christian?", many not knowing what it really means to be one.

Their reasoning would be, that they grew up in a "Christian" culture, and that they went to churches that were "Christian". In addition, they went through a variety of rituals that from baptism to confirmation were identified as "Christian," and they were *not* Jewish. To add to the confusion there are Catholics, Protestants, Evangelicals, Pentecostals, Baptists, Presbyterians, Methodists, Greek and Russian Orthodox, Mennonites, Adventists, Lutherans, and dozens more, all of whom claim to be followers of Jesus Christ. Throw in the word "Gentile", and there is more confusion.

A Gentile is someone who is not Jewish. A Christian is someone who believes and follows after Jesus the Messiah. Often however, "Gentile" and "Christian" are used interchangeably by those who do not fully understand their respective meanings.

If the confusion is great among the so-called Christian community, one can only imagine the perplexity when we are viewed through the eyes of the Jewish people, who have borne the brunt of our persecutions, arrogance, and indifference. A Jew growing up in Spain during the time of the 15$^{th}$ century Inquisition, was surrounded by "Christians". Yet it was these Christians that forced the Jew into conversion, to believe and worship the way the "Christians" did, to be baptized, and to renounce their Jewishness.

Earlier, in the 11$^{th}$ and 12$^{th}$ centuries when the European Crusades were launched, there were many Christians who began in biblical faith to spread the good news about their Savior, but soon succumbed to political agendas which forced people to become "Christians". Good men, deceived and disobedient, followed that which was not of God, but placed His Name on the banner of their cause. The Jewish people and even Moslems were among those who were terribly victimized during these times.

Stepping back several centuries before the Crusades, a terrible reasoning reared its head among Christian leaders. This reasoning eventually became known as "Replacement Theology", and still has its adherents today. In essence, the argument is that God bypassed and broke His covenant with the Jewish people because they did not receive their Messiah, Jesus. The Jews were looked upon as "Christ-killers", and deceived men reasoned that the church became the new "Israel", with God transferring His love from the Jewish people to the Christian church.

"Replacement Theology" has been one of the foundation stones of anti-Semitism through the centuries. It also contradicts the truth of the New Testament that speaks of the Christian church's position as one that has been "grafted in" to the root, which is identified as Jewish. The very re-birth of Israel as a nation in 1948 and the return of millions of Jews to the land is proof enough that God has not forgotten His covenant with His people. Indeed, He has not replaced them.

Moving on to America, this country is historically considered to be a "Christian nation". Many of our forefathers left the European continent because of the religious persecution. State churches run by political and religious despots insisted on liturgies and control which placed many of the clergy and the ordinary worshiper under great persecution. It became a political religion, and God had long since removed His blessing from the human politics, control, and idolatry of the system. It could be considered a parallel of God's removing His Presence from the Temple in Jerusalem because of Israel's sins centuries earlier (Ezekiel 10:18).

As a result of a corrupted religious system, thousands of Christians left Europe in search of a place where they could be free from persecution and where they could worship God in spirit and in truth. Mixed with those who were seeking religious freedom, there were a number of charlatans and rascals. However, America's new leaders were largely believing Christians who acknowledged God even in the foundation documents which chartered the new nation of America.

Throughout church history, many Christians have lived faithful and Godly lives. They have laid down their lives for their faith. Many became lunch for lions in the Roman Coliseum while thousands of onlookers cheered for more blood and gore. Other Christians became human torches, their burning bodies lighting the streets under the evil rule of Nero. Some died burning at the stakes in England, and the hangman's noose of despotic European rulers, or the guillotines of political systems gone berserk. Even today, Christians are being put to death by crucifixion in Sudan, firing squads in China, and gangs of Islamic murderers in the Philippines and Indonesia.

On the other hand, it is also true that Christians have lived not-so-faithful lives. It is here that as Christians we must own up to the tragedies and sins of our history, and make amends to the people that we have harmed. Whenever I have spoken out such a message, either to a group, or individuals, I am often countered with arguments that go something like this: "Hey....I didn't do any of these things to the Jews. Maybe the previous generations did some bad things, but it wasn't *me*. Why should I apologize, for something that I didn't do?" It's a good question, and one that must be addressed.

There is such a thing as corporate responsibility or accountability. God created us with needs. Many of these needs are fulfilled through relationships and community. To have a sense of belonging fills us with a sense of security. The design is that most of these needs should be met through loving families, but these needs are even met in the formation of street gangs, when healthy families are not available. If one of my family members deeply wounds someone else's family member, even if I am not the perpetrator I become involved because I am part of the family.

We see the same phenomenon demonstrated when we cheer our favorite sports team, or an individual player as he or she would represent our nation. If Boris Becker beat his opponent on the tennis court after a close match, thousands of Germans would stand up and say, "We won!" When the amateur American hockey team of the 1980 Olympics, soundly defeated the professional Russians in a hard-fought match, every American who had watched that match on TV suddenly became a hockey fan, and rejoiced ......"*We* did it!!!" We *are* interconnected, and we are part of the wider community of neighborhoods, cities, states, and nations.

The Bible tells us that the "sins of the fathers will visit even unto the third and fourth generations." (Exodus 20:5 and 34:7). That means that what I do wrong today has effect not only upon those around me today, but those who will follow me in generations to come. God also promises that the good that I do today, will plant seeds of goodness for generations to come. It is profoundly important to understand this principle to bring healing to individuals and groups.

Abraham Lincoln stood his ground as a leader and brought forth the Emancipation Proclamation which abolished slavery. This set the stage for racial healing in America, that 140 years later has yet to be fully accomplished. The proclamation was not wrong, but in its implementation there is an inherent requirement that we must let go of the concept of owning people and to embrace the axiom to become our brother's keeper, looking out for one another and offering equal opportunities. Progress, however slow, has been made.

Martin Luther who was a Christian reformer of the 16$^{th}$ century stood up against an incredibly powerful religious system that had, up to his time, crushed and squelched the spiritual life of the ordinary people. His biblical revelation, "The just shall live by *faith,*" ignited the hearts of thousands of European Christians and brought about reformation.

This same Martin Luther, later in his life, frustrated at the fact that he was unable to get the Christian message across to the Jewish population, made some extremely scathing accusations against the Jews. These same remarks were recorded for history, and were brought to life again on the lips of Adolf Hitler when this despot of the 20th century quoted Luther as justification for his persecution of the Jews. Because of Hitler's rhetoric, he deceived many German theologians and pastors, and became effective in seducing the German population into committing many of the atrocities of World War II.

Fellow Christians, remember, it was the Jewish people who gave us our Bible. From the earliest books of Moses right through the prophet Malachi of the Old Testament, we can be thankful to Jewish authors who penned the words under the guidance of the **Ruach Ha Kodesh** (Holy Spirit). Jewish scribes who had no laser printers and reams of copy paper to record and distribute God's word, nevertheless meticulously copied the Scriptures by hand, letter by letter, word by word, and book by book. Moreover, all of the writers of the

New Testament, with one possible exception, were Jewish. The early church was Jewish. They were Jews who endured the persecutions of the Roman Empire and who were scattered throughout the world of that time, and who carried the message of Messiah to others.

Mary, the mother of Jesus, was a Jew in the lineage of the tribe of Judah and the House of David. Jesus' surrogate father, Joseph, was a Jew of the House of David. The Scriptures tell us: "Salvation comes from the Jews" (John 4:22). Jesus' Hebrew name, "Y'shua" means "salvation". "Christ," often thought of by the uninformed as Jesus' last name, is a title. It is the Greek/Latin word for the Hebrew word Messiah, meaning "anointed one". The first Christians then, were "Messiah-ans", Jews who believed that Y'shua (Jesus) is the Messiah of all mankind.

In light of this awareness, we must be extremely grateful and cautious in our behavior, to continue to honor the Jewish people and the heritage that we as Christians have received from the Jews. The apostle Paul, a Jew, and writer of much of the New Testament, cautions us as he uses the image of an olive tree in describing to new non-Jewish Christians, their relationship to the Jewish people.

> "But if some of the branches were broken off, and you, being a wild olive, were grafted in among them and became partaker with them of the rich root of the olive tree, *do not be arrogant toward the branches; but if you are arrogant, remember that it is not you who supports the root, but the root supports you.*"
>
> (NAS—Romans 11:17-18 )

Do we really believe this as Christians? Do we act like we believe it? If not, may Paul's words provoke us all to change any wrongful attitudes that may still fester in our hearts against the Jewish people. There is another very important facet to all of this. At present, most Jewish people do not see the revelation that we as believing Christians want so much to share with others. Again, the Bible speaks:

"What then? What Israel sought so earnestly (a righteous and just relationship with God) it did not obtain, but the elect did. The others were hardened (blinded), as it is written: 'God gave them a spirit of stupor, eyes so that they could not see and ears so that they could not hear to this very day'.

(NIV—Romans 11:7-8)

"Again I ask, did they stumble so as to fall beyond recovery? Not at all! Rather, because of their transgression, salvation has come to the Gentiles to make Israel envious".

(NIV—Romans 11:11).

According to our Christian understanding, there is a mystery in the plan of God. The Messiah, in order to bring salvation to the world, had to shed His own blood as the unblemished 'Lamb of God' to redeem all humanity from our sins. Jesus' death became the ultimate Passover, as He submitted to the will of the Father allowing the very men that He was redeeming to slay Him. The intricate description of the Messiah's crucifixion is rendered by the Jewish prophet in chapter 53 of the Book of Isaiah. The words were penned more than 700 years before the event, an event that had been foreseen and planned by God from before the foundation of the earth. God the Father sent His Servant to live among men and to suffer and die to pay the price for man's sin.

The history of this event documents that both Jews and Gentiles took part in putting the Messiah on the cross. Jewish religious leaders conceived the plot, and the Gentiles drove the nails. It is the very picture of the fact that we ALL put Jesus on the cross and are ALL in need of God's atonement, Jew and Gentile alike, right down to this very day. Paul, the Jew, further pens these words:

"I do not want you to be ignorant of this mystery, brothers, so that you may not be conceited: Israel has experienced a hardening (blindness) in part until the fullness of the Gentiles has come in."

(NIV—Romans 11:25).

Dare we, as Christians drawn out of the Gentile world, persecute and blame our senior brothers and sisters, the Jews? Historically we have proverbially beat them over the head with our Bibles and theologies not to mention the Crusades and Inquisitions. If that is our approach and attitude, we are working against God, who in essence is saying, "I've partially blinded them for a time, until I harvest the full number of Gentiles.

Does it mean that as Christians, we should never share our faith with someone who is Jewish? Of course not. Paul, a devout Jew, educated in the school of Gamaliel, a self-described Hebrew of Hebrews, and a Pharisee of Pharisees, shared with his own people, but he also did so with a deep love and understanding.

Paul, inspired by the Holy Spirit, further instructs us that we as Gentile Christians have been shown mercy by God through the Jewish people, and we are now to show mercy to the Jews (Romans 11:30-31). It is our call as Christians. Not only did our Jewish Messiah die for us, thereby redeeming us, but His followers gave their lives as well. Jesus' Jewish disciples died martyr's deaths to bring the good news of a Savior to all mankind. They did not shrink back from the task at hand. James, a Jew, was put to death by the sword. Peter, a Jew, was crucified upside down. Thomas, a Jew, made his way to India eventually and was put to death there. Paul, a Jew, was beheaded. The only apostle who was not murdered for his faith was the Apostle John, a Jew, who died in exile on the island of Patmos.

As followers of our Jewish Messiah, if we live our lives so as to reflect the very essence of the Jewish One we follow then the ***Ruach Ha Kodesh*** (Holy Spirit) Whom we possess, will flow outward to bring blessing, comfort, and revelation to our root, the Jews. As the Jews have given us our heritage, and been the vehicle through which God has worked His plan of redemption, we, as Christians, are to act as midwives and servants to help bring the Jews and all of Israel into the fullness of their destiny in God.

Israel is presently in the throes of birth pangs. The contractions are becoming more severe and painful. As Christians we must encourage her, wipe her brow, hold her hand, and speak out for her to the Great Physician, and when the delivery is complete, it shall be as "life from the dead". (Romans 11:15)

It appears that we are entering the most perilous days of history. The Bible forewarns us of the things to come, many of which will be anything but pleasant. God is bringing about His plan, and it will not fail. Humanity's archenemy, Satan, is trying to bring about his. It will fail. The ensuing battle will center over Israel and the Jewish people, with fallout for the entire world. Today, as Christians, we must gird our loins for the battle ahead, to stay the course, to finish the race, and in that process comfort God's people, the Jews, and favor Zion, His and their holy habitation.

# 15

# THE WEST, THE EAST, AND THE ARABS

Throughout this book, because of the many stories that have negatively involved the Germans, Russians, and the Arabs, it might be tempting to assume that I or other Christians are anti-Arab, anti-German, or anti-Russian. While there have been many assaults that have come from these nations against the Jewish people, an honest evaluation of history can find extremely damaging testimony against almost all nations as they have related to the Jews. Even my own country, the United States of America, which generally has a good record in supporting the Jewish people, has blood on its hands.

## THE UNITED STATES

It was 1939 when over 900 Jewish refugees left Germany and set sail on the *St. Louis,* a ship owned by the Hamburg-Amerika shipping lines. The refugees were attempting to free themselves from the talons of Hitler's Germany and many had sold all they had to make this voyage. They possessed valid visas for Cuba that had been granted by Cuban Consuls. On arriving in Cuba a change of heart on the part of the Cubans had occurred. These Jewish refugees were denied entry to Cuba despite the fact that many had families and friends waiting on the docks to take them in. After negotiating for days that turned into weeks, money was raised from the American Jewish community to post a bond for each of the weary refugees that would allow them to enter Cuba. The Cubans reneged again, and appeals went out to many nations on behalf of these forlorn Jews in the hope that some country would open its doors and provide haven for people who were merely seeking to save their own lives.

After weeks of failed negotiations with the Cubans, the *St. Louis* sailed north from Havana and continued to send requests by radio to many nations which might be able to offer refuge. The *St. Louis* was only a few miles off the coast of Ft. Lauderdale, Florida, and a U.S. Coast Guard vessel (CG 244) was dispatched to make sure that none of the refugees would jump ship and try to make it to the mainland. Many appeals were made to the United States Government, and all were refused. More appeals went out by radio to other nations, including many Central and South American countries and Canada. None answered the call to provide safe haven for these Jews. After months of negotiations and being held prisoners on a crowded ship, they eventually set sail again for Europe, landing in Antwerp, Belgium where they were greeted by anti-Semitic protestors holding placards that reviled the very existence of the Jews. One such sign said, "We want to help the Jews. If they call at our offices, each will receive gratis a piece of rope and a nail." Most of these Jews were later rounded up by the Germans and executed in death camps.

In the more recent decades, America has been selling arms to both the Israelis and to the Arabs. Where the United States has armed Israel's enemies, money has seemingly taken precedence over principle. In the past, as Arab armies equipped themselves with Soviet made tanks and planes, the Israelis had to play "catch-up". In the early 60's they purchased planes from France to maintain some balance of power against those whose stated desire was to eliminate Israel. Only later, the United States began to sell sophisticated arms to the Israelis so that they could match the capabilities of the nations surrounding her.

According to the Arms Control Association, in the years 1990-1992, starting from the Iraq invasion of Kuwait, America sold more than $33 billion in sophisticated weaponry to Arab States. More than half of the $33 billion in arms was sold after the end of the Gulf War. Almost $15 billion of the arms went to Saudi Arabia to bolster their military capabilities, all while the Saudis were actively subverting America's Gulf security strategy by refusing to allow the United States to base troops and equipment in the Kingdom. America even sold them the very latest in AWACS technology. An AWACS aircraft is a sophisticated airborne command post with the latest in radars, electronic warfare gadgetry, and communications equipment. Such equipment in the hands of capable commanders and officers can give great advantage over their opponents.

Today America is exporting democracy and capitalism to fill the vacuum left by a failed communist system in Russia and Eastern Europe. However, we have forgotten that our capitalism and democracy were built on a foundation of the Judeo-Christian heritage which encompasses a belief in the God of Abraham, Isaac, and Jacob. He is a God who has taught us to be dependent on Him, and expects from us fruits of honesty, integrity, truth, loyalty, perseverance and the like. Without moral foundations no government or economic system can survive for long. Communism itself did not fail because of its purported ideals. It failed because it totally negated God, and presumed that man on his own could produce a utopia. Likewise, capitalism and democracy on their own, in the hands of amoral men will fail just as badly.

Where America is exporting its economic and governmental systems, many results are dismal. While a few of the Russian Mafia "cowboys" have made untold millions, the average Russian is worse off today than he was under communism. America itself is living on the fruits of seeds long past planted by the righteous and God-fearing forefathers of yesteryear. The moral and cultural seeds that America is sowing today are slowly coming to fruition, and the harvest that will be reaped is one that will bring heartache, sorrow, and destruction.

It is not democracy and capitalism that has brought about America's blessings, but it has been a fundamental belief and obedience to God which has allowed Him to bless us through those systems. As America continues down this road of exporting our systems without God, it will ultimately hurt Zion and her people, and America will reap the consequences as a nation. The great dilemma for America today, is that she cannot export what she no longer has, and until there is a deep repentance among Americans leading to a moral and spiritual transformation, the nation cannot offer appropriate solutions to sustain healthy societies.

## THE GERMANS

There is no doubt that the Twentieth Century has recorded one of the darkest epochs of Jewish history, and the German people were largely to blame. Studying the events and decisions of the time, reveals that even some prominent Christian theologians gave full support to the rising false "messiah" of the Third Reich, Adolf Hitler. German politicians, housewives, and youngsters pledged their lives to this high profile demagogue. Almost all of Germany became swept up in the deception which for a few years seemed destined to fulfill Hitler's promise, *"Deutschland Über Alles"* (Germany over all).

Having recently lived in a small West German village for more than four years, I have had a fairly good taste of today's Germany, and it is sometimes frightening to see the roots of hatred that still exist within this nation, often under the deceptive veneer of authority, cleanliness, and order. I lived in Germany when gangs of "skinheads" set fire to tenement buildings in northern Germany that housed Asian immigrants. Sympathizers to this neo-Nazi extreme, longing for prosperity and order, marched through the streets of Berlin chanting *"Ausländer Raus!"* (Foreigners Out!). It was not the demonstrators that caused me such alarm, but the bystanders who applauded. Even one of my own German pilot colleagues, who received much of his professional training in the United States as an *"auslander"*, joined the chanting with fervor from the sidelines, shaking his fist in the air, and giving his voice to the chant from hell, *"Ausländer Raus! Ausländer Raus!"*

During this time, I was a pilot for a small German charter airline. Although there were only a few of these apparent anti-foreigners among the 180 pilots with whom I flew, it was nevertheless disconcerting to walk into flight operations and find stickers on the wall which had the old Nazi black cross in the center with the words, "German cockpits.....German crews!" It didn't seem to matter to those who expressed this sentiment that they were flying American-built aircraft. In contrast, as disconcerting as this was, it was countered by our chief pilot, who upon discovering one of the anti-foreigner pilots, took him to task and made him write a personal letter of apology to every non-German pilot that was among our ranks. Unless I was deceived in my own perceptions, the vast majority of the Germans with whom I worked, held no such animosity toward the Jews and other foreigners, although anti-Semitism and anti-foreigner attitudes were far from being eliminated.

While I lived near the small town of Babenhausen, Germany, the one last Jew who lived there was driven out by local "neo-Nazi" Jew-haters. The Jewish man was continually harassed, his property regularly damaged and defiled. He finally wrote a letter which was published in local newspapers, and he left.

In contrast, I met a wonderful German couple who live in Germany. While visiting their home, they showed me the hundreds of documents and photos that they had collected in their singular search for the truth about the history of their own small town. They had met with tremendous resistance when they began to speak out about the abysmal history of their community and how it had treated the Jewish people during the Hitler era. They even made visits to the small Jewish cemetery in Münzenburg and began to cut the grass and clean and restore the Jewish gravestones that had been desecrated in the past. Even in the 90's they were scorned by fellow villagers who still held hatred for the Jews and who wanted the sins of the past to be forever buried. Fortunately, these German Christians are continuing their fight for truth and are not intimidated by those who inwardly rejoice over the past plight of the Münzenburg Jews.

While there are plenty of negatives from the past and some in the present, I have met some of the most wonderful and warm-hearted people in the world in Germany. I have been treated with the utmost of grace by Germans who housed, fed, and opened their homes to me. I know many who have truly lamented before God over the past history of Germany towards the Jews, and who stand ready today to defend the Jewish people and to honor the State of Israel.

While there were demonstrations in different parts of Germany that were blatantly against foreigners, especially those who were not Caucasian white, there was also a beautiful rising up among the populace of the nation, including those who had personally lived through the dark years of Nazi Germany. Collectively, they were saying "not again" to those in Germany who seemed bent on repeating the Nazi past. Germans by the tens of thousands hit the streets in Frankfurt with placards and candles in a high-profile stand against the philosophies of neo-Nazism. It was a stand that I believe received too little attention. There are large and very significant numbers of Germans who are committed to never repeating the history of the 1930's and 40's, and that is comforting.

There are significant numbers of German Christians who contribute funds regularly and generously to Israel. They have paid for dozens of flights to bring Jewish refugees out of Russia to Zion. These Germans have God's vision for His people and His land. I am friends with a number of German Christians who give freely of their time and money to bring aid and comfort to the Jewish people, and who have opened their hearts and homes to the Jews. There is a wonderful stream of goodness that is flowing within the many churches in Germany. More and more they are meeting their responsibility to bless the Jewish people, not out of a morbid penance, but a deep repentance from past and present sins of the German people toward the Jews.

My friend, Horst, who lives not far from Cologne, Germany has a pastoral and counseling ministry. One day, while visiting him, I noted a map of Germany and Poland on his office wall. On this map were a number of pins which marked several towns and villages. Between the pins was strung some thread which indicated the route that Horst had traveled. I asked one of his staff members what the map was all about.

He explained that Horst discovered that his deceased father had been a Nazi German officer who had been responsible for the deaths of countless numbers of Jews in Northern Italy, Germany, and Poland. His father had never really owned up to it prior to his death, but Horst was determined to find out the facts. He did so, and discovered his father's dark and bloody past which horrified and shamed him as a son.

The map that I was viewing showed the villages and towns that Horst had personally visited. He went to each of these locations, sought out its Jewish, Christian, and/or political leadership, and publicly repented before them for the sins of his father. He went to every place where he had determined that his father had been responsible for the murder of Jewish people. Horst knows the biblical truth that "the sins of the fathers visit even unto the third and fourth generation". He knows that he has the power to bring healing and freedom even to the offspring and the survivors of his own father's sordid past. He is a German on whom God smiles and blesses as he continues to speak and teach on Germany's need for repentance, personally as individuals, and collectively as a nation.

My wife and I were privileged some years ago to join approximately 7,000 German Christians who wanted to express their sorrow to the Jews for the national sins of Germany's past and present. They also wanted to tell to their own populace, of the need for this vision to be caught by the rank and file of Germany.

Young and old, students and truckers, along with housewives with baby carriages assembled at the Lorenkirche (a church) in the center of Nürnberg. Placards painted by household amateurs revealed the heart of this crowd of Germans. Words of sorrow and repentance cried out in the silence of the spirit as people read them. These Germans represented the "7,000 that have not bowed their knees to Baal" (1 Kings 19:18) and who were standing with God's vision for His Jewish people.

Seven thousand Germans silently began their march, walking through the streets of Nürnberg toward the old Olympiad stadium that had been the scene where Adolf Hitler had publicly announced his decrees against the Jews. Tens of thousands of deceived Germans had listened obediently, and willingly took up Hitler's mantle, ready to accomplish their *Führer's* wishes.

On the day of the march it was different. The mood was somber. My friend and Lufthansa pilot, Dieter and his wife Jan, pushed their toddler along in a stroller. They were among the 7,000 who walked. There was almost complete silence among the participants. Their minds were on the past. Their hearts were heavy. It was in these same streets, that Germans had moved their machinery and enabled the horror of World War II. These marchers had been given the gift of repentance, and though ashamed of Germany's past, they were bringing hope for the future as they publicly took their stand.

The only thing heard were the footsteps of the marchers. I observed an occasional curtain being pulled aside on an upper story window of a house or apartment building along the way, and the shadowed outline of a person would appear. Were they remembering those days of the 30's and 40's? Were they the offspring of those that lived those days?

Cars pulled to the side of the road to allow the marchers to pass. There were few pedestrians along the sidewalks. Were they hiding from the message that was being paraded before them? In this city of Nurnberg, there were usually lots of people bustling about at this time of day.

We reached the Olympiad Stadium. The strongly constructed steel and concrete oval had outlasted its builders. My imagination allowed me to think back to 1935 and see a myriad of ordinary Germans lifting their right arms in salute to their *Führer.* I could almost see their maniacal leader standing at the podium and spouting the venom that would lead to the near annihilation of the Jewish people.

Something new was in the air this day. These Germans were different. There were different speakers on the podium today where Hitler had previously stood. There were rabbis representing the Jewish community of Germany. There were Christians who publicly declared their sorrow and publicly asked forgiveness of the

Jewish leaders. A lady Israeli tourist had seen the march and her curiosity got the better of her. She followed the marchers to the stadium. She was astounded. She questioned my wife and me in English. "What is going on? What is this?" Although she could see plainly what was going on, it was as a dream…almost unbelievable. She could not believe her own eyes and ears. She had to have someone else explain it all more plainly and to confirm that what she was witnessing was real.

It was heartening for me to be a part of this. The question however, looms. Will there be enough in numbers to be effective in impacting the hearts of the 90,000,000 other Germans in their nation? Time only will show us, but events like this are encouraging and inspire hope for us all.

No nation has cornered the market on evil or on righteousness. In spite of the fact that Germany had its day of atrocities and is still in need of repentance, hope springs forth. For those of us who are non-Germans, it is easy to point our fingers at their dark history, but Germany's history is a living signpost of what can happen to any nation when the people spurn God and His ways. There are no exceptions to this reality.

## THE RUSSIANS

Even a skimming of Russian history during the twentieth century reveals that much has gone wrong within its borders. From the time of the Bolshevik revolution in 1917 and throughout the years of Josef Stalin, Russia became a land of tyranny, prisons, and death. Not only the Jews were oppressed by the State, but anyone who dared open his mouth with critical words toward the leadership or the idol of the communist State.

Even before communism, Russian Jews were attacked through many *pogroms*, not because they were voicing dissenting opinions against the State, but simply because they were Jews. It is not unlike the many racial injustices that have occurred in America where rebellious and hateful white people have persecuted and killed, just because a person was black.

The numerous "Five-Year Plans" of Soviet Russia finally reached their own demise. The communist system had become so corrupt, that Russia and its satellites rotted out from within. Despite the fact that the nation is blessed with some of the finest farmland in the world, that it has mineral deposits that would rival any throughout the globe, and that it has an abundance of oil reserves, Russia could not pull things together enough to create prosperity for the average citizen. Russia had become enslaved to a political system that excluded God, and for seventy years the one true God had been replaced with the gods of dialectical materialism and the humanism of the State.

Churches and synagogues were closed and some even destroyed. Religious gatherings were forbidden, unless specially allowed by the State at unique times. For the most part, the Russian Orthodox church succumbed to political pressure and through compromise lost their spiritual power.

However, there was a remnant of true Christians who would risk life and limb to gather together in a forest or apartment, just to fellowship and to worship God. Many Jews remained Jewish in name only having lost their spiritual and cultural identity. Others persevered Sabbath after Sabbath, Passover after Passover, and by God's grace have been preserved.

I was brought up in a generation where the "Red Menace" threatened the United States. Upon learning that the Russians had nuclear bombs, civil defense became a significant focus during my school years. I remember the drills in elementary school and junior high where we would have to kneel down in the corridors, put our heads against the wall with our hands over the back of our necks, and wait for the "all clear" signal. It was because America feared that Russia might attack us. We had to be ready.

In my own life years later, elementary school civil defense was displaced by a tour of duty as a fighter pilot with the U.S. Air Force. Much of my time was spent countering the threat that existed from behind the "Iron Curtain". The Russians were my enemy, and where they had influence and control, I could not go and their own citizens could not leave.

At different bases throughout Europe and the Middle East, I sat for long stretches on alert, with a nuclear bomb hung on the center-line of my fighter-bomber. If the whistle blew and we were launched, I would have to be airborne within minutes, fly low-level to a target in the East, and drop my "nuke". This state of readiness went on for decades. The Stalins, Khruschevs, Andropovs, and Bresnevs of Russia kept things this way.

At long last, the "Wall" came down in 1989, and the communist demon was beginning to breathe its last. Doors were opened to countries that had been forbidden territory for most people from the West. In 1991 I made my first trip to Moscow where I was privileged to join with others to minister to as many as 2,000 young people, most of whom were university students. I was part of a ministry team, from different churches and countries. Most of the Russian young people that we served had been told all their lives, that there is no God.

These new Christians had been introduced to Him and had fallen in love with the Messiah who they readily recognized as Jewish . They were eager to learn and often had to borrow another's Bible. They were economically poor, but becoming spiritually rich. They were developing a vision free from anti-Semitic prejudice for Israel and the people of Zion.

To own a Bible in Russia was rare at this time. Bibles were not easily procured, and were very expensive for the average Russian. During the conference, one of our leaders announced that each student would be given his own Bible at the end of the week. A large shipment had arrived. The cheers of delight would rival the noise level of an Alabama-Auburn football game, as 2,000 students leaped to their feet and began praising God for the wonderful gift that they were about to receive. This emotional display demonstrated how important a simple Bible was to these young Russians.

My wife, Hellen, accompanied me on my second trip to Russia almost a year later. We flew on an Aeroflot IL-86 from Frankfurt to Moscow. I was invited to the cockpit as a professional courtesy by the Russian captain. Only a few years ago, this man had been my enemy. Today, we could speak with each other with only vague discomfort. I rode in the cockpit throughout the entire trip. I showed the cockpit crew pictures of my family, and the planes that I'd flown. The walls continued to melt as I spoke with my new airline colleagues. One of the pilots spontaneously opened his heart to me and told me of his failing marriage, and the recent death of his 16-year old daughter. He was a man who like so many others, looked good on the outside, but was dying inside. It appeared that he was looking for spiritual answers for the pain in his life.

Once in Moscow, Hellen and I had the opportunity to minister to yet another 2,000 or so young people who had come from all over the former Soviet Union. There were students from Belarus, Ukraine, Kazakstan, Georgia, and the various independent nations that form today's Commonwealth of Independent States (former Soviet Union). We had the opportunity to address an audience of approximately 600 Jews, most from the Moscow area, who were preparing themselves and their hearts to go to Israel. A few years before such a meeting would have been unthinkable; however, I believe with all my heart that the Almighty has made this window of opportunity available to bring the message of Zion to the Russian Jews, to encourage them to come home. For the Gentile Christians, these meetings taught the need to nurture and bless these Jews and help them to make this journey in their hearts as well as their lives.

Our adventure in Russia continued after the conference in Moscow. We boarded and all- night train and headed south to the city of Orel. We were escorted by some of the young Russians who had been at our seminars in Moscow. They took us to their fledgling church, where we taught for another three days. Our interpreter from Moscow traveled with us. She was a young Russian Jewish girl who believed in Jesus, and who wore herself out interpreting for us. She had to interpret our lessons, and then all of our social conversations with our Russian brothers and sisters.

Through it all, we experienced hospitality in its finest form. My wife and I were introduced to the Russian cultural concept of the "wide heart". We were well received and experienced incredible hospitality through the "wide hearts" of our new Russian friends. Their hearts were able to receive our care and friendship, and returned a fountain of love and acceptance to us, the first Americans that some of them had ever met. Our departure took place at the Orel train station as we prepared for an all night train ride back to

Moscow. The leaders of the small church stood outside the train on the station platform while we viewed them from the train window. They serenaded Hellen, our interpreter Marina, and me. Without restraint, they sang songs to us about the God who loves them and the Jewish people.

Despite the fact that there are many Russians who are repenting for the sins of their nation toward the Jewish people, there are many others who are waiting for the opportunity to once again seize power and bring back the old Russia. We were informed about some "old guard" Russian generals who were just waiting for the chance to seize power and return to the system of the past.

Anti-Semitism is still alive in contemporary Russia today. There are groups that hate the Jewish people, and are dedicated to their demise. One such organization is known as the Pam-Yat, known for its hate crimes against the Jews. Only a couple of years ago, the news broke that the Russian legislature overwhelmingly passed a new law banning evangelistic organizations and efforts to freely distribute Bibles and literature. Boris Yeltsin also signed a pact with Egyptian President Mubarek supporting the Palestinian cause and blaming Israel for the trouble in the Middle East.

Many interpret the Scriptures to indicate that at some point in the future, there will be an attack against Israel and the Jewish people. Taking part in this attack is the nation that many theologians and biblical scholars conclude to be Russia. The attack will end however, not in the demise of Israel, but in the demise of the attacking armies. There is now a window of opportunity (but one that is apparently closing) for all of us to aid and comfort those Jews who are being drawn out of Russia to Zion, according to the Scriptures. No one knows how long this window may be open, but while it is, it is important that the Jewish people come home to Zion.

In spite of the many hardships that the Jews have endured in Russia, and in spite of the Russian history which has often been darker than that of Nazi Germany, there has been a thread of mercy extended throughout the land. For the past decade or so, the Bible has been taught and preached all through the former Soviet Union, and many Russians have come to believe again. There is much hope for Russia as people place their trust in the One who created them.

369

I have found Russian Christians to be some of the most dedicated and loving people I have ever known.

## THE ARABS

In Chapter 16 of the biblical book of Genesis we find a forlorn handmaiden by the name of Hagar. She was an Egyptian maid for Abraham's wife, Sarah. Abraham and Sarah, although quite old, had brought forth no children, in spite of God's promise to Abraham that he would have descendants as numerous as the stars. In normal human fashion, the two became tired of waiting, and thought to take things into their own hands, in order to "help" God to keep His promise. At the urging of Sarah, Abraham had relations with Sarah's Egyptian maid, and this union ultimately produced a child named Ishmael. After the pregnancy became apparent, a jealousy and competition between the two women ensued. The result was that Sarah sent pregnant Hagar away.

Hagar announced to the angel of the Lord who stood before her at a spring, and said, "I am fleeing from the presence of my mistress, Sarah." The angel of the Lord spoke back, saying, "I will greatly multiply your descendants so that they shall be too many to count." The angel spoke further, "Behold, you are with child, and you shall bear a son; and you shall call his name Ishmael ("God hears"), because the Lord has given heed to your affliction. And he will be a *wild donkey of a man, his hand will be against everyone, and everyone's hand will be against him....."* Consulting the Scriptures in Genesis 25 we find the descendants of Ishmael and the lands in which they settled, indicating them as the forefathers of today's Arab people.

The Jews and Arabs, therefore, are half-brothers, each able to claim Abraham as their father. Yet, some of the very worst hatred rages out of the Arab and Persian peoples towards God's chosen people, the Jews. There is probably no rage and hatred that is more destructive than that born out of a close relationship gone sour. When a husband and wife who once had loved each other follow the path of war, the hostility and pain is far greater than that which might ensue between strangers whose paths had crossed in conflict.

America's own Civil War of only 140 years ago brought forth incredible pain and destruction within a family at war with itself. Fortunately, it was resolved, but even today the pain of that war can still be found festering among "Northerners" and "Southerners" as each continue to joke about "Johnny Rebs", "Carpetbaggers", "Yankees", and the Stars and Stripes versus the Stars and Bars of the Confederate flag. An acquaintance of mine wears a T-shirt that depicts the Capitol Building in Washington D.C. with the Confederate flag flying atop the dome. Beneath the picture is the inscription, "I have a dream....." The words are a play on the famous words of assassinated civil rights leader, Dr. Martin Luther King, whose own black people suffered most during and since the Civil War. But, the "dream" of my acquaintance and those that print such T-shirts, is to maintain the spiritual stance that helped cause the Civil War in the first place.

There has been much enmity between Arabs and Jews since Ishmael was brought into existence, almost 4,000 years ago. Through time, the rivalry and hatred has continued to increase instead of decrease. Beginning as brothers, the rift has become seemingly impossible to heal. The Torah ( 1st Five books of the Old Testament) is not wrong when it records the words spoken by the angel of the Lord. Ishmael *"will be a wild donkey of a man; his hand will be against everyone and everyone's hand against him, and he will live in hostility toward all his brothers."* (NIV—Genesis 16:12).

Today, we have the privilege of seeing the long historical out-working of God's Word and His principles, especially as it relates to the Arabs and the Jews. When God speaks through His Word and says that something is going to happen, it *will happen.* The house of Ishmael has truly become like "wild donkeys", according to the Scriptures. A wild donkey as a metaphor depicts an animal that has no domestication, refuses to be yoked to principle, and which demands its own way.

The Arab nations have generally continued in this stance throughout the centuries as it relates to the Jews. This is *not* to say that all Arabs are bad, or that all Arabs hate Jews, but where they can be "broad-brushed" in their national and/or political stances, it is easy to see that there is an incredible hatred towards the Jewish people. In addition, there is intense rivalry and vengeance between Arab tribes and clans, giving more evidence of God's declaration written 4,000 years ago.

On one of my visits to Israel, a young American lady led me to different places in Bethlehem where Arab people were being cared for. In one place, I visited an orphanage, where young Arab children had been abandoned by their parents because they were born with handicaps. There were blind kids, those that were crippled and hobbled around on crutches, some without limbs, but all were being cared for in this institutional setting that was run by some international Christians. The kids seemed genuinely happy and nurtured.

I went to a small house-factory of handicapped adults, who were working at sewing machines and weaving looms. They sat in their various states of handicap and worked industriously to make tablecloths, wall hangings, napkins, and other such items. They bantered back and forth, obviously joking and needling each other, and seemed generally content with their lot in life. Some had been born with their handicaps, but one young lady had been given her handicap in an act of vengeance between two Arab families.

She was as beautiful a woman as one could imagine, and could have easily graced the pages of an international woman's magazine as a model. She had the blackest of hair and eyes, as well as the dark skin of a Mediterranean Arab. She had a smile that would light up a room. She was confined to a wheelchair.

It was explained to me that someone in her family (perhaps one of her brothers) had wronged someone in another Arab family. Someone in the other family took out his rage on this young Arab woman who sat before me. He and some accomplices captured her, held her down, and cut the nerves and tendons in her legs so as to make her a cripple. It was an example of Arab vengeance that seems to fit the prophetic description of Ishmael's offspring. In learning more about the Arab people, I discovered that acts of blood revenge were not uncommon. These types of tragedies happened frightfully more often than one would imagine.

On another occasion, I was wandering along the hillside of the Mount of Olives in Jerusalem. I had my camera and was shooting pictures of the Old City, and some of the trees and wild flowers that graced the dry hillside. Near the top of the hill, I was able to make friends with a 15-year old Arab boy who spoke very good English. He was proud of his heritage, but already had a deep and immature hatred for the Jews. His hero was Yasser Arafat.

An old Arab man watched the hour-long interchange between the teenager and me. Although our discussion was a bit intense at times, it was truly friendly. Nasser, the teenager, agreed to having his picture taken with me, and we left each other as friends. The old man broke off a flower from a nearby bush, walked slowly over to me, and gave the flower to me. No words were spoken, but the language of action said dozens of words.

It would be several years later that I would bring my son, Chris, with me to Israel. I took him to the top of Mt. Olives where we overlooked the city of Jerusalem, and where we found my Arab friend from years earlier. We were invited into his house to meet his father, mother, sisters, and cousin. Nasser's father spoke excellent English. He labored as a diesel mechanic and was a devout Moslem. The entire family treated my son and me with incredible grace and hospitality and fed us a complete meal, though we just "dropped in". The warmth and love shown to us could not be outdone by any that I have received in any country or by any other family. This family was truly a tribute to Arab people everywhere.

I had another occasion to visit with a group of Arabs in Jerusalem. I listened to them intently as each told us their own stories of how their lives had changed when they truly saw the truth of their Jewish Messiah, Jesus. They had been Moslems until they discovered the peace and joy that could be theirs by having a true spiritual relationship with Jesus, the Jew. These were Arabs who were paying a dear price for their faith as well. One of the Arab mothers had her newborn baby poisoned by one of the radicals in her community. Another young Arab boy showed me the scars on his forearm that went from his wrist to his elbow. When his Arab Muslim friends discovered that he was a believer in Jesus, they came to him, held one of his arms down, and cut it viciously with the jagged glass of a broken bottle. He was told that the next time they confronted him, it would be his tongue.

This Arab boy glowed with confidence and love as he told his story through an interpreter. His mother had taught him to pray for his enemies according to Jesus' teaching. While the local bullies of his neighborhood were cutting his arm, he prayed that the Lord would forgive them, because they didn't know what they were doing. He was echoing in action the words of Jesus as He hung on the cross 2,000 years ago on another hill only a mile or two from where we were meeting.

After listening to these Christian Arabs who had a vibrant and living relationship with the God of Abraham, Isaac, and Jacob through Messiah Jesus, one of them said that they did not care anything about the so-called "green lines" (a term used to delineate borders in and around Jerusalem between the Arab and Jewish communities. These were literally green lines drawn on a map that defined territories even by city blocks and streets). They were not interested in the claims to create a Palestinian State within the borders of Israel. They only wanted to grow in the knowledge of God, to enjoy His peace, and to spread this good news to other Arabs and Jews. These are the progeny of Ishmael the "wild donkey" of Scripture who have taken on the yoke of their Creator, whose "yoke is easy and whose burden is light". As they have allowed themselves to become yoked to God and His purposes, their life is one of joy and inner peace. As an added by-product, they have a love for Zion and the Jewish people.

Other Arabs, however, represent their people badly. Their entire reason for living seems to be that of destroying the Jews. They are bent and twisted in their reasoning, and are motivated through rage and hate, rather than love and brotherhood. Many Arabs and Persians in the nations surrounding Israel who are motivated by greed, lust for power, and hatred, have risen to power in those nations, and speak for their people. The obscure Arabs like Nasser's family on the Mt. of Olives, and the group that shared their lives with us in Jerusalem have little to say in today's world of power politics.

From having listened personally to Arabs whose lives and motivations have been changed by having a personal relationship with Jesus, and from knowing how He has changed my own life and many others around me, the conclusion is obvious. It is not being

Arab that brings out the hate towards the Jews, but it is the spirit that prevails over a man or group of men that dictates or encourages any behavior.

Under Islam, it is permissible to lie as long as the purposes of Islam are being carried out. The Islamic principle is **"taqiah"** (Muslims have every right to lie and to deceive their adversaries, and a promise made to a non-Muslim can be broken whenever necessary"). To be anything but a Moslem in that belief system, is to be an infidel, fit only for the fires of hell. Adolf Hitler taught that the truthfulness of a propaganda is of little importance compared to its only valid criterion, that of its success, and a lie will be received as truth when repeated often and loud enough. Murder, terrorism, threats, and intimidation are only part of the descriptions that are acceptable to further the cause of Islam under this mind set. It is this mind set that prevails over many of the leaders of the Arab and Persian nations surrounding Israel. With such thinking, and the allowance for deceit in relationships, is it any wonder that there is no peace in the Middle East?

Islam claims that they worship Allah, and that he is the God of the Bible worshipped by Christians and Jews. Some theologians say however, that Allah was the name of a pagan moon-god to whom temples were built across the Middle East. According to many observers, present day Islam is no more than re-defined idolatry, elevating one of the dozens of other gods of the time to a "one true God" status. The deception is obviously deep and widespread.

Probably one of the most high profile and dangerous leaders in the human chess game of Middle East power politics is Yasser Arafat, the hero of many deceived Arabs. It has not been only the Arabs that have been deceived, but leaders of the Western world. Many in the West have placed their confidence in their own education, their ability to negotiate and facilitate, or to diplomatically twist the arms of others to create a new peace. Mr. Arafat has been given prominence and credibility that has not been earned, and whenever he or others like him are pandered and bowed to, it literally helps him to achieve his end. One of those stated ends is right in the PLO covenant, to eliminate Israel. Arafat has been the chief of the Palestinian Liberation Organization.

There is no real difference between the actions of Adolf Hitler and and those of Yasser Arafat. They come from different cultures, but both believe in the use of lies, deceit, murder and terror. Both had stated aims as it regarded the Jewish people, and that was to eliminate them. Hitler did it through his book, "Mein Kampf" and his laws and ordinances that were blatantly against the Jewish people, his concentration camps and gas chambers. Arafat has done it through terror, murder, the written Palestinian Covenant and now with world politics. The psalmist is not wrong when he penned the words:

"His speech is smooth as butter, yet war is in his heart; his words are more soothing than oil, yet they are drawn swords."

(NIV—Psalm 55:21)

Article 9 of the PLO (Palestinian Liberation Organization) states: "Armed struggle is the only way to liberate Palestine and is therefore a strategy and not tactics. The Palestinian Arab people affirms its absolute resolution and abiding determination to pursue the armed struggle and to work for an armed popular revolution, to liberate its homeland and return to it to maintain its right to a natural life in it, and to exercise its right of self-determination in it and sovereignty over it."

In spite of the fact that Yasser Arafat has been a known murderer and terrorist for decades, the Western nations continue to offer him their red carpets and podiums. Politically, the Western nations (especially the United States) have pressured the Israelis to do the same. Israeli leaders, most of whom are exhausted from the countless attacks against their people, have in their weariness or compromise, too often co-operated.

Arafat's diplomacy is one of double-speak. Remember, it is permissible under the Islamic mind set to lie, as long as it is achieving some end that is promotional to Islam and its cause for world domination. That is why we hear the rhetoric of Mr. Arafat in front of world news cameras, proclaiming a desire for peace and brotherhood. Behind the scenes he says other things to journalists and Arab leaders. Some of his words are quoted below:

"The goal of our stuggle is the end of Israel, and there can be no compromise."

—Yasser Arafat
(Washington Post- Mar 29, 1970)

"Peace for us means the destruction of Israel. We are preparing for an all-out war, a war which will last for generations. Since January 1965, when Fatah was born, we have become the most dangerous enemy that Israel has......We shall not rest until the day when we return to our home, and until we destroy Israel....."

—Yasser Arafat
(El Mundo, Caracas, Venezuela—Feb. 11, 1980)

"O heroic sons of the Gaza Strip, O proud sons of the West Bank, O heroic sons of the Galilee, O steadfast sons of the Negev:.....the fires of revolution against these Zionist invaders will not fade out...until our land—-all our land—-has been liberated from these usurping invaders."

—Yasser Arafat
(PLO Radio, Baghdad, Dec 10, 1987)

"Open fire on the new Jewish immigrants—be they from the Soviet Union, Ethiopia, or anywhere else...I give you my instructions to use violence against the immigrants. I will jail anyone who refuses to do this."

—Yasser Arafat
(Al-Muharar—April 10, 1990)

During the Gulf War: "There is no choice for the PLO but to oppose the Allied force, because it's in the alliance with Israel. Anyone responsible for shedding the blood of Iraqis will be punished."

—Yasser Arafat
(UPI—February 1, 1991)

"We will continue our revolution and our resistance and our uprising until the banner of our revolution flies over holy Jerusalem and the walls of Jerusalem and the minarets of Jerusalem and the churches of Jerusalem."
—Yasser Arafat
(Algiers Voice of Palestine-May 13, 1991)

"The Jews at work! Damn their fathers! The Dogs! Filth and dirt!....And thanks to the rotten Jews with whom I will settle accounts in the future."
—Yasser Arafat
(tape from CNN—January 30, 1992)

"I have no use for Jews.....We now need all the help we can get from you in our battle for a united Palestine under total Arab-Muslim domination."
—Yasser Arafat
(addressing Arab diplomats,
Stockholm—January 30, 1996)

"I now see the walls of Jerusalem, the mosques of Jerusalem, the churches of Jerusalem. My brothers! With blood and with spirit we will redeem you, Palestine! Yes, with blood and with spirit we will redeem you, Palestine!"
—Yasser Arafat
(speech in Tulkarm, Voice of Palestine
April 28, 1997)

It was Yasser Arafat's voice that was intercepted back in March 1973 after he had given the orders to pump 40 bullets into the bodies of U.S. ambassador to Sudan and two other diplomats that were held hostage at the Saudi embassy in Khartoum. Yasser Arafat's "Black September", a faction of the PLO carried out the assassinations under Arafat's orders, and Arafat who was in Beirut at his headquarters wanted to confirm that the violent assassinations had taken place. U.S. ambassador Cleo Noel, and U.S. charge d'affaires George Curtis Moore, were lined up against a basement wall in the embassy and shot. From the book "Inside the PLO" (Livingstone & Halevy—New York: Quill/William Morrow, 1990) a description is given. "The terrorists fired from the floor upward, to prolong the agony of their victims by striking them first in the feet and legs, before administering the coup de grace".

So deceived are our own leaders in America, that Arafat was given the red carpet treatment in a visit to Washington, D.C. in March 1997. He was received by then President Clinton and the Secretary of State, Madeleine Albright. While the murder of our diplomats took place 25 years ago, nothing in Arafat's comportment has changed. He has never been held accountable for these murders, or those of the Israeli athletes at the Munich Olympic Games of 1972. He has not changed his spots, but yet he is coddled by the West.

Other leaders in the region do not have quite the notoriety of Yasser Arafat, but they nonetheless walk the "party line" of the Islamic fundamentalism that would kill all Jews.

"We believe that peace with Israel is a sin."
—Hezbollah
(Voice of Mountain,
Lebanon—August 26, 1991)

"Israel is a malignant tumor in the region. It must be cut off. It must be eradicated."
—Ayatollah Ali Khamenei
(Statement to Iran armed forces staff,
July 31, 1991)

"We must return our Jerusalem to our hands from the hands of Israel the usurper."
—Saudi Foreign Minister,Prince Saud
(Saudi News Agency—Sept. 20, 1990)

"The battle with Israel must be such that, after it, Israel will cease to exist."
—Libyan Leader, Mohmmar Khaddafy
(Algiers Radio—Nov 12, 1973)

"To gather the Jews in Palestine, is to gather them in their tombs....We will hit them with all means and liquidate them"
—Libyan Leader, Mohmmar Khaddafy
(Washington Times—May 31, 1990)

"Our forces continue to pressure the enemy and will continue to strike at him until we recover the occupied territory, and we will then continue until all the land is liberated."
—Syrian President, Hafez Assad
(Radio Damascus—Oct. 16, 1973)

There was a terrible suicide bombing at a Tel Aviv discotheque where twenty young Israelis were murdered, and many more injured. It happened in June 2001. A week after this despicable act of violence, the official Palestinian Authority television station broadcast a sermon calling for more suicide bombings and the destruction of Israel, the United States, and Britain. Sheik Ibrahim Madhi's sermon was broadcast live from a mosque in Gaza. "Allah willing, this unjust state...Israel, will be erased; this unjust state the United States will be erased; this unjust state Britain will be erased – they who caused this people's catastrophe," said Madhi. In addition, Arab children living in Gaza, Judea, and Samaria are regularly taught through the media and in their own schoolbooks to hate the Jews.

Since September 2000, under the guidance of Yasser Arafat, approximately 700 Israelis have been murdered through violence and terror attacks by his deceived minions. Another 5000-plus casualties have occurred during this time and there have been approximately 15,000 attempted attacks on the Israelis.

In keeping with the PLO's covenant to push the Jews into the sea, Arafat continues to procure weapons in any way that he can. The PLO ship, *"Karine A"* was cruising along in the night in the middle of the Red Sea when some Israeli commandos dropped in. The ship was packed with tons of weapons...most with Farsi markings indicating their source...Iran. The captain of the ship admitted working for the PLO. The PLO publicists, including Arafat himself, denied all knowledge or involvement of this mysterious ship filled with weaponry. It would appear that Mr. Arafat employs well, the Islamic concept of *taqiah.*

With leaders like this, the Arab people as a whole are living under incredible tyranny and deception. In metaphorical language, the inmates have risen to power and taken over the prison, and the street bullies of the past are leading the governments of these nations. Worse still, is the fact that the leaders of the so-called "Christian nations" of the West where God has so abundantly blessed, are swallowing the lie, and becoming part of the noose that is being tied to be placed on Israel's neck. Evil compromise always leads to deception, and where the smell of Arab oil or international business profit takes precedence over principle, the immediate gain may be temporarily gratifying, but in the long pull it will be disaster.

> For behold, Thine enemies make an uproar; and those who hate Thee have exalted themselves. They make shrewd plans against Thy treasured ones. They have said, "Come, and let us wipe them out as a nation, that the name of Israel be remembered no more."
>
> (NAS—Psalm 83:2-5)

It has been said that the Arabs have the oil from below, but the Jews have the oil from above. I believe it to be a statement of truth. The Scriptures tell us that God is not a respecter of persons, meaning that His love is a love that crosses all of our human barriers and differences. He loves Arabs, Americans, Germans, Russians, Blacks, Whites, Asians, women and men as much as He loves the Jews. However, God has plans and purposes, and part of His plan as revealed in the Scriptures was to create a people of His own, the Jewish people. He included as part of that plan a nation called Israel, and of all the plans, edicts, warnings, commands, suggestions, and descriptions, none is more apparent and repeated than God's plan to give Israel the land that is in such dispute today.

In the first five books of the Bible, the Lord mentions the land of Israel over 100 times as it relates to being given to the children of

Israel. Throughout the Old Testament this theme is continually repeated another 125 times in such a way that there is no doubt about what God meant. The land was not destined for an ayatollah, a terrorist, a dictator or any coalition of same. No politicians are going to change that plan. Every attempt to go against this plan is to find oneself battling against the Creator of the universe and the Creator of Zion and its people.

Israel does not belong to the Arabs. It belongs to the Jews. Palestine is a name that was created by the occupying armies of Rome in the 1st century A.D. It was an attempt to humiliate and ultimately annihilate Jewish identity in the land. The Jews had already been living there for more than 1500 years, and it was identified as the national homeland of the Israelites.

Even if one were to disregard all of the Biblical arguments regarding the land of Israel, a simple appeal to fairness would seem to settle the issue. If one were to take all of the Arab lands, toss in Israel as part of the lot, and then divide the entire amount by one thousand, the Arabs already have 998.5 pieces, and the Jews have 1.5 pieces. That means that little Israel has only .0015 of the entire lot, or barely ONE TENTH of ONE PERCENT! Israel's adversaries want that as well, and many diplomats of the West are nodding their heads in approval.

Prior to the Six-Day War of 1967, there was no clamor or desire for a Palestinian homeland. In fact, the land that the "Palestinians" are claiming was controlled by King Hussein of Jordan prior to the war. At that time, it was simply Jordanian occupied territory. According to the Biblical account, it was thousands of years before 1967 when the disputed land was identified as Judea and Samaria and given to the Jewish people as an everlasting possession.

Palestine has never existed as an autonomous entity. The area was ruled alternately by Rome, Islamic and Christian crusaders, the Ottoman Empire, and briefly by the British after World War I. There is no language known as "Palestinian". There is no distinct Palestinian culture. There has never been a land known as Palestine governed by Palestinians. It would seem then, that the whole "Palestinian" scheme of today is a diabolical smoke and mirrors land-grab that fits snugly into the Islamic theology of **Jihad**, or holy war. It is birthed out of a perverted hatred for the Jewish people, and its ultimate aim is to annihilate Israel.

Many of the so-called Palestinians of today are people who immigrated to Israel from surrounding Arab nations. They came to the region because their own leaders had failed them within the Arab nations around Israel. These "Palestinians" had been given little to no economic help or acceptance from their Arab brothers. They had been exploited by Arab leaders whose interest was anything but altruistic. In fact, history reveals that the Arabs had very little interest in this territory until the Jews returned to their biblical Promise Land and developed it. As a result, the poverty stricken Arabs in the region were enticed by the economic opportunity created by the Jewish efforts. Those Jewish efforts in Israel have supported and educated thousands of Arab people.

The Palestinian Arabs of today are often spoken of as being exploited, and they are. However, they are being exploited by their own leaders and their own fellow Arabs far more than any exploitation that may come from other sources. Even as I write these words, Yasser Arafat and his Palestinian Authority have been imprisoning and murdering his own people. Some are murdered if they have dialogue with the Jewish people. Palestinian real estate agents have been murdered, imprisoned, and threatened if they participate in any deal that would sell a piece of property to a Jew. Those of the "in-crowd" of the Palestinian Authority are living lives with large estates, Mercedes cars, and bulging wallets, as they squander funds that have been legitimately given by other nations to help the Arab people. This is no surprise however, when we understand *"taqiah"*—the justification of a moral system that encourages lies and deceit to achieve an end.

The struggle which we all face, is not simply one of ethnicity—American, German, Russian, Arab, Black, or White. It is to discover truth and to discern under which spirit we operate as human beings. Quite invisible to our natural eyes, a spiritual war is taking place all over the earth, and is centered round Israel. The Jewish-Christian Bible is replete with explanation about this conflict, expounding on details about the cosmic battle between Satan and God. Mankind is caught in the middle, having to choose which of the two sides he will support. An interesting dilemma about truth is that where it exists, a thousand lies can be spoken about that same truth. It is interesting that the Bible's New Testament refers to Satan as the "father of lies". He is further described as a "liar, a thief, and one in whom there is no truth."

There are some important questions everyone needs to address. This is strategic because we live in a time of "world globalization" and "new world order". Each person has to discern what forces are governing his life. Are you, the reader, being led by the truth or are you following after the "father of lies", expressing himself through deceived or evil men?

History has proven that Adolf Hitler exercised a rigorous and repeated campaign of lies against the Jewish people and deceived an entire nation. Are we now entering into another era of manipulation and lies that will deceive an entire world? Have some lies been told so often and with such volume that they are now believed by even billions of people? Is the so-called "Palestinian" claim to the land of Israel one of these lies? Is one of the most blatant lies of today the one which insists that Zionism is racism?

Are you going to be part of blessing the Jewish people and Israel according to the biblical command of the Lord, or are you going to join in the world rhetoric that is becoming increasingly anti-Jewish and anti-Israel? As a reader, are you going to listen to the evaluations of CNN news, or are you going to seek out God and His truth as revealed in His Word, the Bible? It would seem that once again, the Scriptures have wisdom and warning about the climax toward which the world is racing:

> Why do the nations rage and the peoples plot in vain? The kings of the earth take their stand and the rulers gather together against the Lord and against his Anointed One. Let us break their chains, they say, and throw off their fetters. The One enthroned in heaven laughs; the Lord scoffs at them in his anger and terrifies them in his wrath saying, 'I have installed my King on Zion, my holy hill........Therefore you kings, be wise; be warned, you rulers of the earth. Serve the Lord

with fear and rejoice with trembling. Kiss the Son, lest
he be angry and you be destroyed in your way, for his
wrath can flare up in a moment. Blessed are all who
take refuge in Him.

(NIV—Psalm 2:1-6, 10-12)

The answers to these and other questions are going to label us
from heaven's perspective. There is a statement in the Scriptures
from the book of Genesis. God is speaking to Abram as He is chal-
lenging Abram to leave his country and people and to go where God
is calling him to go. God says to Abram:

"I will make you into a great nation and I will bless
you; I will make your name great and you will be a
blessing. *I will bless those who bless you, and whoever
curses you, I will curse;* and all the peoples of the earth
will be blessed through you"

(NIV—Gen 12:2-3)

I believe each of us needs to answer some questions for ourselves. Are we going to be part of the blessing or part of the curse?
Are we going to take God's side in the battle over Zion, or are we
going to take the side of God's adversary? One's relationship with
God Himself will depend on the answer to these questions.

# 16

# IN CONCLUSION

An old country preacher in the simplicity of his sermon said, "First I tell 'em what I'm gonna tell 'em...then I tell 'em...then I tell 'em what I told 'em". I have purposely tried to maintain this concept throughout the entire book. I have repeated several themes in many ways, in hopes of allowing you, the reader, to grasp these ideas intellectually and emotionally. I must greatly challenge the Islamic concept of **taqiah**, that it is acceptable to lie to achieve an end, and that if a lie is told often enough and loud enough, it will be believed. However, due to our human limitations, we need to continually remind ourselves of truth, lest oft-repeated lies enter our minds and twist or obscure it. By guarding this attitude consistently, we can protect ourselves from deception which leads to war and destruction, proved time and again throughout human history.

Hopefully, through these pages your concept of the Arab-Israeli conflict has been initiated, refreshed or even expanded. You have met a few of Israel's people. You have hopefully felt and empathized in some way with their suffering. It is a suffering, which is not over, but is coming to its conclusion. It is Zion—both the Land, the people, and their God—around which the final battle of this present age is being fought.

It does not take a rocket scientist to observe and conclude from past and recent history, that to join those that have chosen to *curse* Israel and the Jewish people, is to find oneself in opposition to God's plan for all the world. It is to invoke God's promise, that "*I will curse them that curse thee....*"

We can view the more contemporary histories of the Roman Empire, Turks, Germans, Spaniards, and Russians, and we can see that these nations and empires have suffered dramatically as a result of their adversarial behavior against the Jewish people. The Roman Empire is no more. The great glories of Spain and all of its conquests and discoveries have tarnished in consequence of the terrible Inquisitions several hundreds of years ago. The nation of Turkey remains a place of overcrowded cities and a dry economy. The Germans literally had their entire nation split in half, lost their fathers, and nearly starved to death at the conclusion of World War II. Today, the Russian economy is in shambles after seventy years of atheistic communism. Each of these nations in their histories has persecuted the Jews as well as believing Christians.

Even England, a place where only a generation or two ago one could truly say that "the sun never sets on the British Empire", has tumbled downward as a world power. The British took their stand against the Jews at the end of World War II. They opposed the hundreds of thousands of Holocaust victims who were seeking refuge in Israel. Instead of allowing the Jews to go to their biblical home, they interned them in concentration camps in Cyprus. Since that time, little nations around the world have asserted and fought for their independence from Britain. One by one, these nations including India and most recently Hong Kong, have left the family of the British Empire. Britain has become weaker, more insignificant, and an island that has been increasingly laden with social ills.

The little island nation of Cuba reneged on its own promises of asylum toward the escaping Jews of the *St. Louis*. A few years later it found itself in the grips of Fidel Castro's communism which lasts to this day. Cuba was at one time a prosperous and free island, filled with a degree of economic contentment, but today is a wasting slum of dilapidated buildings, miserable roads, broken-down cars, and oppressed people.

Is this analysis a little too simplistic? I think not. While some might point to other corruption, such as economics, poor leadership, or other factors which determine the welfare of any nation, God is still the sovereign ruler over history. His stated laws and principles are unchangeable. Israel is the only nation He called His own and proclaimed the following:

> For the nation or kingdom that will not serve you
> (Israel) will perish; it will be utterly ruined.
>                                          (NIV—Isaiah 60:12)

Biblical scholars tend to believe that these promises will ultimately be fulfilled in a Messianic era for the world. Many feel that the current events around the boiling cauldron of the Middle East are the birth pangs of this new era—a new world order established on God's terms and not man's.

The United States has had a relatively decent record towards Israel and the Jewish people, but I reiterate that it is only *relatively* decent. Our record has been far from pure. America also turned its back on that same shipload of Jewish immigrants on the *St. Louis*. Although possibly well intentioned, the United States today is skating on very thin ice in its constant meddling in the affairs of Israel and the Jewish people, twisting and cajoling her to bow to the "peace" process where there has been no evidence that the other side has interest in anything besides Israel's annihilation. America's latest fighters and AWACS planes are poised on the runways of Israel's enemies and if these and other American supplied weapons are unleashed against Israel, America will have more blood on its hands. As a nation America will reap the consequences of its own corporate greed or misguided decisions.

In the book of Isaiah, penned under the inspiration of the God's Spirit some 2,700 years ago, the Almighty tells us:

"The Lord has established Zion, and in her His afflicted people will find refuge".

(NIV—Isaiah 14:32)

Today Israel is a land of Holocaust survivors, *refuseniks,* and refugees from many nations. If the LORD has established Zion, how dare the world leaders divide it or determine her destiny? Who do we think we are as mortal men to play with Zion as though it was a piece of real estate on a Monopoly board? God's Spirit spoke through the prophet Joel approximately 2,800 years ago:

I will gather all the nations and bring them down to the Valley of Jehoshaphat. There I will enter into judgment against them concerning My inheritance, My people Israel, for they scattered My people among the nations and <u>divided up My land</u>.

(NIV—Joel 3:2)

Recent efforts on the part of American, European, and Arab leaders to create a Palestinian State within the boundaries of Israel, is to provoke and challenge the God of the universe. It is inviting divine judgment on the nations that these leaders represent. I shudder to think what may happen when God keeps His promise and drags nation after foolish nation through the valley of judgment, simply because the people and the leaders of these nations refused to honor the crystal clear warnings of holy Scripture.

At the crux of the entire matter regarding Zion is a very simple but most important issue. The issue is in regard to the Bible. Are the Sacred Writings of the Jews and Christians merely a collection of nice stories, histories, and moral allegories, or is the Bible the very Word of the living God written for men, by men under the inspiration of the Holy Spirit? The answer to this question will dictate an individual's view of Israel, her people, and God Himself. It will also reveal God's view toward an individual.

Someone once said that the Bible is God's "love-letter" to the entire world. Others have described the Bible as the "manufacturer's handbook" on how to operate the human being. I believe that both statements are true, and also that the Bible is much more than these descriptions can convey.

Probably the greatest theme in the Bible is that God LOVES the world and mankind. Many descriptions in its pages reveal God's heart towards us all. He suffers with us. He can be pleased with us or angry with us. He has all of the emotions that we experience as people, not because He is emulating us, but because we have been created in His image and we are like Him except for our fallen sin nature.

Two of God's greatest attributes are that He is merciful and forgiving. If it were not for these special qualities, absolutely none of us as humans could have hope for a relationship with Him. Part of the good news of this love-letter is that any man can come to Him, repent, receive forgiveness, and have an intimate relationship with Him, a relationship which will last for eternity. That's *very* good news for each of us who will receive it. A New Testament cry from the heart of God states:

> The Lord is not slow in keeping His promise, as some understand slowness. He is patient with you, not wanting anyone to perish, but everyone to come to repentance.
>
> (NIV—2 Peter 3:9)

Studying these words, it is clear that the Lord has a promise awaiting us, that He is patient, and that He does not want any man to perish, but this grace extended from Him must have a response. Men must repent (change), stop living by their own rules, and live in relationship with our Creator. This response to God's initiating delivers us from the wrath that He promises for anyone who refuses His offer.

Based on the behavior of nations and their leaders toward Israel and her people, one can only conclude that the vast majority of world inhabitants are ignorant of the God of the Bible and consequently alienated from Him. In the New Testament there are some very significant statements made in the first chapter of the book of Romans concerning this.

"For the wrath of God is revealed from heaven against all ungodliness and unrighteousness of men, who suppress the truth in unrighteousness, because that which is known about God is evident within them; for God made it evident to them. For since the creation of the world His invisible attributes, His eternal power and divine nature, have been clearly seen, being understood through what has been made, so that they are without excuse. For even though they knew God, they did not honor Him as God, or give thanks; but they became futile in their speculations, and their foolish heart was darkened. **Professing to be wise, they became fools,** and exchanged the glory of the incorruptible God for an image in the form of corruptible man and of birds and four-footed animals and crawling creatures. Therefore, God gave them over in the lusts of their hearts to impurity, that their bodies might be dishonored among them. For **they exchanged the truth of God for a lie,** and worshiped and served the creature rather than the Creator, who is blessed forever. Amen.
(NAS—Romans 1:18-25)

No text of Scripture more accurately reflects the situation of mankind today as a whole. Men by the billions have worshiped the creature rather than the Creator. Mankind has bowed to birds, rocks, trees, statues, and philosophies. We have worshiped our homes, cars, children, and possessions. Diplomats of today shuttle back and forth across oceans and national borders, attending this meeting and that conference. They cart with them their advisors, notebooks, computers, and bodyguards. But how many have Bibles and live by the ultimate truth that graces its pages? Only God knows the exact answer to this question, but the answer obvious to all is, not very many. Is it any wonder then, that the world is a proverbial powder keg of deception and intrigue, ready to blow at any moment when the right button is pushed?

While Zion is a physical place on this earth that has been ordained of God, and Zion has its people, also chosen of God, Zion above all, is a place in the Spirit. It is a place where the attitudes of heart have been changed to reflect the oracles of the Scriptures, and where the reasoning of the mind have been disciplined by God's Word. Zion is a place of reflective contentment in the soul and it is where we can meet with God.

> How blessed is the man whose strength is in Thee; in whose heart are the highways to Zion! Passing through the valley of Baca (weeping) they make it a spring, the early rain also covers it with blessings. They go from strength to strength, every one of them appears before God in Zion.
>
> (NAS—Psalm 84:5-7)

This place is not reached without pain and suffering. It requires the death to the selfish part of our human nature, the daily wrestling against our sinful desires, and walking the narrow path of truth and righteousness. It involves daily discipline and living out our lives in the spirit of love, regardless of the cost. This describes the spiritual warfare that rages over each individual who seeks after God. It is also descriptive of the physical suffering endured by the Jewish people to reach and inhabit the land of Zion.

In the New Testament, there is a strong admonition in the parable of the sheep and the goats as it would apply to nations. This story obviously refers to Jesus. He gathers the sheep and goats by nations, and when in this story He refers to "these brothers of Mine", some understand this as referring to the Jewish people as well as believing Christians.

> When the Son of Man comes in His glory, and all the angels with him, He will sit on His throne in heavenly glory. All the nations will be gathered before Him, and He will separate the people one from another as a shepherd separates the sheep from the goats. He will put the sheep on His right and the goats on his left.
>
> Then the King will say to those on His right, 'Come, you who are blessed by my Father; take your

inheritance, the kingdom prepared for you since the creation of the world. for I was hungry and you gave Me something to eat, I was thirsty and you gave Me something to drink, I was a stranger and you invited Me in, I needed clothes and you clothed Me, I was sick and you looked after Me, I was in prison and you came to visit Me.'

Then the righteous will answer Him, 'Lord, when did we see you hungry and feed you, or thirsty and give you something to drink? When did we see you a stranger and invite you in, or needing clothes and clothe you? When did we see You sick or in prison and go to visit You?'

The King will reply, 'I tell you the truth, whatever you did for one of the least of these <u>brothers of mine</u>, you did for Me.'

Then He will say to those on his left, 'Depart from Me, you who are cursed, into the eternal fire prepared for the devil and his angels. For I was hungry and you gave Me nothing to eat, I was thirsty and you gave Me nothing to drink, I was a stranger and you did not invite Me in, I needed clothes and you did not clothe Me, I was sick and in prison and you did not look after Me.

They also will answer, 'Lord, when did we see you hungry or thirsty or a stranger or needing clothes or sick or in prison, and did not help you?'

He will reply, 'I tell you the truth, whatever you did not do for one of the least of these, you did not do for Me.'

Then they will go away to eternal punishment, but the righteous to eternal life."

(NIV—Matthew 25:31-46)

The journey to Zion is to be filled with small drinks of water, outstretched hands, and occasional rays of hope that will spur the pilgrim to keep moving toward the goal. As we Christians continue this spiritual journey through these last and perilous days, we will have an abundance of opportunities to bless and join hands with the Jewish people as they are drawn to Zion. We owe them our prayers and our emotional and monetary support as they make their journey to Zion, first to the land, and then to God's revelation for them. I believe that this message must be received and walked out within the Christian community at large. This message must be sent forth to a lost and dying world. It is a message from which God-fearing people must not back away in the face of diabolical opposition. It is a message that is crucial even to a nation's survival. It is why, for Zion's sake, I will not keep silent.

Printed in the United States
40733LVS00006B/64